LIVING LITERATU

Double Trouble

a story of assisted reproduction

Hazel E McHaffie

Radcliffe Publishing
Oxford • Seattle

Radcliffe Publishing Ltd
18 Marcham Road
Abingdon
Oxon OX14 1AA
United Kingdom

www.radcliffe-oxford.com
Electronic catalogue and worldwide online ordering facility.

British Library Cataloguing in Publication Data

A catalogue record for this book is available from the British Library.

ISBN 1 85775 669 X

Typeset by Ann Buchan (Typesetters), Shepperton, Middlesex
Printed and bound by T J International Ltd, Padstow, Cornwall

Medical ethics – a living literature

In the privacy of general practices and hospital clinics a million people a day in the UK share stories of personal moment with healthcare professionals. Fragmentary and often tangled, their accounts may feature bizarre experiences, unpleasant sensations, weird situations, complex relationships, difficult choices, conflicting interests and extreme emotions.

This refreshingly different series of novels conjures up some of these lived realities, especially their medical and ethical dimensions. The stories draw us deep into moral quandaries alongside people grappling with health issues and difficult choices; they are tales of passion, perplexity and crime that hold the reader spellbound amidst the thoughts, emotions, plans and actions of their characters.

Hazel McHaffie, already an award-winning author, has woven together authentic clinical details and ethical dilemmas with a lightness of touch that transports the reader effortlessly into the world of scientific medicine. In *Paternity*, she addressed the emotive issue of male infertility. In this sequel, *Double Trouble*, she turns the spotlight onto the woman who has problems conceiving. Through a web of interconnected relationships and decisions she challenges preconceived ideas and drives us to reflect on what is done in the name of modern medicine and what, in similar circumstances, we would choose for ourselves.

'Ethics is a complicated matter' writes the philosopher and educationalist, Mary Warnock: 'it is partly a matter of judgement and decision, of reasoning and sentiment, of having the right feeling at the right time, and every time is different'. These novels cogently and evocatively embody that heady mixture of elements, bringing ethics to life. They are accessible and compelling and will be enjoyed by general readers as much as by philosophers and health professionals.

Brian Hurwitz
NHS GP
Professor of Medicine and the Arts, King's College, London
Series Editor
February 2005

Website resource

Medical ethics is a fast-moving, constantly evolving hotbed of challenges. You can stay up to date with current controversies, laws and guidelines by visiting a website created to offer useful background information about the series and about the ethical and medical challenges these novels address.

For those who will use this unique and exciting resource to bring medical ethics alive in their teaching, additional educational material and references are also available free on this website:

www.radcliffe-oxford.com/livingliterature

About the author and series editor

Hazel McHaffie's first novel was published in 1994 and 2005 sees the publication of three more. She began her professional life as a nurse and midwife and later gained a doctorate from Edinburgh University. During her career as a Research Fellow in medical ethics she was the author of almost a hundred academic papers and books. One of her books *Crucial Decisions at the Beginning of Life* was voted BMA Medical Book of the Year in 2002. In her new novels she has woven an extensive knowledge of ethics and moral conundrums into gripping tales of passion and tragedy.

Brian Hurwitz is Professor of Medicine and the Arts at King's College, University of London, and a NHS general practitioner in London. He is a member of the UK Association of Medical Humanities and serves on the Editorial Board of the *Journal of Medical Ethics*.

Acknowledgements

Many people have been involved in the polishing process for this book and I thank them all most sincerely. My long-term colleague and friend, Professor Kenneth Boyd, read the text with an expert ethical eye and gave helpful comment. Dr Martin Lees checked the whole manuscript for medical accuracy. Inspector Stewart Sanderlands gave me the benefit of his extensive knowledge of police work. Professor Brian Hurwitz and Gillian Nineham provided helpful editorial suggestions and periodic injections of enthusiasm during the long publication process. And as always my family offered constant support and enthusiasm for what I was trying to do. I owe a special debt to my daughter, Rosalyn, for her meticulous attention to detail and her patient tutoring in matters technological.

Hazel McHaffie
February 2005

Roberta lay perfectly still in the darkness. Beside her, out of sight beneath the duvet, Dick breathed with the evenness of untroubled sleep. Every instinct urged her to wake him, to seek solace in sharing her worries. Years of training and habit stopped her. But her thoughts would not respond to the same discipline.

Nicholas was already standing at the altar.

The minister was intoning: 'Wherefore if anyone can show any just cause why these two persons may not be lawfully joined together in holy matrimony, let him speak now or forever hold his peace.'

In the token pause, Roberta held her breath. *She* knew a just cause. Could she sit there and forever hold her peace? No, as his mother, she owed it to Nick to save him from disaster.

She slithered forward to the edge of the pew.

The bride turned in slow motion, seeking the source of the sudden disturbance. Puzzled dark eyes scanned the Halley rows, focusing finally on her intended mother-in-law.

Roberta cringed from the innocence of her gaze.

How could she spoil this day? How could she wreck the happiness of two young people, one of them her own son?

No, the time for declaration would be past by then.

She emerged from the dream with a heavy sense of foreboding. Taking care not to wake Dick, she slid out of bed and shrugged into her dressing gown.

Now uncomfortably awake, she was still struggling to banish the images as she paced restlessly, waiting for the kettle to boil. She told herself sternly to take a tighter grip on her common sense.

It was absurd to be so concerned. The chances of Nicholas continuing this romance were slim. Donella was certainly not his first and almost as certainly wouldn't be his last. There was no point in needlessly anticipating trouble.

It had been a shock though, seeing them together. Nicholas didn't usually bring girls to his parents' home. His own flat in town was a much more conducive environment.

Roberta, reliving that moment of introduction, wondered if she had betrayed anything of her inner turmoil.

The girl standing beside Nicholas was tall with chestnut hair and a shy smile.

'Mum, this is Donella.'

'Hello, Donella. What a pretty name. Unusual, but pretty.'

'Thanks.'

'I've only known of one other Donella. Years ago.'

'Judy Robertson's little girl,' Dick chimed in, memory stirred.

Donella and Nicholas laughed simultaneously.

'In that case you've only known one! She *is* Donella Robertson.'

The exclamations drowned out Roberta's sudden silence.

'One of twins?'

'Yes, that's right.'

'Brother Graeme?'

'Yes.'

'Live in Roslin?'

'Yes.'

'Then I held you in my arms when you were just hours old,' Dick said, smiling broadly at her.

'You knew my parents?'

'Your mother, yes. We worked in the same hospital. Is she still a midwife?'

'Yes. Part time. Well, I didn't know she knew you. So are you … a doctor?'

'Sorry, Donella.' Nicholas looked sheepish. 'He's head of the Centre for Reproductive Medicine. You know? Richard Halley? *Professor* Richard Halley?'

Donella looked from father to son.

'Why ever didn't you tell me?'

'I don't want people knowing. Don't want them treating me differently just because he's my Dad.'

'"People"?' Donella repeated with a quizzical look at Nicholas.

Roberta watched her son.

'No, I don't mean *you*,' he said, reaching out suddenly to take her hand. 'I don't mind *you* knowing. Sorry. Force of habit, I guess. I just didn't think to say.'

Donella was looking at Dick again, but differently now.

'Wow. I'd no idea. I suppose I never thought to make the connection. Sorry.'

'No need to be. And here I'm just Nick's old Dad, OK? The butt of heartless jokes and endless criticism.'

'Mum's a doctor too,' Nicholas added apologetically. 'Dr Roberta Mansfield. GP in Melrose.'

'Gosh. A real medical dynasty. You're a dark horse, Nick,' Donella said. 'What else haven't you told me?'

He shrugged.

'Keeping my powder dry.'

Donella's frown wasn't entirely erased by the wry smile.

'Are you a medical student too, Donella?' Roberta chipped in.

'Yes, but not in Nick's year. He's ahead of me – very useful early on when I was struggling with some of the epidemiology.'

'Hmmm,' Dick said.

Roberta couldn't resist a wry grimace at her son.

'Nick hasn't always been the exemplary student, Donella! Well, to be honest there have been times when he's been rather an embarrassment to Dick amongst colleagues who *did* know of the family connection! So it's reassuring to know he's picked up enough to pass on some of his wisdom.'

'Mother! *Please*. It's the medical equivalent of showing photos of me when I was six, sticking a finger up my nose!'

'Oh, I daresay we can rise to that too.' Dick grinned.

The easy banter and shared context had helped them all relax but during the evening Roberta had noted the unspoken messages, the stolen touches, and fear had crept through the cracks in her reasoning.

It was that shapeless dread that churned her thoughts now, the more invidious because it remained silent. But she and Dick had agreed, early on in their relationship: they wouldn't divulge confidential medical information even to each other.

It must be over thirty years since that messy case involving Annabel, her friend from medical school days. There'd been nasty talk, snide comments about 'pillowtalk', 'old boys' networks', 'double standards'. All because Annabel had confided in her boyfriend, second son of the Dean of the Medical Faculty. Offspring of the exalted he might be, but it hadn't stopped him from blabbing during a surgical operation. Unfortunately for him – and the Dean – the patient, not fully under the anaesthetic at the time, had remembered it, and reported his indiscretion. It had all come out. A bright future was suddenly extinguished.

Roberta had watched with horror two promising careers disintegrating. Years later she'd recognised the potential for something similar happening to herself and Dick. They made a conscious decision to avoid trouble. Friends periodically teased them about their notion of trust, colleagues occasionally sniggered about paranoia, but their resolve remained strong. What they didn't know they couldn't let slip, even inadvertently. It grew easier as time went on, and their individual burden of patients' confidences increased. It soon became habitual.

Roberta had suffered momentary qualms of conscience at the time knowing about Dick's friend, Judy. But somehow it had seemed even more imperative that she kept her own counsel.

Until now.

Now Dick's son was involved. Did that alter her allegiance? Did that give him the right to know?

Involved … ah yes, just how involved was Nick? If he moved on, the fear would evaporate. Donella's problem would pass to some other unknowing family to face.

But, try as she might, Roberta couldn't dispel the sense of a mutual attraction which went beyond the youthful skirmishes Nicholas had previously favoured.

Self-reproach added to her unease.

If only she'd given Judy's GP other advice. 'Leave well alone' had been a mature response to an impersonal problem all those years ago, before the Robertson twins were even conceived. But now, when Donella was not only a lovely young woman, but in danger of ensnaring her own son, Roberta cursed her earlier naïvety.

If only she'd had the time to stay in touch with Judy Robertson. They'd met twice at parties given for sets of twins involved in an ongoing study of multiple births at the university when the children were at primary school. They had enough in common to sustain a friendship. Pressure of work had made her decline Judy's invitations to maintain social contact. What did *work* matter?

Perhaps if the children had seen each other at their most obnoxious in the early years it would have been enough to prevent any other feelings emerging.

Perhaps if Donella had befriended Nicholas' younger sister, Alexandra, then, these two would have become more sparring partners than lovers.

Perhaps if Graeme Robertson had been allowed to follow through his fiercely protective brotherly instincts, Nicholas would not have had the opportunity to grow close to his twin sister.

If only … perhaps … maybe …

But it was too late for regret. Now she could only cling to the hope that this embryonic relationship would not survive the period of gestation.

TWO

Nicholas glared from one to the other of his parents.

'But I don't *want* to go to Brazil.'

Mature anger hovered alongside childish petulance.

'You'd be a fool to turn down an invitation as good as this. Opportunities like these don't grow on trees,' Dick told his son sternly.

'I can do other things. I don't want to go abroad at all.'

'Why not? It's the best use of your elective. It'll broaden your horizons.'

'Lots of reasons why not.'

'Name one,' Dick challenged him.

'Donella.'

Roberta's heart sank. The very reason for her 'interference'.

'Nick, you've got to think long term. You can't let a student relationship stand in the way of your career prospects.' She tried to inject a reasonable tone, to make it seem like a casual reference to a casual relationship.

'She's important to me. And besides I owe her.'

'Owe her what?'

'She helped me get down to studying seriously. If it wasn't for her I'd probably have been thrown out of Med School.'

'OK. Fair enough. If she was the reason for your improved grades.'

'She was.'

Dick seemed to have forgotten their strategy. Roberta sidestepped him to take up pole position.

'But if she's serious about studying and wants you both to get on she'll understand,' she coaxed.

'Huhh.'

'And if she's that important she'll still be waiting for you when you get back. It's only a year.' If only Dick knew her hidden agenda. This wasn't the line she wanted.

'And that's another thing – why a year? Why not four months like everybody else?'

'Because it's a special offer. Much more in-depth experience than you'd get in a few months.'

'A year's a long time out of my course,' Nicholas replied sulkily. 'Anyway, Donella's not the only reason I don't want to go.'

'Oh?'

Both parents looked at him, waiting for the other excuses.

'No. I don't want you two – either of you – pulling strings for me. I want to get there on my own.'

'Fair enough again.' Roberta heard her voice, the epitome of reason. Good. Stay cool. 'I can understand that. And we've been proud of you making your own way. *And* we'll stand back and let you do it your way when you get back. But this is too fantastic an opportunity to miss. You'd be mad to let a little scruple like that stand in the way of a brilliant invitation. Dr Leonard is the best authority in tropical diseases you could ever meet and he's said he'll personally show you the ropes and make sure you learn heaps.'

But in spite of their combined entreaties, despite the uniqueness of the offer, Nicholas remained adamant. He was not going to Brazil.

Roberta struggled for three weeks before resorting to the action she'd been doing her best to avoid.

If Nicholas was suspicious of the motive for an invitation to coffee in the Rochester Hotel, he gave no hint of it. Indeed he seemed disarmingly pleased to see her.

Roberta was loath to spoil the moment, almost grateful for the slow service and the incompetence of the waitress. But the delay only added to her sense of urgency and when she did finally launch into her subject it was with less than her usual circumspection.

'Nick, I've got to talk to you.'

'Isn't that what we're doing, Mother?'

'Seriously talk.'

'Oh dear. Why don't I like the sound of this?'

'I'm going to tell you something in confidence but unfortunately I can't give you chapter and verse. You'll just have to trust me.'

'OK. I trust you.'

'And you know I only have your best interests at heart.'

'Blimey, Mum. Sounds like you're going to deliver some ethics lecture!' Her brief smile was half-hearted.

'Why don't you come straight out with it? It's not like you to shilly-shally,' he asked, his eyes suddenly narrowing.

'Well, it's delicate. And you're not going to like it.'

'Try me. I've had lectures before – many times and oft!'

'But this concerns – Donella.'

His smile died. He was suddenly very still.

'What about her?'

'See. I told you you wouldn't like it.' Roberta stalled.

'OK. Go on.'

'You're going to think I'm just interfering.'

'And aren't you?' There was a slight edge to Nicholas' question, but she could only sympathise.

'No. Not in the way you mean. Only because I love you and want to save you future heartache.'

'Hmmm.' He made no attempt to disguise his scepticism.

'I ... know something ... about her. I can't tell you what it is. It's confidential stuff. But it makes her ... unsuitable ... as a partner. Long term, I mean.'

'What on earth are you talking about?'

'In my professional life, I learned something. Something that concerns Donella. And if you knew it, you would agree there's no future for you with her.'

'For goodness sake, I'm not about to elope with her or anything.'

'But you *are* romantically involved with her, aren't you?'

'Yes, of course. You know I am.'

'Well, I don't know how far it's gone.'

'With all due respect, Mum, it's none of your business.'

'I know. But you seem to be more interested in her than the other girls you've dated. And your future *is* my business – if it's in my power to prevent you making a huge mistake. Isn't it?'

'Maybe.'

'And better to say something now before it's too late. One thing leads to another and, before you know it, it's the real thing. The longer you're together, and the deeper the relationship, the harder to call a halt. I think you ought to know this now before you get in too deep.'

'So you're telling me really to drop her?'

'Well, more or less, I suppose I am. But only because there can't be a happy future for you with her.'

'Happy for me? Or her?'

'Both.'

Nicholas was clearly completely bewildered.

'Didn't you like her?' he asked in a boyish voice.

'Oh yes, Dad and I both thought she was charming. And I can quite see why you fell for her. She's lovely.'

'Noble of you!'

'You know what I mean.'

'Yes. She's a stunner! And she's bright. And she's a high-flier. And she's conscientious. And she's kind and generous. And she's the sort of perfectly behaved creature you can safely bring home to meet the parents.'

'Nick ...'

'*And* she saved *me* from ruining my career.'

'But ...'

'But you think I should throw it all back in her face. On your say-so.' His tone was biting.

'That's not fair, Nick.'

'Well, that's what it feels like from where I'm sitting. I'm surprised at *you*, Mum. You always told us boys we should respect girls' feelings and emotions and all that jazz. Treat them gently.'

'And you *should*. And believe me, I wouldn't be saying any of this if I didn't *have* to. And I *still* want you to be gentle about it.'

'Nothing much gentle about being dumped in full flight!' Nicholas said with feeling.

'Is this so serious already that you see your future with her?'

'I haven't a clue. I'm not thinking of settling down for ages yet. Maybe it's for the long haul – this thing with Donella – maybe not. We've never talked about it. But I know she's different. I haven't felt like this about a girl before. That's not to say I'm hearing wedding bells, Mother, so don't read too much into it. I just haven't had a relationship this long or this intense before. That's all. But Donella's that kind of girl. She's not the superficial kind.'

His look and tone gave her all the insight she needed to make her redouble her efforts.

'Nick, I wouldn't be saying any of this if I didn't have a compelling reason to do so. And believe me, even from our parental point of view, on the surface Donella seems perfect for you. But this thing ... I can't *not* warn you. I mean, put yourself in my shoes. If I said nothing so as not to annoy you now, and you got deeper and deeper in this relationship, and ended up making it permanent, and then things went horribly wrong, and you found out I'd known all along and I could have prevented it – well, you wouldn't think I was much of a Mum if I just didn't tell you. Would you?'

'But I can't think of anything that bad. Not that you couldn't tell me about.'

'But this is. Well, not exactly *bad*. But not the sort of thing that makes for happiness.'

'So, let's say I believe you. I can't just dump a girl who's done nothing to deserve it – nothing that *I* know about anyway. I'd have to know why, have a reason.'

'Oh, I'm not suggesting you should – just dump her. Not unkindly, I mean. That'd be quite wrong.'

'So do I just say, "Mum says I've to stop seeing you"?'

'Of course not ...'

'Well, she deserves better than that. And even if I wanted to – which I don't – I can't just drop her.'

'But maybe ... going to Brazil ... would make the break easier ... on you both.'

Nicholas' eyes flashed with anger. He drew back from her with a look which shocked her.

'If this is a ruse to get me to change my mind on *that* subject then *no*! I will *not* do it!'

Roberta looked around anxiously, but his suddenly raised voice didn't seem to be attracting unwelcome attention. She leaned across to speak in a low tone.

'It's no ruse. Come on, Nick. You know me better than that.'

'Do I? Since Donella came on the scene I'm not so sure.'

'Fair enough, I'll come clean. Listen to me – without interruption, yes? Please?'

'OK. But this had better be good.'

'Please don't hate me for this. You know I – neither Dad nor I – have ever tried to use our connections to get you on. Neither of us approve of that sort of thing. And I know *you* haven't wanted it, either.' Nicholas nodded his assent vigorously. 'But because this thing – this thing that I know about, that concerns Donella – is so serious, I did something – something I found very hard to do actually. I broke the habit of a lifetime and traded on my friendship and long association with Jed Leonard. I rang him up and asked him if he could take you for your elective. I hoped you'd just go, and the thing with Donella would just fizzle out, and no-one need be hurt.'

'Talk about conniving ...!'

'Nick, I love you. And I wanted to protect you. I wanted to spare you the knowledge that there was something about Donella you wouldn't like, *and* to make it less hurtful for you to part. It had nothing to do with me wanting to force you into a career path of my choosing. I was desperate, Nick. I couldn't think of any other way to get you out of a predicament you didn't even know existed. But you were stubborn. You wouldn't listen. That's the only reason I've had to tell you – about this thing that I know about Donella.'

There was a long silence.

'Must be very serious information to make you do that, I guess.'

'It is, Nick. It is.'

'Then you should tell me what it is.'

'I can't.'

'Not even on a need-to-know basis? I mean, it affects me personally, so I need to know in order to make up my own mind about the risks.' The appeal tugged at her heart.

'No. It wouldn't be right.'

'Can you not tell me what *sort* of a risk it involves? I mean, if it's medical, criminal, or – I don't know. What sorts of risks are there?'

'It's a combination of things. But I can't be more specific without betraying confidences.'

At that moment the waitress appeared with a pot of coffee. They accepted a top-up without looking up at her. She withdrew from the tense atmosphere as rapidly as she could, spilling the milk as she placed it between them.

'Does Donella know?' Nicholas asked, as soon as she was out of ear-shot.

'I don't know for sure, of course, but I suspect not.'

15

'Who else *does* know?'

'I really don't know. The only person *I know* for sure knows is the family GP – the one who talked to me about it.'

'Does Dad agree with you that it's serious stuff?'

'He doesn't know about it. I wish I *could* talk to him about it – get his advice. But it was confidential information given to me in my professional capacity. And because Dad knows Donella's Mum there's a double reason not to tell him. I never told a soul at the time – nor since. I didn't even tell Dad why I was trying to organise your elective away from here. Apart from our strict rule about medical confidentiality, I wanted to protect Donella from curious thoughts as well as avoid questions I'm not at liberty to answer. No, I haven't told a soul – till now, when I told you – well, just what I've said.'

'Which in reality amounts to nothing. Except that Donella's got a skeleton in her cupboard.'

He looked hard at her. She held her breath. The silence felt interminable.

'There are times when I wish I wasn't so rigid on medical confidentiality. I'd give a lot to be able to share this particular thing with someone else – well, Dad anyway. But especially at this moment – with you and Donella linked – it wouldn't be fair. For your sakes. Not mine. But, believe me, Nick, it's a heavy burden to carry alone.'

Nicholas looked at her closely. She was surprised at the hand suddenly extended to cover her own.

'Thanks, Mum. I know you're only wanting the best for us. But I'm an adult now. I have to make my own decisions, my own mistakes. It's too big a step to take – in the dark, so to speak.'

'I know ...'

'I don't want to do it – for *myself*. But worse than that, I don't want to hurt *Donella*. What would it do to her? I mean, if I don't give her any explanation. It could wreck her trust in men.'

'I see that. But if all she sees is you moving on – just getting immersed in work in Brazil – isn't that kinder than her knowing it's because of something about *her*?'

'Lesser of two evils maybe, but still I come across as an irresponsible, insensitive thug who drops a girl when something more exciting comes along.'

'I'm sorry, Nick. I'd give a lot to spare you this.'

'Well, I can tell you, I hate the idea – totally. And at this precise moment I can't see myself doing it. But I can see it's something pretty awful for you to go to these lengths.'

'It's not a reflection on Donella herself,' Roberta hastened to reassure him. 'I should have said that. She's an entirely innocent part of this whole thing.'

'That doesn't surprise me. She's a real innocent – in lots of senses. But thanks, Mum. Nice to hear that – in one way. Doesn't make it exactly easier to even contemplate dropping her, though.'

'I know. She's a lovely girl. And normally I'd be so happy for you that you'd found such a super girl – whatever the outcome long term. And I know she's been a stabilising influence in your life.'

'She has.' Nicholas was turning his spoon over and over in the saucer, staring at it unseeingly. 'Like I said, if she hadn't come along when she did I'm not sure I'd still be in medicine.'

'Nick – I hope … you're not in this too deep already.'

He shrugged his shoulders, telling her nothing.

Roberta watched him, waiting, afraid to press her point further.

He suddenly braced himself, looked up and said in an expressionless voice, 'OK. I hear you.'

'And Brazil?'

'I don't know.'

'But you'll have to make arrangements.'

'I know.'

'And I'll need to tell Jed Leonard.'

'OK. OK. *OK*! I'll let you know by the end of the week if Brazil is on. Or off. But even if I *do* go, doesn't mean I'm dropping Donella. They're different things. And that's personal.'

'Fair enough. I understand.'

Realising the subject was closed Roberta did her best to return the conversation to a more mundane level but they soon abandoned the attempt and she drove him back to the university on her own way home with a heavy heart.

17

THREE

Nicholas' thoughts were chaotic.

He had to admit to himself, he was tempted by the Brazilian offer. Travel, adventure, new experiences – it was just the sort of package to appeal to him under normal circumstances. A welcome break from the sameness of student life here.

But it stuck in his throat that his mother had pulled strings.

Curious that. She was normally so strongly averse to any form of nepotism. She must have had a compelling reason to break her own rule. But what could there possibly be about Donella to make her feel such an urge to separate them? It had to be serious – at least in her eyes. She didn't normally interfere. So, it was important in her estimation, but would he share the same opinion? Impossible to say without more facts. If only she wasn't such a stickler for the rules of ethics!

On the other hand it was precisely because she was so principled that he trusted her. If only he knew what it was that she feared.

But did he really want to know something unwelcome about Donella?

Donella. Something inside him thrilled at the mere thought of her. She aroused in him such a welter of emotions, feelings that he hadn't really stopped to analyse before. They just enjoyed each other, being together. They were young. They had years ahead of them before they had to ask serious questions, make permanent sorts of decisions. Both of them were determined to do well in their degrees and careers. She would understand if he decided to go. He could encourage her to do something similar for her elective.

But would he?

The thought of her being on her own for a year while he was away was bad enough. No, he had to admit he didn't like to imagine her without him for so long. She was … well, there'd be plenty of other young men only too ready to fill his shoes.

So did he want to commit himself to her? No, he knew he wasn't ready for anything that serious. So why not just go then?

But if he went, on what terms did he leave Donella? He couldn't in all fairness ask her to put her life on hold while he went swanning off to an exciting new life.

Round and round the questions spun. Serious introspection was a novel experience for Nicholas. But he'd promised his mother an answer by Friday.

Four days.

He had four days to make up his mind. Less, in reality, because he was having dinner with Donella on Wednesday. She deserved to know first.

But as he prepared to meet her, he found he was still frustratingly undecided.

Preoccupied with his dilemma, Nicholas was unaware of his own intense scrutiny. He only knew that with Donella sitting opposite him in the little French restaurant, his thoughts were chaotic.

'Have I got food on my nose? Or blotched mascara? Or something?' In spite of her light tone he sensed her embarrassment.

'I'm sorry. Was I staring? No, you look lovely. As always.'

Under normal circumstances he would have injected intimacy into the compliment but today he dared not.

She did indeed look enchanting tonight. Her shining chestnut hair was caught up high on her head, with curls escaping loosely down one side. A string of amber beads twisted through a silk scarf around her throat exactly complemented her colouring and made him want to kiss the hollows on either side of her neck, the creaminess above the scooped neckline …

He dragged his eyes away. Not tonight. This was dangerous thinking. He must stay in control. He must concentrate.

The perplexed frown, the confused glances, told him she was picking up his abstraction. So the tension was palpable.

'You seem distracted. Are you OK? Is it your results?'

He didn't want her to be sympathetic. Not tonight. It was unnerving.

'Sorry. No, it's not the exams. I'm just not good company tonight. Something on my mind.'

'D'you want to talk about it? Or do you need distraction more?'

'Both, I guess. Well no, I *need* to talk about it, but I *want* distraction!'

'Listen first, distract later?' she asked with a teasing smile. 'I'm happy to listen, if it's something you *can* share with me.'

Nicholas plunged before he could procrastinate again.

'I've been offered the chance to go to South America – to Brazil – for my elective.'

He kept his eyes lowered, watching his restless fingers occupied with the pepper mill on the table.

'Brazil!'

He felt her stare, knew she was willing him to look up. He didn't. He daren't.

'Yeah. Once in a lifetime offer. Working with some top notch guy out there – into tropical diseases.'

'And are you going to go?' She was forcing herself to speak evenly.

'I'm thinking of it.'

He glanced up briefly but instantly looked away from the expression in her eyes.

'When would you go?'

'As soon as I get all the paperwork and injections and everything sorted out.'

'How long for?'

'The offer's for a … year.'

There was a long silence.

Nicholas dragged his eyes up to her face. It was veiled, expressionless, guarded.

He wanted to take her in his arms and tell her he couldn't go, not if it meant leaving her behind. He told himself sternly they were both young, only students. It was far too early to let personal things stand in the way of careers.

'What d'you think? Would you go if you were in my shoes?'

It wasn't a fair question and he knew it. He hadn't consulted her, asked her how *she* felt about *him* going.

'I don't know. Depends what the alternatives were, I guess.'

She was giving him the opportunity to say she was one of the alternatives – at least on a par with Brazil in his priorities.

'Nothing else as exotic, that's for sure.'

He concentrated on brushing the tiny pile of pepper dust into a mound on the tablecloth.

'And when have you to decide by?' It was polite. Horribly, impersonally polite.

'I said I'd give my answer by the end of this week.'

'And what does it … depend on?'

She was offering him a second chance.

He wanted to shout, 'You! You! YOU!' Instead he made himself say quietly, 'Just me deciding if it's what I want.'

'Oh.' There was a long pause. 'And is it?'

He dared not look at her again.

'It would certainly be a fantastic experience. Dr Leonard is a legend in his own time. And I've always wanted to travel more.'

'So what's making you hesitate?'

He swallowed hard. The mute appeal in her voice tore at his resolve.

'Well, I didn't think about tropical medicine as a specialty – before this came up. I always fancied doing something in the surgical line for my elective – learning some unusual technique or other.'

'How did you hear about this offer then?'

'Friend of a friend sort of thing,' he said vaguely with a dismissive wave of his hand. He couldn't drag his mother into this. It sounded so underhand, so privileged.

'Friends in high places, eh?' It was a simple remark, completely devoid of sarcasm. 'Could be useful.'

'We'll see. I haven't decided yet. But thanks for letting me talk about it. Now what would you like to do by way of distraction?'

His tone became brisker, he straightened in his chair, and looked across at her with raised eyebrows.

Confusion, hurt, bewilderment jostled for dominance before her gaze fell from his. She glanced at her watch, feigning surprise.

'Gosh, is that the time? I'd better go. I promised I'd phone a couple of friends tonight to chat about a beastly lecture we had this morning on skin diseases, and I absolutely must get my bacteriology assignment printed off before old Jackson sends me another snotty email. D'you mind?'

'No, of course not. If you must. I'll run you home. Just let me pay the bill.'

He waved to attract the attention of the waiter.

'No, please. I'll just get the bus.'

'You most certainly will not! Since when did I allow a lovely young woman to make her own way home at night? My revered parents would have a conniption at the very idea of my forgetting all they ever taught me! Gentlemen do not abandon ladies to an uncertain fate at night.' He strove for a comic air, failing dismally.

The journey back to Roslin seemed interminable. Nicholas racked his brain to think of innocuous things to discuss, but suddenly now everything held undercurrents. It was impossible to regain their old ease. Unspoken questions, half-finished thoughts, hung suspended between them. He stabbed at matters dermatological but could remember nothing of his own two weeks in that department, so was soon forced to abandon even that effort.

He cursed himself for his indecision. What a mess he'd made of it. He hadn't meant to finish things tonight. He'd wanted to just ease off enough to leave a question mark over their future, give them both space to think while he was away. But to backtrack now would be worse. He couldn't rebuild hope only to dash it cruelly later. Misery and confusion tied his tongue and dulled his brain.

As he came to a halt outside her parents' house, he automatically turned the ignition key. Donella sat for a moment uncertainly, the sudden silence seeming to demand action.

'Donella – I'm sorry – it's all so confusing. I've handled this badly,' he began.

She slipped out of her seat and was out of the car before he could even put his arm around her. For the first time she turned to look at him directly.

'I think I get the message.'

'Can I ring you – let you know what I've decided? Hopefully things'll be clearer by Friday.'

'If you like. Thanks for the meal.'

He watched her walk up the path away from him without a backward glance. Only as she opened the door did she turn to give a polite wave before she was gone from his sight.

He remembered nothing of the drive back into town. All he was aware of was the hurt crushing his very being. What could possibly warrant doing this to *any* girl? And more especially *this* one. But he fought off the impulse to ring her and put everything right again.

It was three o'clock on Friday afternoon when he finally got through to her on her mobile phone. She'd been on the wards most of the day or in the library, and kept it switched off.

'Can we meet somewhere?' His request was tentative. He had to try to explain.

'I'm going home early tonight – I've got a dental appointment at five fifteen. But I could fit in ... perhaps ... quarter of an hour?' It wasn't encouraging but it was something.

They met in a small garden fenced in by high tenement buildings.

'So you've decided?' Donella asked, as she took a seat on the bench beside him, a safe distance away.

'I have. It's too good an offer to miss. I'm going,' Nicholas said, but immediately rushed on before his courage deserted him. 'But I wanted to say something. I know I handled it badly the other night. And I'm sorry.'

Donella said nothing, keeping her eyes fixed on her fingers smoothing the knotted fringe on her scarf.

'I'm going to miss you ... a lot.' Nicholas struggled to keep his voice from cracking. It came out scarcely above a whisper. 'But I can't ask for anything. A year's a long time. Maybe ... I don't expect ...' Impossible to go on.

If only he could go, leaving the door open, with the sparkle back in her eyes. But he had to be fair to her too. Things could so easily get out of hand if he weakened now. He mustn't commit to more than he could fulfil.

'It's OK. I understand.'

'I'm so sorry. I wish ...'

'I must dash. Good luck in Brazil. I really do hope it works out for you. And ... thanks for being a ... a friend when I needed one.' He heard the trace of a quiver in her voice.

Instinctively he stood as she rose to leave.

Something beyond their control passed between them. Pain recognised pain. They held one another tightly for a long choked moment before Donella ran from the garden. Nicholas watched her receding figure through sudden tears.

FOUR

Donella kept her dental appointment but remembered nothing of it.

Staring up at the ceiling in her room afterwards her thoughts inched painfully back through the week. None of it made sense. Up until last weekend there could be no doubting Nicholas' affection. Now he was going to South America without a backward glance. Nothing about staying in touch. No token of love. Nothing beyond a vague apology – for what? Raising her hopes? Dumping her? Doing it badly?

Had she just been a pleasant interlude? Conveniently around to be his escort and companion until he moved on? Had he been amused by her responsiveness? She blushed to think of how absurdly gullible she must have seemed. What an innocent abroad!

Well, she'd learned a big lesson.

The hurt was too raw to verbalise and she immersed herself in work to exclude solicitous enquiry. She stayed late in the library; she shut herself away in her room at home tackling her assignments with gritty determination.

Only with her father did she share anything of her bewilderment.

She had always loved time spent alone with him. He had a quietness about him which she found soothing. When he suggested a good brisk walk to counteract the effects of Sunday lunch she found herself welcoming the prospect.

They set out at a fast pace, heading out into the country, conversation superficial and undemanding. Towards the top of a particularly steep incline, Declan begged a break.

'Wowwa. I'm not as young as I used to be. And I don't want to be left to your tender mercies to be resuscitated, thank you very much! Not until you're properly qualified, at least.'

She laughed back at him and stopped. He was panting in an exaggerated way, and holding his sides, as he caught up with her.

For several minutes they stood in silence surveying the tranquillity around them. Then, unexpectedly, Declan moved closer and slipped an arm around his daughter's shoulders, giving her a quick hug.

'I'm sorry, love. I'm so sorry.'

She felt the tears prick her eyes.

'Thanks, Dad.'

It was too much. His grip on her heaving shoulders tightened, but he made no effort to put his comfort into words.

When the sobs were eventually stilled it was Donella who spoke first. 'Sorry. What a baby! I thought I could be adult about this.'

'Nothing wrong with a bit of a weep. It'll do you good.'

'I just don't know *why*, Dad. One minute we were fine. Next minute – wham! It's all over.'

'Didn't Nick give you any explanation?'

'Only that he'd had an offer to go to South America for a year. For his elective, you know.'

'Maybe he didn't want you to feel you had to hang around waiting for him.'

'But he could have *said* that. Given me the option at least. And it didn't seem like that. It felt like he suddenly lost interest. I wasn't useful any more.' She hadn't known there was so much bitterness lurking beneath the control.

'Oh, surely he wasn't using you like that!'

'It didn't feel like it at the time. But why else would he just dump me when something new came along?'

'Well, he didn't seem that type to me – the times we saw you together.'

'Maybe he was more casual about it than I realised, but too well-mannered to let me know it.'

'And it was more than casual – for you?'

She nodded with tight lips. 'I thought it was for him too. He didn't *say* so, not in so many words. But you know – he *acted* like it was important to him too.'

'And nothing specially happened – to make him change? You didn't have a fight or anything? Any sort of disagreement?'

'We never did fight.'

'Well, no. *You're* not the fighting kind!' His smile warmed her in spite of the rawness. It was true though; she had inherited his own even, gentle temperament.

'No. There was nothing – nothing I knew about anyway.'

'He wasn't looking for … more … than you wanted to give – or anything?'

'Well, not that I knew about.'

'It's just that, well, young men can be impatient, you know – sometimes anyway. Specially where a beautiful young woman is concerned.' He gave her an affectionate hug to soften his words.

'Oh, I know *that*. But we'd discussed that. We knew where we both stood. No, I really don't think it was that. I just don't know.'

'So when did you start to notice a change?'

'Not till that evening in the restaurant – on Wednesday night. He'd booked it to celebrate the end of the exams, you know. It was a special treat. We don't – didn't – often eat out … I'm sorry. I'm not usually such a cry baby.'

24

It was abominably hard readjusting. But she was grateful for his silent presence while she struggled to regain control.

'He kept looking at me – but like I was somebody he hardly knew. And when I asked him what was troubling him he just said about going to South America. As if it wouldn't affect me.' She brushed the tears away impatiently. 'It was like we were just casual acquaintances.'

'And no explanation?'

'Well, not then. But when he told me on the Friday he'd decided – he was going to Brazil – he said he wanted to apologise for "handling it badly", as he put it. Said he was confused, didn't know what to think. A year was a long time. He couldn't expect anything.'

'And doesn't that suggest he didn't want to tie you down?' Declan ventured.

'Maybe. But it was … it was like he was acting out a script somebody else had written for him. I mean, you know, you've met him – you wouldn't describe him as slow of speech, would you? And it was one of the things I liked about him, you know – before, I mean – he wasn't afraid to talk about feelings and everything. But this week … well, it just didn't fit somehow.'

'Tough thing to do though, eh, dumping somebody you've been close to? I've never done it personally, but I can imagine it would be.'

'But he could have told me why, couldn't he, Dad?'

'I don't know, love. Depends why, I guess.'

'I'd have understood if he'd been sort of cooling off for a while. But he wasn't. Well, at least I didn't notice if he was.'

'And you couldn't ask him why?'

'Well, I wasn't expecting it. I had to read between the lines that he was dropping me. By the time I got the message it was too late for an upfront approach. Besides, I didn't want to get upset in front of him. It would've made me look a real country bumpkin!'

'You are *not* a country bumpkin. You are a very lovely and very wise young woman,' her father said, giving her another squeeze.

'But too naïve for my own good by the look of things. Better toughen up! Doctoring here I come! Exit wimp, enter tough guy!'

It was the signal for an end to the subject and not until they neared the house did she make any further reference to their conversation.

'Thanks, Dad. I wish all men were like you.'

'Heaven preserve us!' Declan recoiled in mock horror. 'Speak to your Mum some time. She'll tell you about all my weaknesses!'

The shared laughter warmed Judy's heart as she watched her husband and daughter walk up the garden path together.

FIVE

Donella was surprised to find how easily she was upset by unexpected things.

A snatched song overheard as she passed an open window reminded her of Nicholas strumming a guitar, singing a love song, looking straight into her eyes. An exotic waistcoat displayed in a shop window looked like the kind of garment he would have chosen for a student function – something that made him stand out in a crowd. A hearty laugh from a young man standing with friends in Bristo Square might have been Nicholas holding court immediately after an exam in the McEwan Hall, regaling them with ridiculous answers he'd given – or would like to have given.

She turned away from all these reminders with bleak eyes and a weeping heart.

But everywhere she turned there were couples. Young men and women absorbed in each other – on benches, in doorways, in the lecture theatre, in restaurants, in cars – everywhere.

She felt very alone. And utterly miserable. Even work had lost much of its appeal. The huge void in her life – a Nicholas-shaped void – dominated her thinking. But he was in South America, she was here. And between them there was a broken space – a fracture beyond her power to mend.

Her twin, Graeme, coming home for a long weekend, was shocked by the change in her. She had always been a sparkling personality, teasing him out of sulks, making light of difficulties. He was the serious one, the brooding kind. Now he was the one trying to cheer her. She felt his gathering anger.

'Come on, Donella. No bloke can be worth this.'

'I'm sorry. I can't help it. I don't *want* to feel like this.'

'He's a selfish fool – must be.'

'No. That's not fair.'

'He wasn't exactly *fair* to you, was he?'

'But he wasn't like that. Not before. He was kind and … sensitive and … well, really good fun.'

'Well, I don't understand you falling for someone like that, I must say. I thought you had more sense.'

'But he wasn't …'

'Well, *he* didn't love *you* – obviously, even if you thought you loved him.'

'But that's just it, Graeme. He did. He said he did. And he … behaved as if he did.'

'But if he really loved you he wouldn't have hurt you like this.'

'Well, he was probably being cruel to be kind.'

'How d'you fathom that one out?'

'Well, we're both young. He probably didn't want to tie me down. This way we're both free – free to mix with other people, date other people, move on.'

If her brother heard the bleakness in the prospect he gave no sign of it.

'It's probably a good thing he's gone to Brazil or I'd be tempted to do him a mischief for what he's done to you.'

'Pistols at dawn, eh?' Donella tried to laugh.

'Good riddance, I say.'

'But you've always been jealous of my boyfriends ...'

'None of them have been good enough for you, that's why,' he muttered, 'and this just confirms it!'

'Nick was different. Honestly, Graeme. He was. There must be some explanation I just don't know about. I guess I was just naïve, bowled over by the glamour of being dated by someone so sophisticated. I'll get over it. But don't be so harsh on him. Please?' she wheedled.

'Don't tell me you're intending picking up where you left off when he comes back?' She heard the sharp question in his voice.

'I can't imagine that's likely.' If only ...

'He doesn't deserve you, so forget him.'

'I'm trying. Honestly.'

'I hate to see you getting hurt. That's all.'

'I know. And I love you for it. But I've always got you. Nothing like a twin for solidarity, eh?'

She gave him a quick hug which he returned fiercely but perfunctorily, and the subject of Nicholas and his behaviour was dropped.

The unexpected reminders continued for months, but gradually, imperceptibly, the hurt eased. Donella discovered she sometimes had whole days when she didn't think about Nicholas at all. So it came as a shock when she thought she saw him in a queue of traffic. She looked again just as the lights changed to green, and the black Audi drew away. Yes, it was.

Had he returned early? Had Brazil not worked out?

All the careful schooling of her thoughts was to no avail. Her heart beat painfully. She waited breathlessly for his phone call. She imagined him everywhere.

But no message came.

It was another six weeks before she saw him again. This time he was walking along George Street, heading straight towards her. She felt a choking sensation constrict her throat. Should she acknowledge him? Or should she dive into a shop and pretend she hadn't seen him. Her brain seemed like porridge. She couldn't think. He was almost level with her when their eyes met.

'Donella?' The voice held a question.

'Nick.' It came out in a squeak. She coughed, hiding her face behind her hand for a moment. The gesture provided a logical explanation for her red cheeks anyway. When she looked up he was smiling.

'I'm Michael, actually. Sorry. Nick's twin. We're always getting confused. But you *are* Donella, aren't you? Not *her* doppelgänger?'

'That's right. I am. I'm sorry – you must get fed up being mistaken for each other. How nice to see you again.' She took a deep breath. Best get it out immediately before her courage deserted her. 'And how's Nicholas?'

'Fine – as far as we know, anyway. Never a good correspondent, Nick! He's having an amazing time from the little we *do* hear though. You know he went to Brazil – yes?' The deep blue eyes were looking anxiously at her. Did he know her feelings were fragile?

Donella nodded mutely. It felt uncanny standing so close to this man who looked like Nicholas, sounded like Nicholas, but wasn't.

'It's an incredible experience. He's lucky to get a chance like that,' she said.

'Always the kind to land on his feet, Nick.' He laughed. 'Leads a charmed life. Trains and planes wait for him. They've just gone if *I* arrive a minute late!'

She gave him a tight little smile.

'So you're not identical in everything?'

'Far from it. Nick's the colourful one. I fade into the background. He's the life and soul of the party. I'm more the stay-at-home variety. But what about you? You're a twin, aren't you? I think Mum told us once we'd all four met as toddlers – some twin study or other.'

'That's right. As *my* Mum tells it, I was a serious threat to your carefully constructed sandcastles when I was about two!'

This time the laughter was more natural.

'And are you like your twin?'

'Not at all. Graeme is the quiet one; I'm more outgoing. He's a brooder; I'm the positive kind. But we're close for all that. We look out for each other.'

'Funny thing, eh, the twin bond? We're the same. We'd do anything for one another.'

She felt a sinking feeling. Was he telling her he supported Nicholas' desertion?

'Is Graeme a medical student too?'

'No, he's a linguist. *And* he branched out and went down to England to university, to London actually. And you? You did sociology, didn't you? Doing your doctorate now, I think Nick said?'

It was comfortable, moving onto neutral territory. She had space to be impressed by the simple terms in which he described his own PhD work; so many students made what they were doing sound so complicated and high-flown. He seemed very unassuming.

28

'Look, it's lovely to meet up again. And I'd love to chat more but I don't want to hold you up. Where are you heading? Can I come along with you?' He sounded genuine and she accepted his offer with a smile.

It was a disconcerting experience. She couldn't resist a sideways look at him periodically; he was staggeringly like his brother. But it was also comforting to know she could be with this Nicholas-lookalike without crumbling. All good preparation for when it was the real thing.

Even so, when he suggested they meet again, she hesitated momentarily. Was it asking for trouble? His suddenly anxious look changed her mind and she accepted with a smile. Besides, it would be a legitimate excuse to hear more of Nicholas, to steel her against his homecoming.

SIX

The experience was disconcerting for Michael too.

His mind was uneasy. Why had Nicholas ended their relationship?

Watching her now, he felt and saw the hurt. He'd have to tread carefully. The last thing she needed was anything to compound that pain. It'd help to know a bit more of the background so he didn't inadvertently upset her.

She seemed like such a lovely girl – why would Nicholas want to be rid of her?

He emailed his brother.

> *Hi Nick. Bumped into Donella today. She asked after you. I thought I'd take her out for a meal – try to keep things friendly. But not knowing the facts, there's a danger I might make things worse. Can you tell me why you ended it? OK if it's too private. Mike.*

Impressively the reply came back the same day. Nicholas wasn't always near enough to modern technology to collect his mail but on this occasion he'd been actually working on the computer when Michael's message came through.

> *Hi Mike. How was she? Is she still sore with me? I wouldn't blame her. I cringe when I think about all that. Complicated story but basically Mum warned me off. She arranged this trip to get me away. I don't know all the facts myself. But I'm not proud of my part in it. I handled things badly. As a matter of fact I didn't intend to end it – not permanently anyway. Just cool things. But it all got out of hand. And I didn't want to tie her while I was away. But I know I hurt her. I just didn't know how to put things right without promising too much. If you see her again be nice to her for me. Donella's special. She deserved better. Give her my love. Tell her I often think about her. Nick.*

Michael was even more mystified. His mother just wasn't the interfering kind. But she had always been the sort of mother they could talk to frankly.

She was uncharacteristically cagey when he phoned her that night.

'I'd tell you more if I could, Mike. But it's not mine to tell.'

'OK, I understand you can't tell me the details, but why warn Nick off?'

'Because of the consequences if he got too involved.'

'What consequences?'

'I can't say specifically. Unhappy things though.'

'But she seems such a nice girl, Mum.'

'I'm sure she is. We liked her too. I've nothing against *her* per se.'

'So it wasn't that you were being mother hen protecting your chick, trying to keep him all to yourself, then?' He was only half teasing.

'Of course not! You know me better than that,' Roberta retorted briskly.

'I thought I did. But this doesn't make sense. And I can't imagine it did to Donella either. For goodness sake, Mum. What must she think of our family? *I* felt embarrassed I can tell you, even talking about Nick. And it was nothing to do with *me!*'

'Was she ... did she seem to hold it against him?'

'No. She didn't. She was lovely. That made it even worse. Well, she was obviously embarrassed to see me – at first when she thought I was Nick. But once she realised it was me, she was lovely. Asked kindly about him too. Not a hint of bitterness. *I* was the one ill at ease – on her behalf. I felt ashamed to be associated.'

'Maybe it wasn't a serious relationship for her ...?'

'You're kidding! From what I saw when they were together I doubt that. And she doesn't seem like the kind of girl to spread herself around thinly. Besides I could *see* the hurt.'

'Oh. Oh dear.'

'Did you even check though, Mum – before you waded in with your advice? Check how committed they were?' Michael surprised himself with the critical tone in his voice. Donella's pain must have really got under his skin.

'I tried to warn Nick as soon as I knew about Donella – who she was, I mean. But it was only to protect them – before they got too deeply involved. As I thought ...' Her voice petered out.

'But – you can't just *assume*. Even if it *was* early days – they could still have felt a lot. Some relationships start in at the deep end. You know that. And anyway they'd been seeing a lot of each other. For ages. So it wasn't a flash in the pan thing, whatever else it was.'

She was silent.

He ploughed on, his annoyance on Donella's behalf gathering force. 'And just because she's so nice, you can't just ride roughshod over her feelings. Without explanation too. Well, Nick says he didn't give her an explanation. I don't suppose he said *you'd* told him to dump her! You can't trade on somebody's good nature like that. Surely she deserves an explanation.'

'I know. I'm sure she does. But I can't give it. I just can't, Mike. It's not in my power. Other people are involved. It could damage lives.'

'But what about *her* life? This could have damaged her – a lot.'

'I know. And I'm sorry if she's been hurt. But I was genuinely trying to protect everybody.'

Was she? Did Donella's protection come into this? Or was she really protecting Nick? Or the Halley family? The doubts in his mind were pricking uncomfortably.

'Well, if you want my opinion – which you probably don't, but I'm going to give it anyway – medical ethics sucks if this is what it does to a nice girl like that!' he retorted sharply.

'It *does* suck – as you put it – sometimes. There isn't always a right way forward. There was no *one* right way forward then. But I had to do what I thought best in the light of what I knew.'

'And I'm sure you *did* do what you thought was right. But right now it doesn't feel like the right thing to *me*. And I wish you could give me something to go on, so I could do something to repair the damage.'

'Well, you could always blame it on me. Tell her *I* urged Nick to go for advancing his career. Make me the pushy Mum. I can take it.'

'I'll see. Depends how she feels about it. If it's worked out well for her it mightn't need anything. I'll see.'

'Mike ...' There was a long pause. Her voice was low, hesitant. 'Be ... careful.'

'Meaning?'

'Don't get too involved – yourself.'

'Huhh! Not much danger there! Don't imagine she'd trust a Halley again, do you? *I* certainly wouldn't if I were in her shoes! Besides I get the distinct impression she sees me as a substitute for Nick. Not very flattering, eh? But almost certainly true.'

'I'm sorry, Mike. I wish I could be more upfront with you. I really do.'

'OK. I can see there's no mileage in pressing you. I only hope I can do something to say *I'm* sorry, at least.'

He rang off with a sense of pent-up frustration at his own powerlessness.

Meeting him again for their first meal together Donella felt suddenly shy and ill at ease. She struggled just to enjoy his company but doubts and questions seethed below the surface.

What were his motives for asking her out?

Did he feel sorry for her? If so, she was at a disadvantage.

Was he trying to compensate for his brother's cruelty? If so, she felt patronised.

Was he Nicholas' emissary? If he was, he wasn't giving very clear messages.

She dreaded reference to Nicholas. Even when his name didn't crop up, she lived in minute-by-minute fear that it would.

And always there was the nagging anxiety about her own precarious control. She didn't want to betray her hurt and bewilderment to his brother. Besides, it would be wrong to drag Michael into something which was private and between Nicholas and herself, not his quarrel.

She did her best to respond to his infectious smile, his easy good humour, but everything about him was too much like his brother.

Eventually Michael leaned on the table and looked at her directly.

'This isn't working, is it? Can I say something – try to clear the air?'

'If you … think …' She broke off abruptly.

His look was gentle.

'I don't know what Nick did, except that he left you in the lurch. But I feel he's always here between us. And I'm a bit scared to mention him, and you're probably scared in case I do.'

She shrugged sheepishly.

'And you're probably wondering about me too. So it might be best if I come clean. I'd like us just to be comfortable with each other.'

It was comforting at least to know he had gauged her feelings so accurately.

'I'd like that too,' she said, meaning it.

'I gather you and Nick were close – really close?'

She nodded, feeling the familiar surge of emotion riding on a wave of nausea.

'And that he just suddenly called it a day and went off to Brazil?'

She nodded again. The bleakness returned with its old force, the harsher for being vocalised.

'Forgive me. But I think I have to be blunt?'

She shrugged.

'And I think *someone* owes you an explanation.'

Her attention was suddenly riveted. Did he know why Nicholas had just left her? Was she about to hear the information she'd been longing for all these months? She focused on his lips, forcing the image of Nicholas a pace away.

'I suspect that even Nick didn't know how close you'd become until he went away. I had an email from him a couple of days ago – I wrote and told him I'd met you. He sent his love. Said to tell you he thinks of you often.'

She felt the tears prick the back of her eyes and blinked hard. He reached across to touch her arm briefly.

'I'm sorry. And he also said he isn't proud of what he did.'

She blew her nose hard and he waited until she was more composed.

'The only other thing I know is that it was our mother who pressured him into pursuing this foreign thing, working at his career,' Michael went on. 'I don't understand it, I have to say. My Mum is usually great about letting us make our own decisions, learn from our own mistakes. But whatever the reason, she put some pressure on Nick to go. In fairness she probably didn't know how involved he was with you.'

She pursed her lips but said nothing. Maybe.

'Maybe she remembered how he'd mucked about when he first went to uni and nearly blew his chances altogether,' Michael suggested.

'Well, I know about *that*. He did too. But then he really got stuck in. And after that he did well.'

'Thanks in no small measure to your own good influence, as Nick tells it,' he said, smiling at her.

She flushed again, lowering her gaze to hide her own emotion at the recollections his words conjured up. It was how they had become close in the first place, studying together, encouraging each other.

'Anyway, it was Mum who pressed him to go – Nick says so and Mum confirms it. I don't know if that helps?'

'It helps to *know* anyway,' she said cautiously.

'It doesn't excuse Nick if he hurt you though,' Michael said stoutly. 'And for that matter I guess makes him look a bit weak – just doing what Mamma suggests.' The tone was lightly mocking, but how else was he to avoid portraying his brother in a poor light and still be fair? 'Of course, I know Mum can be persuasive – and she's usually right. Irritatingly so at times.' Again he was striving for a lighter touch.

'It probably wasn't all one-sided. Part of it was probably my fault,' Donella said quietly. 'Maybe I read too much into his attentions.'

'D'you think perhaps *he* was scared – about too much commitment?'

'I don't know. Maybe he thought I'd make demands, or want promises or something.' She was shaking her head. 'But I wouldn't have. I really wouldn't have. I wouldn't have stopped him going to Brazil. I just wish he'd talked to me about it. I wouldn't have held him to anything.'

'Maybe he was scared *he'd* make promises – and then not be able to keep them. Is that possible?' Michael was tentative. 'I mean, parting isn't easy. Maybe he was afraid he'd say more than he intended – you know, in the heat of the moment. Perhaps he was trying to protect you both. Being clumsy, I'm sure, but maybe not … cruel?'

'I don't know. I just don't know. I just wish he'd explained.'

'I've no right to ask.' Michael was hesitant now, feeling his way. 'But – if he came back now – would you want him to pick up where you left off?'

'I don't know. I just don't know any more. There's too much pain and too many unanswered questions. It's all confused now.'

'I'm sorry. I really shouldn't have asked.'

'It's OK. You've been very kind.'

'Will you believe me when I tell you that I'm not trying to defend Nick or be his ambassador? But I do feel badly – on behalf of the family – for what he did to you. And I want to be your friend. If you can forgive the Halleys enough for that.'

It was her turn to reach out and touch his sleeve.

'There's nothing to forgive *you* for. You've been lovely. Thank you for persisting. I nearly avoided you ...' – her voice dropped suddenly to a whisper – 'because I was scared.'

After a heavy pause she looked up at him through her wet lashes. 'I'm glad to have had this chance to talk about ... what happened ... with somebody ... who knows Nick. I can't talk to other people. I don't want them to think badly of him. But you *know* him. I can talk to you about it without worrying you'll think the worse of him.'

'I *do* think the worse of him – for hurting you. But I still love him. Whatever. He's my brother. You'll understand that – having a twin of your own.'

She nodded. 'Thank you for making me change my mind – *not* avoiding you, I mean. And I'll *try* not to let Nick come between us. I'll try.'

'I'd like that. I'd like us to be friends for our own sakes not because of the past. Can we start with a clean slate?' His eyebrows were raised in question.

'I'd like that too.'

'Shake on it?' He extended a hand tentatively.

She placed her own unhesitatingly in his and they shook hands solemnly on their promise.

Anxious not to have them thinking ill of Nicholas, Donella shared this new information about the role Roberta had played with her parents. Her mother's reaction surprised her.

'Well, I suspect there's more to it than his career,' she said crisply.

'Meaning what, Mum?' Donella asked.

'There's a bit of snobbery in it somewhere, *I* think.'

'Snobbery?' Donella was completely mystified.

Judy nodded, wrinkling her nose.

'Well, we used to meet periodically when you children were all part of the twins' study at the university – you know, when you two and the Halley boys were all little. I got to know their Mum a bit. We had some nice chats too. She seemed friendly enough, but whenever I suggested we meet up informally for coffee or whatever, there was always some excuse or other.'

'But their mother – she's horrendously busy. I mean she's kept her career going *and* had four kids *and* been a real Mum to them – doing things and everything. And working as a busy GP – it's no picnic.'

'Oh, I know. There was always some really good reason. And I'm sure she *was* busy.'

'She *was*. Genuinely. She *must* have been. Even when the twins were little and she was pregnant, she did locum work to keep her hand in. She worked in the Roslin practice as a locum for a while, she told me.'

Declan's eyes flashed across to Judy. He seemed to be watching her for a long moment. But he said nothing.

'OK. So she was busy.'

'But?' Donella looked challengingly at her mother.

'Well, I wonder if perhaps she didn't want to get involved with us. Not quite in the same league.'

'Mum! I'm shocked! And I'm surprised at you.' Donella frowned at her. 'She's not like that. Not in the least. I went there a couple of times and she couldn't have been nicer to me. They both were. Lovely people. And in spite of their positions they are really nice ordinary folk. They went out of their way to put me at my ease. And the boys – and their sisters – they're all the same. Not a bit self-important. So I think you're being unfair.'

'It's maybe just the tigress instinct,' Declan said soothingly. 'Your Mum doesn't like to think her daughter was rejected so she's looking for an excuse – someone, something to blame it on.'

Judy looked across at him reproachfully.

'So you think she thought I wasn't good enough for her precious son, is that it?' Donella spoke more haltingly, thinking about the idea. It didn't square with the Roberta she had seen. But in any case, whatever the mother had thought, it had been the son who had rejected her.

'No. It was a silly thing to say,' Judy said quickly. 'Dad's right – as usual. I'm just hurt because you were hurt. I have no real reason to think unkindly of Roberta.'

'*I* don't, Mum. I'm sure she had her reasons. And after all, Nick's an adult. He's responsible for his own actions.'

She jumped up suddenly and went to play the piano vigorously before her composure crumbled further.

She was vaguely aware of her father's anxious glances, but pounded the keys with determined force. After a while he got up as if to go to the kitchen, pausing on his way to give her shoulder a quick squeeze.

It was too much. With a crash of discordant notes she jumped up from the piano stool and fled to the privacy of her room, closing the door hard to let them know she did not want company.

Watching her, Declan's mind was in a ferment.

Their previous GP, Dr Farnham had moved on now. She was the only one who knew his secret. As far as he knew no-one else in the practice had been involved. He'd demanded she didn't enter the facts into their notes.

But if Nicholas' mother, Roberta, had worked in the Roslin practice, had she talked with Henrietta Farnham? Did she know? Was that why she'd warned Nicholas off? It made sense. He'd have done the same in her position. But did that mean she'd told Nicholas?

Who else knew? How long before somebody let it out to Donella or … Judy? Even yet, all these years on, Declan dreaded Judy discovering the truth, and his deception.

And if Donella found out – well, who knew what it would do to her? Perhaps it was a mercy really that Nicholas had finished with her. He surely couldn't have told Donella the truth – even if *he* knew it. Her father would have been the first person she'd have challenged.

But there was no way that he could ascertain who *did* know. There might be a number of loose cannons out there, just waiting for the right conditions to be set off. He couldn't even ask Roberta. She might have had some perfectly innocent reason for wanting Nicholas to go to South America. She might not have intended him to drop Donella. It might even be that Nicholas himself was ready to end the relationship, just looking for a way to do it as painlessly as possible.

He was letting this thing get out of proportion again. He must be extra vigilant, not let his own behaviour arouse suspicion for a second time.

SEVEN

Michael continued to see Donella occasionally, choosing active pursuits like bowling or brisk hill-walking over the potentially more fraught situations of quiet meals or evenings in. But he knew too that part of his own interest stemmed from curiosity. It was obvious why Nick had fallen for this girl in the first place, but how could he have given her up in that brutal way? And what was it about her that his mother had objected to? He smiled wryly: forbidden fruit tastes sweet.

For her part Donella welcomed the opportunities to enjoy innocent fun without the necessity to dredge up emotion. She felt her early reservations melting and even started deliberately to introduce Nicholas' name into the conversation. It was all good preparation for the day when she must see him again in person.

At first she had taken precautions: telling herself firmly this was Michael, reminding herself frequently while she was with him. Each new reminder brought a fresh wave of disappointment, of sadness. But as the weeks went by Michael became a person in his own right. She anchored her thoughts on the differences. He was less flamboyant in his dress, quieter in his manner, less volatile in his emotions. She began to feel more relaxed in his undemanding company.

And he knew nothing of medicine. It was wonderfully refreshing to get right away from medical matters.

They understood the arrangement. It was comfortable, uncomplicated. Gradually, imperceptibly, the rawness of Nicholas' betrayal began to heal.

When Michael rang her early one Saturday morning, he seemed in a particularly exuberant mood.

'It's a beautiful day, a day I simply can *not* spend stuck at the keyboard. How about a hefty dose of sunshine and recreation? Go on! Give yourself a day off. It'll refresh the parts the mouldy old books and lecture notes won't – yes?'

'Get thee behind me Satan!'

'Go on!'

'It's all right for you postgrads. You've already proved yourself.'

'Hardly! I've got a thick old thesis waiting to be scribbled, remember, before I've proved anything. But hey, let's not think about work. I'm not in the mood for it. The sun's shining. Come and enjoy it.'

'I've got an exam on Monday. There's a stack of stuff in front of me about hypertension. Yuck! But I've got to get it into my brain somehow.'

'I'll help you. I could test you. Your brain will be the brighter for a blast of ozone, I guarantee.'

'You're tempting me.'

'How about a quick whirl across the water? There's a stately home in Fife I'm itching to see. And then I'll treat you to fish and chips. And I promise you I'll test you on your blood pressure stuff. You can have one of my chips extra for every right answer.'

'OK. You've persuaded me. But if I fail …'

'I'll personally go and explain to your tutor it was all my fault!'

The castle looked imposing in the bright sunshine and they wandered first in the grounds, before exploring the interior with its colourful history, its treasures, its architectural splendour. It was closing time before they eventually emerged.

There was only one place for fish and chips – a shop in Anstruther famous for selling the tastiest portions in the country. They drove to the beach to eat them, and were the only people sitting on the rocks as the sun sank towards the horizon.

As promised, Michael asked Donella questions about hypertension. She laughed at his crazy pronunciation of the complicated medical names. Then, duty done, like carefree children, they kicked off their shoes and frolicked in the water, skimming stones and trailing seaweed through the waves.

'How about our own personal conga along the water's edge before we head back?' Michael laughed down at her. 'It's excellent treatment for blood pressure!'

'Absolutely. Perfect way to end a perfect day.'

She fell in behind him, her hands on his waist. He placed his hands over hers. They danced to the rocks on one side and right back to the other, making their own music, before they collapsed breathless on the sand again, leaving a double snake of footprints behind them.

'I don't want this day to end but end it must,' said Michael rising reluctantly to his feet and holding his hands down to her, 'so up you come, young lady, and I'll return you to your wicked step-sisters before you turn into a pumpkin.'

She screwed herself up in a ball and drummed her heels on the sand.

'No, no, no. Please don't let them turn me back into a slave. I like being a princess. I want to stay in a castle and live happily ever after.'

'And so you shall, my pretty, so you shall, quoth the fairy godmother.'

Michael waved his hand exaggeratedly over her before scooping her up in his arms and running off towards the car with her. She clung on tightly as he jumped unevenly over the rocks, and then sped across the sand. He was quite out of breath when they arrived but held her still while they laughed together.

Their faces were close together when their eyes met and held. The laughter died. There was a long frozen moment. Then suddenly, too conscious of their proximity, Michael put her down quickly, she released her hold abruptly.

They both got into the car, closing the doors, not daring to look at each other. Michael started the engine and the car slid smoothly into the road and headed home. It was several minutes before either spoke.

'I've always loved the sea – always dreamed of living where I can see it every day,' Michael said evenly, eyes firmly on the road. 'Probably stems from happy outings when we were children.'

'Mmmmm. Me too. But even a few hours, like today, leaves you feeling as if you've had a holiday, doesn't it?' She took her cue from him. 'My face feels weather-beaten already.'

'Best cure for study-fever I know!' The smile was back in Michael's voice.

They chatted spasmodically until Donella started to doze.

Noting her drooping eyelids, Michael was quiet, only occasionally glancing across at her.

He was grateful for the silence, finding it increasingly hard to concentrate on idle chatter.

That moment in the car park had taken him by storm. He had told himself repeatedly this was Nick's girl; he was only trying to make reparation for a great wrong. Certainly he enjoyed her company but in an easy undemanding way. They both enjoyed the simple pleasures and could be themselves. There was no need to try to impress her, or compliment her, or treat her as anything other than a comfortable friend. He could tease her and be natural with her.

His mother's voice rang in his ears: 'Be careful, Mike, don't get involved.' He had dismissed the idea as ludicrous. There was no way he would move onto his brother's territory, no chance she would be interested in him. That confidence had given him the freedom to be easy with her, to see a lot of her. It was simple friendship.

He glanced across at her. Her long hair lay tangled on her shoulders where the wind and sand had left it. She hadn't bothered to even brush it out. That spoke volumes for her relationship with him. Effortless. Entirely without artifice. Her face was warmly coloured where the sea air and sunshine had caressed her skin, devoid of make-up. Natural. Her long legs were curled in a relaxed attitude as she slept. This was not the posture of a girl who had anything on her mind but the happy tiredness of a few hours beside the sea.

Yes. He had imagined it. That look. It was merely the product of a light-hearted day together playing like children. But …

He told himself sternly to get a grip on himself, not to start complicating things by imagining … what? What had he imagined? He didn't know himself. It must have been an illusion.

He determinedly avoided looking across at her again.

Donella kept her eyes shut. Deep breathing helped to still her pulse, and even out her breathing.

This was crazy thinking. For one split second it had been Nicholas looking at her with that look he reserved for private moments when he wanted to kiss her. It was alarming that she had reverted to that old feeling of breathless anticipation after all this time.

Michael had done so much to help her relax and forget the hurt. And after a wonderfully happy carefree day, in a twinkling she had almost lost herself in a reckless move.

She told herself again: this is Michael. Nicholas has gone. He's in South America. He's not coming back to me. This is Michael. Dear, dependable, uncomplicated Michael.

She sneaked a look across at him beneath her lashes. Yes, there he was, calmly driving, relaxed, at ease, just himself. She devoutly hoped he hadn't been aware of her momentary flash of lunacy. She closed her eyes again to give herself more time to repeat her mantra.

By the time they arrived back at her home she had 'woken' up and was ready to smile at him happily and thank him for a perfect day out. He even dropped a brotherly kiss on her cheek before she got out of the car.

'You're great company. It's like being on a family day out again, romping on the beach with Nick and the girls.'

'Thanks hugely. And it's my turn to think up something for our next fun day off!'

'Look forward to it.' He grinned. 'Good luck with that blood pressure stuff! And remember, if they ask for the best treatment, tell them, a day out at the seaside. And if they don't like it, just refer them to me!'

She was still chuckling when the car drove out of sight.

Yes, the day off had done her good.

EIGHT

From that point on, Michael was on the alert. He hadn't realised the subtle changes in himself until one of his flatmates, Alicia, who had long had her own eye on him, teased him about being in love. He was swift to deny the accusation, but made a firmer internal resolve to be cautious.

Deliberately, carefully, he began to leave longer gaps between seeing Donella, always scrupulous about explaining to her the necessity to get on with writing up his thesis. Several times he noted her sudden hard look. Not wanting her even to suspect he might repeat his brother's treatment of her, he made a point of telling her later just what sections he had been working on, he discussed the latest breakthrough in the work and spelled out the deadlines he'd set himself to ensure he made steady progress. Whether or not she was reassured that he had indeed been working, he could only surmise. He forced himself to persist in the effort.

Under any other circumstances, had he not wanted the relationship to continue, he would have gradually tailed off his invitations. But this was the last thing he could do with Donella. He felt trapped. Either way the problem was being compounded with the passage of time. Whatever else, he owed her an explanation. The pressure to say something mounted. But his whole intention had been to make recompense for the hurt she had received at his family's hands. He couldn't bring himself to add to that hurt.

When she rang to suggest a hill walk and picnic he could think of no quick reason to decline, although he had intended to work at polishing one of his chapters that day. But then, a tramp outside might provide just the situation to say something, and end this tension.

They set out early to make the most of the daylight hours, arriving at their destination in time to walk first, and return to the car for food later, rather than carry it with them.

It was a grey but still day, just the right temperature for a brisk pace. But as they climbed, the clouds grew darker and an ominous yellowish tinge edged the blackness. Large drops of rain heralded a coming downpour and Michael shouted above the rising wind urging her to run for a hut about fifty yards to their right. They arrived breathless but before the heavens really opened.

Collapsing on the single wooden seat they stared out at the transformed landscape. The noise on the roof of the hut was thunderous as the sheets of rain bounced on the metal. Without warning there was a sudden flash of lightning. Michael was completely taken by surprise when Donella clapped her hands to her ears, curled herself up in a ball on the seat, and sat rigid, waiting. The roll of thunder made the hut vibrate. When she uncurled herself enough to peer out at him, he was grinning at her, thinking she was fooling around as usual. Her parchment white face and hugely dilated eyes showed him her fear was unfeigned. She sat like a frightened animal – tense, ears pricked, waiting. With the next flash she shrank back into herself, wrapped her arms around her head, and curled her body tightly into itself. Her panic was palpable.

Instinct made him move closer and throw his arms around her. She was rigid in his hold. He could feel her trembling. In a sudden lull in the noise of the rain she told him between chattering teeth that she had two horrors – thunder and lightning, and bats. It was irrational, she knew, but she couldn't help it. As she dived down against his chest with the next crash, he looked above her head to check anxiously for bats in the eaves. A combination of both phobias would be too much!

The storm increased its intensity. The flashes and crashes converged. Michael tried to offer comfort, telling her with his mouth close to her ear, above the battering of the rain, how his father used to give him 'scrunches' when he was frightened as a small boy. A 'scrunch' was a very tight hug, with the boy Michael all scrunched up in a ball so that his father's frame surrounded him. It made him feel safe, protected. He knew his parent wouldn't let him come to harm; he stood between the boy and danger on all sides. Michael remembered not being able to tell where his father ended and he began. He was sheltered, secure in the grown man's strength.

Michael tried to laugh as he demonstrated how he could protect her in an enveloping 'scrunch' when she shrank against him with the next flash of lightning. Donella was a long way from laughter but told him she was glad he was there. Michael's laughter too died. This was not the child Michael on his adult father's lap. This was a very well-developed Donella held close to a very disturbed young man.

On his own in the hut under other circumstances Michael would have been fascinated by the effects of nature. Now he was conscious of nothing except the storm within himself. He hoped she, in the agitation gripping her, would not be aware of his own trembling breathlessness. He had no choice; he must see her through this crisis. Instinctively he stroked her head as she hid on his chest, glad not to face her open gaze.

Waves of misery washed over him. He could not exploit this situation. He must not delay this further. He must – today, after the storm, once she had recovered – explain to her he couldn't take it any more. He knew only too clearly that to her he was simply Nick's brother. But he couldn't answer for the consequences if they continued to see each other, and the last thing he wanted was for her to be hurt again. This must be the last time he held her like this. But how to tell her so that she was not left with a second feeling of rejection? He must emphasise it was because she meant *too much* to him, not too little. Just contemplating the break made him groan inwardly as he pressed her close to his body with the next crash of thunder.

Gradually the storm abated, and the rain eased. Donella took a long time to relax, peeping out from under her sheltering arms periodically to check if the danger had passed. Only when the sun came out and the rain stopped altogether did she allow herself to sit back on the seat and give him a sheepish smile. Her face was still ashen and he could see her hands still shook.

'I'm so sorry. What a baby. I know it's pathetic. Thanks for humouring me,' she said in a croaking voice.

'No problem. I'm sure you'd do the same for me if a tarantula ever came within sixty feet of me,' he grimaced. 'We all have our Achilles heel.'

He stood up and walked over to the door of the hut. She still looked so vulnerable; the temptation to take her back in his arms was too great.

'It looks settled enough to venture down again now. Unless you want to go up higher?' he commented without turning around.

'I think I'm too wobbly to risk any more climbing. Sorry. I'm afraid I'm ruining your day out.'

'Not at all. I actually love watching storms so this has been an unexpected treat for me. Sorry it was so awful for you though.'

'I could wait here – if you want to go on up,' she suggested in a hesitant way.

'No, I'll come back down too. We can't have you sitting here terrified out of your skull, can we? Besides, I'm starving, so I'm game for returning to the car and that scrummy picnic you've got stashed away.'

Delicious the food may have been, but Michael struggled to do it justice. Donella was still too shaken to do more than nibble, and they had made little impression on the basket when they packed it away in the boot and turned for home.

It was a full twenty minutes before Donella stopped trembling and again apologised.

'I'm feeling really bad about ruining the walk – and your day out. What a fool to be so scared.'

'Don't be. I understand.' His voice sounded stiff even to his ears.

Silence returned. He felt her occasional close scrutiny, and his fingers tightened on the wheel. He dared not look at her or give a reassuring smile.

'I'm afraid I've made you cross inside. But you're too nice to say so.' Her voice sounded small.

'What makes you say that?'

'You're ... very quiet. But you've every right to be cross. I don't blame you.'

Without answering he swung off at the next turning and drove in silence until he came to a quiet road with a rough stretch of ground under trees. He switched off the engine and sat with his hands still tightly grasping the wheel for a long moment.

'I'm sorry,' she said again.

Taking a deep breath he launched into the most difficult speech of his life.

'Donella, I'm not in the least bit "cross" as you put it. But I *am* about to be the one to spoil the day.' He had to stop to muster his courage. There was no going back now. 'I've been racking my brains for weeks to think of a way of saying this. But there *is* no easy way. So I want you to hear me out – the whole thing. And I hope at the end of it you can find it in your heart to forgive me.'

She sat motionless.

Still he stared straight ahead, not daring to look at her.

'When I first met you – that day in George Street – I felt desperately sorry for what my brother did to you. I just wanted to reach out and show you how sorry I was. You were so generous, you didn't hold it against me. And I felt we became friends. I've loved our times together. You're fun, and you're warm, and you're witty, and, well, I think you're just lovely.' He had to stop and swallow hard several times.

Donella sat unmoving. He felt her frowning intensity.

'But for weeks now I've known it can't go on – seeing each other, I mean. I can't do it. I've tried. I really have tried. The last thing in the world I want to do is hurt you. But I just can't do it.'

The silence was so long that Donella whispered, 'Why?'

He struggled for control.

'First Nick. Now you. Why?' Tears were choking her. He must reassure her.

'Because … because I've stopped thinking of you as Nick's girlfriend. I can't treat you as just a friend. I know you only see me as Nick's brother. And I'm afraid you're going to end up having a dim view of all Halley men. But if we continue like this I'm going to end up ruining everything.'

'I don't understand.' He heard the bleakness in her voice.

'You need friendship – uncomplicated friendship. I can't give it. I've tried to. I've tried to crush all the other emotions. But they won't *be* crushed. Not any longer. I just can't stop myself – from loving you. And the longer it goes on the harder it gets. I've nearly lost the plot – several times. That day at the beach in Anstruther, I realised it first. And today – up in the hut, with you in my arms. It's more than I can handle. I'm sorry. I can't trust myself to even look at you *now*, or I wouldn't say what I know – I've known for ages – I *have* to say. For your sake. You must believe me. It's only because I care *too much*, not because I *don't* care, that I have to say – it must stop. I've tried seeing you less, to see if I could get things back to how they were, protect you from another hurt – but it doesn't work. It just makes it harder when I *do* see you.'

'And do *I* have any say in this?'

'You can tell me what a heartless creature I am, tell me how pathetic I'm being, call me any name you can think of – it won't be anything I haven't called myself.'

'Before I do' – there was a strange note in her voice but he remained resolutely staring ahead – 'will you tell me in words of one syllable what you're trying to tell me. So I'm quite clear where I stand.'

He knew it was fair. In his effort to spare her he'd rambled round and round. Crazy for someone who normally prided himself on his command of language.

'I've fallen in love with you. I can't help myself. So we have to stop meeting like this.'

'And *now* can I call you names?'

He nodded mutely.

'You adorable idiot.'

He didn't move.

'Michael. Will you look at me?'

Her eyes were alight with an expression he hadn't seen before. In her still pale face they looked even larger and darker than ever.

'Loving is not a punishable offence. Thank you for telling me. I am so relieved. I thought – I was afraid – it might be … all one-sided.'

'You mean …?' He hardly dared ask.

She nodded.

'At first I was afraid I might be getting things confused – you're so like Nick in some ways. But I knew – deep down – it wasn't that. I tried to tell myself it wasn't there. I was imagining it. I didn't want to lose your friendship by expecting more than you could give.'

He moved towards her but she stopped him. A sudden overwhelming thought had wiped the half smile from her face.

'We can't. Much as I want you to – we can't. Whatever it was your mother had against me for Nick – won't she have it for you, too? We can't let this happen. It would only be harder in the end. I can't bear – not again.'

'I *can't* let you go – not if you feel the same way.'

'I do. I love you too. But I won't be responsible for doing anything to come between you and your family.'

He looked at her for a long moment.

'I don't know what it was. Mum wouldn't tell me when it was Nick but I shall ask her now. Tell her about us. And if she can't give me a satisfactory explanation then I won't give you up. I absolutely *won't*.'

Their eyes held.

'And I won't go along with any form of torture either! So will you get out of the car?'

His stern instruction puzzled her but she obeyed. He took her hand and led her into the trees. Shielded from sight, and without a word, he drew her close. There was nothing tentative, nothing fraternal, about the kiss they exchanged. Neither thought of Nicholas, or Roberta, or the future. The present was enough for this moment.

It was much later that they began to remember the complications.

Was there an element of sibling rivalry here? Might they be mistaking a need to comfort each other for something warmer? Was Michael's wish to make amends for past errors motivating his emotions? Was he some sort of substitute for Nicholas? Could Donella really trust him – another Halley? Could they handle the reaction of their parents? Of Nicholas when he found out?

But through the frankness, they found increasing conviction. There was no doubt. They had both consciously willed this *not* to happen – because of the past, because of the possible complications in the future. Love had grown in spite of their efforts, not because of them.

NINE

Michael found he was surprisingly reluctant to see his mother.

Why had she intervened to separate Nick from Donella? The girl seemed perfect – for Nick *or* for himself. What could his mother possibly have against her? He knew he was procrastinating because he didn't *want* to hear anything which could come between himself and Donella.

When he eventually called at his parents' house he found them enjoying a glass of port and a Wagner opera. The room was lit only by side lamps and he smiled to see them sitting hand in hand. After all the years they had been together, in spite of all the demands made on their time, they still made time for each other. He wanted this for himself.

'To what do we owe this unexpected pleasure?' Dick asked brightly, turning down the volume.

'Hhmmmm. Outcast from the parental abode now, eh? Have to make an appointment. Disturbing a little romantic interlude, am I?' Michael teased.

'It's always lovely to see you. Ignore Dad,' Roberta said warmly, giving her husband a dig with her elbow.

Dick doubled up as if hurt.

'Always takes the kids' side rather than mine,' he grumbled through exaggerated groans. 'No romance left to kill!'

He staggered to his feet, limping to the drinks cabinet. Michael took the proffered glass of port with an affectionate smile.

'So *did* you have a specific purpose in coming tonight?' Dick asked.

'Well, I did actually.' Michael shifted in his seat so that he could face them squarely and gauge their instant reaction.

'Ahha, I smelt a rat from the outset!' Dick replied, wagging his finger. 'How much this time, lad?'

'Fine thanks I get for staying within my budget!' Michael retorted laughingly.

'So, trouble of a non-financial variety. Hmmm. Opting out of university, methinks? Ceiling fallen in at the flat? Or girl trouble?'

'Dick!' Roberta was quicker to see Michael's reaction.

Dick was instantly contrite. 'Sorry, Mike. Go ahead.'

There was another long pause. Michael felt his pulse thudding.

'Remember Donella? Nick's ex-girlfriend.'

They both nodded. He saw his mother's face tense.

'Well, I need to know why you scared Nick off her.'

His father's look spoke volumes.

'Didn't you tell Dad?'

She shook her head. Dick turned to look at her.

'Tell me what?'

'That I set up the Brazilian thing – to try to get Nick away from becoming too involved with Donella.'

'Well, I didn't know it was a set-up. But fair enough. He was very young – still a long way to go before he qualified. And with his track record for skiving, he probably didn't need the distraction of a pretty girl,' Dick said easily.

'But it was something more than that. Wasn't it, Mum?'

Again she nodded.

'Yes. It was. Something more serious.'

'Would somebody please enlighten me? I feel as if I'm walking in a thick fog here,' Dick protested.

Roberta was choosing her words carefully.

'I found out something – when I was working as a locum – something that concerned Donella. It had – has – implications for her in the future. I didn't want Nick to get embroiled in it. I thought they were at an early stage in their relationship, better to steer him away from trouble before it was too late.'

'And what was this something?' Dick was intrigued.

'I couldn't – I can't – say. I learned it in confidence.'

'And – just on that basis – Nick ended it?' Dick sounded incredulous.

'Well, he didn't *want* to, but I persuaded him – and you helped, you may remember – to encourage him to go to Brazil. It was a fantastic offer.'

'Indeed – but I didn't know about the ulterior motive. Presumably Nick wasn't that infatuated if he just took your advice.'

'It wasn't infatuation,' Michael said sharply. 'He really cared. But I think he was confused too, by Mum. Didn't know what to think. But I know he's regretted it – a bit anyway – since.'

'And the girl?' Dick asked, looking hard at his son.

'Donella.'

'Donella. What did she make of it all?'

'From what she's told me, she blames herself quite a lot,' Michael said quietly, watching Roberta. 'She thinks she maybe misread the signals, read too much into Nick's intentions. She was hurt pretty badly, actually – more than she admits. But I've seen the pain. She's OK *now* – I think – but it left her very insecure at the time. And I didn't know enough to give her anything like a decent explanation.'

'And d'you think Nick did lead her on? Too much, I mean?' his father asked.

'No, I don't. I think it was mutual. They were both in pretty deep. But I suspect Nick was scared – not just because of what Mum knew, but probably a bit because of the potential commitment. You know Nick. All show on the outside but not as confident on the inside. And like you said, he was young. Still a long way to go before he'd think of settling down.'

'So it all left a bit of a mess.'

'Exactly. More than a bit,' Michael said emphatically. 'I met her by accident at first. She thought I was Nick and she was obviously distressed. So I tried to be friendly, help her put herself back together again, you know. I didn't want her to think we were a rotten sort of don't-care family.'

The expression on both their faces showed they were disturbed by this interpretation.

'I knew she wanted some kind of explanation, but I didn't know anything, so I asked Nick. He told me a bit about what happened. Mum told me a bit. But I couldn't really make sense of it myself. So I couldn't excuse him totally, though of course, I tried to put a better gloss on it, to make her feel better. But gradually she seemed to come through it and she relaxed. And we – we just became good friends. We had a lot of fun together actually – you know, just … fun – innocent fun. She's good company; a nice, natural kind of person. She likes simple things.'

He felt the need to emphasise how uncomplicated it had been, how he'd tried to keep it on an easy undemanding footing. Roberta's expression was very still but her eyes never left his face.

'But then it changed – for both of us. We pretended it hadn't to begin with. But well …' He shrugged. 'Anyway, now we both know how we *really* feel. And that's why I came. I need to know, Mum.'

'Are you saying …?' Roberta's words dragged out slowly.

'That we're in love. Yes.'

'Oh, Mike!' Roberta said.

'I know, Mum, you warned me – but it just happened.'

'So?' Dick was mystified. 'Nice girl. No problem, is there? Or is it Nick?'

'Nick doesn't know. Yet. No, it's Mum. She warned Nick off – for some reason. So I need to know – this thing *you* know – would it affect me too?'

'Yes. It would.' She sounded so … desolate.

'So you'd try to dissuade me too?'

'I would, if I could.'

'You know, Donella herself told me I needed to check with you before she'll let this go any further. Imagine that! Lots of girls would have written you off as – well, interfering, to say the least. But not her. Doesn't want *me* to be hurt, she says. Damn it, what about *her*?! Between us we've done enough damage to last her a lifetime.'

'I'm sorry, Mike. It wasn't my intention to hurt her. I was only trying to protect Nick.'

'Well, I'm *not* Nick. And I'm not going to South America, and I'm old enough to make up my own mind, so I'll need an awful lot of persuading that *I* should give her up. So if you've anything to say, speak now or forever hold your peace, as they say.'

'For once I've nothing to say.' Dick ventured a comment to break the long silence. 'I haven't a clue as to what this is about at all. Roberta?'

'I can only say again, I'd rather you didn't get involved.' It sounded so lame.

'Too late for that! I *am* involved. Over my head, as it happens. But tell me. This thing you know, Mum – would it be any worse if she was involved with *me* – I mean, *me* rather than some other bloke?'

'Well for *you*, yes.'

'No, I don't mean me. For her.'

'Not that I know of. Not that anybody could say at this moment.'

'So the risk is just mine then.'

'Well, in a way, yes.'

'So if I'm prepared to risk it, no-one else will suffer?'

'Not really. No.'

'Then that clinches it. If you still can't tell me what it is, and as long as I know *I* won't harm *her*, I'll take that risk.'

'I really don't like the sound of this,' Dick interposed. 'It doesn't seem right for Mike to be taking a risk with his future, without even knowing what that risk is all about, if *you* know what it is and you *wouldn't* take it.' He was looking directly at Roberta. 'Isn't it better if he knows?'

'No. I don't think it is. Not on this occasion.'

'Could you tell *me*? See if I think the same,' Dick asked.

'I wish I could. I told Nick I wanted to tell you but I felt I couldn't – shouldn't even – because it was confidential stuff. But then he took my advice in the end, so I decided it *had* been best not to share the information – even with you. But now it's Mike, I need to think again. Do I share it? I guess it depends a bit how serious your intentions are.' She turned her full attention to Michael.

'Like I said, Donella won't move on at all until she knows what you say. So I haven't discussed the future with her. And in any case it's early days. But I know my own intentions.'

'And they are?'

Both parents looked hard at him as the question dropped between them.

'This is the real thing for me. I have every intention of marrying her – if she'll have me. Only I'd rather have told *her* first, so keep that under your hats.'

Dick whistled. 'Serious indeed.'

'Deadly.'

'So maybe I *should* tell Dad,' Roberta said hesitantly, as if thinking aloud.

'But if you can tell *Dad*, seems batty that you don't tell *me*. I'm adult and it affects *me*, not Dad, after all,' Michael protested

'I totally see your point,' Roberta replied, 'but in the first instance, would you settle for me telling Dad? And if he agrees we *should* tell you, well and good. He knows about medical ethics and all that stuff. Confidentiality, all that. But if he thinks you're better not to know, then will you accept that it's for your own benefit? We know you're adult. And you're strong. But sometimes it just isn't appropriate to pass on information that affects other people. People quite outside our family, in this case. *I* think you'd be happier just not knowing. But I'd be glad of a second opinion. Dad would be a good person to share it with because he loves you too and has your interests at heart. And the information wouldn't affect him in the same way as it might you – being a doctor and all that jazz. He'd understand it in a different way.'

This got more and more bewildering.

'Looks like I don't have much choice,' Michael said with a hint of bitterness. He stood up as he spoke.

'Oh, I didn't realise. You want an answer – right now.' Roberta stabbed her finger downwards to emphasise the immediacy.

'Too right I do! I'm not going back to Donella, only to leave her in limbo again. It's not fair. I'll go up to my old room. Just shout when you're ready.'

As soon as he had left, Dick turned to Roberta with a strained look on his face.

'This feels bad. No wonder the lad's feeling steamed up.'

Roberta leaned forward, her hands gripped tightly together.

'Just before Alexandra was born, d'you remember going to see Judy Robertson and her husband?'

'Yes. They'd recently lost a baby.'

'That's right. A baby with an autosomal recessive condition.'

'Yep. They wanted to talk to me about their options.'

'Well, I was working as a locum in Roslin around that time, as it happens. And their GP talked to me about their case. I didn't realise it was anyone you knew at first. But bit by bit the jigsaw fell into place and I realised this was the couple you knew.'

'And?'

'Henrietta Farnham – the GP – was concerned. She knew things about them that they didn't know themselves. Worrying things. And she didn't know what to do.'

'So she asked you.'

'Yes. You have to bear in mind this is ages ago, so I might not get all the details exactly right, but as I remember, she'd found out a number of things that, put together, spelled trouble.' Roberta checked each item off on her fingers. 'One: they'd had a baby with an autosomal recessive metabolic disorder – I don't just remember exactly which one. Something rare. But anyway it meant they were both carriers of the same gene. Two: they both had Gilbert's Syndrome – as you know, an inherited dominant condition. Three: they were both the product of artificial insemination by donor. Oh yes, and I seem to remember Declan's mother came up here for the insemination for some reason – I vaguely recall that it was something to do with keeping it secret but I might be wrong on that. Oh, and Henrietta was also struck by the physical resemblances between Judy and Declan – and she's right on that at least, I do know. They both have really unusual large dark eyes. Donella's eyes.'

Dick let out a slow whistle.

'You see? See why I didn't want Nick to get involved?' Roberta urged.

'Do Judy and Declan know?'

'They know the individual facts. I don't know if they put them all together and realised what it meant. They certainly didn't know when Henrietta talked to me about it. But she was still trying to decide whether she should tell them. The geneticist – Keith Galloway – had strongly advised against it. But she thought they had a right to know.'

'And you said?'

'I said I'd listen to Keith. He's very experienced. Leave well alone.'

'And the outward signs would suggest she didn't tell them.'

'Inasmuch as they went ahead and had more children – Donella and her brother – yes.'

'And now ... Good grief, Roberta, you've been carrying that around on your own – first for Nick, now for Mike – without sharing it with anyone?'

She nodded mutely.

'Phew.'

'So did I do the right thing by Nick? Tell me honestly, Dick. I've worried myself sick over this.'

'Hard to say for sure. In Nick's case ... you probably did. As Mike says, Nick couldn't have been too certain of the relationship, or he'd have ignored your advice anyway. Must have been some doubts in his mind. In any case that's all water under the bridge.'

'Well, it's not if Nick holds it against me. Or Donella either, come to think of it.'

'Hmmm. Donella. If she's eventually going to be our daughter-in-law we don't want her thinking we know some dreadful secret about her.'

'But we do!' Roberta cried. 'And she probably hates me already for influencing Nick.'

'She won't hate you when she gets to know you better. Nobody hates you.'

'Mothers-in-law are different! You have to tread extra carefully. This is *not* a good start.'

'It certainly feels uncomfortable, I agree – us knowing this thing, but neither of the youngsters knowing it themselves.'

'But if we tell Mike, he has a secret from Donella. And it's pretty obvious her parents – if they know – didn't tell *her*. If *Mike* tells her, what would it do to her? It's a pretty big thing to know something like that about your origins, eh? And maybe her *parents* don't know. She might go storming off and confront them. What a mess! Whether or not they know.'

'And we don't know if they do – and we can't find out,' Dick mused.

'Exactly. We don't know for sure if *anyone* knows except that GP, and Keith, and me – and now you. Oh I know I can trust *you*. But don't you see, Dick? Already the circle's getting bigger. And it gets more and more worrying the more folk who know.'

'Remind me again – what exactly did you advise the GP to do?'

'Say nothing. Hide behind Keith. Best left alone, I thought. It could wreck their lives knowing something like that.'

'And now it could wreck the life of our boy,' Dick said quietly. 'Funny how different things look when they affect somebody close to you.'

'Tell me about it! Our children. Our *grand*children!'

She saw Dick's brow contract.

'So what should we do?' she asked in a small voice.

'Well, my instinct is to check this out. Not divulging any details, of course, but I could contact somebody at the BMA or one of the guys in the Law department, and find out where the Robertsons stand officially. And maybe somebody in genetics.'

'D'you think that's advisable? I mean, if you know for sure won't you be under some sort of obligation to act on it?'

'Possibly. Is that what stopped you?'

'Partly, yes.'

'OK, I'll give it some more thought before I do anything.'

'And in the meantime, what do we say to Mike?'

'I think you're right. Better if he doesn't know. She can't wheedle out of him what he doesn't know. We can play this medical tolerance card you introduced: it's all right for me to know because I'm a doctor, but it's the sort of information best not shared because lay people might get it all wrong. That sort of line.'

'I hope to goodness they never do find out. I can't imagine what either of the boys would feel about us if they knew what we'd kept from them.'

'Don't underestimate them. They'd know you did it for the right reasons.'

'Maybe. Eventually. But it hurts, Dick, to have them talking to me in a way they've never done before. We've always had such a good relationship.'

Dick nodded, understanding.

'It's bound to rattle them when we meddle in their love lives, though.'

'I know. And I do sympathise. But it's tough all the same.' He reached across and placed a comforting hand on hers.

'Thanks, Dick, I feel so much better sharing the responsibility with you – not because you agreed with me, but just not being alone in it.'

Michael looked hard at them both as he resumed his seat.

'Mike, I think your Mum's right on this one,' Dick began in a steady voice. OK, it was very 'Dad': authoritative but reasonable. 'She's told me the medical stuff and it's not the kind of thing to divulge. Because of its effect on other people – not our family – but other people. It *is* confidential stuff and she's right not to have let it go any further. I know it seems ridiculously secretive behaviour to people outside the medical profession, but we do have our code of professional ethics. So I think you have to trust us on this one.'

Michael sat looking from one to the other in silence for a long moment.

'I can tell when I'm beaten. So I won't even try to persuade you any more. But one thing more, Dad, knowing what you know now, would *you* try to persuade me to give Donella up?'

The answer was a long time coming. Hah! So his father hadn't anticipated that.

When Dick did speak it was slowly, without any of his usual breezy style.

'Given everything that's happened, and taking into account the seriousness of your involvement, no, I don't think I would. Not now. But I can sympathise with Mum's reservations, and if you weren't in this for the long haul I'd probably try to dissuade you too.'

'Thanks, Dad. Thank you, *both* – for trying to be honest with me.'

'Mike – you know it's not because we don't trust *you*. Don't you?' Roberta's voice was pleading.

'I know, Mum.'

She jumped up and walked across to give him a warm hug.

'And from the bottom of my heart, I hope you'll be happy, Mike. If Donella is the girl for you, then I hope she makes you truly happy.'

'Thanks. She is. And I plan to concentrate on making *her* happy. She's one in a million,' he said, returning the hug with interest.

Roberta and Dick talked long after Michael had left to return to his own flat.

Roberta was far from easy about the outcome of their discussion. Oh yes, she knew Donella herself seemed a fit and healthy young woman, mentally as well as physically. But who knew what genetic bombshells she was incubating?

And if the young people ever discovered what had been hidden from them, what would it do to them individually as well as to them as a couple? To the whole family.

The following morning Dick told her that he'd decided against checking things out with the BMA – at least for the time being. The less people who even knew such a situation existed, the better. Roberta let her breath out slowly and simply nodded her agreement.

TEN

Donella, impatient for Michael to confront his mother, had earlier toyed with the idea of asking her own parents if they knew anything. But this was confidential medical information, Michael had protested. What if they were completely unaware of it themselves – and happier in their ignorance? Just alerting people to the fact that such information existed, and was known to others, was potentially damaging.

Still she had fretted.

Michael, doing his best to calm her fears, had reassured her: his parents had nothing against her as a person; they thought she was lovely. This concerned other people. His mother had said that. But her unrest had forced his hand; he'd had no choice but to talk to Roberta.

Worries turned next to Nicholas.

Michael promised to email him.

> *Hi Nick. Thought you ought to know that I've been seeing a lot of Donella. And we've fallen in love. You'll understand that at least! Hope it isn't too hard for you to find out. Mike.*

It was a week before Nicholas received the message. His reply was short and to the point.

> *Hi Mike. Congrats. You deserve her. I didn't. Be happy. Nick.*

For very different reasons, Donella hesitated before phoning Graeme.

He said the token right things but there was a conspicuous lack of excitement or enthusiasm in his response, and Donella felt curiously deflated. It grieved her that they seemed to be drifting further and further apart as the years went on. His obsessive jealousy made it hard for them all to be together, and everyone was less enthusiastic about family reunions because of it.

But worries about Michael and Donella were eclipsed in a most unexpected way when Michael's sister, Alexandra, discovered a lump in her breast. She was at Aberdeen University studying law but instantly came home to the support of her parents. On this occasion neither had any compunction about pulling strings to get her an urgent consultation. The real threat of this alarming experience drove imaginary future problems out of everyone's minds. When a needle biopsy proved impossible, tension mounted.

Donella was working in an adjacent ward in the block where Alexandra was admitted for excision of the lump, and dropped in both prior to and after the operation to cheer her with girlish chatter, fashion magazines, the latest CD, and the newest perfume she had discovered. Alexandra welcomed her visits, finding her refreshingly relaxed about the medical reason for her hospitalisation. She found she could talk to this young woman, and ask the brutal questions she kept from her parents. In her artless enthusiasm about Michael's girlfriend, she did more to endear her to Dick and Roberta than any effort of Michael's could have produced.

The lump proved to be benign but by the time the crisis was over, and Alexandra had been dispatched back to her studies, Donella had become very much part of the family.

Their feelings for one another now openly declared, Michael and Donella increasingly resented time spent apart. It seemed a natural step to decide to get married. They had no doubts about their love; they wanted security and permanence.

But in the welter of preparations, as the day approached, misgivings stirred within Donella at the prospect of seeing Nicholas again, for the first time since that awful afternoon when they'd parted. He'd said he might not be able to get back for the wedding, but if he did, how would she feel?

It would be better to clear the air before he came. Just an email.

Hi Nick. Surprise, surprise! I know Michael has kept you posted. But I thought I'd just write to make contact before we meet again.

Last time we parted on uneasy terms. I felt very confused and didn't understand what was going on. But I'd like to clear the air before we see each other again. After all, we're soon to be related!

My only excuse for that awkwardness is that I was very young – and, as you know, inexperienced. I just wasn't prepared for what happened. But I probably should have seen it coming. If I made it difficult for you to dump me, I'm sorry. Hopefully I've learned to be more adult about things since then!

And I just wanted you to know there are no hard feelings. Michael and I are so happy together; I know now things have worked out for the best. I just feel a bit embarrassed that I was so naïve before, and hope you can manage to put all those memories behind you and accept me as a sister – older and hopefully wiser!

With affection, Donella.

Nicholas sat staring at the email for a long time.

Memories rushed at him like an express train. But the overwhelming feeling was one of guilt. He had left her feeling *she* was at fault. It was unforgivable. She had been entirely innocent throughout. He had to set the record straight, restore her self-esteem, correct the error. But how to do so without betraying what he knew? – well, half knew.

It took him hours to think of a suitable response and he was still not satisfied that it captured the right feelings. He dispatched it in the end before he lost his nerve altogether.

Dearest Donella. It was wonderful to hear from you. I've thought of you so often since I left but didn't dare contact you. Congratulations – I'm thrilled to hear you're going to be part of the family. Well, if I'm honest, thrilled at one level, but hugely envious of my brother on another one.

I too am glad of an opportunity to clear the air. But you have absolutely nothing to reproach yourself with about our parting. You did nothing wrong – apart from being too sweet, too forgiving. The fault was all mine – I handled it all so badly. I'm not at liberty to divulge the things that were going on when I withdrew from our relationship – any more than I was then – but I want to tell you, it had nothing whatever to do with you personally. You were never anything but adorable and mature and altogether wonderful. I shall always treasure the time we were together.

That evening in the restaurant, I was hurting too. But I had to be cruel to be kind – to both of us. Believe me, I've wept – literally! – remembering that night. And that awful ten minutes in the garden when I told you I was going to Brazil. I don't think I shall ever forgive myself for causing you so much pain.

I wish with all my heart things could have worked out differently. There has never been anybody who has meant as much to me as you did then. I know now that I loved you more than I realised. And I also know I should have told you how much I cared – but I was young and trying to be cool and sophisticated about these things. Brash young fool that I was! But this will be the last time I can say this to you because I must learn to love you as my sister-in-law from now on.

I'm so glad you've found happiness. And with someone I know you can trust absolutely. Mike is the best. A far more worthy mate for you than I could ever be. And I know he loves you devotedly, so I'm content for you both. Be happy.

Yours always, Nick.

If Donella was surprised by the tone of Nicholas' response, Michael's response reassured her.

'Very Nick' was all he said. 'Are you OK about it?'

'As you say, it's Nick. But kind of him all the same. It'll make it easier when we meet.'

She wrapped her arms around his neck and Nicholas was forgotten.

ELEVEN

Two days before the wedding, the church rehearsal over, Michael and Donella worked late at the flat, packing his possessions ready to take to their new home the following day. The discovery of two bottles of a very good Merlot generated an impromptu celebration and neither was in any state to drive, so it seemed sensible for her to stay the night at his flat rather than trek out to Roslin, only to come in again a few hours later.

Weary from the physical exercise as well as soporific from the wine, she fell instantly into a deep sleep. The clock told her it was three thirty when she woke and groped her way to the bathroom, keeping her eyes almost closed. Odd, someone had left the light on over the wash-handbasin. But the dim light was kind on her sleepiness.

The sudden splash made her start, and her eyes shot to the bath in time to see the young man suddenly sit bolt upright in the water.

'Donella.' The voice came out as a hoarse whisper.

She stared from him to the door and back in disbelief.

'The door was open …'

'Sorry. Force of habit. I assumed everyone was in bed.'

For a long moment they held each other's gaze.

'It doesn't matter to me – but sorry I startled you,' he said in a low voice.

She giggled and instantly stifled the sound.

He looked at her hard.

She giggled again and, lurching slightly, moved towards the bath. She slid down onto her knees and reached forward to kiss him. His fingers slid through her long shining hair. She closed her own hand on his and brought it down to kiss his palm.

'Donella …' His voice was stilled by her lips meeting his.

The cold hardness of the bath pressed against her body. She shifted a little to relieve the discomfort. With his mouth on hers, she felt his hands lifting her to her feet as he rose out of the water himself, reaching blindly for the towel. She was suddenly enveloped with him in the thick towelling, as they stood together on the damp mat, her skimpy T-shirt sodden, her reason drowning.

He started to speak again.

'Don –'

'Sshhhhh,' Donella whispered, pressing her fingers against his lips. 'Don't say anything.'

The caresses, exploratory and tentative at first, increased in intensity, became more intimate. She clung to him, breathing fast. The fire ignited.

It was a long time before they finally drew apart. She felt his fingers tenderly tracing the contours of her back, his lips dropping kisses in unexpected places.

'I guess we'd better get out of here – before someone else comes hammering on the door,' he whispered.

She pulled a face at him, registering the predicament that would pose, but released her hold reluctantly. She took three uneven steps towards the door, but instantly returned to kiss him lingeringly. Then, without taking her eyes off him, she moved more purposefully, slipped the bolt silently, and was gone.

Nicholas stood unmoving where she had left him. He was under no illusions; she had assumed he was Michael. The deceit was all his.

He had traded on the dimly lit room, her sleepy, inebriated state, her innocence. His attempts to tell her of her mistake had been half-hearted. He hadn't wanted to embarrass her, he told himself feebly. She would have felt so foolish.

No need for her ever to discover her mistake. No need for Michael ever to know.

Michael. She was Michael's girl now. The thought was searing in its intensity.

Why had he done it? Was it simply his unresolved love for this girl? The unexpected opportunity? Or had there been a tinge of revenge driving him?

His conscience smote him briefly later as he stood for a long moment looking down at his sleeping brother before slipping into the adjoining bed, but he fell asleep with a smile on his lips.

Next morning Donella was up early and breakfasting when Michael entered the kitchen. She smiled shyly at him but he seemed his usual relaxed self, sliding an arm round her as he passed, dropping a kiss on her upturned face. His flatmate, Dan, was in the room crunching toast so she didn't expect him to make reference to the night before, and the potential awkwardness of that first encounter passed.

Michael had his head in the fridge searching for orange juice when he casually mentioned his brother.

'Oh, by the way, Nick arrived late last night. Still sleeping, of course. I don't suppose he'll surface very early. He never was an early riser. And he's been travelling for ages. But at least he's made it in good time for the wedding.'

'Nick? Oh brilliant. I didn't think he was coming until tonight.'

'I didn't say about the change of plan in case he couldn't make it. I didn't want to raise hopes and have folk disappointed.'

'I'm so pleased that he could get away. It wouldn't have been the same – without your twin.' Donella's pleasure for her fiancé was genuine.

'You'll have yours, I'll have mine. The square will be complete,' he said laughingly.

'Has he changed, d'you think? It's ages since we last saw him.'

'Can't say, really. We went to bed pretty much as soon as he got here. He was knackered.'

Nicholas emerged just before midday full of apologies. Donella was sitting at the table with Michael, making a list of things they still had to do for the wedding, jotting down times by which each must be done. They both looked up as Nicholas entered the room.

'Mornin' all,' he said with a mock salute.

Donella rose instantly, holding her hands out to him, a wide smile lighting up her face.

'Nick, how lovely to see you again. Michael didn't tell me you were coming early. I only heard this morning. What a lovely surprise.'

He strode over and gave her a warm hug. It was all so simple. So natural.

'What? Take a chance on missing this big event? No way! I only have one twin. I couldn't let him lose his freedom without me to hold his hand now, could I?'

They all laughed.

It was uncanny how exactly like Michael he was still. Until you saw them side by side. Then Michael's face was slightly longer. And now she could see the lines around Nicholas' eyes were etched more deeply after his stay in the Brazilian sun. His look flickered from one to the other, whereas Michael's gaze was steady and more intense.

'So tell us about Brazil. What's it like? What do you do?' She was genuinely interested.

Nicholas helped himself to a coffee before taking a seat opposite his twin. He talked of a life they could only half understand. It was evident that the experiences had shocked the impressionable young student and for a time his passionate defence of the underprivileged lent a sombre air to the conversation. Gone for the moment was the ebullience they associated with the young carefree Nicholas who had left Edinburgh so abruptly. In its place was a maturity, a concern which explained better than words why he'd stayed on to work there rather than return as soon as he could to his studies here.

Donella wanted to know all about the medical conditions, availability of drugs and treatments. Michael probed the social conditions, political constraints and availability of humanitarian aid. The three were so absorbed they failed to notice the passage of time until a phone call from Judy reminded Donella that she had promised to meet her mother at the flat she was soon to share with Michael. There were last-minute seating arrangements to be altered, and wedding presents to be collected from various newly arrived guests who wanted to deliver them in person … where was she?

She reluctantly began to gather her things together. This would be the last time she would see Michael before the wedding. Her mother had insisted she spend her last single night at home, not seeing the groom again until she walked down the aisle.

Michael excused himself to Nicholas and caught her round the waist, drawing her into the privacy of the hall, where he took her in his arms. It was a further ten minutes before he let her out of the door to return to his brother.

Nicholas' expression was enigmatic as he looked hard at his twin.

'You, brother dear, are a lucky beggar!'

Michael grinned at him sheepishly. 'Sorry. Didn't mean to desert you.'

'There'd be something amiss if you didn't take advantage of every moment!' Nicholas replied.

TWELVE

Outwardly the event was masterminded to perfection. The church was vibrant with bright colours, elegant outfits, glorious music and huge banks of fresh flowers. All the principal players were too well-bred to allow anything of their inner disquiet to show on this day of all days: the first family wedding on both sides this generation.

But the thoughts occupying the minds of the family in the front pews were not easy thoughts. For Dick and Roberta there was the knowledge that their son was entering a marriage which could have unexpected and distressing consequences. The fact that they had tried to dissuade him did little to ease their anxiety, and indeed had added to the tension as the day approached. It was hurtful seeing Michael guarded in what he told them, in how much he involved them. They had always been so close to their children.

Judy, resplendent in champagne-coloured silk, felt very alone without Declan at her side. In spite of her resolve, the sight of Nicholas in the church was a powerful reminder of the harm this family had brought to her beloved daughter. The knowledge that Roberta had warned him off – for whatever reason – made it hard to meet her too in an open and friendly way. Oh, she would certainly go through the motions, but her heart was at odds with her smile.

For Graeme, sitting beside her, the wait seemed interminable. He sat only feet away from the two men who had done more than any others to separate him from his twin. He could not find it in his heart to forgive Nicholas for giving her up, or Michael for keeping her. Both had eroded that special exclusive bond he had treasured and needed. How could either of these – these *strangers* – ever understand her moods, her needs, as he did? How could they love her unconditionally, as he did? He felt the same urge to smash sandcastles he had experienced that day when they had first met the Halley brothers, when he was two. He averted his eyes from the groom and his best man, and concentrated instead on his sister. She looked so beautiful walking down the aisle on her father's arm. But she didn't once look at him; her eyes were fixed on Michael. He gritted his teeth.

Declan walked tall. No father could ask for a more beloved daughter to escort. And he knew that Donella would always be close to him. He wasn't losing her. He could still protect her – as he'd done in very special ways since before she was born. The thought of his other daughter, Bethany, flickered unbidden into his mind – his firstborn, the daughter who did not grow up to be a bride. His eyes sparkled with unshed tears as he looked at Donella, and he clasped the hand lying lightly on his arm for a brief moment before they began the slow walk to the front of the church. She smiled brilliantly at him before turning to look forward – to where Michael stood waiting. As he saw the look of undisguised adoration on Michael's face, Declan found himself wondering if this young man would be strong enough to support her if – when – the secret finally emerged. Would his new and untried love endure the revelation?

Of all the immediate family, only Alexandra and Josephine, elegant in their forest green wild silk dresses, watched Donella's progress through the church without a qualm. It was their first time as bridesmaids and they were enjoying every minute. They had been spared all the discussions which haunted their parents and brothers, and both girls were warm in their welcome for their new sister-in-law who had already become an ally and confidante.

There had been no competition in the choice of a best man. No-one else came close in Michael's affections.

But seeing them standing together at the front of the church, dressed identically in their morning suits, both watching her approach, Donella was struck by the fascinating picture the twins presented. A mischievous smile played on her lips; what fun they could have impersonating each other. But as she neared them, she felt a sudden surge of doubt: would Michael approve the close-fitting Maid Marion style dress, the simple spray of orchids? She focused on his face and watched his expression answer her question.

The service safely over, much was made of the twinships. The photographer traded on the unusual angle, taking shots of Michael and Nicholas in identical poses, alone or with Donella between them. Then he worked at a series of both sets of twins. On all sides they heard the exclamations. Donella saw with surprise and pleasure that even Graeme smiled for the lens. Attention reverted to the groom and best man. Donella herself had to check which was which, sometimes only a flash of wedding ring identifying Michael.

Nicholas laughingly said in his speech that he'd been congratulated so many times that day that he felt he'd got married himself. As they had predicted, his speech was witty and entertaining and Dick and Roberta learned about a number of occasions when even they'd been hoodwinked by their resourceful sons. He ended with a reassurance to the newly-weds that though he'd had years of enjoyment from changing identities with his brother, by getting married they had beaten even his ingenuity.

As the couple prepared to leave that night Nicholas gave Michael a bear-hug and a gruff, 'You're a lucky dog. Wouldn't mind changing identities right now.'

'Not a chance this time, bro!' Michael slapped him on the back with a laugh. 'This is one act you *don't* get to come in on!'

Donella received an enveloping embrace before her new brother-in-law looked straight into her eyes as he said, 'Remember, I'm the understudy if you ever need one.'

She laughed as she returned his hug with genuine affection.

That night in their hotel room, Michael was a shy lover. It was Donella who encouraged him, and she who set the pace. Afterwards he propped himself up on one elbow to look down at her.

'You are so beautiful.'

'And you are a wonderfully sensitive husband. I liked it being so gentle.'

'I know you didn't want us to wait. But thanks for humouring me. It was only because you're just so special. I wanted this to be special too. I can't tell you how much I've been looking forward to this first time. But it was even more magical than I ever imagined.'

Donella's eyes flickered from his mouth to his eyes. First time? Had he forgotten the night before last – in the bathroom? Had it meant so little to him?

He smiled deep into her eyes before lowering his lips to hers, his body moving to align itself more comfortably with her curves.

'I have every intention now of making up for lost time,' he said in a sultry voice.

In a blinding flash the truth hit her.

THIRTEEN

When her period failed to materialise Donella told herself it was just the excitement of the wedding, and the stress. And going abroad for their honeymoon – that often upset women's cycles. She reassured Michael it would be OK, she'd used the contraceptive as per instructions, she knew what she was doing. She was a *doctor*, for goodness sake – well, almost.

When she missed the next one, it was harder to convince herself all was well.

She went into the chemist three times before she could summon up the courage to buy a pregnancy kit. On the way back she called in at four other shops, though there was nothing else on her list, before she walked slowly home. She made a pot of tea and drank it all, deliberately delaying the moment.

There was no mistaking the blue line. She felt physically sick.

Michael was later home than usual that night, with an evening seminar to attend. He took one look at her and strode across the room to take her in his arms. She hid her face on his shoulder.

'What is it? What's happened?'

'You're not going to like it.'

'What?' He turned her face up to his. 'Tell me.'

'I'm pregnant.'

She watched his eyes widen in disbelief.

'But you *can't* be.'

'I am.'

'But you said …'

'I must have got it wrong. I thought I was OK. But you know …'

'Pregnant? Now?! Hell, Donella – we're *students*! How can we think about a kid at this stage?'

'I know.'

'Bloody hell! Bloody, bloody hell.' It was uncharacteristic language for Michael. But this was no ordinary situation.

'I know.' Her voice ended in a wail of anguish. She'd been over and over the choices for hours and could see no way out of their dilemma.

'How long have we got to decide?'

'Well, if it happened – the earliest – on our wedding night, I'd be two and a half months on now. At the *most*, that's ten weeks. So …'

He flopped down in the chair, his agitated fingers leaving his fair hair looking unruly, absurdly youthful and carefree.

'Hell, after all Dad said. He'll think we're so irresponsible.'

'For goodness sake! Your *Dad's* the least of my concerns! What about *us?*'

She glared at him, tapping her chest as she emphasised the word.

'I didn't mean ... Sorry. Yeah! Of course. What about us? Should we – try and work out – pros and cons?' He was tentative, unsure of his role.

She watched him rummage for a pen and paper, and sit down at the table. His eyes were raised again to hers. Then he abruptly leapt to his feet and came to take her face gently in both his hands.

'Don, I'm sorry – how are you *feeling?*'

'Physically? Fine. Emotionally? Like a combine harvester's driven right through my middle and churned up my entire insides!'

'Did you suspect?'

'Well, when I missed the second time I did. But I didn't want to believe it. So I didn't do the test till today.'

'And do you *feel* pregnant?'

'What does pregnant feel like? I don't know. I feel just great – physically.'

'I can't take it in. Us – pregnant!' He looked as uncomprehending as his words implied. 'We never – ever – calculated on this.'

'So much for being intelligent, responsible people, eh?' She smiled ruefully for the first time, touched by his vulnerability.

They wrote two lists. One for continuing the pregnancy, one for terminating it. Top of the *'against termination'* list Michael wrote 'OUR KID' in capital letters. Donella shivered, wrapping her arms around herself as she stared at the letters. There were persuasive arguments on both sides but her eyes always returned to that line. A new person had been created; could they just discard it without long-term effects?

It was late that night when they finally ran out of items to add to the list. Michael laid it aside with a sigh.

'I think we should sleep on this and see what we think in the morning,' he suggested. 'I know we're in this together but you have the casting vote, Donella. You're the one who stands to lose most – either way.'

Three times he had promised to stand by her decision whatever she chose and to try to be as supportive as he could. She felt only an increasing sense of isolation. Was he protesting too much?

Sleep eluded them both for a long time that night. They held each other tightly, but they spoke little. Donella was grateful. She needed peace to sort out her raging thoughts.

They gave themselves a week to think through the issues. She was sitting up in bed scribbling furiously, when he woke next morning. It was scarcely light and far too early to get up.

He reached out to touch her.

'You OK?'

'Yeah. I think I've decided. What about you?' She brushed her fingers lightly across his cheek as she spoke. He caught her hand in his, pressing it to his lips.

'I know what I'd prefer – personally – but I still think you're the one who should say.'

'And are you ready to tell me? Or d'you need more time?'

'No, I think I'm ready. You?'

'Yeah, me too.' She shivered suddenly. 'This is scary.'

'Come here.' He reached up to draw her down into the bed beside him. 'I want to hold you tight while we do this.'

Grateful as she was for his warmth and understanding, she was only conscious of a sick feeling of apprehension.

'You go first,' he whispered.

'Promise not to just say the same?' She looked into his face searchingly.

'Promise.'

'I think we should continue with the pregnancy.'

She lay with her eyes screwed up tightly, waiting.

'Me too.' His response was so low it was barely audible.

Her eyes flew open. 'You do? Honestly?'

'Honestly. If you can cope with it, I'll do everything I can to help. I've already started looking for a proper job. I'll be more single-minded about getting one sooner, that's all. The thesis is nearly finished anyway. I can titivate it in the evenings, if necessary – get it out of the way. We'll soon have a proper income and we'll manage.'

She burst into tears. He cradled her tenderly.

They talked for over an hour about the changes it would involve before they had to get up and leave for work. As they parted, Michael placed a hand on each of her shoulders and smiled into her eyes with a look she hadn't seen before.

'Tonight, Mrs Halley – almost *Dr* Halley – you and I are going out for a slap-up meal. Don't forget. Best bib and tucker job.'

'We are?'

'Indeed we are. It's our celebration.'

'Celebration?' She looked at him questioningly.

'We're having a baby. Remember?' He grinned at her. 'So far we haven't even congratulated ourselves! See you later – Mummy!'

By the end of the month they had taken in the implications of the pregnancy and were able to allow themselves a sense of wonder at the miracle of conception. But they were not robust enough yet for negative reactions so they kept their secret for several more weeks.

Donella's first trip to the antenatal clinic was a tense one. Michael had intended to accompany her but at the last minute had an interview for a job to attend instead. Her spirits were unaccountably low, and she feared at every turn that staff who knew her father-in-law might become involved.

When the midwife gave her the expected date of delivery, calculated from the scan, Donella instantly corrected her. The earliest date of conception was a fixed point, she emphasised; it *couldn't* have been before that. The midwife accepted her categorical assurance, scribbling something in the notes.

The thought of telling their parents loomed large. Donella was touched by Michael's protective instinct – let him be the one to tell both sides in case of adverse comment – but she declined. The best course of action would be for each to inform their own families, she said.

Michael's own experience was not easy. The silence was unnerving.

'You bloody idiot,' Dick said, shaking his head.

'Dick!' Roberta remonstrated. 'These things happen. You know they do.'

'Yes, I know. But I expected *my own son* … But too late for all that. When's she due? What're you going to do?'

Dick seemed somewhat mollified when he heard that Donella would still finish her course. Roberta immediately offered to help with the baby to make it all possible.

Telling Nicholas was a straightforward matter. Just a statement of fact. Michael simply added a postscript to his normal email message.

By the way, Donella is pregnant. Accident, but we're going ahead.

Back came an instant response.

Wow! You don't hang around! Honeymoon babe?

Donella found it harder to summon up the courage to tell her own family. She was all too aware of her new vulnerability, her volatile emotions.

She decided to test the reaction of her twin before telling her parents. In their youth he had always understood her and been her chief ally, before jealousy of her boyfriends had hardened his attitude. She adopted a cautious approach.

But Graeme was unprepared for this particular bombshell and was silent for a long moment.

'Good grief, Don, didn't you take precautions?'

'Of course we did – but something went wrong. It happens.'

'Well, rather you than me!'

She felt curiously deflated by his dismissal of something so important to her.

'Your husband'll have you right where he wants you now – chained to the house, attending to his creature comforts.'

'Graeme! It's not like that at all, and you know it! I shall finish my course and work as a doctor – as intended. And Mike will take his share of the load.'

'Well – it's your problem, not mine,' he said curtly.

She felt more distanced from him than ever.

Judy and Declan reacted to Donella's news with the same stunned silence at first. But it was quickly replaced with concern for how she was feeling and keeping. Swift and sincere offers of help, to enable her to qualify on time, reassured her that they might be less than enthusiastic but would certainly be supportive.

It was curious, she thought, having children was such a personal decision, but in these circumstances everyone else seemed to think they had a right to judge. But in keeping the decision to themselves, Michael and she had asserted their independence and established themselves as a separate entity.

As the pregnancy advanced, reactions thawed. She had never looked more radiant and healthy. And in spite of her other preoccupations, she applied herself to her studies with energy, gaining distinctions in the exams.

Michael had three interviews in quick succession and was successful in the third one. The post of Research Fellow in the university's Social Policy department carried sufficient flexibility to enable him to complete his doctoral thesis on schedule and graduate as they had originally planned.

But the highest point in the whole experience was the warm commendation of his father on graduation day.

'Well done, Mike. Brilliant work. Not many students finish in that sort of time normally, but you've done it in spite of everything that's happened. I'm proud of you.'

'Donella deserves a lot of the credit, Dad. She been terrific; freed me up to stick at it. And knowing I'd have to support a family, well, that kept the old nose to the grindstone too. It was now or never.'

'Point taken. I take back what I said.'

Dick was generous in his apology, and insisted on taking the whole family out to celebrate Michael's doctorate in style at a plush country house outside the city. He raised a special toast to Donella, warmly acknowledging her role in her husband's success.

Rachael Nicola arrived exactly six days before the official due date, slipping into the world after a short labour and no necessity for analgesia. All four grandparents and both her paternal aunts visited with pride, and Donella breathed a sigh of relief.

Nicholas, completing his medical training in London where his Brazilian mentor had connections, sent effusive congratulations and an enormous basket of roses. He rang Michael to say he'd certainly be up to inspect the latest addition to the Halley family while she was still 'squeaky new'. Graeme sent nothing but a second-hand promise to visit when he could.

It took almost three weeks for Nicholas to arrange time off, and Donella was increasingly aware of very mixed feelings about his impending visit. It would be the first time she had seen him since realising that he was the one who had made love to her in the bathroom. No word had been said on either side.

When he arrived by taxi an hour earlier than expected, she was on her own feeding the baby, and still clutched Rachael to her breast as she opened the door.

'Oops, sorry – bad timing,' he whispered, bending to drop a light kiss on her cheek. 'Away you go and sit down, I'll get the door.'

She returned to the nursing chair beside the hearth, gesturing to Nicholas to come in and sit down.

'I'll just finish this side and then you can take her while I get you a coffee – if you'd like to, that is?'

He nodded vigorously. Watching her absorbed in her task, he was silent.

But he had eyes for no-one but the baby as Donella laid her in his arms with a quiet, 'And this, Rachael, is Uncle Nick, Daddy's twin. Meet your niece, Rachael.'

Motherhood clearly agreed with Donella, and the rest of the family looked on with pleasure and pride as she juggled her responsibilities calmly and competently. There was no word of criticism when two more babies followed in due course, both girls: Fiona and Emily. A part-time research job in the Medical Faculty gave Donella the flexibility she needed and Michael found he could often work from home when he wasn't physically needed at the university.

FOURTEEN

They rarely saw Nicholas. With a low boredom threshold, and his taste for foreign travel stimulated, he had found the excitement of medical relief work abroad suited him perfectly. Privately both Roberta and Dick worried constantly about his safety as he moved from war zones to disease-ridden emergency intervention centres, but to him they expressed nothing but pride and support.

It was more than five years after Michael and Donella's wedding before Nicholas was ready to make such a commitment himself. Heidi, a Swiss administrator with Médecins Sans Frontières, first caught his attention in Cambodia. The calm and efficient way she organised the distribution of humanitarian aid, her uncomplaining acceptance of their spartan living arrangements, her apparent fearlessness in the face of lurking danger, were curiously at odds with her air of gentle femininity. Wanting to know at first-hand what the medical team needed she asked to watch operations, attend makeshift clinics and listen to the doctors' personal assessments of what they most needed. Nicholas, observing silently, was intrigued. He continued to watch from a distance until one night he found her weeping at the cotside of an orphaned child dying from septicaemia. He drew her outside and told her gently she needed to distance herself or she'd 'burn out before you're a day over twenty!'. He mocked his own 'brutal' approach to life and death and offered to help her harden up too. His friendship helped her to regain a more robust perspective and, she later acknowledged, stopped her from withdrawing from the work prematurely.

When Nicholas was posted to the Sudan, Heidi went too. Although surrounded by thousands of displaced people suffering from the ravages of malnutrition and dehydration, juggling titanic need against insufficient medical assistance, and daily witnessing the deaths of women and children as well as men, she flourished, and for the first time felt she was fully integrated into the tight-knit medical team. And in the midst of squalor and deprivation love blossomed.

It was Heidi, with no close relatives still alive, who insisted they should return to Scotland for the wedding. Nicholas, absorbed in a very different culture, left his brother to attend to the local detail. Just a simple affair, he said, small, so Heidi didn't feel overwhelmed: no frills; register office service; family meal afterwards. Nothing lavish.

The bride and groom flew over for the minimum length of stay required before the ceremony and made a whirlwind tour of the family to introduce Heidi. She was five years older than Nicholas, but her petite figure and blonde hair gave her a youthful air only belied by the intensity of her conversation. Her understanding of English was good but she spoke it with a strong German accent, and curious inflections.

But Nicholas was puzzled by the Heidi who arrived in Britain. She seemed strangely subdued, keeping close to his side and making little effort to get to know his family. The customs of the British were strange to her, she explained. His family, naturally warm and demonstrative, drew back in the face of her polite correctness.

Even at her own wedding she seemed to be a shadow of her usual self. In her national costume she caused a sensation not only within the bridal party, but with passers-by who stopped to stare and admire, but her increasing bewilderment was very evident. Torn between the easy camaraderie of the Halleys and concern for his bride, Nicholas began to look anxious himself. He did his best to explain the jokes and references to past events; he kept his own speech short. But it was with genuine amusement that he enjoyed his brother's colourful anecdotes of their youthful escapades masquerading as each other. Michael told Heidi she need not run out of conversation on their honeymoon – she could simply instruct Nicholas to fill her in on all the stories he, as best man, had neither time nor permission to recount fully today. Heidi only smiled superficially.

But it was Michael's final suggestion which brought the most thunderous applause.

'Five years ago when Nick and I were in reversed roles as bridegroom and best man, he ended *his* speech by saying that, by getting married, I had taken a step which excluded him from taking my place as we had so often done as boys. It occurs to me that today he has opened up new opportunities for us to return to our old tricks of impersonating each other. If any of you see a Halley twin out and about with a tall, beautiful brunette you will assume it is me – or *I*, for the purists and linguists amongst us! On the other hand, if you see one of us out and about with a petite, beautiful blonde you will assume it is Nick. But here we have the makings of the perfect crime, the perfect alibi. You have been warned!'

Under cover of the applause Nicholas bent to whisper a brief explanation in Heidi's ear. She looked hesitantly from him to Michael. Nicholas glanced at Donella. Her face was hidden from view as she bent to kiss her eldest daughter, curled up on her lap.

'But I have to admit that we have still to consult our wives about their willingness to enter into such an open *mariage à quatre*,' Michael went on as the laughter abated, turning from his sister-in-law to his wife with a grin. The eyes of the family followed from Heidi to Donella. The bride looked up at her new husband enquiringly. He was looking at Donella. She was laughing but keeping her gaze on Michael.

The years slipped by and Nicholas and Heidi, busy in their professional lives, did not return home to Scotland. They moved from the Sudan to Fuerteventura where they established an emergency intervention centre to receive the thousands of immigrants coming in from sub-Saharan Africa. Nicholas, appalled by the condition of the people arriving at the Canary Islands after twenty hours packed so tightly into boats that they could scarcely move, worked tirelessly to set up a field hospital and mobilise a medical team out of Gran Tarajal harbour. Heidi matched his hours and energy, co-ordinating the distribution of blankets, food and drink. Nicholas made vague promises to his mother about taking a break but she recognised the token nature of his assurances and contented herself with an occasional visit overseas to see them in their changing situations, subdued by the sheer size of their challenges, awed by their courage and commitment.

As time passed and Heidi failed to conceive, Nicholas found he had new problems to contend with in his personal life which began to dominate those he faced elsewhere. Signs of a certain inflexibility emerged in Heidi hitherto unsuspected, and tensions developed which strained their relationship for the first time. It took all his powers of persuasion to get her to submit to preliminary gynaecological investigations. The discovery that her ovaries and uterus had been extensively damaged by endometriosis was bound to be profoundly disturbing, but he was disconcerted by her implacable refusal to talk to him about it.

Reluctant to add to her distress, he initially did his best to respect her silence, but his anxiety mounted as the months ticked by. He began as sensitively as he could to try to coax her into discussing their options but he found himself unable to get beyond or understand her pained expression. When he finally insisted that they *must* talk about their problem, Heidi obediently sat down and waited for him to speak, but the sight of her primly upright figure and passive face was frankly inhibiting. Only desperation made him persist.

'Heidi, are you sure you really do want children?'

'You know that I do.'

'We could just forget it; concentrate on our work.'

'Work is not the same.'

'No, of course it's not. OK then, but you know IVF is a long, drawn-out business with no guarantees, don't you? And it's a pretty taxing business – especially on the woman. You'd have to be very sure you wanted to go down that route.'

She shuddered and closed her eyes.

'I do not want this.'

'OK then, what about adopting a child instead? There are hundreds of kids out there desperately needing someone to love them, as you know only too well.'

'But that is not *our* baby.'

'Not exactly, no, but ...'

'Is it what *you* want? The child of somebody else?'

'Well, no, I admit, it wouldn't be my first choice.'

'So, we do not do it, no?'

'OK. In any case, I suspect the authorities wouldn't be too enthusiastic about us as adoptive parents. No fixed abode; living abroad; wrong side of thirty already. And on top of that it can take years to set it all up.'

Nicholas let out his breath slowly. One step at a time.

'But, Heidi – no, don't look away. Are you quite, quite sure you do want us to have a baby?'

'Yes. And you?'

'Yes, if we can. But if you don't want IVF and you don't want to adopt – what *do* you want?'

'What else can we do?'

'Well, that depends how far you're prepared to go. We'd have to have tests, find out if your eggs can be harvested, if my sperm are up to speed ...'

He broke off seeing her face close, her nostrils flare, her lips tighten. Perfectly at ease with the language and concepts – both natural and assisted – from an early age, Nicholas was taken aback by her reaction. Gently, tactfully, he did his best to introduce the choices, but her responses only succeeded in making *him* start to feel uncomfortable, and somehow lacking in refinement.

Repeatedly frustrated in his efforts, Nicholas withdrew emotionally.

But the problem would not recede. Needing an anchor for his relentlessly circling thoughts he started to jot down the challenges and questions on cards, making notes underneath of possible answers or problems each presented. The exercise helped to clear his brain, to think through where he stood himself, and to identify the things he must try to find out from Heidi. In some ways it was easier than trying to formulate questions in careful English or stilted German, he discovered. He could scribble his thoughts without reference to good grammar or potential ambiguity. The paper had no sensitivities.

The basic facts he'd known already from his father's conversations and his own early exposure to obstetrics and gynaecology, although from the outset he'd personally steered well clear of that specialty because of Dick's position. But he found the questions and options had a new and poignant challenge now he was considering them in relation to himself and Heidi.

An early question he recorded was: '*Is it right to try to have a child when we can't produce one naturally ourselves?*' To his surprise he found he could marshall far more arguments in favour of them trying than not. It seemed undeniable that having children was a good and special experience, a pleasure worth having. The evidence of his own eyes told him that it was.

But just because they wanted a child, did that mean they should be given one? Plenty of people in the world wanted essential things but didn't get them. They both knew this first-hand. They had watched whole families *dying* for want of basic food and hygiene. No, just wanting something wasn't enough. A child after all might be classed as a luxury. They wouldn't die for want of one.

No, but their lives would be the richer *with* one. And in the developed world, if the resources and availability were there, wouldn't it be wrong of other people to deny them that experience? They would be good parents after all: more – much more – than 'adequate'. They certainly wouldn't abuse a child, or neglect it, or mistreat it in anyway. Those might all be legitimate reasons to deny couples access to fertility services. He and Heidi would give any child of theirs a safe, secure home and a surfeit of love and protection. They were well equipped to provide the best. It had always seemed to him unfair that adoptive parents, or those who needed help to conceive, were subjected to closer scrutiny than natural parents. OK, his father had explained that when professionals got involved *they* had responsibilities to the actual or potential child, but in their case …? Even given such scrutiny, he and Heidi would come through with flying colours. Wouldn't they? Well, maybe the purists would baulk a bit at Heidi's age. But – no, any discerning observer would agree, they'd make excellent parents. He knew they would.

A second question which he tackled head on at an early stage disturbed him more. It challenged him at a deep personal level. It questioned his relationship with Heidi as well as his own inner needs. '*Would it matter to me if I could never father a child myself?*' He was equipped to do so. He knew it. Indisputably. The early tests they had both undergone had proved that. If he had married a normally fertile woman he would have had children without even thinking along these lines.

He knew the answer. He did want a child of his own. It surprised him just how much. But, with the acknowledgement of this fact, came anxiety about Heidi's inner feelings. She could never know the delights of natural motherhood. Never. Was it fair to even contemplate having a child of *his* own when she was forever denied the equivalent emotion? Would the inequality in the biological make-up of the child fester? Could their own relationship stand up to that strain?

If only he could get her to talk to him about her real feelings. He had to find out. Somehow. Perhaps someone else – someone who was not part of the emotion of it all – might get her to open up. He noted in pencil on a separate card: 'counsellor' – on reflection adding a question mark.

Thinking about fathering his own child brought him to the options. '*How far would we go to have a child by assisted conception?*' he wrote on a new card. He got no further with the list than IVF. Heidi's rigid form, her outrage, were so vivid, he smiled ruefully and scored it through with a

heavy pencil. There was no way she would undergo the intimate procedures such processes involved. She had hated the simplest of
investigations; she couldn't even bring herself to mention bodily parts or
functions – even to him. There was no point in wasting time considering
treatments which involved her. No, if he wanted a child of his own it
would have to be via some process which excluded Heidi from physical
involvement. Someone else would have to undergo the indignities, the
invasion of her privacy, the discomfort, the emotional and physical strains,
not Heidi.

The first time he allowed himself to think this thought Nicholas smiled
benevolently. It was just Heidi. It was part of who she was. But his brain
would not let it rest there. The analysis he was undertaking denied him the
comfort of staying at a superficial level. A voice in the recesses of his mind
whispered, 'Is this fair? Why should someone else do the suffering?' In spite
of his resolute attempts to thrust the thought away he was compelled to look
at it again. And again. Until he addressed it honestly he could find no peace.
No, perhaps it wasn't quite fair, but life had not been fair to Heidi in denying
her natural parenthood. He must allow her to be herself, not force her into
something that violated her finer feelings.

'*What do I think about having a child via some other woman?*' Nicholas
felt disloyal writing the question. He added, '*i.e. assisted conception*'. Put
down in black and white it shouted at him to simply write, 'I don't like it!'
But the situation demanded that he look at his feelings more closely. A
picture came unbidden into his mind of himself being handed a child
looking exactly like him, hearing someone call him 'Daddy'. Somewhere
in the background was a hazy picture of a woman. Any woman. She wasn't
important.

But, of course, she was. She had carried the child, borne all the ailments
of pregnancy, the pain of labour, the stress of relinquishing the child. All
he had done was supply the sperm. He couldn't ask someone else to do
that and then take the child away from her. He couldn't.

But what if she was volunteering to do this thing? If it was a woman
who just wanted to help childless couples to know the joy of having a
baby? If she did it gladly? A picture of a woman in a Sunday paper who
had been a surrogate mother for three couples came into his head. She
was a big, rounded, Earth Mother figure, exuding warmth and domesti-
city. And she was smiling, hugging her own three children, in the picture.
Didn't look as if she felt exploited. So they did exist – such women. She'd
told her own story in the article. She loved her own children, loved them
to pieces, she'd said. Her heart went out to a couple who appealed for
help. Her husband had backed her all the way, she said. It had been a
success. She'd felt good. Done it again. And a third time. It was only the
risk to her own health that stopped her repeating it. The childless couples
had remained her friends and they stayed in touch, but she was content to

leave the children in their care. She didn't think of them as hers, she'd insisted. They belonged to the fathers.

How would he feel about such a woman having his child, Nicholas wondered. He reached for another card. '*How do I feel about surrogacy?*' If it was that happy Earth Mother, and she did it as cheerfully as she declared she did, and for the motives she described, perhaps it wouldn't be so bad. And afterwards it would be his – his and Heidi's – child. And he'd know it carried his genes.

But how could you know the surrogate would be as pure in her motives, as altruistic, as that woman sounded? You couldn't know. And where would you find such a person? How did one go about it? And who else would be involved in the conception process?

Nicholas repeatedly drew a blank. He didn't know anything about the logistics. But he knew a man who did. Before he started any more cards he needed to fill this one in.

Dick was surprised to get an international call from his son during working hours. He was intrigued further by the nature of what sounded like an urgent request for information.

'Yes, Nick, of course I know about surrogacy.'

'I know the basics – I think anyway – but what I need is up-to-date facts, more detail.'

'OK.'

'I've had a look on the net but can you recommend any good literature, something dealing with the pros and cons?'

'Yes. There's a pretty comprehensive text: *Assisted Conception*. I use it myself for reference purposes sometimes. I've got a copy somewhere in the office.'

'And does it deal with the ethical issues as well as the medical?'

'Well, it's got a chapter at the end on the moral side of assisted reproduction in general. But if it's that side of things you're looking for, there's a more expansive book on those questions called *The Ethics of Artificial Reproduction* which has a whole chapter dealing with surrogacy. It lists questions people sometimes ask, stuff like that.'

'That sounds exactly the kind of thing I need.'

'It deals with all the other kinds of procedures we use too, not just surrogacy.'

'OK.'

'D'you want me to photocopy the surrogacy stuff and send it out to you?'

'Please. That'd be brilliant. And the one on ethical issues – is it colossally heavy?'

'No, quite a slim volume actually.'

'Could I borrow that? I'll post it back as soon as I've read it.'

'No problem. No hurry to get it back.'

'Thanks a lot. I knew you'd be able to help.'

'But Nick …' Dick's words stopped him from ringing off.

'Yes, Dad?'

'Go cautiously if you're thinking of getting involved with anybody going down that route. There are a lot of potential pitfalls. Make sure you know what's inside and what's outside the law. Specially in a foreign country. We don't want to read "British doctor struck off for selling babies" in the international press!'

'Point taken. Thanks for the warning.'

FIFTEEN

It took a week for the package to arrive, but Nicholas knew as soon as he flicked through the pages that it was what he was looking for. He placed the book and papers in the drawer of his desk beside the cards, anxious not to leave them where Heidi might see them. Perhaps later – when he himself was more ready – perhaps then he'd steer her towards some of the literature – once he'd screened it – maybe.

It was late that evening before he could begin the task.

He decided to begin with the chapter on the medical facts of surrogacy, then he'd tackle the ethical challenges. He'd be in a better position to ask relevant questions once he'd got the details of the particular processes straight in his mind. How astonished his father would be to see him reading about obstetric matters with such attention!

As Dick had said, the ethics book was laid out under subheadings which represented the questions people tended to ask. To concentrate his mind, Nicholas took out a pile of fresh cards and wrote each question at the top of a new one. He would assemble the arguments which held any power for him in two columns – the pros and cons – to help him get an overall view of how the balance fell.

Is it a violation of human dignity? he wrote. Apparently some critics saw it as on a par with prostitution. Did he? Surely not. Other body parts were used in medicine – blood, bone marrow, eyes, livers, kidneys, hearts – he'd seen them all. Were they a violation too? No, he couldn't see that they were. So was a womb different? He could find no convincing argument to suggest it was. And the prostitution thing – was leasing a womb akin to prostitutes selling their bodies for sex? From where he stood, it *felt* very different. Wanting to use a woman's womb in order to have his child felt very different from wanting a women's body for his own sexual gratification. But he put a row of three asterisks against the point to remind himself to revisit this question, in case his desire for a child was clouding his judgement.

Is it degrading to the child? the book went on. His card noted only one point: alternative is non-existence.

Some people argue that surrogacy does not represent a proper approach to pregnancy, Nicholas read. He stopped, wondering what 'a proper approach' was. He struggled to understand this point. The practice was as old as the hills after all. The book said it happened in biblical times. Apparently Sarah gave her slave-girl Hagar to her husband Abraham to have a child for her. Ah yes, but then when the going got tough, it was her own younger

– *natural* – son who took precedence, not the surrogate child. So it looked as if – back then anyway – the surrogate boy didn't come as far up the pecking order as the fully legitimate offspring of both parents. Was that a warning? But then those were different times. After all, what was marriage then? Seemed to be a matter of going into a tent and sleeping with a woman. Abraham had *chosen* Sarah so that seemed to make her a wife. He'd done exactly the same physical thing – had sex – with Hagar, but she wasn't. Nope. There was no mileage down that track, he decided. Probably dangerous to extrapolate too much from bygone times.

So back to this question of 'proper pregnancy'. OK, he told himself, let's start with the premise that a proper pregnancy is one where a woman conceives a child through normal sexual intercourse. How is surrogacy *improper*? Because the woman isn't the man's chosen partner? Because the sperm get there by different means? Or because the pregnancy is so much more scientifically or emotionally planned? Or what? Well, if you started thinking like that you could argue that the pregnancy was *ultra*-proper! How many couples embarking on spontaneous sex really anticipated fully the results of that union? He thought ruefully of one of his own youthful experiences – a careless encounter that might very well have ended up in a pregnancy. Those agonisingly long days while he waited for Jess to have a period. How 'proper' would that have been?! In the surrogate pregnancy, everyone concerned was carefully scrutinising all aspects of the act of conception, *and* the results, *and* consequences. They even often drew up contracts! He decided this 'proper' argument held no force for him and was on the point of tearing up the card, but decided in the end to leave it in with 'No argument' scrawled across it.

The next point preoccupied him for a very long time. *Problems of secrecy and deceit. Does it have a harmful effect on the family and society?* the book put it. The subject came alive as he thought of his own situation. Supposing – just supposing – *they* went for surrogacy. You just couldn't keep something like that secret. The family of the surrogate mother would know. The doctors and staff at the clinic, or wherever they arranged it, would know. Their own families would have to know. Anyone who knew Heidi, and saw that she was not pregnant but suddenly had a baby, would want an explanation. And the child – when and what would they tell the child? What would be on the birth certificate? Even if they left the area as soon as they got the child, and moved somewhere where they were unknown, some of these people would know. The potential for trouble from this source grew larger with each line he wrote on the card. So for them as a family – yes, this was a live issue. If it involved deceit it could undermine family trust. He underlined the heading with red ink – up to 'the family'. He'd have to think this through very carefully if they ever came to this point themselves.

And what about the harm to society? Would deceiving anyone about his child's origins undermine *society* and the fundamental importance of truth-telling on which it was built? He could think of lots of different situations – isolated instances in his own experience even – where there had been an element of deceit. Where people had been less than honest or frank with each other – for very good reasons usually – for the greater good. They hardly constituted a threat to society. Nor would this harmless deception about his child. No, he didn't buy that one. Perhaps if it was on a very large scale it might be different. But it never would be. And even if it became so, there'd be laws written and it would be properly debated, and the rights and wrongs, and harms and benefits, all worked out.

He took another card and wrote the next heading: *It denies the child knowledge of its real genetic background.* Well, that applied to a lot of people, he thought instantly. Children of mothers who slept around or just didn't know who the father was. 'Hidden paternity', the book called it – nice turn of phrase, he thought with a grin. Most babies born through assisted conception wouldn't know either. Or adopted children. So whatever route he and Heidi opted for, they might not know what genes the mother was providing. Would that matter? Maybe. Maybe not. But there again, if the assistance came through a professional organisation they might well be able to supply the essential information; they'd screen the woman. And if they met the donor or leasing mother they might learn even more.

The next point he'd already made a card for, so he shuffled through his existing pile and drew it out, changing the title slightly to make it conform to his current thinking. It concerned the *suitability and motives of parents*. The familiar surge of irritation welled up. How many acts of unprotected intercourse were subject to close scrutiny for the couple's suitability as parents? Why should *we* be? But this time his thoughts were focused on surrogacy, and his thinking moved on. It moved to the mother.

He saw again that buxom Earth Mother in the paper. It made sense to check her suitability as a *surrogate* – not as a parent. They'd need to know if she had the stamina and right mental attitude to go through with it. You heard of women chickening out at different stages. He shuddered to think what that would do to him, or to Heidi. Imagine getting that far, and then not having the child! Knowing he had a son or a daughter out there somewhere but not ever seeing it, knowing it. It crossed his mind to wonder what those children in the picture thought. This was their half-brother or -sister. They'd watched their Mum through the pregnancy. Then – wham! Nothing. Did they do suitability screening on the siblings? He jotted it down – he should search for more information.

As he scanned the card his eyes returned to the top section on the suitability of social parents. What about if somebody in the chain thought he and Heidi were unsuitable for any reason? What a cheek! But if they did? Was there anything to stop them just making a private arrangement? The actual conception bit was pretty simple; shouldn't require specialised help, surely. He flicked back in the book. Nope. Easy peasy. Anybody could do it. It just needed a kitchen baster and a bit of common sense. And even if Mrs Earth Mother objected to the corner-of-the-kitchen feel, surely his father would know of someone … Nicholas shuddered. That was a hurdle best deferred until they came to it – if they ever did. He wasn't sure how much he could tolerate his father knowing what they were doing. Smacked of taking your mother on your honeymoon! Of course, it would depend exactly what they were doing. Unbidden, a mental picture of his father flashed into his mind, taking his semen, examining it, passing judgement on its quality. He shivered at the thought. Perhaps not.

The last point in the book asked, *Is it a form of selling babies? Should surrogates be paid?* He heard his father's voice warning him to be careful. Too right. The whole idea of payment for children was abhorrent to Nicholas. They just weren't saleable commodities. But if Mrs Earth Mother gave up a year of her life, needed maternity clothes, incurred travelling costs? Well, perhaps she should be *reimbursed*. And if she'd given up a job? Well, she could receive payment in lieu. Imagine she had a high-powered job, though – demanded an exorbitant replacement 'salary'? He could see it might be difficult to see where costs ended and payment began.

And if it wasn't Mrs Earth Mother? Supposing it was some devious scheming creature who was all sweetness and light on the outside, who fooled everyone into thinking her suitable, but in reality wanted the money. She might conceal potentially adverse information, mightn't she? How would you know how far you could trust her? Would he always have his doubts?

Better if she wasn't paid then – did it for altruistic reasons. No need for deception then. They'd be on the same side.

It was already very late by the time he got to this card and he felt mentally drained. Enough was enough for one night. He gathered the cards together, slipped them inside the book and closed the drawer on them.

Heidi had fallen asleep before he joined her. He gently removed the book from beneath her hands. As he stood looking down at her, the prospect of what lay ahead filled him with an overwhelming sense of sadness for her. He wanted to shield her from further pain, protect her from all the things he knew she found so abhorrent. In spite of her inner strength, she was vulnerable when it came to the subject of reproduction. But how could he do that if he knew so little of her inner thoughts?

He stared for a long time at her face – that inscrutable face veiled now in sleep. What would she make of all those questions? Would she have an opinion? Or would she just once again beg him not to talk about biological processes but just use his medical knowledge to find a way for them to have a baby. He sighed. It felt very lonely grappling with such fundamental choices on his own. And might she not come to resent a unilateral decision later?

His own thoughts were far from ordered as he slid under the cover beside her. She didn't stir.

The need to return his father's book forced Nicholas to raise the subject with her sooner than he would have chosen. He methodically went through the points on his cards with her, one by one. She listened passively. His hopes rose when she agreed without protest to reading the ethics book before he posted it back to the UK.

But, try as he might, he could not persuade her to talk through their treatment options, or to even consider a preliminary meeting with their doctor.

'Well, then we'll just have to give up the whole idea,' he cried in exasperation. It was the first time he had ever lost patience with her.

'No, please, no,' she replied, wringing her hands in her agitation. 'You decide for us. I know you will choose the right thing.'

'But it's not just about *facts*. It's about *feelings*. How you feel *inside* about these things.' Nicholas tapped his own chest as he tried to emphasise the extra dimensions he needed.

She shrugged.

'Seriously, Heidi, I think we should forget this whole idea of having a baby at all,' he said despairingly, moving to the door. 'Nobody will take us seriously if you won't even talk about it.'

She jumped to her feet at that. Clutching at his arm she spoke vehemently. 'You *must* not. No, you *must* not. We must have a baby.'

He was taken by surprise at this unusual display of emotion. '*We* – yes. That's the whole point. It's both of us. So *you* have to be involved in the choices, too.'

Seeing her expression he softened his tone. 'I'm sorry I was cross,' he said contritely, dropping a light kiss on her forehead. 'But if you can't talk to me we need help to sort out what's best for us.'

Her eyes grew wide with a haunted look which made him sit down and pull her onto his lap. She shook her head wordlessly.

'What distresses you about that? Tell me.'

'I do not want people to – to … come into our private life. It is for us. It is not for them.'

'I understand that. Believe me, I *do*. I don't want anyone else involved either. But unless you can talk to me, I can't *keep* it private.'

'What do you need me to say?'

Carefully, gently, he explored her limits. If it was possible, did she want a baby enough to endure the rigours of IVF? She confessed haltingly that much as she wanted a family she just could not bring herself to contemplate physical involvement in fertility treatment. She just could not. Full stop.

But she wanted his child? Oh yes, she did. She *did*!

Even if it wasn't biologically hers? She loved him, she would love his child.

And did she think she could cope with someone else having the baby for them? She could.

'You could arrange it so?'

'I don't know, Heidi. But I'm prepared to start making enquiries if you're sure that's what you want.'

'I do. I do!'

'We'd have to go and talk to our doctor. He'd ask us lots of questions Probably want to do more tests. They'd start with …'

She laid a hand over his mouth, her eyes wide and fearful.

'*Please* do not talk about such things. I do not want to know what they do. I just want a baby.'

In spite of her revulsion, he knew he couldn't afford to lose his advantage. Tightening his arms around her, but holding her gaze steadily, he pressed on.

'Look, I'm sorry to keep pushing this. I know you hate it. But if we try for a baby by any of those means, *other people* will need to talk to you about these things, Heidi. They won't take *my* word for it that that's what you want.'

'That is why I think we should go to Scotland. Your father – you say he knows these things. He is the expert. *You* could tell him I want it too. Then he could just arrange it. And we could get a baby. *Your* baby.' She nestled up to him as she emphasised the pronoun. 'And Edinburgh would be a good place to have a baby, I think. It is a place of good reputation, you always say. It is better than here, yes?'

Her solution took him completely by surprise. So much for taking one's parent on honeymoon, he thought wryly. Since leaving Scotland he'd been increasingly less reliant on his parents emotionally as well as physically and financially, and he'd known a quiet satisfaction in asserting his independence in the decisions he'd made for his career and personal life. Marriage had further strengthened this sense. Painful as their ongoing childlessness was, Nicholas had nevertheless felt no compulsion to involve his family in something essentially his and Heidi's private business, but now she was leaving him with no viable alternative.

And, of course, she was right: Edinburgh would indeed be a far more suitable place for infertility treatment than these Médecins Sans Frontières outposts. Especially perhaps now. The most recent appeal had come for a surgical posting in Haiti. Doctors were urgently needed to treat the escalating numbers of war wounded as well as the victims of demonstrations and other violent uprisings. But hearing of the danger and particularly threats to the staff themselves from armed men, in spite of appeals for their neutrality to be respected, Heidi had begged him not to transfer there. He, for his part, had told her emphatically: Haiti was no place for foreign women, and he would not countenance her exposing herself to those particular dangers, even if he decided he should do a stint there himself.

And so it was that they left their nomadic life behind them and returned to Scotland in search of parenthood. Nicholas had no difficulty in securing a post in a busy Accident and Emergency Department; Heidi stated her intention of finding something useful to do once they were settled. They left the Canary Islands with hope in their hearts and a promise of accommodation with Nicholas' parents until they could find a suitable place of their own.

SIXTEEN

Dick was flattered on one level when Nicholas explained their reasons for coming to him, but he was only too conscious of the pitfalls in keeping something like this in the family.

He did his best to explain to Heidi that he would happily talk to them about the options and explore the issues, but when it came to physically managing the case it would be better to ask one of his colleagues to take over. He watched her expression close. She needn't worry, they were all to be trusted, they'd be the soul of discretion, he said. She turned away with a bleak look.

Troubled more than he could admit to Nicholas, he suggested they discuss the realities of assisted conception. Heidi simply refused.

'Fair enough, Dad,' Nicholas said. 'It isn't something a girl discusses with her father-in-law, is it?'

'But I thought you said it was her idea.'

'Well, she wants you to *organise* it. But it's a different thing actually talking about it face to face with you. You must see that.'

Dick shrugged, looking hard at Nicholas.

'There's not much I can do if she won't even talk about it.'

'Could *we* – just you and me – talk about it? As a first step.'

Dick was silent for a moment. It wasn't ideal but perhaps he'd get a better feel for where Heidi's most acute sensitivities were this way.

Both Nicholas and Heidi were finding the adjustment to British life a complex experience. They missed the close camaraderie of the relief team; but they felt secure surrounded by the warmth of a loving family. Nicholas looked back nostalgically at the daily buzz of unknown medical challenges, of pitting his wits against hostile administrations and insufficient resources; but he observed with pleasure Heidi starting to relax in the safety of a country at peace. Heidi herself was relieved that her husband was no longer working absurd hours and was already losing that look of a driven man; but secretly she struggled with the need to share him with his family and watched with some alarm the independent self-assured man she had married revert at times to the cosseted son of strong parents.

When Roberta suggested she should take Heidi to visit Donella and the girls, leaving Nicholas to discuss medical matters with his father, Heidi felt the familiar sick feeling in her stomach. She fell in with the plans without comment but the conspicuous absence of enthusiasm was obvious to Nicholas. He contrived to draw her to one side and whisper an explanation which sent her on her way with a better grace, but he sensed something deeper still troubled her.

Dick was conscious of a strange sensation of tension within himself as he ushered Nicholas into his study.

'OK, this is potentially a bit tricky – confusion of roles and all that. So let's establish where the limits are at the outset, right?' he began.

'Fair enough.'

'I'll try to stick to being the professional fertility expert, talking with a patient. You just tell me if I encroach on territory too sensitive for a father's ear.'

'Don't worry, Dad. I'm just hugely grateful you're willing to have a go with this. I just felt we'd got to an impasse.'

'Yes, but being grateful doesn't stop *you* having no-go areas,' Dick said, looking seriously at him.

'I know. Not the kind of things one normally shares with a parent. And believe me I wouldn't be here now if I had any choice in the matter! But you've given me good training since I were a lad,' Nicholas said with an attempt at lightness.

'It's different when it's your *own* sex life, your *own* gametes, your *own* wife we're talking about though.'

'Yep. I see that. And I must confess I feel a bit queasy thinking about it. But heck, I'd feel like that *whoever* waded into my private life. Rather you than anyone else, I guess. I know you're on my side. *And* I know you're the best in the business. So let's go for it, Dad. If either of us gets out of our depth, we can just say. We'll both understand. Yes?'

'Actually, before we go into doctor-patient mode,' Dick said, 'I'm going to do something I *never* do with other – real – patients. It's bound to feel a bit uncomfortable for you to talk to *me* about these sensitive things, so it might help if you remember that, ancient as I seem to you, I'm a fully paid-up member of the male race too. Same anatomy, same feelings, sex drive, taboo areas, private thoughts. I do understand!'

'Thanks, Dad.' Nicholas grinned at him. 'I'll try to believe it!'

Dick pulled a pseudo-stern face at him but adopted a self-mocking tone.

'I don't say that to real patients, of course. I always want them to see me as a creature from another planet, completely asexual and carved out of stone. But with you, well, it might help a bit to think of me as a fellow man!'

'Rather than as my Dad. Who shouldn't know what I get up to, eh?'

'Something like that. And of course – you know this, but I'll say it anyway – it's all absolutely in confidence.'

Dick adjusted his glasses, leaned back in his seat, and put on his professional voice.

'Let's start with the business of finding out about the infertility, shall we? How are you both coping with that?'

'Heidi – she seems to have taken it on the chin. Just says it's life. I think she's OK about it. Remarkably OK actually.'

'And you?'

'I'm – well, I didn't think it'd matter as much as it does.' Dick saw that Nicholas' jaw was tight. 'I'm desperately sorry for Heidi, of course. But I do feel – I don't know – cheated?'

'Mmmhm. It's a big thing to come to terms with. Especially when you know you *could* have kids yourself.'

Nicholas shot him a grateful look. He nodded but said nothing.

'And your relationship – has it affected that, d'you think?'

'Sex life, you mean? Nope. Still eleven out of ten.'

Dick hadn't meant this but he took his cue from his son.

'And outside the bedroom?'

There was silence for a moment as Nicholas thought about the question. His eyes remained on his forefinger tracing the design on the arm of his chair. His words were more halting.

'Yes, it has ... affected us. Before, we were ... more carefree, more relaxed together. Now I'm more wary – about what I say, what I do. I'm afraid of doing something that'll make her feel worse. And she's not as ... spontaneous. But I guess the thing that's surprised me most is ... she's become much more dependent on me. She wants me to make all the decisions – well, about this anyway. Perhaps not everything else. She used to seem more her own person.'

'And are you OK with that?'

'I don't mind her being dependent. But I wish I could get her to tell me what she thinks on this. Seems to me there's a good chance she might not be totally happy with a decision I make on my own. And if there's a baby involved – well, it has to be right for her too. But I can't get her to open up and talk about it – tell me how she really feels.'

He looked up, and Dick saw the expression in his eyes.

'It feels disloyal to talk about her ...'

Dick cut in quickly.

'I know. But it's strictly between you and me, Nick. And I'm only asking because somebody needs to try to help you towards a solution. And if Heidi can cope with me being involved – as you say – then I do need to know some basics. Can you deal with that? I know it's awkward. But believe me I'm only asking the sorts of things I'd ask any couple. Try to think you're just telling me what she would say if she were here. She wants you to speak for her, doesn't she?'

'I know. But some of this stuff, I mean, *she* doesn't know it worries me. I don't want to add to her burden. And as I say, *I* don't know how *she* feels on a lot of it either. It'd be OK if she was here and heard what I said, what

I feel. And if she had her say too. But it doesn't feel right, me – on my own – you know?' He shook his head slowly.

'I see that. And I appreciate your reservations. But it's an issue from my point of view too. In my professional capacity, I'd be worried if a woman just wouldn't even talk about it.'

'I know you would. Any doctor would. But that's partly why we've come to you. Heidi thinks you'd take my word for it that she thinks what I say she does. That's the only way she'll agree to us moving on this at all – my talking to *you*.'

'OK. It's a problem. I would really need to know how she feels from her own lips if I were to give any real advice. However, I know you need to move on so let's just record that as an area we can't ignore, but we'll put it on one side for the moment and move onto something different. And Nick, just say. If it doesn't feel right. I do understand, you know.'

'I know. Thanks. But can I just say – it sounds as if we just don't communicate. It's not like that really. It's only on the issue of treatment for her infertility that she clams up. I don't want you to get the wrong impression.'

'Fair enough. It helps to know that.'

Nicholas shifted his position to curl one leg under him in the chair. His father waited until he was settled.

'Have you asked yourselves whether you really do want children?' Dick went on evenly.

'Yes. That much I do know. We both do. Very much.' It was confident. Good.

'Are you equally sure you want them for themselves?'

'Sorry? I'm not sure what you mean.'

'Finding out about infertility comes as a huge shock to a lot of couples. It can become an obsession just to solve the problem, or to be pregnant, or to be a parent – just like everyone else they know. Have you considered that aspect of things?'

'Not quite like that, but I'd say … Yep, we do want the children – or *a* child anyway – for its own sake. Certainly I know it's not because Heidi wants to be pregnant. She doesn't! Not by the means available to her anyway. But she definitely wants us to have a baby.'

'That's helpful,' Dick encouraged him. 'And you?'

'I know I just love kids. I love being with Mike's three. That's what I want for us. A family of our own. Children we can love.'

Under other circumstances Dick would have raised the question of the wish simply to please the spouse. Was Heidi sure she wanted children for herself? She wasn't here to ask. It was not something to ask her husband.

'How important is it to you to have a child of your own? You say you don't want to adopt. But does the child have to be genetically yours?'

'If I'm honest – OK, I know I have to be, or this is all a waste of time –

sorry. I know I *do* want it to be mine. Given that I know I'm fertile, seems crazy to use somebody else's sperm.'

'And Heidi?'

'I *do* know what she thinks on this. She doesn't seem bothered about it being hers but she insists she wants it to be mine. She seems to want it to be like me! Crazy, huh?'

Dick shot him a warning look. They must preserve a more formal approach if he was to be able to probe for delicate information.

'That would, as I'm sure you've realised, make the relationship unequal – if it was biologically yours but not hers. Is she all right with that?'

'I've tried to talk about that with her. She *says* she's OK with it. She wants it to be mine, but she definitely doesn't want to be involved in the physical bit herself.'

Dick kept his gaze steady.

'D'you know what's behind that resistance?'

'No. I can't get anything more. She freezes when we start to talk about anything biological, functional. But I don't know why or what's behind it. No.'

'D'you know if there's anybody she *would* talk to? Anybody professional? Anybody in the family?'

'She's adamant she wouldn't. Nearest I got was she said – she *suggested* – you. But it was more a case of you might take my word for her opinions, not that she'd be willing to talk to you yourself. In fact, she goes really scared just thinking about talking to anybody else about all this. It seems like a big bogey to her. It was only when I suggested we dropped the whole idea of having kids that she talked to *me*!'

'And d'you know what scares her?'

'It's two things really. She seems to be really squeamish about biological functions. And she hates the idea of our private lives being paraded before strangers. But heck, I can understand that! I do myself. But I suppose I try to see it as a means to an end.'

'So we've got a problem from the outset. The first step is to do tests, find out what's possible. If Heidi isn't willing to go through those we're going to fall at the first hurdle.'

'Not if we take her involvement out of the equation.'

'But we can't ignore her. You're both in this together.'

'Not ignore her, no. But we can respect her feelings and bypass her for the physical bit.'

'Meaning?'

'Go for surrogacy.'

Dick started. There was a long pause as the two men looked at one another.

'Surrogacy,' Dick repeated slowly.

'Yep.' The word was crisply decisive.

Dick was silent.

'Well, Heidi seems to have least problem with it as an option. We get a child who's biologically mine; she doesn't have to be physically involved. And it seems to *me* there are definite advantages. Like it poses the least risks to the mother. And involves the minimum of medical intervention.'

'The notion of intervention sounds like a major problem for both of you.' Dick placed the tips of his fingers together and looked at his son over his linked hands.

'Too right it is!' Nicholas shot out. Then, as if suddenly remembering the terms, he moderated his tone. 'Sorry. Yes. I can't say I'm keen on having a crowd of strangers dabbling in our most private lives. And having to talk about things – do things – that, well, you don't usually involve anybody else in.'

'It's perfectly normal – to feel like that,' Dick said with an understanding smile. 'Not many men relish the prospect!'

'I *will*, of course – do it. If that's what it takes.'

'OK. So you see surrogacy as a way of circumventing medical intervention?'

'Well, possibly. Not entirely maybe. Depends how we arrange it and how willing you are to get involved.'

'And I take it you've read up on all of this? Hence the request for my book.' So it wasn't for some patient Nicholas had wanted the information. It was for himself.

'That's right.' Nicholas nodded. 'I couldn't tell you then. We hadn't talked it through enough ourselves at that stage. I've done a few literature searches and read a stack of stuff. But it's no substitute for hands-on experience, I know, and to be honest, I haven't the first idea of how we go about arranging it.'

'Well, I'd better come clean and say, *I* haven't got hands-on experience either. I *don't do surrogacies*.' Dick said it with heavy emphasis on each of the last three words.

'No? But you know about them.'

Nicholas again rearranged himself in his chair. He leaned forward with his arms propped horizontally across from the arms of his chair, hands loosely linked, looking earnestly at his father as he spoke.

'Can I check with you the facts as I understand them? I know these things change and I might be out of date.'

'Most certainly.'

'As I understand it, it's allowed in this country, provided no money is given or received – other than expenses. Correct?'

'Correct.'

'And the husband or partner of the surrogate – if there is one and providing he consents to the procedure – would be the *legal* father. Correct?'

'Technically, yes.'

'So would we need to legally adopt the baby?'

'No. If it's properly arranged and unchallenged, your names could be put on the certificate and thereafter you would be the legal parents.'

'So as long as the surrogate or her partner don't dispute the validity of the certificate, it's straightforward.'

'*If* they don't – but therein lies one of the problems inherent in surrogacy arrangements.'

'OK. Point taken. But we can medically, legally, ethically, do the whole thing ourselves. There's no need to involve a clinic or doctors or anyone. That right?'

'Well, it all depends really on what type of surrogacy you're talking about. There's *full* surrogacy – that's where eggs are recovered and fertilised outside the uterus and then the embryo is implanted in the surrogate. That, of course, requires medical intervention. But in your case, as I understand it, even if Heidi has usable eggs she doesn't want them used?' Nicholas nodded. 'So you'd be talking about *partial* surrogacy. If the surrogate's a young woman – a fertile woman with naturally produced, good eggs – then all you'd need would be to introduce your sperm. And that requires no medical skill whatever. Some surrogates, it must be said, prefer to make the insemination a clinical procedure. But there's no *medical* reason why it shouldn't be done by a relative or friend. Or the woman herself if she's competent.'

'OK. That's what it sounded like when I read it, but I couldn't see why folk would involve doctors at all, if they didn't need to. So it's really about making it feel right for the surrogate.'

'Well, it's a bit more than that. It's partly because people prefer it to be clearly a treatment and not some kind of kinky variation on sex. But it's also because you need to be sure the people concerned know what they're doing. You'd be surprised how many people just don't understand basic anatomy and physiology!'

'I can believe that!' Nicholas smiled.

'And it's also about ensuring that it's done hygienically. And that nobody abuses their position. There's a huge potential for people to exceed their limits in this process.' Dick felt it was time to sound the first warning bells.

Nicholas' interruption stemmed the flow of his arguments.

'Just before we come to the downside, can I just ask you one more thing – before I forget it?' Dick nodded. 'Your reference to kinky sex … What about the morality thing? One of the articles I got off the net said it was a form of adultery. It isn't – is it?' Nicholas looked so concerned that Dick was quick with his response and more emphatic than he might have been with someone else whom he knew less well.

'Well, you'll have detected I personally am *not* in favour of surrogacy, but *that*'s not one of the reasons why I'm not. I fail to see how it *can* be classed as adultery if it's condoned by all parties – if they all consent and are involved. And it's done properly in controlled conditions. It's simply a form of treatment. But I know that the morality thing *is* a real worry to a lot of people. But then if we're honest the whole business of artificially creating babies is a worry to a lot of people. So it's not just surrogacy that raises this issue. Although,' Dick added as a thought struck him, 'I guess, if you're introducing fresh, warm semen into a woman's vagina in her own bedroom, it might seem more like adultery than a doctor in a green mask introducing an embryo into a woman, in the lithotomy position, under the eye of a team of professionals, under clinical conditions. Yes?'

Nicholas grimaced. 'Put like that ...'

'But no. I don't personally see that as a valid objection,' Dick clarified.

'Have you ever heard of a case where one of the parties accused anyone of adultery – after the event?'

'No. I haven't. Is that something that bothers you?'

'Well, it scares me a bit how much we'd be in the power of the surrogate and her husband – or partner – if she has one.'

'You're right to feel scared – of that, and of the whole thing. D'you want to talk a bit about the things you personally find scary?' Dick was gentle. This might be a more persuasive method of warning Nicholas off this idea, rather than him scotching the idea too heavily from the outset.

'Lots of things really. Where to start?' Nicholas leaned back in his chair again, unconsciously copying Dick's pose. 'Well, for a kick-off, I mean, we don't know this woman from Adam – or should that be Eve? Yet we're relying on her to carry *our* baby – *our child*. We're depending on her to take care of herself during pregnancy, and then give the baby up to us. There are so many places it could all go horribly wrong. What control have we got over her behaviour? *Zilch*, it seems to me.' With the word 'zilch' he cut through the air with a slice of his hand. 'Even if we have contracts and all that stuff, we can't *really* stop her doing her own thing.'

Dick was nodding as Nicholas spoke.

'All legitimate concerns. You are entirely without control.'

'And at the end of the day we might go through all that worry and she might change her mind and not want to give the baby up to us.'

'Absolutely. And it happens. Even when you think everyone's intentions are honourable. And when *they themselves* thought they were. Emotions, instinct maybe, take over.'

'And I must confess, in the cold light of day, my sympathy is with the surrogate on this. Hang it all, if she's done all the hard graft, I don't think I *could* insist she gave the baby up to us – not if she didn't want to. When you compare her part in it with mine – well, it just wouldn't be fair. And in this case, it'd even be half hers *biologically*.'

'Indeed. That makes it even more weighted in her favour. But either way, her eggs or somebody else's, she gives up the best part of a year and takes a lot of risks – both emotional and physical. And that, of course, is another reason why the courts would usually give her precedence in the event of dispute.'

'Quite right too. I think the law's right there. But having said that, it'd be horrific. And I'm not sure I'd be as sympathetic in reality if this woman was waltzing off with *my kid*!' Nicholas' voice grew more fierce.

'And all this business of couples keeping it official, involving third parties, drawing up contracts, and so on, it's all because there *is* such a real potential for things to get messy.' Dick felt that Nicholas was doing a good job of talking himself out of this idea. He started to relax.

'I had another look at some of those high-profile cases that were splashed all over the papers a while back. It gave me cold feet, I can tell you! Bad enough to have a few *doctors* involved in your sex life – imagine the press and the public knowing about it all!' Nicholas shuddered. '*And* on top of that, not having a baby at the end of it all too. Doesn't bear thinking about.'

'You're very wise to think through all these things, Nick. I'm impressed. You've certainly done your homework on this one.' Dick smiled warmly across at him.

'It feels like a horribly big decision to make.' Nicholas sounded so vulnerable. 'We'd have to be sure we could handle it.'

'Absolutely. But not everyone is as mature about it all – or as well informed – as you.'

The sudden shrilling of the phone interrupted their discussion. While Dick answered it Nicholas went to the kitchen to pour two long cold drinks.

SEVENTEEN

'But you're about to tell me there are another forty-five problems I haven't even thought about,' Nicholas said with a wry grimace when they had settled back into their chairs.

Dick noticed he was clenching and unclenching his clasped hands. He must be gentle. Nicholas was extremely vulnerable here; he didn't need the door slammed shut too abruptly.

'Well, not forty-five. But one or two. There are potential problems in the other direction too. I don't know if you've thought of that. What, for instance, would you feel if the baby turned out to be defective in some way? Would you be willing to go through with the arrangement then? Have you and Heidi discussed how you feel about a child with problems?'

'Well, to be honest, no, we haven't. But I take the point. We should.'

'Don't blow it up out of proportion. It's just another thing to think about.' It was always difficult to steer a course between giving the facts and burdening couples, Dick knew. 'And there's the issue of your relationship with the surrogate.'

Nicholas suddenly stood up and wandered over to the window. After a long pause he turned to face Dick again.

'She's the weak link in all this, as I see it. How do we know she's somebody we can trust?'

'You don't. There are no guarantees. With anyone. No matter how good she sounds on paper.'

'And that's one of the reasons why folk often choose relatives to do it for them, presumably.'

'Well, you probably have a better idea of the risks involved in those cases, but still no guarantees. And there are extra dimensions – like relationship issues – to worry about there.'

'We don't have a suitable relative anyway. But if it's not a relative, is it a good thing or not to meet the woman? So you know a bit what she's like? And she knows what you're like?'

Dick watched him closely as he answered.

'Advantages and disadvantages. For example, if she's a dishy, outgoing girl you might think, "Good-oh, we should have a nice-looking, easy baby." But – and it's a *big* but – you might find yourself fantasising about her. Oh, don't look at me like that! You might. It happens.' Dick couldn't help smiling at Nicholas' scornful expression. 'Ask yourself what that would do to your relationship.'

Nicholas inclined his head to show he had mentally recorded the point.

'And Heidi might feel jealous of her being inseminated by you, having your child.'

'Yes?' The young man's attention was arrested by this thought.

'It's possible.'

'If you say so.' Nicholas shrugged his shoulders and looked away again. 'Don't see why she would. She knows I love her. Ain't no way I'd love the surrogate.'

'Well, think about it, Nick. Heidi sees this lovely, leggy blonde. Not only physically attractive, but a *fertile* young woman too. And she knows that you and this girl are linked in a particularly intimate way. Your sperm are being carried in her, successfully fertilising her egg. Her body's nourishing your child. She's giving birth to your child. Not only might she think you'll be fantasising about this other woman, but she might well be jealous of the girl herself. Because she can do something that she, Heidi, can't. She can have a baby. And – I don't wish to make things harder for you than I know they are – but women are hurt at a very deep level by being unable to do something that's so much part of womanhood – of being female. Being unable to have a child for the man they love.'

Nicholas' eyes registered the pain he knew was Heidi's. Time to introduce a lighter note.

'On the other hand, of course,' Dick moved on swiftly, 'if the surrogate's a plain, homely girl with thick waist, pock-marked skin, crooked teeth and cellulite, *Heidi* might feel less resentful, but *you* might think, "Hmm".'

He was relieved to see Nicholas manage a faint grin.

'But that girl might be much better at physically having kids and relinquishing them.' Nicholas finished off the thought.

'Indeed,' Dick agreed. 'Capacity to have children is not linked to physical charm. Nor is altruism.'

'No. It's not.' The sadness in his son's voice told Dick he was thinking of Heidi, who for all her attractiveness was denied this chance.

'To return to the advantages and disadvantages of seeing the woman,' Dick went on. 'It works the other way too, of course. The *surrogate* can fantasise or make snap judgements or whatever. If she *doesn't* see you, she might imagine you as a Robert Redford lookalike. That probably shows my age – substitute whoever the latest heart-throb is. Or she might think of you as a squat, middle-aged chap with a squint and a pot-belly. Who knows? If she sees you and Heidi she might, or might not, like the look of you. She might, or might not, like the idea of you bringing up her child. See what I mean? Swings and roundabouts. So there's no easy answer to your question.'

'Yep. I see that.'

'It's such a special bond – the one between a man and woman creating a child together. It has a huge effect on everyone concerned. And because surrogacy is so close to the natural process it's all the more hazardous.'

'I see that. But because it *is* closer to the real thing, it doesn't have the same horrors that the test-tube stuff has.'

'True. Different drawbacks.'

'Coming back to the surrogate – whether or not the different parties meet – d'you think it's right for a commissioning couple to keep in touch with the surrogate? Let her know how the child's doing?'

'Obviously it's nice for her to know that things are going well, I think. And natural compassion might say, keep in touch. But again there are real disadvantages. It does lay the couple open to being contacted in ways they don't want. They might not want to be tracked down at all. They might not want to know the woman's having second thoughts. They might not want to risk unheralded visits. They might not want her to have the facility to contact the child. All those kinds of things. And that's again another reason why people operate through an agent or third party, to try to minimise the risks from and to either side. But they are very real risks.'

'Presumably unless they know a surrogate personally, they don't have much choice but to go through an agency. Do they?'

'Well, there's nothing to stop them advertising directly for a surrogate.'

'You mean, as in the paper? In the ads column?'

'Yep.'

'Blimey. What a gamble!' Nicholas sank back into his seat, clearly appalled at the thought.

'Indeed.'

'Oh, I nearly forgot. And this is one of the big questions, as far as I'm concerned. I think I've sorted most of this out in my mind, but this one I keep coming back to. What do folk do about telling people?' Nicholas frowned as he spoke. 'I mean, it's not something you can conceal, is it? Not like when it's the man who's infertile. You can get away with *nobody* else knowing if it's a case of artificial insemination of the woman with donor sperm. But when you need to involve another woman it's a whole heap more obvious.'

'Absolutely. It's a thorny issue – just who needs to know what, and when you tell them. And there are no textbook answers. It depends on the family. But it's a minefield.'

There was a long silence. Nicholas had dropped his head in his hands and was sitting with eyes closed, sorting the whirling thoughts in his mind. Dick remained motionless, watching him with tenderness. When the younger man raised his head his eyes looked directly into his father's.

'Thanks, Dad. I appreciate your honesty. And making it as easy as you could for me to talk about all this stuff.'

'You're welcome, Nick. I hope it's been useful to talk it all through. You can see why I can't help you go down that track.'

'But you *can*.' Nicholas spoke with energy. 'You're the one person who *can* help.'

Dick frowned.

'I don't see ...'

Nicholas smiled lopsidedly as he asked, 'I presume you don't personally have tame surrogates in your vast circle of friends and acquaintances, do you? Somebody you could feel pretty sure about for the job?'

'No. You presume correctly. As I said, I *don't do* surrogacies, Nick.' Dick again emphasised his position.

'This is one occasion where I'd settle for a spot of string-pulling!'

Dick gave a half smile, unsure where this was leading.

'But if we find a surrogate, *you* could do the necessary. And we know you'd be trustworthy. Because that's the key, it seems to me – basing it all on trust – real trust.'

'Hang on a minute.' Dick leaned forward towards his son as he spoke slowly. 'I don't think you've heard me. I *don't do* surrogacies. The problems are too great. The potential for the whole thing to fail is enormous. I thought I'd made that clear. I don't do them because they're a bad idea. For *anyone*. Not specifically *you*.'

'Yep, I heard you. I know you're not normally in favour of them. And I can see why. I know that there are potential problems. Loads of them. I knew that before I talked to you, and I've thought about them for hours – weeks! And you've just gone over them again. But this is *us* we're talking about. You know us. You know we'll be trustworthy, and be good parents, and all that. We know *you'll* be trustworthy. So we only have to find a trustworthy surrogate and we've eliminated almost all the risks.'

'Nick ...'

'Besides, we don't have a choice, Dad. It's this or nothing,' Nicholas interrupted, leaning forward again, his voice and his look intense. 'You say you want to help. Well, you *can*. You're the one person we can trust to set this up in a way that minimises the risk of all these problems we've been talking about.'

'And just how do you propose that I do that?' Dick's tone was sharper. It looked now as if he'd been too gentle.

'Well, you must know somebody who knows somebody in this line. Somebody trustworthy who could put us in touch with a reliable surrogate. And then *you* could be the agent who makes sure it's all carried out in the right way so it's fair to everybody. And that way we'd keep it private, and ensure everybody was properly protected. And knowing what *you* know, with all your specialised knowledge and experience, you'd be *better* than an agency.' Nicholas was loading his appeal with emotion, not all of it consciously.

'Look, I'd do anything I could to help you. You know that. You kids mean the world to me. But I won't do something that I feel is stacked with problems that spell disaster. This is one of those things. I'd be going against everything I think and know to be in your best interests.'

'But isn't it up to me to decide what's in my best interests – our best interests?' Dick noticed the hasty correction but, not wanting to antagonise Nicholas, he refrained from comment on Heidi's strange reluctance to even talk about this issue.

'Normally, yes. But if I'm asked to be involved, it's my right, and my *duty* to make a decision myself.' Dick heard the Director of the Centre for Reproductive Medicine speaking. 'I can't – I *won't* – be forced to do something I believe to be a wrong.'

'So you're saying you won't, full stop? Even for us?' There was a hard edge creeping into Nicholas' voice. His eyes were watchful, veiled.

'You're making me out to be some kind of despot. I'm only saying I won't do this particular thing because I believe it to be a pathway to disaster. I'm more than happy to start the ball rolling for another course of action.'

Dick saw Nicholas watching his last hope disappearing.

'Why do you always think you know what's best for us? We're grown-up now! We're not your little boys any more. I've been thinking this through for ages – considering all the pros and cons, reading a stack of stuff.'

'I know. And as I've said, I admire your mature approach to this whole thing. I do. Really I do.'

'But I'm still wrong, huh?' Nicholas was glaring now. 'You know what I'm hearing? I'm hearing you have a problem. You and Mum. Mum telling me, "Don't get involved with Donella. It would only spell trouble. We parents know these things. I can't give you a full explanation but I know things you don't. I only have your best interests at heart. Run along and work at your career."' His voice caricatured his mother's. 'Funny thing, though. Mike's been with her all these years. Not much of a disaster, was it?'

He paused, looking at his father challengingly. Dick said nothing.

'No. Indeed. And now it's *you*. "No Nick, you shouldn't have a child. I know things you don't. I only have your best interests at heart. Run along and be a good doctor."' Again the caricature, the mocking tone. 'That's what I'm hearing. I'm hearing you and Mum, you have a problem with me growing up. Or you have a problem with my sexuality. Or something.'

'Nick, I know you don't really think that ...' Dick began, placatingly.

Nicholas rose from his chair and flung over to the window. He looked scornfully back at his father.

'Don't I? You know that, do you? Well, I'm not so sure. Look at it from where I stand. You have it in your power to help us. But you won't. Ask yourself: why not?'

Dick breathed deeply, slowly. The boy needed somewhere to vent his frustration and pain. His anger was natural. And the messenger of bad news had to be a legitimate target. He was used to it.

He had to admit, though, it hurt this time – when the shots were fired by his own son. But stay calm. It would pass.

Nicholas, probably misconstruing his silence, drove home his advantage.

'I never did understand why Mum made me give up Donella. But I was young then. I trusted her. I wasn't ready to settle down with anyone, anyway. But I …' He suddenly stopped speaking, gritting his teeth. Turning abruptly on his heel, he stared out of the window. With his back to his father he continued. 'But now, I'm not an impressionable young student, dependent on you for support. So if you won't help us, then I'll find some other way.'

'Nick, I understand your anger. I do. And I do want to help. But this is not the way.'

'No, of course it's not!' Nicholas spat out. 'How could I possibly know what's best? Ridiculous of me to have thought for one moment that I could work something out for myself.'

'This just underlines how dangerous it is for doctors to try to keep these things within the family. You'd be far better talking to someone else about it, someone you can just see as a professional. Keep other emotions out of it. I can ask one of my colleagues to take you on. Get someone to talk to Heidi, find out what's stopping her from considering other more appropriate alternatives.'

'You know perfectly well, we can't. Heidi won't talk to anyone else.'

'But Nick, she won't talk to me either. And with the best will in the world no-one will feel able to help when only one partner will talk about it.' Dick tried to be gentle, but he knew this would be wounding, spelled out so clearly, so accurately.

'And that's exactly why we came to you. We gave up our jobs and everything else to come here to get help – your help. You *know* us. And Heidi trusted you. She trusted you to listen to me speaking on her behalf.'

'I know. And I'm touched that she did. And I've tried to listen on that basis. But even putting that reservation on one side, I can't do what you're both asking me to do – go against my better judgement.'

At that moment they heard the front door opening and the sound of Roberta and Heidi returning. Nicholas turned to look again at his father. He tried one last appeal.

'So you're telling me I must go out there and tell Heidi she was wrong to trust you? You aren't willing to do the one thing you could do to help us?'

'No. I'm telling you I *am* willing to help. I *want* to help. But just not in this way. I think you should ask her to trust me by talking to me – with you, of course, if she prefers that. And we'll try to find some other way to resolve the problem. I can't offer anything specific right at this moment. I'd need to know far more, do more tests.'

'She won't. I just know she won't.' His voice was flat, final.

'Nick, isn't that worrying? In itself?'

'The whole bloody thing's worrying. It must be hell for her. But she's been so strong about it. I've *got* to do something. I owe her that.'

Dick, looking hard at him, saw he was close to breaking point. He rose to his feet and moved to throw an arm around his son's shoulders. When the anticipated rejection didn't come, he tightened his hold, pressing the young man close. His voice was tender.

'Nick, this is a killer. I know. It hurts like hell. And I haven't helped by telling it like it is. I know that too. But I wouldn't be doing you any favours if I glossed over the problems. Give yourself time to think about what we've talked about. Try to talk to Heidi again about everything. Let me help you.'

'Thanks, Dad.' Nicholas' voice wasn't quite steady. He swallowed hard, opened his mouth to say more, but couldn't trust himself. 'Sorry.'

Dick gave him another hug.

'Why don't you go and stomp around the garden for a few minutes. I'll ward off the women.'

By the time Nicholas returned to the house he was in control again although Dick's eyes took in his pale face and restless eyes. Before long he heard Nicholas suggest to Heidi that they went for a walk down to the river.

He saw Nicholas draw her close to his side, and her smile as she glanced up at him and slid her arm around his waist. The outward trappings of love and companionship. But he watched them walk away with a heavy heart. It was a lonely path for this son he loved so dearly.

Unknown to the two men Roberta had seized an opportunity to talk to Heidi herself.

Their time with Rachael, Fiona and Emily had been cut short by the arrival of one of Donella's friends, but as they drove back home, Roberta talked about how calm Heidi was with the girls and how much she admired her gentle ways with them. Heidi smiled but said nothing.

Roberta told her how she worried that being with the girls might be hurtful sometimes for her. Heidi simply reiterated how well behaved the girls were, what a good mother Donella was.

Roberta tried again. Approaching cautiously, introducing each idea gently, inch by inch she moved towards assuring Heidi she shouldn't ever blame herself for her inability to have a child. Heidi agreed.

Roberta gave up. It was clear Heidi just could not, or would not, talk about it.

She too watched the young couple walk away towards the river. Her eyes too were troubled. She too grieved for her son.

EIGHTEEN

A few days later, seeing a wan-faced Nicholas slipping out through the garden gate, Roberta seized the moment. She gave him a ten-minute head start and then followed him, confident she knew where he would be heading.

She found him down by the stream where he and Michael had played for hours as small boys, building dams, racing sticks, creating miniature underwater worlds. Now the adult Nicholas sat on the big stone promontory staring into the depths below him.

The sound of the water muffled her approach and he started when she suddenly appeared beside him. He smiled but not before she had seen the unguarded look on his face.

Roberta sat down, her legs dangling over the edge, both hands on the ground behind her to keep her balance. There was a long silence before she spoke.

'Feel like talking, Nick?'

'About what?'

'Hey, doesn't take a genius to know it's a bad day.'

'GP instinct, eh?'

'Sorry.' She smiled at him sheepishly. 'Do I sound like my professional self?'

'No. *I'm* sorry. I didn't mean to be rude. I guess I'm defensive right now.'

'I'm daring to intrude – as your *Mum* – not as a doctor. But you can tell me to mind my own business if you don't want to talk to me. I'll understand.'

'Thanks, Mum. Presumably Dad told you what I told him the other day?'

'Only that you wanted him to help organise a surrogacy, and he doesn't feel he can. No details. You know us and confidentiality.'

It was true. Dick had kept his own counsel, respecting Nicholas' confidences absolutely.

'I was pretty rude to him.'

'He didn't tell me that. But even if you were, he'd understand. He's been dealing with this particular pain for a hundred years. He knows what it does to people.'

'Doesn't excuse my rudeness.'

'Nick, I'm not trying to muscle in on this. And I genuinely don't know what you told Dad or what he said to you – beyond what I've just told you. But my old maternal heart worries about you.'

'Why do I get the feeling I'm not going to like this?' She heard him struggling for his old teasing tone. His dismal failure only saddened her further.

'No, it's not like that. It's your call. If you want to offload I'm here. I know you're all grown-up now but you're still my boy, and I hate to see you hurting. That's all.'

'I just don't know, Mum. I'm so confused about all of this.'

'I know.'

'So, you going to tell me what you think?'

'Oh, it's not my place to do any such thing. It's your decision.'

'But you have an opinion, I bet.'

'No. I don't know enough of the circumstances. But I *can* see what it's doing to you.'

'It stinks!' Nicholas spat out, throwing a stick fiercely into the water.

There was a long tense silence. It was Roberta who eventually broke it, her voice low and cautious.

'Nick, can I ask you something?'

'You *can*; the real question is, *may* you?' Nicholas was casting her own repeated correction of them as children right back at her, stalling for time.

'*May* I?' She smiled at him, recognising the quote.

'You may certainly *ask*. I may not answer. Depends.' He was clinging onto the whip hand, needing to stay in control.

'Is everything OK – between you and Heidi, I mean? Are you happy – together?'

'Yep. What makes you ask?' He didn't look at her, though she was watching him closely.

'Nothing specially. But it's just that ... well, it's important ... how you two are ... if you're going to go for treatment.'

'We're happy really. It's just this baby thing. Gets to us sometimes. We're OK really.'

The flat tones made Roberta's heart sink. But she took a deep breath and ploughed on. It was now or never.

'Forgive me – but do you love her – really love her?'

She saw him swallow hard, twice. Her hand slid across to cover his. She waited.

'Depends what you mean by love. Aren't there different ways to love?'

'I think there are, Nick. I think there are.'

She sat for a long time in silence, waiting, giving him space.

'I *do* love her. I respect her, I admire her. If you'd seen what she did in Cambodia, in Darfu ... she's incredible.' He broke off and there was another long silence. 'I love her in a quiet, steady sort of way, you know? I want to make her happy. And she depends on me. She seems to need me. I'm arrogant enough to think I'm good for her. We're good together.' He stopped suddenly and then added in a harder voice, 'But if you mean that crazy, mad, passionate, on-fire kind of love, then no, I don't love her like that.'

He broke off abruptly, turning his head away so that she couldn't see his expression.

'But you've known that kind of love?'

'Once.'

'But?'

'She married someone else.' The words came out tight, flat, without emotion.

She wriggled across until she was close enough to put an arm around him.

'I didn't know. I'm sorry.'

'All water under the bridge.'

'But it still hurts?'

'Not normally. Only when I'm depressed and when people like you dig it up! And I already wish I hadn't told you. Besides, I'm not at all sure that's the sort of love that lasts.'

'I'm so sorry, Nick. I honestly didn't know there had been anyone else.'

'Well, for goodness sake keep it to yourself.' She heard the more abrasive tone, and the undercurrent of tears. 'You have a beastly way of winkling things out of a chap! It was a long time ago. And it doesn't have anything to do with how I feel about Heidi. I *do* love her. Just in a different way. She's a different kind of girl.'

'I won't breathe a word. Promise. There, it's forgotten.' She tightened her hold for a moment as she used another childhood expression, blowing the thought off her hand as she had done years ago.

Taking a deep breath she continued. There was no point in coming thus far and chickening out.

'The only reason I asked is – well – you're not using having a baby to – sort of – shore up your marriage, are you?' She knew she was treading on very thin ice.

'I don't think so. No, I really don't think I am, Mum. It's something we *both* want. We want to be a family.'

'Sorry, Nick, but I've been worrying about that since you told us about the infertility. If the relationship isn't stable, having a baby – especially in these circumstances – isn't the answer. You have to recognise that.'

'I do know that. Believe me, I've questioned my motives – our motives – over and over. And I don't honestly think that's an issue. I think what we have is strong enough. And Heidi's very different when she's on her own with me. It's not easy for her being here, you know? I mean, out there she had a responsible job and she was very much her own person. This part-time job with Oxfam here, well, it's not exactly stimulating, is it? It's way beneath her abilities. And staying with you and Dad – I mean, we're very grateful and all that, of course, but hang it all, Mum, the Halleys are an intimidating bunch *en masse*! In fact, I'm ratcheting up the search for a place of our own. We should have moved ages ago. I should have seen that. It's not fair on Heidi.'

Roberta was relieved to hear the conviction in his voice.

'Fair enough. As long as you two are all right. Sorry, I asked …'

'It's OK, you're right to point it out if that's what you think. We have to be doing this for the right reasons. It wouldn't be fair on a child otherwise.'

'Sorry if I seemed to doubt. It's just that – sometimes people aren't able to see things as clearly – when it's them.'

'I know that's true. There's so much stuff hanging around. You start to doubt yourself. That's the only reason I'm sitting here letting you ask these impertinent questions. Somebody's got to ask them. Better you than some stranger, I guess.'

Nicholas threw a leaf towards the water. The wind caught it and it blew back into his face. He picked it up, staring at it, tracing its veins with his finger, lost in his own thoughts.

'Is it helpful, Nick? Somebody asking?'

'Well, I don't *like* it. I want to tell you to mind your own bloody business – sorry, Mum – slipped out. But I know *somebody's* got to.'

'I know I said it's already forgotten, but on that basis, sounds to me like you've got some other baggage – serious stuff – hanging around. Would it help to tell me about the other girl?'

'No, not that. I can't, Mum.' He turned his head away to look unseeingly downstream. 'I can't.'

'But you … still have feelings for her?'

Silence.

'I don't know.' The low reply was full of suppressed emotion. 'I try not to think of her. And before all this, when we were abroad, Heidi and I were so happy … I didn't think about her – much – at all. It's just … feeling low … well, it makes you doubt yourself. And … OK, I guess a bit of me always will think of her … sometimes.'

'Oh Nick, I'm so sorry.'

'Don't, Mum. Just … *don't*.' The choking words brought tears to her eyes. He was clearly very low today. It was rare to find him tearful. She blinked hard.

There was a long silence.

'Even if I do still think of her sometimes, doesn't mean I can't be happy with Heidi,' Nicholas said in an intense voice.

'No, dear, it doesn't. You're right. And there are compromises to make in every relationship.'

'Like I said, it was fine before all this stuff about a baby came along. I'm just depressed. Normally it's not an issue.'

They sat again in silence. She searched for the right tone, the right subject. She knew an opportunity like this would not easily present again without seeming too contrived, too manipulating.

'Nick, the surrogacy thing. Dad's the expert, but would it help to talk about the emotional side of it all, the non-specialist side of it? Would it help to sort it out in your head? I can listen if you want a listening ear?'

'I don't know. It's all such a mess.'

'Is it really what *you* want?'

'In my brain – I feel it makes sense. Looking at the options available in our case, it's the one that fits. OK, I know it's potentially fraught with problems but I can't see anything else is an option in our case.'

'But in your heart?'

'In my heart? Sometimes yeah, I feel it'll be OK, once we're on our way with that. I know I'd like it to be *my* kid. But other times – gee, Mum, other times I freak out thinking about it.'

'It's natural. It's a big thing.'

'I *hate* the idea of other people meddling in something – so – *private*, you know? And that's what I always come back to. I mean, you'd think I'd take it in my stride, wouldn't you? With Dad doing this kind of thing. All my life knowing about it all and everything. But when it's personal – when it's *you* … By gum, it's a different thing when it's you!'

'I know. It is, dear.'

'If we could just do it all *privately* – it wouldn't feel so bad. But the thought of other people dabbling in our …' He shuddered at the mere idea.

'I can understand that.'

'But don't let Heidi know that! She thinks it's no big deal for me.'

'Does she? Does she really?'

'She's got a really big block about this whole thing. Squeamish about intimate things being exposed to other people's scrutiny. But you know that. You must have felt that.' He looked at her briefly. She nodded without speaking. 'I can understand it, but in her case it's *big* time. She'd hate it if she thought I wasn't too keen on my bit either. No point in freaking her out. I think she thinks because I can talk about it all, that it's no big deal for a man.'

'You *have* grown up,' Roberta said gently.

'I owe her that. Besides I'll get over it. Probably won't be as bad as I'm building it up to be. But …' He shrugged his shoulders, dismissing the subject. Then in a more brisk tone he said, 'Hey, what I really need is some fairy godmother to magic a lovely altruistic person to volunteer to do it for us out of love!'

Roberta smiled in response.

'But of course, given the said fairy godmother, I'd get her to magic Heidi's ovaries and uterus back into shape instead. Solve all the problems.' The pain was back in evidence in his face.

Roberta turned in slow motion towards him, words dragging out in time with her thoughts.

'But ... if it's surrogacy ... maybe ... you *could* ... just arrange it ... privately. If you knew someone personally who'd do it for you, you *could*.'

'Exactly. As I was saying, Mother dear.' He leaned across and tapped her on the head. 'Hello! Earth to Mother! Are you receiving me?'

'Sorry, love. I'm listening really, but I'm thinking along a slightly different channel.'

'*That's* partly why we came down this route to surrogacy. It's the least invasive course of action. Least interventionist.'

'But who do we know who would do such a thing?'

'No-one. And there's the flaw in our perfect plan. It'd have to be someone pretty special to do *that* – for nothing!' His cynical tone sounded much more like the old Nicholas. 'I don't think so. *I* certainly don't know anybody *that* altruistic! A nice idea but a non-starter.'

'*I* would,' she said stoutly.

Nicholas shot round to stare at her in astonishment.

She felt suddenly flustered, embarrassed.

'But you probably wouldn't want an old woman ...' Her words were lost as he enveloped her in a tight hug, nearly toppling them both into the stream.

'You're the best, Mum. You would too! Bless you for the thought. But I couldn't let you. Too risky at your age.'

'And of course, you'd have to use a young woman's eggs.' She pursued her point, thinking aloud of ways to overcome obstacles. 'I'm physically fit, though, even if I'm hormonally over the hill. So once it was at the implanted stage the rest of it could be between ourselves.'

'Just being pregnant, giving birth, it'd be far too risky. I couldn't cope with having your ill health on my conscience, just because I want kids.'

'Oh, I'm a tough old bird, you know.'

'Well, even if you were willing, Dad'd do his nut if we suggested it.'

'Would he? I don't know. I'd be willing to work on him. I told him once, years ago, I might go in for surrogacy. I *loved* being pregnant.'

'And? What did he say – then?' Nicholas turned to face her fully for the first time, his mouth smiling though she noted the laughter didn't reach his eyes.

'Told me he'd put a reserved ticket on that space and if I persisted, he'd make sure it was occupied until I was on the biological scrap heap, as I recall!'

'Sounds like the Dad we know and love!' They both grinned at each other. 'So that's where his hang-ups come from!'

'Has he got hang-ups? I didn't know he had.'

'Yep, I'd say so.'

'He loves you though. He'd do anything for you children. He might well change his tune – if it was for *you*.'

'Thanks, Mum. That's a brilliant offer. You're a star.' He gave her another hug before releasing her. 'But I don't think Dad *would* change his tune. Even for us – even if you could do it for us.' He shook his head slowly. 'No. He "doesn't do surrogacies", and I quote. And in any case, Dad notwithstanding, I think it would be a mighty confusing thing for the kid to have his Gran as his birth mother.'

'And not at all seemly for *me*, your old *Mum*, to be impregnated with *your* sperm – from your point of view too, I guess.' She grinned up at him.

'Well, it does make a chap feel a bit queasy. You must admit!'

'True. I do admit it has its dodgy side.'

'You're a Mum in a million though. I mean – how many chaps could even *talk* about this kind of stuff with their mothers? Not many, I bet.' He was looking at her with deep affection. 'I must say, I've always valued that. We could always talk to you – and Dad – about anything, no matter how – *delicate*.'

But he couldn't talk to his wife, she thought sadly. Or at least she couldn't talk to him. And he'd never told his parents about this other love in his life. Or the hurt she'd left behind. And if he hadn't been so low about the infertility, he probably never would have. She felt sick at heart for him. And for Heidi.

'Well, that's nice to hear, dear.' She kept it light. 'Probably because we're both doctors and deal on a daily basis with the stuff of people's souls – and intimate parts!'

'Not just that. You're just such *open* people.'

They smiled warmly at each other.

'But now you need more than talk, I know. What's next on the agenda? Dad helping you to move on?'

'Not really. It's an impasse. Dad's against surrogacy. Heidi's against anything else.'

'And you're stuck in the middle. Oh, Nick.' She reached out to put an arm around him again.

'Don't get me started again. I must get a grip. This isn't doing anybody any good. I don't know why I'm so down today.'

'Don't be too hard on yourself, dear. It's natural to feel low. You've got a lot on your plate. And as yet, no solution on the horizon. But one will come.'

'Will it, Mum? Will it? I'm not so sure.'

'You're disappointed because the thing you thought was the way through hasn't worked out as you hoped. It's only natural to feel down about it. Give yourself a bit of space. Then think again. Something will present.'

'Thanks. Sorry to be so pathetic. So much for being all grown-up, eh?'

'You're not pathetic. I'm really proud of you. Dad is too. The way you're handling this whole thing. It's matured you. And we do notice – and we admire – your gentleness and your strength with Heidi. We don't say much – don't want to interfere – but we've noticed. She's lucky to have you. Lots of men wouldn't have been as supportive. So hang in there.'

'Thanks.' He gave her a shaky smile but looked away quickly.

'D'you want me to go? Give you some peace?'

'Please.'

She scrambled to her feet. Stooping to drop a kiss on his head, she said quietly, 'Remember I'm always here if you want to talk, Nick. But I don't want to intrude.'

'I know. Thanks. I'll be OK. But … thanks.'

She left him sitting unmoving on the rock. Something of his low spirits hung around her as she retraced her steps back to the house.

NINETEEN

When Donella, Michael and the children came for a meal that weekend, Nicholas went instantly into uncle-mode. He began by becoming a space-ship swooping after the girls, who ran from him shrieking with delight. As he caught up with first one, then another, he scooped them up in his arms and made zapping noises as he propelled them through the air and deposited them in strange places from which they must extricate themselves. The house was suddenly full of noise and laughter.

But when the girls clamoured for their favourite game Roberta saw the unguarded expression on Nicholas' face.

The game was one devised by the twins, known in the family as 'Is it Daddy?' At first when the children were toddlers, it simply involved one or other of them appearing, whereupon everyone else would sing out: 'Is it Daddy? Is it Uncle Nick?' If the girls got it right everyone would shout 'Hooray!' and clap their hands; the youngsters would shriek with delight. If they got it wrong everyone would shout 'Boooooo!'; the girls would still shriek with laughter.

As the children grew older the two men would present only a part of themselves – half a face around the door, a hand waving above the back of the settee, one eye peeping through the curtains. It was a great favourite, but today Roberta was aware for the first time of the tension around Nicholas' mouth. How his heart must ache.

Roberta glanced at Heidi. She sat to one side watching silently. After a while she rose to her feet and without a word walked out into the garden, where she sat in the sun with her eyes closed. Roberta caught Dick's eye. He raised an eyebrow.

Was Heidi cut out to be a mother? Would she adjust to the noise and the mess and the demands of children?

Answer came in an unexpected guise.

The girls were in bed. The menfolk were poring over a brochure show-ing the latest model of a car Dick was contemplating buying. Roberta was dozing in the rocking chair and Donella and Heidi were playing whist.

A sudden roll of thunder produced an effect which clearly astonished Heidi. Donella froze in her seat, eyes dilated, the colour draining visibly from her cheeks. The cards slipped from her fingers and scattered over the carpet.

'Whoops! Excuse me,' Michael said and leapt across to the settee where his wife sat rigid.

He dropped down beside her and she threw herself in a ball against his chest. Over her head Michael explained to his wide-eyed sister-in-law about her terror of thunder and lightning. Heidi smiled sympathetically and quietly packed the cards away.

Roberta watched her move over to the window to look out at the heavy clouds and the flickering flashes, a small lonely figure. Presently Nicholas came to stand behind her, wrapping his arms around her and bending his head to drop kisses on the top of her head. She twisted in his embrace to look up and smile into his eyes. They were both startled at the brilliance of the lightning seeming to fork into the room. The noise of the torrential rain and the approaching storm prevented conversation and drowned out the symphony playing in the background. Roberta, stealing glances, took in Heidi's peaceful expression as she stroked the hands that held her so tightly.

After a while, she saw the girl stand on tiptoe to whisper in his ear, and then leave the room. She watched Nicholas' eyes follow her, flicker to where his brother cradled Donella against her terror, then turn back to the deluge outside. His thoughts were impossible to read but she felt some unknown fear stir within her.

She gave herself a mental shake. The eerie darkness and suspense of the storm must be getting to her. Time to make a cup of tea.

An unusual sound arrested her attention as she stepped out of the kitchen. Knowing the girls were supposed to be asleep, she took the stairs two at a time. But on the landing she stood spellbound. A rich contralto voice singing a lullaby sent shivers down her spine. She could see Heidi perched on the bed, cradling Fiona in her arms and rocking her in time with the music. When the lullaby finished and another song began she crept downstairs and beckoned to Dick and Nicholas to follow her.

All three stood motionless as a Swiss folk song filled the air with its soothing melody. At the end of it they watched through the half-open door as Heidi moved gingerly to place the sleeping child in her bed, pressing her lips to the damp curls.

Only when she emerged from the room did she notice the listeners. She smiled self-consciously, closing the door quietly before she said simply, 'She was frightened by the storm. I heard her crying. I hope you do not mind.'

It was Roberta who found her voice first.

'Heidi, *where* did you learn to sing like that?'

'My mother, she always sang. At home with her I learned the songs. And then when I am bigger, my music teacher, she trained me.'

'You have a *fabulous* voice.'

'Thank you. You are very kind. I like singing. I like music.'

'Did you know about this?' Roberta demanded of Nicholas.

113

'Naturally. She sings to me.' Nicholas gave Heidi an intimate smile. 'But I was under strict instructions not to tell people.'

'Why ever not?' It was Dick's turn to look incredulous. 'You have a major talent, Heidi. That was absolutely, stunningly beautiful.'

She smiled shyly, inclining her head slightly.

'I do not like to think Nicholas would boast about such a thing. I did not make it so. I was born with it. From my mother.'

'Even so … Wow! I don't know what to say,' Dick breathed, looking at her with amazed respect. 'I don't think *I'd* be so modest if I had the voice of an angel!'

'And thank you, thank you *so* much, for soothing Fiona. You were lovely with her,' Roberta added, touching her briefly on the arm. 'We didn't even know she'd woken.'

Heidi smiled warmly back.

'As I told you before, I think they are very lovely children. I like to do things with them. Quiet things.'

When the thunder ceased, there was a clamour for Heidi to sing for the adults. At first she shrank back into her seat, shaking her head vigorously. Nicholas, who had been standing behind her chair, leaned down to whisper something in her ear. She looked up at him with a startled expression. He drew one hand softly down her cheek, raising his eyebrows in a question. She nodded slowly, rising to walk across to the piano.

She sat for a moment with her hands in her lap thinking, then her fingers rippled over the keys as she played the first bars of a Tyrolean song her mother had taught her. The audience sat spellbound. The liquid notes soared effortlessly, the singer soon lost in her song. Their rapturous applause made her blush and start to rise from the piano stool, but they insisted she continue. She agreed to do so provided they join in. Her hands deftly changed to a bright melody they all knew and they sang along with her – all, that is, except Roberta, who stood watching her daughter-in-law with an enigmatic expression on her face. She looked so happy, so energised. It was a different girl.

'But you do not sing,' Heidi reproached her.

'I do not sing, my dear, because I should ruin the whole thing. I have a terrible voice and I wouldn't profane your glorious sound with even a mumble.'

'But it does not matter. We sing to be happy. To enjoy each other,' she cried.

'Believe me, it *would* matter! But do go on. I'm enjoying *you* enormously right now. I've never heard a beautiful voice like yours at close quarters before. So please don't stop.'

Heidi turned to the eager faces gathered around the piano.

'Tell me what you know. What would you like to sing?'

They sang two more songs in unison and then by popular request they all fell silent as Heidi introduced them to the songs of her homeland. When she sang her own particular favourite unaccompanied, Roberta felt emotion choking her throat. There was an ethereal quality to her voice, which touched deep chords. But more than that, Heidi had suddenly lost the pinched and lost look which seemed to have become habitual, and Nicholas couldn't drag his eyes away from his wife.

When she declared she absolutely could not utter another sound, he moved close behind her and in front of them all bent to kiss her full on the lips. She was blushing again when she eventually emerged from his embrace, but all around her Roberta saw with satisfaction the approving faces.

That night marked the beginning of a new chapter in the lives of the Halley family. Fiona, having been sung to sleep by her aunt during the thunderstorm, clamoured for more of the same. Heidi introduced all the children to singing games. She became a firm favourite. Although she had always hated boisterous play and shrank from the riotous activities Nicholas initiated with the girls, she was in her element with creative or musical activities.

Under her guiding voice they learned to sing the alphabet and the notes of the scales, to play tunes on the piano and guitar, and to identify the opening bars of famous concertos and symphonies. Encouraged by their responses, she introduced them to culinary and domestic pursuits. She taught them how to make sweets, to embroider, to make Swiss delicacies. The rest of the family looked on in wonder. There was not a shred of doubt left in Roberta's mind that Heidi would make a wonderful mother. Her love for her nieces was transparently obvious.

Roberta began to see the Heidi Nicholas had married, the girl she had been before sorrow stole her peace of mind. And she discovered with some surprise that it had taken her own tunelessness to help Heidi feel part of the family. She had entered the house overawed by the strength of these talented people, all so intelligent, so articulate, so capable, she felt intimidated, Heidi explained. The strong bonds which united them left her on the fringe. The more they worked to include her, the more excluded she felt. But Roberta had shown her that she too had skills which set her apart, a talent they could never hope to emulate. Their genuine enthusiasm for her voice and creative skills showed her that their reaching out to her had not been in any way patronising or polite. They just wanted to draw her into the love of this big-hearted family. Roberta watched with a growing peace, as she nestled in that heart gratefully, her sadness softened because of it.

Donella's children innocently helped that process, encouraging her just to be herself. Heidi reached the ultimate pinnacle of their admiration the day she yodelled through the glen near where they lived; the echoes of her sounds entrancing old and young alike. They tried to copy her movements as she explained them step by step, but no-one else could produce the right noise, never mind the perfect cadences she emitted so effortlessly. She laughed helplessly at their concentration and the strange results, and they were all infected by her simple unaffected pleasure.

TWENTY

It was during this time of adjustment that Nicholas made a sudden and unexpected appeal to his brother for advice.

It was rare now that they were alone and Michael had welcomed his brother's suggestion of a pint in the local pub. Autumn was already turning the leaves but the warm evening sunshine was enough to tempt them to sit outside until the light faded.

Without warning, without preamble, Nicholas suddenly launched into treacherous waters.

'What would you do, Mike? If you were in my shoes.'

'As in?'

'As in having kids.'

'Blimey, I don't know,' Michael said, staring at his twin. 'No easy answers. It depends. I'm not really in a position to say, am I?'

'No, you lucky blighter. Had it easy, you.'

'I know. And that's why it's kind of hard for me to say anything. You must see that. Be pretty insensitive of *me* to go crashing in.'

'But I'm asking you.'

'Well, since you mention the subject, I feel for you, Nick. I really do. Believe me. I'd give anything to help if I could. It must be hellish.'

'That – and more.' Nicholas' voice was tense. 'But it'd help, if you could bear it, to talk about it. I need to sort this stuff out. It drives me mad these questions going round and round in my head.'

'Well, sure. Fire away. So long as you understand where I'm coming from on this.'

'I've been watching you a lot lately – with your girls. It's special, isn't it? Having your own.'

'Absolutely.'

'And you're really good with them.'

'So are you! They go overboard with excitement when they know you're coming.' Michael smiled warmly at him as he spoke. It was the truth.

'But that's different. I just lark about with them. But for you – I mean, it must be different. D'you think – what you feel – that bond – does it come from them being yours? Genetically, I mean, yours?'

'Goodness, I don't know. Can't say, really. I guess mostly parents don't separate out the two things, do they? Social, genetic. They just *are* yours.'

'Well, no reason to, normally.'

'That's right.'

'Funny thing really, though, for a bloke, huh? I mean, you can understand it when it's the Mum. She's felt them growing inside her, and given birth, and she feeds them and everything. But our bit, well, it's over in a jiffy. But having children, it's obviously special for a Dad too.'

'I must admit, I hadn't really analysed it, but I see your point.'

'D'you think it's because of – how you feel about the woman who's carrying them, that makes you feel like that?'

'Well, in my case, I guess it's all part of it. I mean, because I love Donella, and because we wanted to have children together, we both love the ones we've made together. But lots of men love their kids even when they can't stand the mother! Don't they? So it can't really be that. Must be something to do with them being yours, I guess. I don't understand the mechanics though.'

'Would *you* have wanted children if you couldn't have had them normally, d'you think?'

'I don't know. Not for sure. Before we got married we discussed having a family, of course – like you do. We knew we *did* want them – eventually. But we didn't get to the stage of wondering if we ever would. Well' – Michael looked at his brother rather sheepishly – 'you know Rachael just happened – *way* before we planned a family. So the question never arose really.'

'*Super*-fertile you two!'

'Looks like it! Sorry. That doesn't help you.'

'D'you think – if you'd *had* to have help – d'you think it would matter if, say, Rachael was yours but not Donella's?'

'Pros and cons, I'd say. It'd be nice knowing she had *some* of our own genes, I think. But I could see it might be tough on Donella. She might feel resentful or guilty or something. I suppose it's something like a step-child in the family. You'd have to do some serious talking and be very honest, I guess. Sort it all out. See where your limits were. Is that a problem for Heidi?'

'She says not. Insists she *wants* it to be my kid. Trouble is, Mike, you don't know what will come out of the woodwork years down the line, do you?'

'I know what you mean. But hey, none of us do. I mean, in years to come will Donella hold it against me that we had Rachael so soon, or that we didn't have a boy, or that we had three children and it was her career that suffered? Who knows? You just have to do what seems best for you both at the time, don't you?'

'I guess so.'

'Is the jury still out on this for you two?'

'Well, we think surrogacy's our best bet.'

Michael did a double take.

'Surrogacy, eh? Wow.' He was silent while the information was absorbed. 'So? Anything stopping you?'

'Only about sixty-five worries! And Dad. It fairly keeps a chap awake at night, I can tell you.'

'I can believe that! Dad giving you grief, is he?'

'Well, not exactly grief. He's been good about talking to me. And he gave me all the facts, all the options, all the pros and cons. But you know Dad. Gives it to you straight. Tells it like it is. Thing is, at the end of the day, he doesn't approve of surrogacies. Doesn't want to get involved. And he won't budge.' Michael heard the grit in his brother's voice.

'It can't be easy for him – you know – when it's *you*.'

'Oh, I appreciate that. And to give him his due, I must say, he made it dead easy to talk to him. You know, about the intimate stuff. But he still won't do it.'

'Is that a problem?'

'Yep. We were relying on him to make sure it was all as good as we could make it. Minimise the chances of disaster, you know.'

'And he won't budge?'

'Nope.'

'And Mum?'

'Mum? She's a star. D'you know what she said?' Nicholas' voice changed. Michael shook his head slightly.

'*She'd* be our surrogate!'

'Blimey! Did she?' Michael stared at his brother. 'But yeah, that's Mum. And you said?'

'Thanks, but no thanks. Of course!'

'Gives you goosebumps thinking about that one!' Michael shuddered.

'I think Mum saw that.' Nicholas laughed. 'But it was dead good of her to offer. She meant it the right way.'

'She *would* do it too. What a mother! Not as squeamish as the rest of us mere mortals, I guess. But *you* … and *Mum* … Nah! No way!'

'My sentiments exactly.' Nicholas grinned at him.

'Pity though. It'd solve a few problems.'

'Some maybe. You'd know she'd go through with it, give it up to us at the end, all that. But it'd cause others. Could be tricky for the child if its birth mother was its grandmother, don't you think? Pretty confusing!'

'Indeed! But women do it for relatives, don't they? I guess the ones you hear about are usually young women doing it for sisters or cousins or whatever though, huh? It's a pity Heidi hasn't got a sister. Somebody the right age. With kids of her own. Somebody who'd do it for love. All that jazz.'

'Yep. But we can't conjure one up!'

'Pity. Even the first bit could be private then – if it was a young person. If it was *Mum*, you'd still have to go through the old IVF stuff, wouldn't you? Have those colleagues of Dad's poking their noses into your most intimate affairs.'

'Absolutely. Double horrors!'

'Alex and Jo don't qualify, I guess. Since they're still having their own kids.'

'Besides you couldn't have *them* – my own sisters – having *my* child!'

'True. I didn't think that one through! Sorry!'

Another long silence fell.

'It's not just what we want. We have to think of the child – growing up,' Nicholas said slowly. 'Hell of a thing for a kid. Even if *we* can accept it. Wouldn't want to find out I'd started that way myself. How about you?'

Michael thought about it before responding.

'Would it be so awful? I mean, if it knew you loved it and you'd gone through fire and brimstone to get it?'

'I just don't know. That's my problem – who knows?'

'I think if it felt totally secure and loved it'd take the news in its stride in the end. I mean loving them, protecting them, caring – that's the kernel of parenting. More important than the actual conceiving. Isn't it?'

'D'you think so?'

'Yep, I do. I mean, our three – it doesn't matter one iota to *them* just how they were conceived. But they'd know from early on if they weren't loved, wouldn't they? It's much more – I don't know – *fundamental* to their welfare.'

'But what about when they're older – eighteen, say?'

'Who understands the workings of the teenage mind? Certainly not me! But I think, even at that crazy stage, if they'd had a loving, secure home-life it'd be a head start in them accepting facts about their conception.'

'Mmmmhh. But say they were surrogate kids: would it make a difference if they knew you were their natural Dad – or not – as the case may be?'

'Depends on what kind of rebellious creatures they were, I guess. But on balance, I'd say, it'd be a bonus if they knew they were at least half ours biologically too.'

'D'you think so? Honestly, Mike? Tell me what you really think. Don't just say that because you know it's what I'm contemplating for us. It'd be good to hear a few blunt truths.'

'No, I'm not. Well, kids like to know their roots, don't they? If I was their natural father, they'd know half of it at least. My side. And presumably we could fill in a *bit* about the surrogate. So they're not totally up the creek without a paddle, are they?'

'Yeah. That's the way I see it. But then there's the missing bit. OK, I guess you'd know *basic* details, but what would it do to them knowing their birth mother was a woman who gave them away? I can't get my head around that bit of it.'

'Well, it's not quite like that, is it? I mean, their mother's actually a woman with a great big heart who loves kids and wants them to have happy homes and be really wanted. You could say she's extra special.'

'If you get one of that variety. But how d'you know she is?' The expression on Nicholas' face said what words could not capture.

'Well, I don't know. But I believe there *are* altruistic women in the business – from the little I know, anyway – those who know what it's like to love kids and who want to help other folk who aren't as fortunate.'

'Yeah. There must be. But how do you know you've got one of those?'

'Pity you don't know somebody – you know, a bona fide surrogate. So you'd know where they're coming from. I suppose Dad doesn't know somebody he could vouch for?'

'Nope. Won't touch surrogacies with a barge pole.'

'And Mum? No contacts there?'

'Nope.'

'Pity. Specially with Dad in the trade, so to speak. So what are your thoughts at this moment?'

'At this moment? I feel like I'm in a maze. Just think I'm on the home straight and know where we're going and there's another impenetrable barrier in the way.'

'So are you going to pursue the surrogate thing?'

'Probably. D'you think I'm mad? Is Dad right? Should we just accept we can't have kids and sublimate our needs through other channels? Go back to somewhere dangerous, get ourselves killed for a good cause instead?'

'Well, don't go and get yourselves killed, that's for sure! But as to whether or not you have kids, only you can say. I wouldn't presume to advise you.'

'We talked about that from the outset. I mean, we had a pretty exciting life before we came home. There's loads of work to be done out there; they're crying out for folk without domestic responsibilities. But Heidi's adamant she wants kids too. It's not just me.'

'Well, all I would say, Nick, is don't let other people get to you, or persuade you. Nobody else can know what's right for *you*. Even folk in similar situations – they're not *you*. And certainly not those folk who breed like rabbits but think they have all the answers to infertility. It's none of their business.'

'Thanks, Mike. You're right, of course, but the comments do sort of creep under your skin.'

'I know. They always do when you're vulnerable. No matter how much you *pretend* not to notice, or not to care what folk say.'

They sat in silence for a long moment.

'Must be hard to know what to say to Heidi,' Michael began softly. 'It's tougher on her in a way, eh? At least you know you *could* have kids.'

'Yeah. She's strong though – inside. She's not the overly emotional kind – you'll have noticed that!' Nicholas gave a small smile as he spoke. 'But she's strong. She seems to just accept it. It's happened.'

'Good for her. No merit in weeping all over the place. Doesn't get you anywhere. But it must be tough, all the same, having all this going on, and no family of her own and everything.'

'Well, she's had to be pretty self-sufficient. She hasn't looked to family for support for a long time. Hasn't ever had our kind of support behind her. But she's taken a shine to *our* family. And she adores your kids.'

'Well, as you know, they adore her.'

'She's also got a sort of blind trust in Dad. She's averse to seeing anybody else professional, but reckons Dad's top of the tree – he'll work some miracle.'

'Heavens! Don't let him know that. Not good for his humility!'

They laughed together.

'So has she got anybody to talk to about how *she* feels about all this?' Michael asked.

'Only me. And I have to confess she doesn't say a lot – about *this*, I mean – even to me. She finds all the biological stuff hard to talk about.'

'Not surprising. It must be especially hard for her to talk to *you* about it. I mean, it's *you* it affects most – her infertility.'

'I know. You're right. I must admit I didn't realise that at first, and I just tried to get her to tell me honestly what she felt. But when the penny dropped, I wanted her to see somebody independent she could talk to – somebody outside the family who hasn't got a vested interest in this. But she freaked at the mere suggestion. Doesn't help, of course, that she's in a foreign country now. But I suggested it before we came over here – going to Switzerland, finding somebody good there. She wouldn't even consider it. Even if I set it up for her.'

'Mum? She any help?'

'She tried, but nope, Heidi didn't want to talk.'

'Tricky.' Michael shook his head. Then turning to his brother, he said quietly, 'But you, Nick. If *you* need a listening ear any time, remember I'm available and I'm willing.'

'Thanks, Mike. Thanks for listening tonight, too. I can talk at a different level to you. It helps.'

TWENTY-ONE

Not until late that evening did Donella learn anything of the twins' conversation.

Michael was stretched out on the carpet staring up at the ceiling, while Donella read the paper. She became aware gradually of his inactivity.

'Are you OK?' she asked tentatively.

'We are *so* lucky, Don.'

She sat forward in her chair and waited.

His own sorrow for his beloved brother pervaded the story, and it was not until he reached the point of Roberta's offer that Donella interrupted the flow.

'She's brilliant, isn't she? A one-off. And what did Nick say?'

'Well, he was terribly grateful of course, but he couldn't let her do it.'

'Why not?'

'Nick having a baby – with *Mum*? Nah. He *couldn't!*'

'But she's only offering to carry his child to term, and give birth to it, not have sex with him.'

'Well, it doesn't feel right.'

'I think that's because you're thinking about this all wrong. Your Mum'd be the incubator hatching out the chick for Nick and Heidi. If you look at it like that, Mum's the very best person to do it. Except that I'd be worried about what it'd do to her health, now she's older.'

'Well, whatever. It wouldn't work because they'd still need eggs from a younger woman. And they want to avoid the medical intervention bit. Seems Heidi's got a block about it. Well, in fact, Nick's none too keen.'

'That's rich coming from a family of doctors, eh?!'

'Good point. I hadn't thought of it like that. What does that say about your profession, Dr Halley?'

She saw Michael's sudden questioning look and realised she was supposed to respond to the taunt. But her thoughts were already moving on.

'So they need someone young, preferably close, and who's happy to do it for them,' she mused aloud.

'That's about the size of it.'

'Pity Heidi hasn't got any young eligible female relations.'

'That's what Dad and Nick both said. And on Nick's side, Alex and Jo don't qualify because you can't mix their genes with their brother's.'

'No, of course you can't.'

There was silence. They both remained unmoving.

'Are you thinking what I'm thinking?' Michael's voice was a whisper.

'Probably …' Donella's thoughts were turbulent. 'But …'

He rolled over and sat upright, cross-legged, looking directly at her.

'Would you want Heidi to carry your child?' she asked suddenly.

'Mmmmmm. What a question! I don't know. I don't feel I know her well enough to say. And I don't know how she'd cope with pregnancy or having a child. So probably not.'

'But you think *I* should do it for *them*?'

'It's completely different.'

'How so? The relationships are the same.'

'Technically maybe. But completely different feelings. They'd want *you* to do it.'

'*You* might think so, but *they* might not.'

'Well, Nick would anyway. I'm sure he would. Why wouldn't he? You're like a sister but not genetically related. He's known you for years – hang it, longer than me! He's very close to you. *And* you're a fantastic Mum. He knows you'd do all the right things. *And* you produce gorgeous babies. *And* we know your genes are compatible with the Halley genes. *And* you're a gorgeous creature yourself. So what could he possibly object to?' Michael was warming to his theme.

Donella gave him a hard look.

'Me being your wife, for a kick-off!'

'Meaning?'

'Well, put it this way, how would *you* feel about me carrying *his* baby?' She held his gaze steadily.

'But you said yourself, you're only incubating it.'

'No, I said your *Mum* would only be incubating it. The genes wouldn't be hers at all. If *I* did it, it'd be half mine, half Nick's. Not at all yours. *Now* how do you feel?'

There was a long silence.

'You pregnant. With Nick's baby.' He spoke slowly. 'I think – I *think* I'd be OK with that. If it was for Nick.'

'Nick might not be so sure you'd be OK with it, though.'

'But if it was done – you know – like a treatment – it wouldn't be like you and Nick … Would it?'

'Having sex, you mean? No, of course it wouldn't. But you'd need to think of all the worst-case scenarios and work back from them. It's dodgy stuff this. You'd have to be absolutely sure. Everybody in this thing would have to be sure it felt right.'

'Does it feel right to *you*?'

'I haven't a clue. I'd have to think about it a lot more before I could say one way or the other.'

'But you're not ruling it out?'

'No, I'm not ruling it out. But I'm not ruling it in either.'

'Makes sense. You're the perfect choice really.'

'Don't, Mike. Don't try to make me feel it's my responsibility.' She drew away from him.

'Oh, I didn't mean it like that.'

'Well, whatever you meant. I won't do it if it's out of duty. I'd have to *want* to do it.'

'Fair enough. And I wouldn't want you to do it for any other reason.' She shrugged.

'Well, I need time to think about this, and I'd have to read up more about it before we even *think* of suggesting it to Nick and Heidi. If we ever do.'

The search for information, the complex emotions involved, robbed Donella of sleep as well as mental rest. Should she talk to a colleague at work about the subject? Although she worked in oncology research she had ready access to all the other disciplines and departments at the university as well as the local hospitals; the benefit of their expertise might help her to sort out her own thoughts. But something made her draw back from sharing anything of her own emotions unless and until the idea became a possibility. Should she talk to her own parents about it? After all, Nicholas had consulted his. But she knew the dynamics within the two families were very different. Much as she loved her mother, it was a long time since she had relied on her for guidance; they saw the world differently now. Her father was closer to her but he would intuitively defer to her better understanding of medical matters. Besides he would not have thought through an issue like surrogacy, and this was no time for knee-jerk reactions or emotional appeals. No, Michael was the only person with whom she could discuss this – it was too personal for other ears.

It was Michael who again raised the subject ten days later. They were lying in bed and his eye caught the title of her book as she laid it down under the lamp: *Family Patterns*.

'How are you getting on finding out about surrogacy?'

'Well, I've got a whole lot more factual information but I still haven't a clue if it's something I could cope with myself.'

'Would it help to talk about what you're thinking up to now?'

'Probably not. I haven't got enough of it sorted out in my head. But what about *you*? What do you think? You'd need to be one hundred and ten per cent certain *you're* OK with it.'

'Me? I'd be pretty peripheral to the whole thing, wouldn't I? Just be there for you.'

'Absolutely not. You're not peripheral. What you think is crucially important. People forget the psychological side of this sort of thing. It's not just some surgical operation that the woman just has to recover from.'

'Sorry. I didn't mean to make light of it.'

'OK then, you want to move on? Let's just concentrate on your side of it – for now? I'll need to think heaps more about how *I* feel – but it'd be good if you were working out where you stand too.'

'OK. Looks like I need a bit of help to ask the right questions. You'll know all the ins and outs.'

'Well, I don't know it all by any means. But I can see it's not nearly as simple as you seem to think it is.'

Michael turned onto his back, the better to concentrate on her words and not be distracted by her body.

'Fire away.'

Donella felt relieved not to have to meet his eyes as she began to outline the practicalities. It certainly wasn't easy to think about these things when your emotions were so much engaged with the people concerned.

'This is very much off the top of my head, but let's go through the procedure first. Nick has to produce semen first. It has to be inserted inside me.' She waited for him to visualise the steps. 'Where do we do it? In our bed? In their bed? In a hotel room? Who does it? Do *you* want to be actively involved? How would you feel knowing someone else was sticking the turkey baster inside me? Sorry, sounds crude but you've got to think it all through, Mike.'

He was lying with his eyes tightly shut, lips pursed, trying to see the events and gauge his reaction. At this his eyes flew open. He turned a wide stare on her.

'The *what*? What's a *turkey baster* when it's at home?'

'The syringe thing you use to baste meat. You know – the thing I use to suck up the fat and juices and trickle them over the roast while it's cooking.'

'Oh *that*! And that's what you'd use?'

'Yep.'

'Not a syringe or something?'

'Baster's better, apparently.'

'I guess I see why. OK. Not exactly competition! Sorry!'

'Typical male!' She grinned briefly.

He turned back and closed his eyes again.

'Where were we? Oh yes. The baster. OK, the deed's done. Now I'm lying for half an hour waiting for the sperm to swim up towards the egg. How would you feel then looking at me, knowing that it's not your semen, it's Nick's. And that I'm willing it to work? And Nick's *thinking* about me lying there like that?'

She saw his abdominal muscles go taut. She knew she wasn't making it easy. But he hadn't begun to think what it would be like.

'OK, it works. I tell you I'm pregnant. Remember what that felt like before. But this time it's not yours. How will you feel about this growing fetus? Will you want to feel it moving, kicking, stretching, inside me? Will you start to love it – like you did with Rachael and Fiona and Emily? And if you do, will you be able to let it go?'

He was frowning in concentration now.

'How will you feel watching me getting bigger? Knowing we'll have nothing ourselves at the end of it? And what about if this time I'm not as fit as I was before. What if I keep being sick, get varicose veins, stretch marks, look done to death, have thinning lacklustre hair, heartburn, lose interest in sex?'

'I'm rapidly going off the whole idea!' he said without opening his eyes.

'Will you resent Nick for being responsible for all that?'

'I hate him already!'

'And then there's the question of sex. For you and me, I mean. I'd have to come off the pill while we were trying for the pregnancy. You'd have to use a condom. Or abstain. Or be sterilised! It wouldn't be the same. How would you feel about that? Would you resent Nick for that? Or me?'

'Gee whizz, Don. Pile it on, why don't you?'

'And we see a lot of Nick and Heidi. He's always been easy with me. Affectionate too, sometimes. You know. It's just Nick. It doesn't mean anything. But how will you feel seeing him with me if I'm carrying his child? Will you wonder what he's thinking about me? Will you hate it if he's all anxious about me, like *you* were when I was pregnant the other times? He might well be. He's sure to feel protective about *his* child. You know Nick. And will you feel in competition – *you* wanting to protect me, *him* wanting to protect me? Will you read things into my responses?'

'And to think I said I was peripheral to all this! Good job you're here to keep me right.'

'And then, if we survive all that, the birth. Are *you* there? Is Nick there? Is Heidi there? How do *you* feel about them being there, watching that, seeing me stripped of my dignity? Do they take the child away out of the labour ward, leaving me just with the bleeding and the after pains and the leaking breasts and the fourth day blues and the postnatal depression. And I might be depressed. Because I *had* a baby, but I haven't got one now. And will you still feel happy for them when you're left to mop up the tears and the mess and cope with my crazy moods?'

Without opening his eyes he reached across to pull her back close to him. She felt the fierceness of his hold. But it was no time to relent. He had to think about this realistically.

'The baby is with Heidi and Nick. It's theirs. But we see it. Of course. How will you feel when I hold it, play with it, look at it lovingly? How will you feel when I cry at night because it doesn't know I'm its mother? Will you still be happy for Nick? And for Heidi? Or will you resent them for making me unhappy?'

'I do already.'

'Will you always have to check how I'm feeling when it starts to talk and calls someone else Mummy? Heidi'll be a first time Mum. She'll do things differently. Will you be able to cope with me being uptight because I want to intervene and do it my way – but can't? And will you come to resent Heidi because she made all that stuff necessary – put us both through it?'

There was a long silence. When she spoke next Donella's voice was thick with emotion.

'And what about our girls? Will you want them to know this child is their half-sibling? They'll have to know. They'll see me pregnant; they'll know there was a baby. And Aunty Heidi wasn't pregnant but she's got a baby. Will you worry about what they will think of me giving away my baby? When they ask you when I'm going to give *them* away?'

There was a breathless pause as Michael waited for more. But Donella had finished for now. She couldn't deal with any more of this kind of thinking herself at this moment. Slowly he raised himself on one elbow to look down into her eyes.

'For someone who is so beautiful I still feel weak at the knees looking at you, you do a very effective hatchet job on a chap!'

'I'm sorry, Mike. I have to be brutal. Now's the time, not halfway through the process.'

'I take it it's a no.'

'No, not necessarily. As I said, I haven't ruled it out – or in. But don't let's pretend it's a simple we-want-to-help-Nick-we'll-do-it. It has colossal implications. And we have to think long and hard before we even suggest it – if we ever do.'

'That message has gone home loud and clear. Sorry I was so naïve.'

He remained propped up beside her, his finger caressing the skin of her neck and shoulder.

'That's OK.' She smiled up at him. 'This time.'

'Underneath that oh-so-calm exterior, are you feeling in the least bit disturbed yourself?'

'Disturbed? At this moment I'm thinking we must *both* be seriously disturbed to be even *contemplating* doing this!' she retorted.

'Well, that's a relief! I try to hang on to the illusion that you are human somewhere underneath that professional façade! But you medical folk never cease to astound me. You just don't think like us ordinary mortals.'

'I can tell you, if I'm honest, the whole idea scares me to death at this moment. But that's a gut reaction. And I'm wary of gut reactions. I need to think about this for a long time. Don't expect an answer for a least a fortnight.'

Michael was suddenly very still, holding her gaze squarely.

'While we're being so honest – there's one thing you didn't say.'

'Uhhuh?'

128

'Nick fancied you – before I did. You were keen on him. Would that affect any of this?'

She returned his look steadily.

'I don't know. It's something we'd have to talk about. Together and even perhaps with Nick.'

'He's always been a bit soft on you, I think. OK, maybe he's never said so in so many words. But I think he is.'

'You've never mentioned that before.'

He shrugged.

'Thought it though.'

'No. I think you're wrong. OK, we're close, easy with each other. We have lots in common, we speak the same language, both being doctors. He's naturally demonstrative – we both are – but he knows I won't take it seriously. He knows I love you. No, it's nothing more. Not now. And especially since Heidi came on the scene. You've seen how he is with her.'

'But it *was* special – for both of you. Once.'

'Yes, it was. I don't deny it. You know it was. You saw what it did to me when he went away. But that was all a long time ago. He was my first real love. But you know that what *we* have – you and me – it's much more than that.' She reached up to take his face in both her hands still holding his gaze. 'I love you, Mike, in ways that you can't compare with that young headstrong kind of love. You know that. You must do. You and the girls – you're everything to me.'

'I know. But sometimes I've thought, if Nick hadn't gone away, if he hadn't let you down, you might have been with him now.'

'Who knows? Maybe. Maybe not. But then you wouldn't have ever been involved with me, so it wouldn't have hurt you.'

'But if you had his kid – would I worry about it in that way?'

'That's for you to say. I don't know. I only know you don't have a shred of reason to worry on that score from my point of view.'

'No?'

'No. And if you come here … I'll show you just how much I love you.' She reached up to slide her arms around his neck.

'Thank goodness for that,' he said in an altogether different tone. He dropped down onto the pillow and nuzzled into her neck. 'I do *not* like to be kept at arm's length in bed for anything in excess of two minutes so I expect you to redouble your efforts to put me in a good mood with you.'

TWENTY-TWO

The following fortnight was a long and difficult one for Donella. The issue of surrogacy was ever present in her thoughts. It was hard to concentrate at work; household chores seemed ridiculously trivial; the children's artless chatter and demands irritated her uncharacteristically.

Again she was tempted to talk through the issues with a colleague but as before she turned away from including anyone outside the family in her dilemma. She briefly toyed with the idea of talking to Roberta about it. She was so calm, so level-headed about things, so easy to talk to. And she'd know the medical consequences. And her integrity was beyond question. But ... it felt wrong. On this subject Roberta had her own vested interests. Her allegiance would surely be to her son: his need, his interests. Well ... maybe ... but ... there was no way of gauging how sympathetic Roberta would be to such an idea. And Donella knew from Michael that Dick had been opposed to the very idea of surrogacy.

No, she had to accept this was her decision. She was an adult, a doctor, a wife, a mother. She did not need to lean on anyone. The facts, of course, she could find out; the emotions she must sort out for herself. It was her decision and she must arrive at a conclusion without pressure from either direction. No-one else, except perhaps Michael, should share any part of the responsibility for what she might or might not do.

She found herself slipping into the girls' bedrooms one night to stare at them, wondering what life would have been like for her, for Michael, if they had not been born, if she had been infertile. And wondering what it would do to the children themselves to know their mother was the kind of woman who could give away her own child.

She looked down at the baby, Emily, flat on her face, bottom in the air, her breathing noisy in the silence of the night. The flushed cheek was warm and soft to her kiss. She smelt again the familiar baby smell, and felt the yearning love surge through her. There could be no substitute for this.

She drew back, trying to look at the child through different eyes. What if there was another baby lying in a cot – like Emily – but this one she could *not* keep? She'd been so sure that three was her lot. Her career was gaining ground now. But if she had another one – carried it, gave birth to it, held it – would she have the strength to hand it over to Nicholas and Heidi? To keep her distance, let Heidi take over? Heidi in all her inexperience, her emotional tightness? How would she feel seeing her own child, from the distance of an aunt? Not breastfeeding it. Not being the one to make decisions. Perhaps not approving the way it was disciplined or brought up.

But at least she'd be able to watch it growing up, legitimately take an interest. And it would be told – eventually – that she was its biological mother. That she had simply given it back to its father. Simply? Nothing was simple in this! But she would be able to tell it herself how much she loved it. Make sure it knew how special it was.

Rachael lay spreadeagled in her bed, one foot poking out of the covers, long lashes sweeping the flushed cheeks. Donella stared down at her eldest daughter. But the thoughts were too chaotic. She left the room precipitately.

In the dimness of the unlit drawing room, she picked up a photograph of the three girls. Would they understand if she did this thing? They were so precious. They loved her so completely now. Would that change? Were they secure enough to accept her motives for giving away their brother or sister? Would they be able to accept the confusion in relationships without being traumatised themselves? How would they respond to her pregnancy and then the information that she was giving the baby to their uncle?

Deliberately she let her mind travel back to her pregnancies. She had felt fantastic throughout all three of them. No, the physical effects held no fears. But what about the psychological implications? Would she be able to cope with other people's comments? The ones who didn't know the truth, congratulating her, asking when she expected the happy event? *Happy* …! Or the reaction of those who had to know the truth. The sudden silences. The stunned disapproval. The cold condemnation. The voluble criticism.

Would she be able to explain convincingly that she had done it out of love? Love for her husband's brother? You could explain doing it for a sister, even a daughter … but … a *brother-in-law*? How would she react to their sudden looks, the unspoken thoughts, the veiled innuendoes? The jokes about *how* they'd done it. She held her hands over her ears and closed her eyes to shut out the horror.

It still left the thoughts inside her own head. How did she feel – really feel – about having Nicholas' child growing inside her?

He had always been special to her. He was still special. But just where did the boundaries lie? Even Michael had had doubts.

But of course he was special; he'd been her first real love. It had broken her heart when he'd left her and gone to Brazil. But that was before Michael – Michael who had replaced Nicholas completely in that way. There wasn't a shred of doubt – she'd told Michael so. But … was it true? Even in the furthest, darkest, totally unseen corners of her heart? Was it true there too? Because if there was anything of that crazy, all-consuming love left, might it not sneak out if she held his child within her?

But she had. She knew – no-one else did – not even Nicholas – but *she* did. She knew Rachael was his. That one night in the bathroom was the only time she'd not used her barrier contraceptive. She'd given herself spontaneously, no thought of pregnancy, just of loving. Oh yes, she'd known, even before the midwife had revealed her dates, she'd known the baby was her brother-in-law's. But no-one must ever know.

No, no-one *would* ever know. Not even a DNA paternity test could tell – not with the two men identical twins. But it cut her to the quick to see the pain in Nicholas' eyes – the pain of childlessness – and not be able to tell him he was the father of a beautiful, laughing child who adored him, but only knew him as uncle. If she could give him another baby, would that help to assuage her guilt? He would be the one to listen to it calling him Daddy; she would be the one to hear Aunt. It would be her way of giving him back his own, without destroying the lives and wrecking the happiness of so many other people.

She must find a way to do this thing. She realised, with a sharp jolt this was why she had avoided consulting anyone else. There was really no question about it; she had to do it. She owed it to Nicholas.

It would surely not take much to become pregnant. A couple of attempts should do it. Her fertility was proven; she knew Nicholas' was too. A couple of quick goes at most. Not much to ask. And since he was Michael's identical twin their genes were almost certainly compatible. So it was a matter of steeling herself to view this whole thing as a medical procedure which would give Nicholas what was rightfully his. She resolved to keep that thought firmly in the forefront of her mind. She would repeat it like a mantra every night before she went to sleep. She was strong. She could do this thing. She had it in her power to right a great wrong. And in the end, she too would feel the cleansing of this act of love.

It was another whole week before she again broached the subject with Michael.

Had he come to a decision himself?

He had. Had she?

She had.

They agreed to write their answers on a piece of paper and hand them to each other simultaneously. They would give themselves ten minutes on the clock to sit without comment, thinking about the word on the other's slip of paper. Only then would they speak.

They both wrote one word, exchanged the slips of paper. The ten minutes extended into infinity.

When Michael dared to raise his head the tears were already running down Donella's face. Without a word he took her in his arms, shivering inside as he held her.

She confided: her biggest anxiety was the girls. They would both have to be extremely vigilant and ensure the children felt totally secure in their love. Michael surrounded her with his promises.

TWENTY-THREE

When Nicholas took the phone call inviting them to dinner two nights later there was no hint of a hidden agenda.

But as the evening progressed he became increasingly aware of the little intimacies passing between Donella and Michael. There was something in the air. Ahhhh. That would be it. They were having another child and were fearful of breaking the news. He consciously steeled himself.

'Nick, Heidi' – Michael looked from one to the other as he spoke – 'Donella and I have something to tell you.'

There was silence.

'It's rather delicate, and it's important that we all remember we're family. Everybody must be honest and say what they really think on this one.'

Nicholas saw his brother needed encouragement to drop the bombshell.

'Wow, heavy-duty stuff for a post-prandial conversation, bro! But don't mind us. Fire away.'

'Well, yeah. It *is* a pretty heavy-duty proposition, I guess.' Michael looked at Donella with his eyebrows raised. 'Over to you, Don.'

Donella looked directly at Heidi as she spoke.

'Would you consider me – as your surrogate?'

Nicholas and Heidi both stared at her, too stunned to register any emotion. The air was thick with their silence.

'Are … you … serious?' He heard his own stunned voice but it seemed to come from someone else.

'Never more so.' She smiled hesitantly at him.

'I just … don't know what to say. That is the most generous offer anybody could ever make.' Nicholas' voice cracked. He stopped abruptly.

'If the whole idea appals you, you can just say. We'll understand. But we just wanted to help – if we could.' Donella looked suddenly shy.

'*Appals* us? You must be kidding. You're a fantastic mum. I can't think of anyone better. But what about *you*? Both of you – but especially you, Donella. It's a huge thing to ask of you.'

'But you're not asking. I'm offering.' She looked again at Michael, smiling at him as she added, 'We're both offering.'

Nicholas' eyes went to his wife.

'Heidi?'

She was sitting motionless.

'I do not have the words to say. You are very kind. Very, *very* kind. And you would be a very good person to have a baby for us,' she said, her command of English unequal to the moment. 'You make beautiful children. I think I would like to have children like your children. But I did not expect such a thing and I think we must talk a lot about this – Nicholas and I. But thank you very, *very* much.'

Donella smiled across at her.

'You mustn't feel you have to say yes, just because we offered. I won't be offended. But if you think it might help, then we'd be glad to do it for you. And if you think it's right for you, we can talk more about the arrangements and everything, then.'

'You're something else, you two. It never entered my head that you …' Nicholas was lost for words again.

Donella looked away quickly and focused on her sister-in-law.

'You must take your time, Heidi. It's a big thing to contemplate. Mike and I have talked for hours about it, but we've just dropped it on you, so give yourselves time. Just let us know when you're ready to talk some more about it. You two are the most important people here. It has to be what you want. We just want you to know we're willing.'

She smiled quietly and rose to pour more coffee.

It was difficult to steer the conversation into normal channels after that. Long silences punctuated the evening. Eventually Nicholas sat forward in his seat.

'I think we should go. It's obvious none of us can think of anything much except your amazing offer. Heidi and I have a lot of thinking to do. And I don't think we'll get much sleep tonight if we don't go home and start talking.'

He stood up, Heidi following his example. Slipping an arm around her waist he smiled down at her.

'Ready for an all-night session?'

'If we must talk so long, I will do it.'

'She'd probably outlast you.' Michael laughed.

Nicholas watched him move to give Heidi a farewell kiss. She caught his hand in both hers.

'You are a most kind and generous man. Tonight you make me feel you care about us very, very much – to do *such* a thing. I think Nicholas is very lucky to have such a brother.'

'She's right there. I am indeed lucky to have such a brother – and sister-in-law,' Nicholas added as he embraced Michael.

Donella's hug was spontaneous but her expression was unusually soft as she stood looking down at Heidi.

'I mean it, Heidi, don't be rushed into anything. We won't mention it again until you're ready to. You just let us know. And if it would help to talk to me, or to Mike, or both of us, just say. Whatever you need. You let us know. It's a big decision. Best to think about it really carefully now – not have doubts halfway through.'

Nicholas smiled to see the hug returned with enthusiasm. It hadn't always been so.

'You are so very, very kind,' Heidi said earnestly. 'I do not know how to thank you. But tonight I feel like you gave me a very special present. And I think you must have the biggest heart of love. I *would* like to talk to you some more about this, but first I must talk to Nicholas.'

When it was his turn Nicholas himself held Donella close.

'I always did think you were special. But this eclipses everything. Bless you. We'll let you know as soon as we've decided.'

As the car turned out of the drive, he glanced in the mirror. Michael stood behind Donella, his arms protectively round her. They were exchanging a kiss, not watching their visitors leave.

TWENTY-FOUR

Neither spoke as they travelled back to their flat in the West End of Edinburgh. Nicholas, always a fast driver, exceeded even his own record in his haste to get home.

It had been a good move leaving the parental nest. In her own abode Heidi had begun to relax and become herself again. They still saw the family frequently but it was now on their terms.

And the independence had brought a return to her more decisive self. Until they had made up their minds whether or not to try for a baby, whether or not to return to their overseas work, she declared, she wouldn't take on a full-time job. An administrative post working three days a week for Oxfam suited her purposes meantime, leaving her free to exercise her undoubted skills at home-making. The flat was quickly transformed into a home, and both derived pleasure from its welcome whenever they returned to it. But tonight neither saw anything of her creative flair.

Quite deliberately Nicholas seated himself opposite Heidi. It was imperative that he knew exactly what she was trying to convey. Sometimes words alone were unequal to the task.

'Wow!' he said in an awed tone.

'It is hard to know what to say. It is such a big thing they would do.' Her bemused expression spoke more eloquently than the simple statement.

'Indeed. I'm absolutely staggered by it.'

'And what do you think about it?' she asked.

Nicholas, with no idea of what she thought, proceeded with caution.

'If we're sure we want to go for surrogacy – *if* we still are – I don't see how we could ever get a better chance than this.'

'Donella is a very good mother. And she would give us a beautiful baby, I think.'

'Yes. I'm sure she would. It would probably look a lot like the girls, given that Mike and I are identical. But how would *you* feel about that?'

'I should like to have a beautiful baby like her children.'

'And how do you feel about *Donella* doing this for us?'

'I like her. She is very kind to me. And she loves you.'

He was suddenly still, watching her closely.

'I'm not sure … what you mean.'

'She has known you a long time. You are very much like her husband. You tease her. You can touch each other. And she likes it all. She loves you like her family. Me she does not know so well and I am not so … comfortable?' Did she still feel herself to be an outsider?

'And does it trouble you – that she's close to me?'

'No.' Her innocent open look seemed to confirm the truth of her response. 'I think it must be very nice to love the new family of the husband as well as the old one.' Her strange constructions told him she was tired – or emotional. Probably both.

'It is. And *you'll* come to love them too, when you get more used to them, understand them better. It's harder for you, joining the family later. I've known Donella for ever – since we were students at Medical School. She's always been easy to be with. And she just slotted into the family naturally.'

'But she is a friendly person too. Me, I am not so warm to them. I am not used to the touching and the jokes.'

'But they love you too. And especially since you started to do things with the children more, you're becoming more and more one of the family. The girls think you're wonderful. You know they do.' He leaned closer, willing her to feel the truth of his words. 'And that's helped the others to see more of the real you. You're more relaxed with the children.'

'I do not think all the time *they* will be watching me. They will not be wondering why you married me. For them I am just me.'

'And is that how you feel with the adults?' Nicholas asked in astonishment.

'Perhaps they do watch. They are all so … *clever* people.'

'But so are you!'

'I cannot talk so.'

'Only because you're speaking a foreign language. You *are* in your brain.' She shrugged.

'*And* you have loads of fantastic abilities none of them have. And look at all the work you've done overseas – things they've never even seen. They are terribly impressed by you. Believe me,' Nicholas insisted. 'They are *definitely not* criticising you. They just want to love you. They *do* love you. They just aren't as used to you yet as they are to Donella who's been in the family for years. And the touching thing you mentioned, that's just part of it.'

'But it is not what I am used to at home. I do not know how to be when your brother hugs me. I do not hold a man like Donella holds you.'

'It's nothing. I'm a huggy sort of a person. So is she. We just hug to show we are happy – we like each other. Like I hug my mother. My sisters. And Mike too. But it's not like I hug *you*. Is it?'

A slow smile curved her lips.

'That is not the hug for the family to see. No.'

'No, indeed. Definitely not for *anybody* else to see. But the hugs for Donella – those *are* OK for the family to see. She's family too.'

'Thank you. I think I understand.'

'Good. So if I hug Donella, or Mike hugs you, or Dad hugs you, it's just because in our family we all love each other. They are hugs anybody can see. You can hug them too. You have nothing at all to worry about there. But I wish you'd said this before.'

'It is not easy to understand the different ways people are – what to do, how to do it.'

'I know. But you do really well. You're even getting the hang of the jokes. And that's *really* difficult – understanding jokes in another culture.'

Nicholas was still synthesising this unexpected revelation. There was a long silence before he brought them back to consideration of Donella's offer.

'Where were we with the baby thing? Oh yes – how would you feel about Donella doing it for us? So we've established you like Donella.' Nicholas counted off the items on his fingers as he spoke. The thought flashed through his mind that he was sounding like an estate agent summing up the things they liked about a house. 'You like the babies she has. We know certainly that she has babies easily. We know she doesn't want any more of her own too, so presumably she wouldn't want to keep the one she had for us. So I guess we need to think, how would *you* feel about *her* having *my* baby – I don't mean it wouldn't be yours too. It would, of course. But it would be my genes.' As he hastily corrected himself, Nicholas realised how careful he must be in his choice of words.

'You talked to me before about … about … how it is done. At first. I do not like to think about it.' She'd made no secret of her discomfort with the idea of insemination.

'I know. I understand.' He smiled gently at her.

'*You* would not do it to her – no?'

'Inject it, you mean? No! I'd imagine Mike would. Or Donella herself. But not me, no.'

'So it would be just the family? We do not need doctors?'

'Well, since most of the family *are* doctors …' Nicholas stopped abruptly. This was no time for teasing. 'I'm sorry, Heidi. No, we wouldn't need to have anybody else involved. We could trust Donella and Mike. They could trust us. We'd have to work it all out carefully, of course – where, when, how, who does what. But we're all sensible. We know the risks. We'd make sure it was all done properly, and sensitively, so that everybody feels right about it.'

'This is the thing you said would be best? Some woman you could trust. No doctor. No agency. Yes?'

'It is. But I never in my wildest dreams thought of *this* as a possibility!'

'But Donella – she makes it possible.'

'Donella and Mike. But Heidi …' Nicholas sat forward in his chair leaning towards her. '*You* must feel OK about it. Remember all the things we talked about before when we thought we'd have to find a surrogate through the paper or some agency? Now you've got to ask yourself all those questions but think how you feel if it's *Donella.*'

She turned wide eyes on him. It was a long time before she spoke.

'I think it is different if you know her. It feels different. She knows you. You know her.' Her pointing finger told him she was thinking of him specifically. Not just anyone, not even them as a couple, but he, Nicholas, knew Donella. She knew him. It was clearly not a comforting thought to her at this moment.

'It is. Different in a nice way in some senses. But different in an uncomfortable way in other senses.'

She was nodding slowly, staring at him but not seeing him. Seeing instead the potential for trouble.

'We trust her,' she said, thinking aloud. 'We know she is a good person to have our baby. But is it OK if she has your baby inside her?' The words fell between them. This was something she must grapple with alone.

'In a nutshell.'

'I think I must think about this a lot.'

'You must indeed. And so must I. But I want to say one thing before you go away to think on your own. Well, two things, maybe.'

He slid off his seat and knelt beside her, taking her hands in his, looking directly into her eyes.

'The first thing is that I want to emphasise, it matters *hugely* what *you* think. It's more important to me than anything else. And I don't want to influence you in either direction. I'm not going to tell you what I think until I know how *you* feel. If *either* of us doesn't feel this is right, we won't do it. Definitely. No matter how much we want a baby. We have to feel right about it. And it must be right for *us*, not because we're thinking of other people. So we mustn't say yes so as not to hurt the feelings of Donella and Mike – tremendously generous though the offer is. It has to be right for you and me. It's something we have to live with for the rest of our lives. And we're not talking about buying a new car, or a new picture. We're talking about the possible creation of another human being – a child whose happiness would be all important to us. Yes?'

'Yes,' she whispered.

'My second point – and remember this isn't an attempt to influence you – but I want you to remember – when you're thinking about all the things it would involve, especially the bits you don't want me to talk about – that it's a form of treatment. Donella and I are both doctors. It would be a kind of medical procedure for us. It is nothing – *nothing* – to do with making love. Just as family hugs aren't like our hugs. OK?' He squeezed her hands gently in his as he asked the question.

'I will try to remember. But I must think.'

'Of course. You must.' He sank back on his heels. 'But not now. You must be exhausted. Come on. Let's get to bed. Leave the thinking till the morning.'

But they both knew this was not something they could forget at will.

Heidi lay still in the darkness. She could hear Nicholas' steady breathing and assumed he was asleep. But for her there could be no such escape from the riot of thoughts disturbing her peace.

When she had first met Nicholas he had seemed to her a larger than life figure, successful, popular, full of vigour and fun. She knew he was energetic and skilled, but his compassion and caring had caught her attention more: a spontaneous hug for the grief-stricken mother of a Cambodian boy of twelve who had just died from gunshot wounds; a long day in the operating theatre and then a night's vigil beside a malnourished and orphaned teenager who had abandoned hope of life, with an expression on his face that tore at her heart. His passion for helping the underprivileged and downtrodden was beyond doubt. But away from the medical environment he was a boisterous and charismatic person who charmed the ladies and amused the men in equal measure. And alarmed her.

She'd been cautious, at first, doubting the seriousness of his intentions. He'd shown surprising sympathy and understanding the night he found her in tears because she could not persuade officials to forward essential supplies for an unexpected influx of refugees. She was wary, half-prepared for ridicule. But little by little he revealed his softer side. She came to realise that with her he could be himself. There was no need of the endless banter, the façade of confidence; he allowed her glimpses into his doubts, his fears.

Marriage had served to strengthen her self-confidence and further soften his exuberance. Only the discovery of her infertility had cast a shadow over their quiet happiness. Her habitual pragmatism faltered in the face of the fleeting pain she occasionally glimpsed in her husband's eyes, and awareness of her own responsibility for it eroded her self-esteem as well as her happiness.

But now she'd been offered a way back to fulfilment. An impossibly perfect plan which answered all the problems Nicholas had so painstakingly spelled out. But ... first the hugging ... now this. Was he right? Had she got it all wrong? Could people see the same thing and interpret it so differently?

Heidi curled herself up, hugging her knees close to her body as she steeled herself to think about what it meant. It had been one thing to think about it in a fairly abstract form. Now it assumed the proportions of an overly magnified cell: beautiful seen from afar, somehow too naked, too functional seen at close quarters. Her every instinct was to close her mind to the pictures flashing through her brain. She knew she could not ... must not.

141

Donella. Would it be right for her to bear their child? She had been kindness itself. Her open-hearted welcome, her generous sharing of her children, her sensitivity to Heidi's feelings – in every way she had been everything Heidi wanted in a sister. But …

She was beautiful. She was clever. She was capable. She was warm and loving. And this was the girl who was offering to do this amazing thing. *Offering*! Because her heart was big enough to love them so much, and give of herself for them. But …

She was secure in her own marriage. Michael clearly adored her. She had finished bearing her own family. She knew what was involved, knew from a medical point of view as well as from a woman's – a mother's – point of view. But …

What was it? What made her question this offer? What made her creep down into the darkness of the bed and seek to hide from her thoughts? Heidi knew she must confront these goblins.

Donella was a full woman. Conceiving, being pregnant, giving birth – these things were part of the essence of womanhood, the ultimate expression of femininity. They singled women out. They were things men could not do. They gave women power. And Donella had these things in abundance. Such abundance she could offer them to someone else as well as her husband.

An overwhelming sense of emptiness surged within her. It was as if there was a hollow space, a black hole where these things should have been. Scalding tears trickled down her cheek. If Donella did this thing for them would she, Heidi, end up feeling jealous and bitter and angry against her saviour? She did not want to feel such things against a woman who had been so good to her, a woman she both admired and loved.

Perhaps she could school herself to recognise the fact that Nicholas had so recently reinforced – they all had different talents. Donella included in her repertoire the capacity to have children. It was simply part of her, just as Heidi's exceptional voice was part of her, God given.

Why was it so hard to think that *Donella* was the one who might do this thing for them? They had agreed – Nicholas and she – that surrogacy was the answer. And that was in no small measure Nicholas' response to her own aversion to involving doctors. She must remember he was making compromises. So must she. They wanted to eliminate outside agencies. This way they could do so. So why the doubt now they had this specific chance?

If she had had a sister of her own, someone who lived in Switzerland still, who would come over for this thing and then go back again – yes, that would seem right. A sister would do it for love of her. So why not this new sister? Heidi forced herself to look at the question starkly. It was because Donella was doing it for *Nicholas* not her. Her love for her husband's brother was so strong that she would do this thing for him. *Want* to

142

do it for him. Heidi was his wife, so indirectly it was for her, but otherwise she would not have made this offer.

It was too big a gift to accept from someone who was not close enough to *her* to do it for her alone.

Ah yes. That again. *They* were that close. She knew it, she saw it, they admitted it. It was a closeness she could not fully understand. Was it because Nicholas was so much like her husband? Michael was not so close to her, Heidi, though he was identical in appearance to *her* husband. Was it because Donella had known him so long? That would not of itself make them automatically so close. Was it just because they were doctors? Or because they were both demonstrative, affectionate people? Nicholas said so. When he said it, so openly, looking directly into her eyes, she knew he was believing it. But still she felt it was more. There was a bond there. It was palpable. And it made her shrink from doing something which would unite them in a most intimate way.

There it was. She was facing it. She did not want to share Nicholas in this way. Not with someone he was already so close to emotionally. Not in that part of their lives that should be so exclusive. These things were not to be shared. Nicholas was hers. He had chosen her; she had chosen him. His body, his gametes, they belonged to her. Exclusively. It would be a violation of the sanctity of their relationship to have him share them with Donella. But … she'd been prepared to share them with an unknown woman – a surrogate!

She believed – she trusted – that Nicholas was entirely faithful to her. She believed he held their marriage as sacred and inviolable too. He would never have *contemplated* this thing if she had done her part – been able and willing to share her eggs as well as her body. It was only because the rightful result of their union was denied to him that it was being considered. Only because there was no alternative. And he had assured her it was not a form of sex with Donella. He had emphasised it, singled it out as the one thing he must tell her. He'd known she'd see it like that. But he didn't. He'd *told* her he didn't. Nor did Donella. Was it her sick mind? They said it was just a medical procedure. They wouldn't be sharing their bodies; they'd only be placing his sperm where they could do the work needed to make the baby they craved.

And it was only what they had decided was right for them. She remembered again her relief when he'd suggested surrogacy, after all the other repugnant possibilities. And it even had all the elements of trust she had looked for when she had suggested they involve Nicholas' father in the process. It was exactly what they had come to this country for. And it was being handed to them voluntarily – no need for adverts in the newspaper, interviews with strange women, talk of payment, worries about it all going wrong. No need even to ask. It was perfect. Foolproof. She'd even be able to watch the pregnancy, share in the development of their baby.

And Donella would be there to help her learn the skills needed to care for this child.

The thoughts swirled around, mixing and separating like the coloured crystals in a kaleidoscope. She struggled to stay focused. The crystals coalesced – the baby, the pregnant abdomen, the act of conception, the face of Donella ...

She saw Nicholas' face close to hers. He was leering at her. He was walking backwards, still with that mocking look. She was trying to make him come to her but he was retreating faster than she could keep pace with him. In spite of her imploring, he kept getting further and further away.

Then he was standing behind an invisible barrier. She couldn't touch him. He had his hand stretched out, dropping something into a transparent bowl. She strained to see what it was. Sperm. Giant, wriggling, red-hot sperm. They were swimming around in the bowl struggling for space. There were so many of them. He was dropping them head first into the bowl. They writhed and thrashed furiously as he held them by their tails, as if they were desperate to get away. When he had filled the bowl to the brim he looked up at her again. He was grinning. He picked up the bowl and walked away from her. He vanished ...

She woke in cold terror, her whole body trembling violently. Without moving her head she looked out of the corner of her eye. Yes, Nicholas was still lying there. He was quietly sleeping, relaxed. But the dream had been so vivid. She told herself it was the strain. Her fevered imagination was getting things out of proportion. But the images would not leave her.

She slid out of bed and went to make herself a hot drink. She felt so cold. While the milk warmed she wrapped herself tightly in the thick dressing gown she had flung around her. She still trembled. Her hands closed around the mug. The warmth crept into her fingers.

Nicholas padded sleepily into the kitchen.

Peering through heavy eyelids, he yawned as he mumbled, 'Y'OK?'

'It was a bad dream. A very bad dream.' She shivered as she said it.

He wrapped his arms around her, sinking his head on the top of hers.

'Wanta tell me aboutit?' His slurred speech told her he was still drowsy.

'I will tell you. But first I will finish my drink. I am cold. You go to bed. I will come soon.'

'S'OK. If you're cold, I'll warm y'up.' He held her closer, rubbing her arms to generate heat, enveloping her inside his dressing gown too. 'Hmm, you do feel cold. You're trembling. Snuggle into me.'

Back in bed she shared her nightmare. He was awake now, feeling her fear.

'It's been the shock,' he soothed. 'All these weeks of thinking about it and bracing yourself for disappointment. Now we've finally got hope it's too much for your brain to take in. Don't think about it now. There's no hurry. Remember Donella said – take your time. No hurry. No pressure either way. We won't decide anything until you're a hundred per cent sure. Just put it out of your mind. Think about something else.'

'I am all right now. It is all all right when you are holding me.' She had stopped trembling but stayed curled up tightly against him.

'Then you stay right here. You're perfectly safe. I've got you.'

His calming tone surrounded them both hypnotically and he drifted back into sleep.

TWENTY-FIVE

There was no time for further discussion for two days. Nicholas was on call and had to remain at the hospital at night as well as through the day. Phoning Heidi to check she was all right, and to let her know he was thinking of her, he was reassured by her bright account of her busyness.

It was a shock when he returned on Monday evening to find her pale and withdrawn, to learn that she had spent much of the night painting the inside of a cupboard. His heart sank.

'Let's go for a walk. You look as if you could do with some fresh air. Help you to sleep tonight,' he suggested, keeping his voice light.

They took the car to Cramond and walked along beside the water. A light breeze brought the salty air inland and Nicholas, in spite of his worries, felt some of his own tension ease. Hand in hand they strolled for some time talking of nothing more serious than the soaring of a gull or the silvering of a cloud. But loath as he was to break the illusion of calm, Nicholas knew he must seize his opportunity.

'Heidi, I can see you're struggling with this surrogacy thing. Do you want to abandon the whole idea? I'll understand if you do. Would you prefer to go back overseas?'

'No. Please no. I want us to have a baby.'

'But it's making you so unhappy. I thought it was because you hated the idea of doctors intervening. But now I can see it's more than that. I think it's the whole thing that upsets you. It's OK to say.'

'No. It is not that. I am sorry. I did not sleep much. That makes me quiet.'

'Quiet – yes. Miserable – no. Come on, Heidi. You must talk to me.'

She did not respond for a long time. Nicholas grew impatient.

'Are you saying you want a baby just to please me? Because you think it's what I want?'

'No. It is not so. I want a baby too.'

'Truthfully?'

'Truthfully.' Her eyes told him she believed what she said.

'So what is it that's troubling you?'

'I do not like what is in my head.'

'Share it with me. I want to help. I need to know how you're feeling, and what's troubling you. I know you *are* troubled and I'm pretty sure it's to do with Donella and Mike's offer. Yes?'

She nodded.

'Just tell me what's in your head – and your heart. Don't worry about the sentences. Don't worry about hurting my feelings or anything. Just let it out.'

'I will try. I know we must share what we think. But it is hard for me to say it.'

'I know, darling.' The endearment was deliberate. He reserved it for special moments. She held his hand more tightly.

He listened in silence as she tried in her halting English to explain how much she wanted it to be right. How her head told her it was the answer to their prayers. How much she liked and admired Donella. How grateful she was to Michael too.

'But …?' He looked down at her with a smile. 'It's OK to have buts. We all have them. We have to talk about those too.'

'You have them too – still?'

'Of course I do!'

'Ahh, then it is all right.' She visibly relaxed her shoulders.

Nicholas stopped suddenly and turned her to face him. With his hands on her shoulders he asked, 'You thought this was all plain sailing for me?'

'You make it seem so.'

'Only because I want to protect *you*. Oh dear. I think this is all my fault. I was trying to protect you because I know it's hardest on you – harder than for anyone else. I didn't want to burden you with my concerns too.'

'But I think it would be good that I know it is not easy for you.'

'Fair enough. When you put it like that …' He caught her hand in his again and they started to walk. 'I'll tell you why it's not easy for me. Then you must tell me why it's not for you. Fair?' She nodded. 'Promise?' She nodded again.

But what he had to tell her was too intimate for arm's length. He drew her close to his side and, holding her tightly against him so that their hips moved as one with each step, he shared his doubts and fears. He told her how much he disliked the thought of masturbating to order, of handing over his semen, of having it mixed with anyone else's eggs but hers. He spoke of his desperate wish that she should create the child with him, of how much she was central to his life and hopes, of how it hurt him to know the child would not be biologically hers too. He had pictured a little girl, a miniature of her: blonde hair, grey eyes, beguiling smile.

At that point she smiled up at him and told him she'd be more than happy with a tall, fair, blue-eyed boy just like him. He was relieved to see the tense lines relaxing momentarily. But he knew he must tell his story even if it meant banishing the smile.

He revealed his own questioning of himself – how he would feel about Donella, how he would worry about his brother's feelings. He disclosed his additional worry about his father's reaction when he learned what they had done, that they had gone against his advice. He shared his anxiety about how they would deal with telling people.

No, he told her, it was certainly not easy for him either. She was silent throughout, leaning towards him so as not to miss the words on the sea breeze.

'And yet ... you still think maybe it is possible we will do this thing?' she asked in a surprised tone.

'It's *possible*.' His reply was guarded. He didn't want to force her into a position just to please him. 'If you are quite sure you want a baby. I'm prepared to go through a lot to make you happy. You're my number one person. But it depends on *you*. How much *you* want a baby. How much you're prepared to pay for it.'

'We have to *pay*?'

'No, not in money! I mean what it costs us in terms of our feelings, our doubts, our worries, our peace of mind.'

She tramped along in silence before responding.

'I know I do want a baby. I do not want doctors to do this thing to us. And I think ... to have it in the family is a very special thing. Yes?'

'It is, of course. But only if it feels right for you.'

'But it is what we came to your father to do. But better. Because they offer and because we trust them. It is so, yes?'

'It's an incredible offer. So much so I keep looking for the hidden snags! It can't be this easy!'

'But it is *not* easy. You say tonight. It is not easy for you too.'

He realised he had said too much; he must wait for her to tell it her way.

'You're right. It isn't at all easy. And it's hardest for you. I've told you my worries. Now it's your turn. Sometimes it helps just to say them out loud. I feel better for sharing mine with you. Otherwise they just go round and round in your head.'

'It is true. That is what happens to me. But I look at them again and again and again – these worries. And always they come to one thing.'

'And that is?'

'I ... I think ... maybe you will come to love Donella more than me.' The words came out in a rush.

Nicholas was taken completely by surprise by the bald statement. He stood stock-still staring at her.

'I'm totally thunderstruck.' He stared down at her in silence for a long moment. 'I have no idea where this idea is coming from. You'll need to explain it to me.'

'She is beautiful on the inside and on the outside. I am not right on the inside. She can have a baby for you. I cannot. You will make this baby with her. It will be hers, and it will be yours, but it will not be mine. You love her already because she is so nice. If she does this thing you will love her more.' He could only dimly guess what it cost her to make this speech.

He caught her in a crushing hold, closing his eyes to blot out every-thing but the feel of her. They stood silent, still, fiercely together in their pain. Then slowly he released her enough to be able to look into her eyes. They were uncertain, questioning.

'This isn't really the place, but it's definitely the time. There is no way I shall love Donella more than you. You are the most special person in the world to me. You are my wife. I chose to spend my life with you. I didn't marry you in a hurry, did I? It took me ages to summon up the courage to ask you. Because I had to be sure this was for ever. And I don't intend *ever* to stop loving you in the most special and wonderful way two people can love one another. OK?'

She nodded her head slightly. He saw the uncertainty. It was fair enough. Intentions were one thing … thousands of people pledged undying love every year. But they didn't keep those pledges. Not when the going got tough.

'We've been through a hard time lately,' he said quietly. 'We haven't been as happy as we used to be. It's made me ask myself a lot of questions about us. And about my feelings. I've been unhappy inside too because you're so unhappy and because things aren't like they used to be between us.'

Heidi looked gravely at him as she nodded her agreement.

'But because I've thought long and hard about us, I can tell you for sure – all this – the infertility, the worries about a family, surrogacy – everything – it hasn't changed how I feel about you. I want to be with you. That's more important to me than having a baby. If it's a choice, you win. Every time.' He smiled tenderly, waiting for her to assimilate the fact. 'And you're no less lovely to me because you've got this problem inside you. None of us is beautiful on the inside! And I've seen lots and lots of insides, remember! It's not your fault. And if you stop to think calmly and rationally, you *know* you are utterly, wonderfully lovely, and desirable to me. You *know* how I feel about that.'

He tightened his hold on her, willing her to acknowledge the truth of his statement. She could be in no doubt.

'Perhaps.' She was cautious.

He gave her a small shake.

'No perhaps about it. You *do*! You *must*.'

'You are right. I do know.' Again she nodded. But there was still no smile in her eyes.

'How I feel about Donella is completely different. As I told you ages ago, I loved her once when we were youngsters at Medical School. She was my first serious girlfriend. She was special to me. But you know that. Maybe, though, that's why you're thinking these things. I do still love her – but not in that way any more. I love her because she's lovely and warm and kind and fun, and because she's my brother's wife, and because she's part of the family.' He hesitated. 'You want me to be brutally honest? Tell you what I've been thinking? Even the painful bits?'

149

Heidi nodded, a fearful look returning to her eyes.

'Well, I'll tell you. Since she offered to have our baby for us I've been thinking again about what she means to me. Asking myself does she mean more to me than I've just told you – anywhere deep down inside my heart? Because if she does I think it would be too dangerous to let her do this for us. If I'm honest, I know that if I'd been more mature when we were younger, we *might* have stayed together. She's a lovely person. But I don't know. No-one can know. But if we ever had a chance of that, I was the one who blew it. That doesn't say a lot for the stability of my love back then, does it? And now? Now it's completely different. I'm certain – without a shred of doubt – I don't feel that way about her now.' He looked down at her steadily, willing her to believe him.

'No?'

'No. What I feel for *you* is a grown-up love. It's deeper, more mature, more lasting. Nobody could persuade me to leave *you* – as I left her – in the lurch. I share things with you I've never shared with Donella. I talk to you about things that are really deep inside me. You make me feel safe. I can show you bits of myself nobody else knows about. I know you'll understand, be there for me. And you bring out qualities in me Donella never did. You make me want to protect you. You make me feel good about myself.' A brief, faint smile flickered across Heidi's face, the intense look replacing it all too quickly. 'Even now, talking about these really difficult things, I'm feeling good inside again because I *can* talk to you like this. It hurt before because you couldn't talk. I felt shut out. And because we weren't sharing things, I started to doubt the strength of our relationship. And that made me look again at how I feel about you, how I feel about Donella.'

'And did you think ... I wish I had married Donella?' Heidi's voice was not quite steady. She swallowed hard. 'She would not be like me. She would talk about these – difficult things.' Her earnest enquiry made him caress her face for a long moment.

'No, darling. I did not. I did not.'

She gave a small smile, not breaking her steady gaze. He held it as he spoke again.

'Donella, because she's the girl she is, is offering this thing because she knows how we're hurting. She wants to help us. She *wouldn't* offer if she still felt that kind of love for me. I know she wouldn't. She'd know it would be too dangerous too.' He spoke with absolute conviction. 'And Mike – he knows what Donella and I were to each other then. He's bound to have asked her about that. He wouldn't let her do it if *he* had any doubts. So you see, there's nothing for you to fear.'

'So you all wonder about it?'

'We *have* to. We have to think of everything.'

'I thought it was just me.'

Nicholas smiled gently.

150

'But you all think it is OK.' She was clearly still reflecting on this.

'Yes. That part of it is definitely OK.'

'But will it be different? If you do this thing with her?'

'If we do go ahead with it – please note, *if* – it won't make me feel as if Donella is mine. Not like you are mine. She belongs with Mike. She is just lending us part of herself to have the baby. She'll still be living with Mike, doing all the things they do as a couple, all the private things that they share. I'm no part of that. Having to give her my semen – that's just a form of treatment. I won't be … neither of us would be thinking we're having sex together.' He saw her flinch, knew he had hit a raw nerve. 'Are you still feeling that's what it's like?'

She nodded mutely, tears welling in her eyes.

'I think it makes me a not nice person to think this.'

'No, it doesn't. It's natural. I can see why you feel like that. I shouldn't want you to have some other man's sperm in you. I know I wouldn't. But it's just a means to an end. I confess, it still makes me feel uncomfortable knowing it has to be done, but it's a quick procedure and we can soon forget all about it.'

'Yes? Even for you it is uncomfortable?'

'Even for me – hard old professional that I am. I wish with all my heart it wasn't necessary.'

'I am so sorry – so very, very sorry, I make it so.' Fresh tears ran down her cheeks. He took her face in his hands and wiped them away with his thumbs.

'Heidi, I didn't mean that. I don't blame you. It's not your fault. It's just one of those things. I'm only saying this because I want you to know, if we do this, this will be *our* baby. Yours and mine. I don't want to share a baby with anyone else. I shall – we both will – be eternally grateful to Donella for making it possible – but she is like the midwife – bringing the child to *us* – to you and me. For *us* to love. For us to bring up. For us to be a real family.'

'I like to hear you tell it like this.' She placed her own hands over his.

'Yes, but even so, you mustn't feel pressured into doing it. If you still have doubts we won't go through with it. You have to be absolutely certain. If it feels wrong at all, we'll give up the idea. We'll devote ourselves to each other, and to our work helping people who need us. It'll be OK.'

'Tonight, when you are here, holding me so, I think it will be OK.'

He bent to kiss her tenderly, lingeringly.

She clung to him as the breeze gathered strength and brought a discarded crisp bag and an empty drink carton bowling past their still figures.

Over the next few days they returned to the subject again and again. Nicholas was so relieved that Heidi was talking the issues through that he felt he could ask her gently if it would help her to hear first-hand from Donella what her feelings were for him now.

Heidi was swift to decline this invitation. She did not want Donella to know she had harboured such thoughts, she said. It might spoil their easy friendship if Donella felt she had to watch for signs of jealousy and be anything other than her normally spontaneous self with him. It was agreed. She assured him he himself had convinced her that her fears were ground-less.

But he still watched her carefully. It was with a growing sense of relief that he saw her regain her calm demeanour, start to sleep soundly again, and even sing as she worked. The sound of her beautiful voice always thrilled him; now it moved him at a deeper level than usual, speaking of an inner harmony.

He had told her she must take her time, look at all the issues, share her doubts and fears no matter how 'silly' she feared they might be, but he thought it prudent to monitor development until they came to a decision. It would not be wise to let her brood alone without sharing her questions, her doubts.

On Saturday morning Nicholas woke first and lay looking at her, savouring her sleeping peace, her air of fragility. Gently, once she was properly awake, he asked her if she was ready to share her current thinking.

'Must I say first?' she asked.

'I think you must.'

'You will tell me honestly too?'

'Promise. It's desperately important that we're totally honest with each other. I promise I will tell you honestly what I'm thinking.'

They lay for a long moment waiting.

'I think ...' Heidi began slowly, 'I think that, if it is not too hard a thing for you, I think we should say yes please to Donella.'

'You do?'

She nodded.

'But you want longer to think some more?' he asked.

'No. I do not think I will change. Unless you say no. You said we must both say yes if we are to do this thing, yes?'

'I did indeed. But you think you would say yes.'

'I *know* I would say yes – for myself. And you?'

'If you can bear it then I would say yes too.'

'Not for me only?'

'Not only. For you, yes. But for me too. I think it's the best way we shall ever find to have the baby we both want – for us.'

They held one another tenderly as the decision settled around them as the fingers of a man settle around the fluttering feathers of a fledgling bird before he can transfer it safely back to its nest.

Donella confessed to Michael that she felt uneasy asking Dick and Roberta to babysit for them on the night they were to hear the verdict. Given their personal reservations it seemed somehow underhand.

A powerful silence followed the quiet statement of the decision.

It was Donella who suggested that as a first step it might be helpful if each couple drew up a list of points to cover and their own ideas on how the practical details would be managed. Then they would meet to work out a plan and together decide whom to tell, and just what the child would know of its origins in time. For now, though, it would be their secret – a planned pregnancy between the four of them.

On only one point was there any real difference of opinion. Donella and Michael were adamant they wanted no reimbursement of their expenses or her loss of income. They could not bear any suggestion of payment for a child.

This was a gift of love.

TWENTY-SIX

When Nicholas bought a house in the north side of Edinburgh, more spacious than the city centre flat, and surrounded by its own garden, Roberta and Dick watched with pleasure the indications that a second son was putting down roots so close to them. He seemed to have settled confidently into his job, confessing he liked the thrill of a busy Accident and Emergency Department: there were few routines; it was challenging to receive unconscious patients who tested his diagnostic skills; he liked to help put badly damaged people back together again; what he did counted and he wanted to make a difference. On the domestic front he discovered a flair for DIY. Heidi put her undoubted skills with colour and fabric to good use and between them they began the process of converting the house into a family home.

Nicholas' conscience smote him when his father tentatively asked if they had resolved the question of their infertility, but he kept his counsel, merely replying that yes, he thought they had.

There was little time to dwell on the deception given the approach of the date for the first attempt.

Tension mounted.

It was Nicholas who suggested that he and Heidi should stay the night at Michael and Donella's house.

'I don't want to take over but I think it would help. I'd like to have Heidi with me – especially immediately afterwards. I want her to feel involved in the conception.'

'No problem.'

'Actually that's a really good idea,' Donella added. 'Then if one of the girls wakes up – at a tricky moment – there'll be somebody available to see to them.'

It all sounded so matter-of-fact.

But Nicholas was all too aware that it was much more than that, and declined an invitation to dinner that night. Instead he took Heidi out to a small French restaurant about four miles away from Michael's house. They ate little, said nothing of the purpose of their visit that night, but instead devoted themselves to the gentle art of flirtation.

The bedroom prepared for them was softly lit.

Showered and in his dressing gown Nicholas looked around him. What care Donella had taken. It was exactly right.

Heidi closed the door quietly behind her, standing for a moment in the half-light looking across at him shyly. Then, untying her pale pink robe slowly as she went, she glided across to where he lay watching her every move. He felt again the breathless wonder her femininity created in him.

She melted into his arms. His hands slipped over her body, savouring her softness, her shape, her responsiveness. He had tried not to think about the transition from foreplay to providing semen for Donella, but Heidi unexpectedly made it seem natural and right. Without a word she simply moved aside at the appropriate moment to allow him to complete the final part of the process while she knelt behind him, her arms holding him tightly, her face, unseen and unseeing, pressed against his shoulders.

Again without a word, she slipped off the bed, wrapped herself tightly in the discarded robe, and carried the covered plastic container carefully out of the room.

Straining his ears, Nicholas heard her quick footsteps, the light tap, the door opening, a whispered word, the door closing again. He dragged his mind away from the room at the opposite end of the landing and waited for Heidi to reappear. As if she had just tripped along to the bathroom, she returned, discarded the robe for the second time, and slipped into bed beside him.

He scanned her face anxiously. It was calm, impassive. He took her fiercely in his arms, holding her so tightly she could hardly breathe. They lay still, silent, neither sharing their most secret thoughts at that moment poised between worlds.

It was she who eventually broke the spell. With her first move he relaxed his hold, ready to take his cue from her. She raised herself up on one arm to look down into his eyes, shadowed by the light from the lamp still burning beside the bed. Her look was inscrutable. He waited for what seemed like an eternity, holding his breath. Then a gentle smile curved her lips, warming her eyes.

Tonight he had the luxury of time. The slowly mounting excitement, the generosity of Heidi's giving, the freedom from anxiety, now lent depth and richness to their lovemaking. It eclipsed the best of the best.

Cradling her in his arms afterwards he felt unusually wide awake. A strange sense of suspense hung in the air. Somewhere in the recesses of his mind his thoughts were with that first ejaculate, but he forced himself to concentrate on the fragrance of the second.

'That was – fantastic. You are a magician,' he breathed in her ear.

She snuggled closer on his chest.

'I love you – so very much. And you make me feel … so … special.'

'You *are* special. Wonderfully, uniquely special,' he responded emphatically, stroking her skin tenderly, 'and never more so than tonight.'

'It was not so hard as you expected?' she asked tentatively.

He started. Then drawing back slowly to look at her, he whispered, 'You knew? You knew I was scared?'

'But of course. I love you,' she replied simply.

'You never cease to amaze me. There was I, worrying – in my incompetent male way – how I could make it up to you, and all the time you are calmly and beautifully, making it right – for both of us. You are …' Words failed him. He let his lips speak for him.

It was a long time before either broke the silence.

'Heidi, can I ask you something?'

'Of course.' She ran her fingers lightly over the fair, tightly curled hair on his chest.

'How come you are so brilliant at all this' – his hands on her body told her what he meant – 'and yet you hate to think about the … *biology* of it all?'

'I do not understand.' Still the fingers moved, relaxed, tender, caressing him.

'You are a fantastic lover.' He saw the pleased smile. 'But you hate to talk about what happens inside us.'

The tension was instantaneous. The smile died. The movement of her fingers ceased. Her words when they came were stiff.

'Making love is a wonderful thing. I love you. I think you love me too. It needs us to be *so*.' She pressed her hips hard against him to show him what she meant.

'Close. Intimate. Yes, my darling, it does.'

'But it is all very private. Secret things happen nobody sees. *We* do not see. It is better so. They should be hidden. I do not like to talk of them. It is better we make love.'

She wriggled herself into a position which effectively stopped him worrying about her inhibitions and they settled themselves for sleep.

TWENTY-SEVEN

As Michael closed the door on Heidi, he felt the warmth through the covering cloth. The baster was cold in his hand as he drew up the liquid, but by the time he reached Donella it had taken on something of the heat it held.

They had used the waiting time as they had agreed, to quietly enjoy the proximity of their bodies. By the time he was ready to introduce the semen, insertion was painless and easy. She had already – calmly, professionally – talked to him of the best technique, of angles and danger points, and he was careful now in the silence to obey her advice to the letter. On matters medical she was the undisputed leader.

As he emptied the instrument deep inside her, he forced his mind to concentrate on the mechanics of the instructions echoing in his head. Carry the baster through to the bathroom. Rinse thoroughly. Leave it to dry overnight, covered with the cloth. Ready for next time.

Pray God there would be no need for a next time.

On second thoughts he moved it higher up – out of sight of his daughters' inquisitive eyes if they should chance to wake in the night.

Donella was lying still on her back where he had left her, her bent knees making a mound in the bed which cast a shadow over his side. Slipping out of his dressing gown and putting off the light, he slid under the duvet beside her. She turned instantly to take him in her arms, to be enfolded in his. But there were no instructions for this phase.

He was glad of the darkness, not wanting her to see the turbulence of his thoughts. Though she'd done all she could to prepare him for this, he knew in that moment he was not truly ready for the reality. He told himself firmly, he just needed time. It would pass. But he wanted so much to make love to her, to reclaim her as exclusively his. He could not. He wanted to exclude the shadow of Nicholas from the room. He could not.

As if sensing his confusion, his frustration, she began to stroke his back, holding him close against her.

'We are so lucky, Mike. We have three beautiful children. It's right.'

He dared not speak but held her tenderly like a fragile treasured possession. In the silence his thoughts were rebellious. For Nicholas things were already back to normal. Even if this worked first time, for him they would not be as normal for at least a year. He and Donella were now in limbo: they could not go forward as instinct demanded; they could not go back as his mind willed them to. They hovered on a pinnacle of uncertainty.

He forced himself to picture his daughters, adorable in sleep, waking up with big smiles, cuddling into him, telling him they loved him, their Daddy. Priceless joys. What must it be like to be denied that pleasure? And it was his own beloved brother – closer even than that – his other self, his twin – who craved those simple emotions. Yes, it was right. It was right that they should be the ones to do this thing. His own pain now was as nothing to the suffering his brother had endured. It would pass. This feeling would pass. He could grow to be glad he had given of himself to ease that heartache in Nicholas. It would not be only Donella's offering, her sacrifice.

'Thank you. Thank you for being there. Thank you for loving me.' Her words whispered in the darkness.

'Help me with this, Don.' The aching appeal seemed to echo in his head.

'It'll be OK. You've been brilliant. It'll pass.' She was like a mother soothing a child after a bad dream. 'I love you all the more for minding.'

'You warned me, I know. But I thought ...'

'When it comes, it's not about facts. It's not about reason. It's about emotions. I'm glad you care enough not to like it.'

'Care enough? *Care* enough?!' Michael was lost for words. 'This is the hardest thing I've done in my whole life. And ... I haven't really *done* anything!'

'Oh, but you have. And the way you're feeling right now proves you have.'

'Bless you, Don. For understanding.'

She drew a hand softly down his cheek.

'*I* should be the one helping *you*. Not the other way round,' he said, perplexed by the chaos.

'Oh, I've always told you women are the stronger sex.' He heard the smile in her voice.

'And you are. I've always known you are. Just don't like to admit it.'

They were back in control again. Donella stretched herself out in the bed, her body sliding through his hands as she did so. Then she curled herself away from him for sleep, keeping tight hold on his arms around her.

He moved in to surround her with his body, savouring the contact inch by inch. The shadow faded from the room and they slept.

Michael and Donella were the first to rise the following morning. They were busy giving the children breakfast when Nicholas appeared. The girls instantly claimed his attention and he shared both Fiona's proffered toast, and the edge of Rachael's seat, with a solemnity which made their parents smile. Emily grinned at him benignly.

As he dramatically slid off the eighth of the chair allotted to him onto the floor with a great commotion, he could see all three children's faces peering down at him. He informed them amidst groans that he feared he was now totally unable to go to work and that the whole day would have to be spent listening to stories and playing games. The girls began to giggle.

When Heidi entered the kitchen a few minutes later it was to a scene of such infectious fun that the potential embarrassment of their meeting was entirely bypassed.

There was only one awkward moment, and that an innocent one.

'Uncle Nick?' Rachael asked, ladling cereal into her mouth.

'Uhhhuh?'

'Why did you sleep in our house last night?'

The breathless immobility was palpable. Then Nicholas leaned close to her with a conspiratorial air.

'Well, it's a great big secret, but I'll tell you if you *promise* you won't laugh,' he replied, looking at her solemnly.

'Promise. Promise,' she sang out.

The other three adults stood absolutely still.

'Well, last night Aunty Heidi and I went out for dinner. We had lots of scrummy food but best of all were the carrots. Lovely, juicy, bright orange carrots cut into tiny little matchsticks. And they were so scrummy that Aunty Heidi had *two whole* helpings. Mmmmmhhmm, she did! But I had *loads* more than that – loads and loads and loads and LOADS of carrots – so many that I could see in the dark like it was daytime. And when we'd finished eating I thought it *was* daytime. So I thought, what shall we do now? I know what I'd like to do. I'd like to go and play games with my favourite girls – Rachael and Fiona and Emily!' He stabbed his finger towards each in turn. 'So we got in the car and we drove here. But' – his voice dropped for maximum dramatic effect – 'when we got here the carrots had worn off and I found it was night-time in this house. And my favourite girls were all tucked up in bed.'

Nicholas pulled a very sad face. Rachael, absorbed in his story, looked sad too.

'But Mummy and Daddy were sorry we didn't get to play games, so they said, "Why don't you stay here tonight and you can play games in the morning when the girls wake up." So here we are!'

'And *can* you play games? Don't you have to go to work today? Can you stay *all* day?'

'I'm sorry to say I do have to go to work, but I think I can fit in one special game before I go. So hurry up and finish your breakfast or there won't be time. And if you finish before me, you get to choose which game.'

The child applied herself energetically to emptying her bowl and

Nicholas made exaggerated movements to show he was hurrying with his toast. They were soon absorbed in a game of 'Is it Daddy?' which had the girls shrieking with laughter, and all four adults laughing with them.

TWENTY-EIGHT

The waiting seemed interminable.

When her period started two days later than anticipated, Donella felt as if she had failed an important exam. But outwardly everyone moved carefully into the next stage of the process. It had all been rehearsed. The next date was agreed. Without this schedule they knew they would be spinning unharnessed in a maelstrom of emotions.

Secretly Michael was forced to admit that his father was right: this was a dangerous game.

Four days before the scheduled repeat, Michael was taken aback by Donella asking him if he'd prefer to absent himself from the actual insemination.

'I'll understand. I'm quite capable of doing it myself, you know.'

He was sorely tempted. But in the end his conscience drove him.

'Nope. It was my choice too. I can't let you down now.'

'You wouldn't be letting me down.'

'Besides it's for *my* twin. You're already planning to take the lion's share of the strain. No, I'll be there.'

'Well, OK. But remember, if you change your mind – I shan't think any the worse of you. As long as you're there to support me through the pregnancy and relinquishing the child, you don't need to put yourself through unnecessary pain.'

'I'll be all right.'

In reality he found the procedure no easier the second time around, but he was better prepared for the emotions and more confident that the resentment would pass. And this time he could remind himself how committed he was to this plan – his strong sense of disappointment when it hadn't worked the last time confirmed it.

Donella forced herself to stay calm.

But she had reckoned without the artless chatter of her eldest daughter.

Rachael was busily putting her dolls to bed when she commandeered her uncle's undivided attention.

'I'm the Mummy. You're the Daddy,' she explained patiently.

Donella's eyes flew involuntarily to Nicholas. He flashed a glance at her. She mouthed 'sorry' and smiled apologetically.

'You must kiss the children good night, OK?' Rachael said.

'OK.'

He watched as she wrapped each doll with care.

'You have to say "Night night, sleep tight."'

'To *all* of them?' he asked in mock horror.

'Yeeeees. Don't you *know?*'

'I'm afraid I don't know much about putting babies to bed. Sorry. But just tell me and I'll do my poor best.'

'Uncle Nick.'

'Uhhhuh?'

'Why aren't you a Daddy?'

'Well, I'm afraid I'm just not. But if I *was* a Daddy I'd like to have a little girl exactly like you.'

Donella was glad he didn't look at her again. A wave of emotion swept over her that could not be entirely hidden.

'Would you?' Rachael replied.

'I certainly would.'

'Will you be a Daddy when you're all growed up?' chimed in Fiona.

'I hope so, sweetheart.'

'I'm going to be a Mummy when *I* grow up. You can be the Daddy then,' Rachael said.

'Thank you. I can't think of a nicer Mummy to have than you.'

'But I won't be all grown-up for ages and ages and ages.'

'No?'

'So would you like to be my *pretend* Daddy now?'

'I'd like that very much.'

'OK. You can be my Sunday Daddy.'

Nick looked across at Donella with a questioning look.

'"Sunday" as in special, occasional. Sunday clothes, Sunday games, Sunday treats,' she replied lightly.

He turned back to Rachael, engrossed in her task. She handed him another doll to kiss.

'Mmmm,' he said, 'I think I'd like to be your Sunday Daddy.'

It was decided. The last doll was tucked up in bed.

'OK, all you children, off to sleep!' Rachael called briskly to the row of uniformly wrapped dolls. 'Sweet dreams. Your Sunday Daddy has to go to work now.'

Nicholas feigned dismay.

'Do I *have* to go to work, Mummy? I'd rather stay here with you.'

'No. You must go to work. We need the money to feed the children.'

He dutifully rose to his feet, kissed her goodbye, and left the room. She waved solemnly to his retreating figure.

As the days refused to hurry Donella forced herself to make excuses. It could be the tension of the experience. It could be the strain of knowing three other people waited with bated breath. Three days. A week. A fortnight. Still nothing.

It felt strange knowing other people, not just Michael, were tracking her menstrual patterns. Watching her. Waiting for her to say something.

The line on the pregnancy kit confirmed it. She sat on the edge of the bath feeling physically sick. There was no going back. Nicholas' baby had embedded itself deep inside her. For the next eight months she must carry that knowledge with her. She had done it before, but this time it was different. Other people knew; others still would have to know.

She hunched herself up, rocking back and forth in the isolation of that moment. For the rest of that day she would hug the secret. Tonight she must tell Michael, then Nicholas and Heidi, but for a few hours it was hers alone. She needed that time for herself – for the child. Ahead lay all the doubts, the questions, the accusations, the stunned reactions. For now she wanted this child to feel the full force of her all-enveloping love. For today it could be exclusively, intimately hers. Then she must steel herself to stay at a distance – a safe distance – from it.

From this evening onwards it must become Heidi's baby.

Michael stood motionless, staring at her. She had done it. Three times they had faced this moment before. He had been totally unprepared for news of Rachael's conception; the shock had reverberated for weeks. But with Fiona and Emily he had gloried in the news. With this child he was at a loss to know what he felt.

Her hesitant, anxious look brought him out of his self-preoccupation. In one stride he reached her and took her in his arms. Words might not be adequate but they had another language they both understood.

They stood together in silence facing the enormity of what they had agreed to do. There were no congratulations, no excited wonderings about gender, names, looks; there was only a blank undefined feeling.

But he had to admit, one predominant emotion was surging to the forefront of his reaction. Relief. Yes, it could not be denied. Never again would he be forced to impregnate his wife with his brother's semen.

He held her tighter, finding his voice at last to assure her of his love and support.

It was Nicholas who answered the phone. Donella felt an instant sense of relief, but made no attempt to analyse it. She heard instead his breathless silence.

'Hi, Nick. It's good news. You're going to be a dad.' It was carefully rehearsed, even-toned.

She waited, understanding. He hadn't dared anticipate this.

'I don't know … what to say.' His voice was choked. 'Donella …'

'I know.'

'You're … wonderful. I can … never thank you … enough for this.' He stumbled over the words.

'Please don't, Nick. I need you to be strong … for me.'

Another long silence. She regained control.

'Will you tell Heidi? Or do you need me to?' She was pleased her voice sounded so steady, so normal.

'I'll tell her.'

'Congratulations to you both.'

'Bless you.' Another long pause. 'Are you … OK?'

'I'm fine. See you soon.'

She had to ring off before he heard her crumble.

They had created a new life together but there was a greater distance between them than there had ever been before.

Donella always kept a supply of cards in a drawer of the desk. She had added a specially selected one some weeks earlier to her collection. That night she took it out. It was blank inside – 'for your own personal message' – but had a photograph of a tiger curled around a cub on the front.

Inside she wrote, *Congratulations! Just heard you're expecting a baby. Very special love.* She slid it across the table for Michael to sign before adding her own name and three kisses. They went together to the post box just yards from the house to post it.

A huge basket of roses arrived the following afternoon. The card said simply, *You're a girl in a million.*

The news came as a complete shock to their parents.

But not until the young people had left did Dick and Roberta allow themselves to fully address the enormity of what lay ahead. Roberta did her utmost to cling to the reassurance that both couples were eminently suitable, level-headed parents; there would be no question of anything less than optimal conditions during pregnancy, a stable and supportive environment later for the child. There was such a depth of family love, such commitment to this joint decision, there would be no last-minute breach of trust.

But even as she rehearsed these reassurances, the doubts crowded in. How would these loving people cope when the relational ties were confused, as they inevitably would be? How would they handle the reactions of the rest of the family, friends, colleagues, children? How would they withstand the powerful emotions within their foursome? Were they strong enough for all of that? Only time would tell.

Roberta thought wryly of her own offer to do this thing for Nicholas – how he had felt about her carrying his child. But how did he feel about Donella? There was no blood relationship but there were deep emotional ties – ties that went back longer than with Michael. She shivered inside.

Her heart went out to Michael and Heidi. How would they each deal with their own exclusion, the knowledge of this shared bond – a shared child – a constant reminder?

And … she felt the cold clench of past dread … yet again she must silently worry about the outcome. It was unbelievable. A *fourth* grandchild born with a frightening secret in its ancestry. Two sons, four grandchildren, all inextricably linked to one girl – a girl with a past about which she knew nothing.

Donella herself insisted on telling her own parents.

It was easy to allay their concern for her welfare: she felt wonderfully fit and energised as she had done each time before. Their cautious comments about the psychological impact on the four people most closely involved she found harder to handle: she could only assure them they'd all thought through the consequences carefully.

She heard their promises of support: they would help her through her pregnancy; they would be there for her when she gave the baby away. But only then in the hollowness of their words did she glimpse the enormity of their suffering. It would be their loss too. They must stand by while she gave their grandchild away – away to the man who had broken her heart all those years ago. She knew in that moment they had not forgotten; they could not begin to understand her actions.

It was Judy who suggested she should spare Donella the trauma of telling Graeme. Donella needed little persuasion but she was adamant on one thing: her mother must report what he said. She must know, she insisted; he was her only brother. And it must be an unvarnished account.

The truth, modified though it probably was, hurt more than she betrayed. To her vulnerable mind, listening to the account of his reaction, Declan's own averted gaze and the look in her mother's eyes seemed to condemn her too.

Graeme's open scorn of her actions reinforced her awareness of a widening rift, a chasm she was powerless to bridge until this thing was over. His cruel words about those she loved killed her desire to make the first attempt. What kind of a hold was it these Halley men had over his sister, he demanded. He would never be able to accept the fact that she – his twin – could give away her own child. What kind of a monster had she become?

Would he ever come to understand that, in her eyes, she was simply returning it to its father? No, not when that father was Nicholas, the man whom he had never forgiven for hurting her so cruelly all those years ago.

She tried once, in a letter, to explain something of her reasons, appealing to him to be supportive in her difficult task. There was no reply.

TWENTY-NINE

Donella continued to radiate health and energy. She laughingly suppressed the instincts of both Michael and Nicholas to leap to do things to help, but inwardly she was touched by their protectiveness. It was only the threat of generating unwelcome speculation that forced them to accept that she must be allowed to act normally. Quietly and methodically she drew up a timetable for her research that would enable her to work as long as possible and take the minimum of time off for the birth.

She made a concerted effort to involve Heidi in the progress of the pregnancy. Together they kept a diary of when she felt movement, what it felt like, how big the child now was, when its limbs were first discernible. The scan pictures were handed over to Heidi on the very day they were taken. Donella even asked the ultrasonographer to simply write '*Halley*' on the photograph and leave off the initial '*D*'.

Quite deliberately she chose to be cared for by a community midwife rather than attend the hospital where she was known, and where her other children had been born. The fewer people intimately involved in this transaction the better.

Including Nicholas in the practical realities felt more awkward. But she resolved in the later months to ensure he and Heidi together felt the movements and talked to the child.

She felt the watchful scrutiny of the entire family. But outwardly her composure cracked only twice.

Heidi was appalled to be the instigator of the first storm of tears in the fourth month of pregnancy. The two couples were sitting in the garden one evening when Heidi told her they wanted her to choose a second name for the baby. Completely unprepared for such a thought, she rushed indoors and locked herself in the bathroom for twenty minutes. Eventually Michael coaxed her into letting him in, and she sobbed in his arms, trying to explain it was nothing, she was just suffering from turbulent hormones.

Seeing Nicholas and Heidi's distress, she was instantly reassuring. They could not have predicted the idea would trigger such sad connections, she explained. But thoughts of her own sister had come into her head; a sister who had died in infancy, before Donella was even born. She admitted at the moment she was particularly vulnerable to ideas of children dying. But if this was a girl, she'd really like her to be called Bethany, after her sibling – the sister she had never known. As for a boy's name, she'd give it some thought. The tension eased but everyone became more wary.

The second moment of weakness came a week later but her family knew nothing of it. Christine, a colleague of Donella's, was leaving to have a baby, and a party was thrown on her last day to wish her well. Cries of 'Speech, speech' forced Christine into the limelight. She spoke excitedly of the activities she had planned for her maternity leave and how she'd probably get so hooked on motherhood that she'd never come back.

Crushing comparisons crowded into Donella's unguarded mind. She hid in her office, slumped on the floor, hugging herself piteously in the force of her emotions.

The demands of work and the return of the party-goers forced her to resume her usual calm exterior and she resolutely pushed the feelings from her, but she knew now she must redouble her efforts to distance herself. She would repeat on the hour every hour, 'This is Heidi's baby. This is Heidi's baby.' A voice deep inside appealed to her not to let this innocent child be deprived of maternal love even before it was born. Outwardly she told herself sternly, the forthcoming adoration of its parents would more than make up for any potential deficit now.

She felt the first warm trickle start without warning when she was carrying an armful of files down the long corridor of the hospital. She instantly thrust the papers at a passing janitor with instructions as to where they should go, and dived for the nearest toilet. Yes, it was blood.

Forcing herself to stay calm, she immediately took a taxi straight home and went to bed, contacting her midwife only when she was safely horizontal. It took only thirty-five minutes for the midwife to reach her, but it was clear to them both that there was to be no reversal of the process which had established itself so inexorably. It was all over within the hour.

What made her ask to see the fetus she couldn't say. Dry-eyed she looked down at it, absorbing every detail. What should have been Morag Bethany Halley.

Donella phoned Michael herself, and in spite of her protestations, he came straight home. Not until he entered the bedroom did she give way to the convulsing sobs. Again and again he countered her cries of guilt about letting them all down: she was not to blame; these things happened; everyone's concern would be for her. But she was inconsolable.

He rang his parents, asking them to take the girls, before ringing his brother.

Nicholas' first thought was for Donella – could he and Heidi come over? Michael agreed. It would be best for her to see them sooner rather than let the prospect of meeting get out of perspective.

Donella was sitting in the drawing room, red-eyed and pale, when they arrived. One look at her was enough. Heidi watched in silence as Nicholas abandoned all he had rehearsed on the journey across the city, dropped on his knees beside her and enveloped her in his arms. They clung to each other in full view of their spouses, oblivious of all except the need for comfort.

Heidi became aware of Michael's arm sliding around her shoulders, and looked up at him questioningly, but what she saw in his face made her give him a spontaneous hug.

Her eyes returned reluctantly to her husband. He called this a family embrace? Oh, she knew this was no time for jealousy or doubt. These two people had both lost a baby – their own baby. They needed to share their sorrow. But …

Eventually Donella raised her tear-stained face, and held out her arm to take Heidi too into her embrace. Heidi knelt silently as both included her in the circle of loss. Through her confusion she heard Donella's broken voice, over and over again telling them all how sorry she was. She seemed beyond hearing their assurances that she was not to blame.

Though she made a determined effort to put what had happened behind her, Donella's recovery was slow. Outwardly she restructured her research timetable and brought all her deadlines forward, but her mind refused to be so disciplined and she grew increasingly frustrated and dejected.

She sagged too under the oppressive concern of the whole family – the solicitous enquiries, the anxious looks, the protective behaviour. Intellectually she knew they were driven by love; nevertheless she found herself increasingly burdened by the constant surveillance. They had not approved her action in the first place; their sympathy now must surely be edged by relief and a sense of vindication.

She felt an aching need to deflect attention away from herself onto the new life, the promise of which had been snuffed out before it was even realised. Nicholas and Heidi, their loss too, should be the focus of their concern. But no-one seemed to hear her.

It was six months before she mentioned to Michael the possibility of another pregnancy.

'You have to be kidding!' he exploded.

'No. We shouldn't leave it too long.'

'No! Absolutely, categorically … *N… O*. This is madness. Look at you! You're in no fit state – to make such a huge decision, never mind go through with it.'

'I must. You have to see that. It's the only way I can get rid of this awful feeling of guilt.'

'*You … are … not … guilty.* How many times do I have to tell you? Nobody blames you. It's just one of those things.'

'*I* do. I blame myself.'

'But that's not a rational thing. It's your hormones, the shock, grief, everything. It's been an incredibly stressful experience from beginning to end. You're not yourself.'

'But I want to try again.'

'Maybe. But I have absolutely no intention of letting you, so just forget the whole idea. You gave it your best shot. It didn't work out. But that's life. I simply won't stand by and watch you go through this little lot again.'

Donella felt totally alone. If Michael would not support her, she must forever carry a burden which she was convinced would grow heavier with every passing month. She turned from him with a crushing sense of desolation.

But it was not until Nicholas dropped in unexpectedly one Saturday afternoon, when she was on her own, that the real source of her oppression escaped unbidden.

Nicholas was surprised to find her alone, working at the computer.

'Mike's taken the girls to the zoo. But I'm so far behind with work – I can't seem to concentrate these days – so I decided to use the time to get on with some analysis.'

'Where are you now with the research?'

'All the data are collected but I've only just started with the proper analysis. I must admit, it's my least favourite bit so I have to force myself to stay at the computer. But I think I'm starting to get the picture and I suspect we're going to find a difference between the five-year outcomes with the two therapies.'

The words were right but the lacklustre tone told its own story.

'Oh yuck! I don't know how you stick that academic stuff. Give me the thrill of a motorway pile-up any day!'

'Ghoul!'

'And as for choosing chi squares and probabilities over the zoo – no thanks! Give me monkeys and penguins any day! Even the odd reptile'd be more attractive than statistics on a Saturday afternoon.'

She barely smiled. He looked at her more closely. For the first time he saw the unguarded grief.

'Sorry. I'm disturbing you. I only called to see if I could maybe take the girls off your hands for a while, give you and Michael a bit of peace.'

'Don't apologise. And don't go on my account. I couldn't concentrate on this stuff anyway. I'm glad of the interruption.'

Her bleak expression, her flat voice, were more distressing than any tears. He moved across to sit beside her, wanting her to feel his aching concern.

'Donella, I hate to see you so low. I feel most horribly responsible.'

'It's not your fault. It's just life,' she countered mechanically.

'But it *is* my fault. We shouldn't have let you do it.'

'I chose to. You didn't make me. You didn't even ask me to.' She kept her eyes down, shredding the tissue in her hand.

'I know we can't go back and make things right for you. But is there anything – *anything* – we can do to help?'

'Let me have another baby for you.' Her eyes were suddenly lifted, the appeal heartrending.

The shock made him physically recoil.

'You *can't*. You *mustn't!*' he stammered.

'Then you can't help me.' The hopelessness nudged against the foundations of his certainty.

She looked away from him.

'But ... Look, I'd do *anything* to spare you this pain. But I *couldn't* – not *that*. Donella, you must see that.'

'You don't understand. None of you do. Michael doesn't. You don't. You just don't know what it feels like.' It sounded so empty.

'I know we don't. We can't. But we *can* see what this is doing to you.'

'If you understood, you'd let me do it.'

'You've told Mike that's what you want?'

'Yes. But he says no too.'

'Only for your sake.'

'It'll never be right if you don't let me.'

Nicholas reached across to turn Donella to face him.

'Donella – listen to me. No, don't look away. You must hear me.'

He waited until she dragged her eyes back again.

'It wasn't your fault. It just happened. You have nothing to blame yourself for.'

'But I *do*.' Her face crumpled and the bitter tears fell over his hands.

Instinctively he pulled her close, rocking her against his shoulder like a child, until she was still again. She buried her face in a handful of tissues.

Holding her head against him still, he said in a low voice, 'Tell me. Help me to understand what it's like for you.'

Haltingly she tried to tell him how empty she felt, how she couldn't get the picture of the baby out of her head.

'Was she ... OK?' he interrupted in a hoarse whisper.

'She was perfect, yes. Well, she looked it anyway.'

'I didn't like to ask.'

'I know. But I looked for you too. I knew you'd want to know. She was perfect in every detail.'

'I'm glad.' He held her tightly again. 'Sorry, I interrupted. You were telling me how you feel.'

She told him how she felt such a failure, how much she had wanted to do this thing – needed to do it for him, owed it to him.

'You don't owe me anything,' he soothed, stroking her head gently. 'And I wish with all my heart we hadn't let you do it before. I can't bear to see you hurting like this.'

'I *had* to do it. I had to repay you.' Her words were muffled by the wodge of tissues.

'Repay me for what?' he asked softly, humouring her.

'For keeping Rachael.'

'Rachael? What's she got to do with all this?' Nicholas was completely mystified now. She was clearly seriously disturbed by all this.

'She's ... yours.' It was only a whisper.

His hand stopped its caressing movement.

'Say ... that ... again.'

'That night in the bathroom ...'

'That's when ...?'

'I didn't know it was you. Not till after we were married. I never would have done it. Not if I'd known.'

'I know. It was unforgivable of me – taking advantage. I tried to stop you – half-heartedly – but you didn't want to listen. And I didn't want to embarrass you and ... well, you know how it was. You were mildly drunk. I hoped you'd never realise.'

'But that was when ... Rachael ... happened. Mike and I, we took precautions.'

He sat motionless trying to take in the truth, unaware that he still held her in a vice-like grip. Only when she eventually stirred in his arms and raised her face to look at him did he release her.

'So you must see this was my one chance – to right that wrong.'

'Does Mike know?' He hardly dared ask.

'No. And he *mustn't*. You do see that, don't you? It would kill him to know. Oh, you *couldn't* tell him. *Please* tell me you won't. I never meant to tell *you*.' She was clutching at him in her agitation.

'No, of course I won't. But ... Rachael ...' He couldn't take it in. That adorable child who had adopted him as her 'Sunday Daddy' – she was *his*. His daughter.

'I know it's not fair on you. I know it's not. But don't you see? If I could give you a child now, and you'd have it but I wouldn't, that would be ...' She broke off, her look imploring him to understand.

'You don't have to put yourself through any more. I understand. *I* was to blame. Not you.'

'But I kept her – pretending.'

'Of course you kept her. I understand that.'

'So I'm to blame. I must make it up to you.'

'Donella, listen to me. *You ... don't ... owe ... me ... anything.*' He emphasised every word slowly and carefully. 'I was the one who left you so heartlessly. I was the one who took advantage of you. *I* knew it was me. I was the one who agreed to let you have a baby – for me. If anyone is to blame it is *definitely* me.'

'But now you know – about Rachael, you do see? I *need* to do it. *Please.*'

He held her gaze for a long moment.

'I don't know what I think any more. I need time. Everything is so confused. I never dreamt ...'

'But you will think about it – not just say no?' she begged, her tear-filled eyes more eloquent than her words.

'I'll think about it – all.'

'It's the only way I'm ever going to get over this. I know it.' The forlorn appeal was more than he could bear. He must get away.

'I need time. I have to think this out calmly. I can't think. Not here. Not seeing you like this. It's all I can do not to howl like a baby myself. It's all – *all* of it – my fault, not yours.'

He stood up abruptly. Standing above her he said unsteadily, 'I'd give my right arm to spare you this pain. You know that. But what you're asking ... I don't know.'

'You can help me, Nick. Remember. You *can* help me.'

He saw the flicker of hope in her eyes and turned away. This was too big a decision to be dictated by any unguarded emotion.

THIRTY

Nothing more was said of Rachael's paternity but the next time the children clamoured for a game of 'Is it Daddy?' Nicholas' eyes flew involuntarily to Donella's. He scooped Rachael up in his arms and dropped a kiss on her curls, before shooting off with her to deposit her behind the curtains under strict instructions 'not to peek!' But it was time spent with the children more than anything else that helped the adults to settle back into a more normal relationship again.

Gradually the tensions eased. Only Donella's dogged insistence that when they were all ready, she wanted to repeat the process, kept the issue alive.

Heidi was scandalised by the idea, and bewildered.

'It would not be fair on Donella, why does she insist so?'

'It's something very deep seated. She feels guilty,' Nicholas told her.

'But it is not her fault. We all tell her so. And *she* must know it is so.'

'You know that, I know that, everybody else knows it. But she just won't believe it.'

'But why? What does she say to you?'

'She feels she's failed us.'

Heidi shrank back into an old shell she had thought long discarded. If this was failure how did Donella view her own inability to conceive at all?

The family watched with mounting dismay as Donella continued to limp through her life.

It was Michael who first admitted to his brother that trying again would probably be the only thing that would drag her up out of her despond. Time just wasn't having the desired effect.

But his eyes were sombre as he surveyed the subdued and visibly uneasy group who finally gathered to discuss the subject of surrogacy again. Both he and Nicholas reiterated their strong reservations. But watching Donella closely, hearing her conviction, he was persuaded. It was the only way to erase the pain of her loss.

They began, tentatively, to discuss arrangements. There would be a maximum of three more tries – definitely, *emphatically*, no more than three, Michael insisted. If she was not pregnant by then they would abandon the attempt. Donella smiled at him: of course, they were right to set limits.

Both men emphasised, if she had *any* misgivings at *any* stage she must say. Everyone would understand. She wouldn't, she said simply, but thanks.

But it was Heidi who expressed the feeling of them all when she suddenly crouched down to take Donella's hands in both her own, holding them tightly as she spoke.

'Donella, you are a very strong person. I do not think I could be so strong. You are doing a wonderful thing for us. We cannot ever say a thank you big enough. But it is *you* we care about. You *must* tell us if this thing is too much that you would do. You are very special to us. We love you very, very much. We do not want you to hurt any more just because you want us to be happy. *We* want *you* to be happy too.'

Donella bent forward to hug her warmly. They held each other for much longer than Heidi usually tolerated.

'Thank you for that, Heidi. You've all been fantastic supporting me already. And I know I *will* be happy if you let me do this thing for you.'

Michael saw his brother swallow hard, and choked back the sensation in his own throat.

Donella was under no illusions about her husband's reservations. He would not actually prevent her doing this thing for his twin but he was appalled at the prospect of the insemination itself. He could not disguise the fact. Indeed he had admitted his abhorrence of it in the rush of relief following the successful pregnancy last time.

She sympathised. But she didn't require him to torture himself, she told him, she just needed his loving support. He berated himself for being 'pathetic' and 'weak'. She bargained with him. She would accept the finality of three attempts without complaint if he would accept he had limits too.

On the day appointed, Nicholas and Heidi came for the night and repeated their part in the proceedings much as before.

For Heidi there was now a new dimension, a confidence which lent an air of calm to her demeanour. Having had her dream snatched away from her so harshly, she now knew beyond question how much she wanted a family of her own. In sharing the pregnancy with Donella she had become so attached to the growing fetus that it had taken all her determination to conceal her personal grief when her expectations had been shattered.

But nothing prepared her for the emotion that shook her when it was to Donella instead of Michael that she handed the semen. This time there was no smile, no eye contact. She turned abruptly on her heel and returned to Nicholas. He held her tightly for a long time but she could not bring herself to explain her tension, only grateful that he made no effort to unravel it.

Michael, alone in his office, found his mind would not stay tethered to the thesis he was reading. The work was actually well-written and on a subject close to his own interests – the integration of ethnic minority groups into rural communities – but he found himself skimming the pages without a word of it going into his brain. Aware of the deadline by which it must be examined, he applied himself with renewed effort, reminding himself that the peace of a silent building late into the evening was so much more conducive to concentration than the hubbub of normal working hours. But it was to no avail.

Every instinct cried out to him to go home. How could he have left Donella alone with this burden? Heidi would have Nick to reassure her. Donella would have no-one – no-one even to hold her close.

He reached for the phone.

'Don, it's me.'

Her voice was calm, almost sleepy.

'Mmmmhhm. All done.'

'You OK?'

'Absolutely.'

'I feel terrible leaving you to do it yourself.'

'It was no problem. In fact I worried less doing it myself. I knew you hated it. That made me feel tense. But this time I was quite relaxed.'

'I don't know how you do it.'

'It's just like a medical procedure. Just doing it to myself. And I knew *this* patient wouldn't moan about my cold hands or my brusque manner! So no problem. Honestly.'

'You make it sound so straightforward.'

'It was. Honestly, Mike. I'm fine. In fact I feel more at peace inside myself than I have done since ... since the miscarriage.'

'Yes?'

'Truly. I *know* this is right.'

'You're amazing.'

'No, I'm just a mum. A very lucky mum. We are so lucky to have our girls. And I'm lucky to have you supporting me – allowing me to do this. Thanks, Mike – for everything.'

'I love you.'

'Love you too. You coming home soon?'

'Right now.'

'Good. I really need a cuddle.'

This first attempt proved unsuccessful but confirmed to her watching family the wisdom for Donella of pursuing this course. The partial return of her old sparkle was in itself a positive outcome.

For Donella there was more at stake. She had only three chances. With each attempt she was reducing those chances of completing her task successfully. She worked at maintaining a positive frame of mind, her first priority to provide the most conducive environment possible for conception.

She experienced a bitter sense of disappointment when her period started four days late after the next attempt. There was no restraining the immediate silent tears which fell in the privacy of her own bathroom, but she then resolutely applied every technique she knew to restore her inner peace. This was her last chance; she had to give it her best effort.

Never before had she prepared so single-mindedly during the preceding week. On the agreed night, with Michael away from home speaking at a conference in Belfast, she gave herself over to total relaxation of body and mind as she waited for Nicholas and Heidi to arrive.

When the phone rang an hour before they were due, it was an effort to answer and her voice sounded distant even to her.

'Hello.'

'Donella? Are you OK?' It was Nicholas.

'I'm fine. I'm just totally relaxed.'

'You sound mildly drunk!'

'Not a bit of it, cheeky. Just concentrating of staying completely calm.'

'I'm afraid we've got a slight complication this end. Heidi's got a splitting headache – she can't lift her head off the pillow without being terribly dizzy.'

'Oh, poor thing. I hope she's soon better.'

'Nothing to worry about. She gets these migraines every once in a while. But what about you? I feel bad about postponing tonight.'

'Why postpone it … unless you …?'

'Oh, it's not *me* I'm bothered about.'

'Can you leave Heidi?'

'Well, yes. She says I should just come if you're OK with that.'

'Is *she*?'

'Yep. Says you'll be totally psyched up to it and it would be really hard for you to have to put it off.'

'Perceptive woman – your wife.'

'Mmmmhhuh.'

'So I'll see you soon?'

'You will indeed.'

When he arrived, Donella was still perfectly tranquil, sitting in the candlelit drawing room listening to sounds of the ocean. Deep resonating tones, womb sounds. Unfathomable.

The room he was to use was prepared with the same care and sensitivity. Without Heidi's feelings to concern him Nicholas allowed himself to take in the detail. What an amazing girl Donella was.

He was in the bathroom when a sudden tap at the door seemed too loud in the hush of the house. Wrapping a towel around his waist, he peeped outside.

Her face was pale in the dark, her forehead creased with a small frown.

'What's up?' he whispered, instantly concerned for her.

'We've got a crisis! I was moving the baster from the high shelf, and it slid out of the towel and into the wash-handbasin. The glass thingy on the end has completely broken off.'

'Damn!'

They looked at one another questioningly.

'Hang on a sec. OK if I borrow this bathrobe of Mike's?'

'Sure.'

'I'll be out in a tick. And we'll think about this.'

'Come along to my room when you're ready. We don't want to wake the girls.'

It was the first time he had been into their bedroom and he instinctively wrapped his brother's bathrobe more tightly around him. It felt easier looking at the room than at her. His eyes took in the lovely blend of colours: the shades of cream through to a deep olive green creating a muted background, the more vibrant touches of gold and bronze adding definition and character. Heidi would love it.

Donella, stretched out in the bed, the quilted cover drawn up to her neck, was patting the side of the bed. He perched beside her. Quietly and methodically they considered their options.

Should they try to find someone with a baster? At this time of night? Who? What excuse would they give?

OK, a syringe then? That would involve a trip to the hospital. What reason would they give? And if it was their last shot, was it fair to have it less than optimal?

Maybe they should postpone it. Nicholas saw the effect of this idea on Donella. Could she handle more disappointment, the strain of waiting another month? Could they alter their work patterns again to accommodate yet another appointment?

What about Heidi and Michael – what would they think?

The first cry suspended thought.

'Mummy!'

They remained motionless.

'Mummy!' It was louder. Nicholas looked at Donella.

'Just leave her. She'll probably go back to sleep in a moment,' she whispered.

'*Muuummmmy!*' It was much more insistent.

'Shall I go?' Nick made as if to rise from the bed. 'You stay and work at that deep breathing. And think of a solution!'

'D'you mind? She probably just wants a hug or a drink of water.'

Rachael was sitting up in bed scrubbing her heavy eyes when he slipped into the semi-darkness.

'I want Mummy,' the child wailed when she saw him enter.

'I know, darling, but Mummy's tired. She's in bed,' he said soothingly.

'But I want Mummy.'

'Cuddle?' He put his arm around the hunched-up child.

She snuggled up to him and he held her close, rocking her gently.

'Now can I go to Mummy, Daddy?'

The name took him so much by surprise that he was slow to respond – too slow for the waiting child.

'Daddy!' She wriggled out of his arms to pound his chest with her little fist. '*Now* I want to go to Mummy?'

'OK, just for a kiss. Then back to bed. Yes?'

'Promise.' She nodded, her curls bobbing vigorously.

He scooped her up in his arms and carried her along to the bedroom. Donella must be alerted.

'Mummy, Rachael just wants a cuddle,' he said in a stage whisper as they approached the door. 'Then she's going to be a good girl and go straight back to bed.'

'OK, darling.' Donella held out her arms to the child. Rachael wriggled down inside the covers and snuggled in to her mother. Donella dropped tender kisses on the flushed cheeks, the damp hair, the heavy eyelids.

Nicholas stood looking down at them, with a strange tight feeling in his chest.

'And you, Daddy. Family cuddles.' Rachael held out one imperious hand to draw him into the circle.

He lay down on the other side of her and felt her arm encircle his neck. He slid his own hand around her slender body and lay motionless, heart racing, acutely conscious of the intertwining of all of their limbs.

'No, Daddy, right inside.'

He obediently slid underneath the duvet. She wriggled down further drawing them all closer. Neither adult spoke.

Nicholas' thoughts surged recklessly. This was his daughter. Innocent of the turmoil she was generating in him, she lay between her parents for the first time. She had called him Daddy. But tomorrow, in the cold light of day, he would be Uncle Nick again. His brother would take over as before.

He wanted this moment to go on and on.

Donella was the first to move.

'Back to bed now, darling. Sweet dreams.' She planted a soft kiss on the child's forehead and eased her over to Nicholas.

He lifted Rachael up out of the covers and held her close against him as he carried her out of the room.

'Night, night, Mummy. I love you,' he called softly, mimicking her young voice.

'Love you,' she echoed, before snuggling back against his chest. It was the first time he'd been aware of the shortness of the landing. Telling himself he must check she was safely asleep he lingered beside her, tucking her in, holding her, kissing her goodnight, watching as the eyes closed and stopped fluttering.

Outside Donella's door he paused. Rachael mustn't hear him tapping, or her mother granting permission for him to enter.

Inside the room he leaned heavily against the closed door, suddenly needing the support.

'She called me – Daddy.' His whisper cracked as he uttered the word.

He saw the suddenly outstretched arms and, dropping on his knees beside the bed, laid his head within the circle of their embrace. Tears choked him.

For a long time neither spoke. Then, her fingers caressing his cheek, she whispered brokenly, 'Nick, I'm so sorry. I'm so sorry.'

He reached up to place his hand over hers, taking it to his lips in a long kiss.

'Don't be. I'm sorry I broke down. It's the emotion of all of this ...'

'I know. It's affecting us all.'

Just how it happened he never knew but one moment Donella was dropping soothing kisses on his face, the next their lips were touching, returning, lingering. He was on the bed again. Inside the covers. They clung together each seeking and giving comfort.

The enveloping fragrance of the scented room, the warmth of the shared bed, their mutual distress, each reaching out to the other's pain, the emotions Rachael had unearthed – everything swept them along on a tide of need they seemed powerless to resist.

They lay for a long time, fearful of speaking. Nicholas was the first to find his voice.

'We must forget this ever happened.'

'For everyone's sake.'

'It will have to be … just another … part of the process.' The words were jagged, jarring with his emotions.

'The last part. The last time,' she breathed. There was a sense of closure given.

'But …'

'No, Nick, don't.' She reached up to lay her hand on his lips.

'I *must* … tell you …' Dare he put it into words?

'It's better not said. I understand.'

'You've always been special to me.'

'I know. And you to me.'

'But …'

'You love Heidi. And I love Mike. And …'

'I never intended …'

'I know. Nor me. It's just the emotion – everything.'

'I'm cursing myself.'

'I was just as much to blame. But it's happened.' She sounded so calm, so reasonable.

'It never will again.'

'I know. And we must carry on as normal. No-one must ever know.'

'Could you – could we – think of it – as a solution to the broken baster?' he asked tentatively, searching desperately for a construction they could live with.

She was silent. He lifted his head to look at her for the first time.

'I'm not trying to diminish what there is between us. You know I wasn't just … using you. You know it was more than that for me,' he said looking full into her eyes. 'But it can't be. And we must get this into perspective before we meet again, before we go back – to what we were.'

'We must, but … Nick, if it works this time – it will have been the perfect solution. If it doesn't, we will know we gave it our best – so much better than the baster.' She paused, adding in a whisper, 'I hope with all my heart it does.'

'I can never thank you enough. But after tonight I can't speak of what you mean to me.'

'But – after tonight – if I can give you your own beautifully created child, I shall come closer to making peace with myself than I ever dared hope.'

'Help me to be strong enough to go back to being as we were?'

'We'll be strong for one another. It's what we both want.'

He bent to kiss her gently before he slid out of the bed and went to get dressed.

When he returned she was lying as he had left her. Her face was serene. She smiled as he sat on the edge of the bed.

He took her hand in both his and sat looking down at her in silence.

'Mmmhh. You have a lovely soothing bedside manner, Dr Halley,' she said teasingly.

'I'll stay with you – if I may – for the full half hour – as per the manual. Just in case the girls need anything.'

'I'd like that,' she said quietly.

'Will you be OK then? I hate to go and leave you on your own. But Heidi will wonder if …'

'Of course you must go back to her. I'll be fine.'

'Shall I take the baster and dump it in the bin?'

'Please do. You can ceremoniously smash it to pieces on my behalf!'

'Thank you for putting up with … all that – for us.'

She smiled up at him.

'It'll have all been worth it, if it works tonight.'

'But promise me – no guilt if it doesn't? You couldn't have given it any more than you have.' He increased the pressure on her enclosed hand as he spoke.

'I know that this time. And I promise.' He believed her. She was at peace with herself.

It was unbelievably hard to leave.

'Thank you for staying,' she said quietly. 'But you must go.'

'I know.'

'It'll be OK. There'll be no awkwardness. Tomorrow it'll be as it's meant to be.'

'Thanks entirely to you. It's been an incredible evening – Rachael – and you – us – but I shall lock it away in a secret compartment of my heart. You've nothing to fear from me.'

'I know that.'

He knelt to take her once more in his arms, kissed her softly, and then left.

The broken baster he wrapped in two pieces of newspaper and dumped in a bin at the end of the street. It was empty and there was a sound of smashing glass as it dropped from a height but the newspaper stopped the package from revealing its contents.

Heidi was sleeping when he got home, the medication she had taken to ease the pain deepening her unconsciousness. He let his breath out slowly.

THIRTY-TWO

When Michael rang the following morning Donella bought herself some time, asking him: how was Belfast? Any sign of the troubles? How had his presentation gone? By the time he had opportunity to ask about her evening, her voice was perfectly under control. She assured him she was fine. It was all over. Heidi hadn't been well enough to come but they had managed perfectly well – consummate professionals that they were, she said lightly. And Nicholas had taken the baster away to dispose of it, so that was the end of the attempts.

She heard his sigh of relief. It was over.

To her surprise she found no difficulty in being herself with him, and it was three days before the next bombshell hit her.

'Don.' Michael sounded very odd.

She swung round to look at him, suddenly fearful.

'Uhhhmm?'

'You're not going to believe this.'

'What?'

'The condom – it burst.'

She stared at him in silence, backing slowly towards a chair. They were within an ace of the finishing line – and now this?

'We never even *thought* of this possibility,' she said in a voice devoid of emotion.

'What do we do now?'

'We must stay calm here. Let's think about it. If I'm *not* pregnant – it won't matter at all.'

'But if you are …?'

'Well, if I am … what if it's yours?'

'Would we have to have tests – DNA or something?'

'That wouldn't tell us. You're identical twins.'

'Oh, of course – same DNA.'

'Yep.' She paused looking at him closely. 'The scan, even if it's done at a *very* early stage, is only accurate to within three days. So that wouldn't tell us either.'

More silence.

'Mike, would it matter to *you*? … if it might be yours?' The ramifications were hitting *her* like hailstones.

'No. I couldn't let it. Oh no! Not after all *you've* gone through.' He sounded totally confident.

'You'd pass it off as Nick's?'

'Isn't it most likely to be his kid? The other night – that was your most fertile time. Wasn't it?'

'Yes,' she confirmed slowly. 'But what if …?'

'It *has* to be his. Hell, Donella, we can't stuff it up at this stage. After all you've been through.'

Indeed. After all that had happened. It would be too cruel.

'Need they know?' Michael asked cautiously.

'You mean – say nothing – just let them think – no question?' She was tasting the thought.

'Would that be … honourable?'

Donella's conscience smote her. If he but knew how dishonourable *she* had been, he wouldn't be chastising himself. Or would he? He had always been so scrupulous about integrity.

'I don't know about honourable – but I think it might be kindest,' she said gently.

'Could you live with that?'

'*I* could. But hey, this isn't about me. Not this time. After all, I'm giving away my child whichever of you fathered it. But what about you?' The same question – but he'd had a bit more time to think about it. The answer was less instant, less confident.

'I think I'd learn to. I think I'd learn to convince myself it was Nick's. And I *couldn't* tell him – not now. Not now we've come this far.'

'It would be pretty hard, I agree.'

'I'm so sorry, Don.'

'It's not your fault. Hey, don't look so guilty. Let's wait and see if I'm pregnant, eh? Worry more about it if I am. If not, there's no point in beating ourselves up over it.'

But she knew both of them would berate themselves internally.

The days dragged by as all four waited.

The nausea told them. It was a new experience, and it was constant.

Michael seeing her vomiting day and night was under no illusions. His emotions churned as he faced the prospect of another child – a child to be given away in spite of all it had cost them. And this time it might even be his own child. But his first concern was for Donella's welfare.

She smiled wanly.

'I guess it's my turn for a few complications. Not many women have disgustingly good health all through pregnancy. And I sailed through the first three.'

The thought of the outcome of this one flashed into his mind unbidden. He said the first thing he could drag into his mind.

'It must be a boy.'

'You've been listening to too many old wives' tales!'

He grinned in spite of his turmoil.

'It's all Nicholas' fault. *My* babies were better behaved!'

The responsive smile vanished as she rushed for the bathroom again. It gave him time to think.

'Mike, what if it is yours? Will you be OK?'

'If you can handle giving it up, so can I.'

'Sure?'

'Sure. Besides, like I said, no kid of *mine* caused this much trouble. Nick's always been the one to stir things up!'

A fresh bout of vomiting interrupted them.

'We've got a new problem here,' she said wanly.

'Oh? What now?'

'If Nick and Heidi see the vomiting they'll draw their own conclusions. If I make excuses not to see them, they'll think I'm not coping again.'

'Could you just keep away from them till you've done the test, know for sure?'

'It's the only way, I think. They'll have to know pretty much straight away.'

Nicholas stared at the email Donella had sent, asking them to call that evening.

He knew exactly how many days since her period was due but he had no idea if it had come or not. Was she summoning up the courage to tell them that in spite of everything, they would not now – ever – know the joys of parenthood? Or …?

No, he mustn't let himself even think of the alternative. The last thing she needed was a disappointed face. She mustn't go through that terrible guilt again. She'd done everything possible.

His thoughts went involuntarily to that last attempt. Incredible. How could they have so lost themselves as to *both* forget their allegiances, their commitment to others? Why had all their careful precautions been forgotten?

It should have been simply a fifth and last attempt to create a child. But … this time they were alone. This time he'd had no wife to stop him being drawn into the ambience Donella had created. This time there was no impersonal baster … This time Rachael had innocently stirred their emotions, given them permission to acknowledge their connectedness.

The proprieties had dissolved. The safeguards had slipped. There was room for the reality of what they were doing to creep in through the cracks in their defences. It had ceased to be a medical procedure.

If only Michael and Heidi had continued to be actively involved it would not – *could* not – have happened. Could they too share the blame? No, he couldn't stretch even his own credulity that far. Heidi especially, he knew beyond question, had been above reproach – strong, calm, committed – in spite of what this must have cost her. And he could only dimly comprehend what toll this whole infertility experience had taken of her. She had found the courage to be intimately involved, even to handing over his semen to another woman. He shuddered at the thought. And in spite of her earlier anxieties and doubts, she had trusted him enough to send him alone to Donella – with her blessing – rather than cause Donella a moment's extra pain of disappointment. And he had repaid her trust by ... It didn't bear thinking about.

But he *had* to think about it. He had to deal with it if he was to behave normally with them all.

How would he respond when Donella told them the news tonight? Would he – *could* he – naturally hug her as he had done so many times before? If he did not, what message would that convey? That he was blaming her? How unfair would that be? That he was ill at ease with her? What possible explanation could he give to Heidi or Michael for that?

But if he held her again, what would that do to him? Could he keep a rein on his emotions? He could find no absolute assurance now.

Mercifully Michael and Donella had been too busy to see them as frequently as usual. It had given him breathing space. Or ... was Donella unable to face seeing him? Tonight would give him a better measure of her feelings.

It would be harrowing to have her distancing herself now. But it might be necessary, at least for the time being, until their old relationship was restored. Could it be ... could it ever be as it had been before?

What was it ... before?

He now no longer knew.

The sound of his pager summoning him to a crisis in the department drove the thoughts into hiding. Six casualties were on their way, serious burns from an explosion in a local factory. Amputated limbs, head injuries, crushed chests ... he went into instant action.

By the time he arrived home that night, two hours later than he'd expected, he was too physically exhausted to start to apply his mind to the questions. But there were things he had to say to Heidi.

'Heidi, I'm sure you've been preparing yourself for this. We both know it might be the end of the road. And because she's calling us so soon I very much fear it's not good news.'

'I think it will be very hard for Donella to tell us so,' she replied quietly.

'Exactly. And I want to tell you that, if I seem to concentrate on her feelings tonight, it doesn't mean I'm not thinking about you – what it means to you. I shall be. But I can comfort you in private.'

'I know. It is right we think of her first. She has done so much for us.'

'Indeed.'

'But we must not let her see it hurts.'

'She knows it will. But she mustn't feel she's to blame. It was so tough for her last time.'

'I know. I saw it. I hope it will not be so hard if the baby does not start.'

She didn't need to tell him how tense she felt – her strange choice of words betrayed her.

'I hope so too. It was harder for everyone – you especially – and Donella – to get so far last time and then lose out. But I know it will be a bitter night for you tonight if she says it hasn't worked.'

She nodded.

'When we get home you and I'll talk about where we go from here, yes?' he said.

'There is time for that. Tonight it is Donella's time.' She was unconsciously giving him permission to be himself with her sister-in-law.

As Michael let them into the house, Nicholas searched his brother's face. It betrayed nothing.

Donella's welcome was exactly as it had always been – warm hugs for them both, cheery greetings. Nicholas let out his breath slowly.

Michael took his seat close to Donella on the long settee. Nicholas glanced at them once but had to look away quickly.

'Congratulations – you're going to have a baby.'

There was a stunned silence. No-one moved.

'Not what you wanted to hear?' she teased.

'Not what we *expected* to hear,' Nicholas said in a breathless voice.

She stood up suddenly, held out her arms and said, 'Come here, both of you.'

They jumped to their feet and all three held each other tightly as they half-laughed, half-cried in their relief. Michael was smiling broadly and, after a moment, joined the huddle of arms and bodies.

Not until they were all seated again did anyone say anything coherent. Donella was the first to speak.

'There's something I want to say. I know it's terribly early days and a lot can happen between now and then but ... I want to give this baby the best possible chance. I'm going into this with as much positive thinking as I can muster. It will make it harder, I know, if it goes wrong again, but I don't want us to be always anticipating trouble. So please ...' – she looked from one to the other – '*please* don't try to warn me, or worry about me, if I seem too optimistic. I know. I know it might all go pear-shaped. I haven't forgotten. But we stand the best chance if we think positively. So I want you all to try to stay calm and enjoy each day as it comes.' Her voice changed suddenly to a pompous one. 'I shall not tread this path again!'

'Well, that's a relief!' Michael said, grinning at her. 'Spoken in front of two independent witnesses, too.'

She grinned back at him, but Nicholas saw the long look they exchanged. What courage. How could she voice such thoughts?

'You're brilliant' was all Nicholas said aloud. '*We* haven't forgotten either. And you must remember that we aren't underestimating what you're doing for us. But I agree, it would be great if we could be happy together. It will be *our* last time too.'

Heidi's eyes were full of tears as she added her own thoughts.

'It is not possible to tell you what is in my heart. But what you are doing and how you think to make it good – for the baby – and for us – and for you – it makes me feel ... very small. I think it is a very lucky baby that you will have it.' Her voice crumbled and she stopped speaking abruptly.

There was not a dry eye in the room.

'I shall have it for only nine months, Heidi, but it will be a very lucky child to have a real mum who's so strong, and so courageous, and generous, to bring it up,' Donella said gently.

'You girls,' Nicholas said, openly wiping his eyes, 'you sure know how to crack a chap up.'

It was Heidi who volunteered to invite Dick and Roberta to her own home for a meal, Michael and Donella joining them to present a united front for the revelation of the pregnancy. Watchful in her silence, Heidi knew her parents-in-law were totally unprepared for what was coming. It was a relief when Donella spoke.

'We have something to tell you. You might not like it at first but we've all given this a lot of thought – a *lot* of thought.'

Dick and Roberta looked at her; the rest of the family looked at them.

'I'm pregnant. We're having a baby for Nick and Heidi.'

Their faces said it all.

Donella rushed on.

'It was my choice. I needed to do this. I felt so guilty last time when it all went wrong. This is right – for us.'

Their silence was unnerving.

'Oh dear' was all Roberta said.

'I just don't know … what to say.' Dick's first words were accompanied by an expression it was hard to read.

'Well, that's a first, I guess,' Nicholas said flippantly. 'Dad lost for words.'

Heidi knew it was nervousness speaking, but she was grateful for the warning look Michael shot at his twin.

'Sorry,' he muttered contritely.

'I think, under the circumstances, you should say what you're thinking. Get this out into the open,' Michael said quietly. 'We know you won't approve. But we had our reasons.'

'What I'm really thinking is,' Dick said slowly, looking from one of his sons to the other without a glimmer of amusement in his eyes, 'how could you possibly go along with this? After all that happened – what it did to Donella last time – how could you risk it?'

They both looked crushed.

'But honestly, Dad'– Donella leaned across towards him, interrupting before the men could respond – 'it wasn't their fault. They did their best to stop me. They really did. They were as shocked as you are when I suggested it. They both insisted – no way would they do it. But I knew it was the only way I'd get over last time.'

'Time would have healed last time,' he said. 'Eventually. And support.'

'No.' Her voice was low but final. 'It wouldn't.'

Heidi watched Michael slip his arm around her waist, Donella's hand covering his in acknowledgement.

'They saw what was *really* happening,' Donella went on. 'They knew how deeply it affected me. They came to see it was the only way.'

'It's true, Dad,' Michael confirmed. 'You didn't see how badly she was hurt. She put on a show to protect you. But as soon as we agreed to give it another try she started to recover. It was a deeper need than any of us realised.'

Heidi saw the look that flashed from Nicholas to Donella. What did that mean?

'And if it goes wrong again?' Dick asked. 'Will you keep going? Keep compounding the pain?'

'No.' It was Nicholas' turn to deflect the fire. 'It's over. We agreed. Three tries and that was it. No more.'

'Hell's bells,' Dick shot out. '*Three tries*! Each time you put her through this ...' Words failed him as he stared from Nicholas to Michael.

The long silence was painful.

'I'm just staggered by you all,' Roberta interjected quietly. 'If you've been able to cope with three tries, without us even *suspecting*, you're made of sterner stuff than Dad and I are.'

Both her sons cast her a grateful look.

'We didn't tell you, Mum, because we didn't want you worrying,' Nicholas said. 'We knew you and Dad didn't approve – at all. And we sympathised with how you'd feel if you knew. I don't mind telling you, I was dead against it. We all were – Mike, Heidi and me. So we *do* understand. But Mike's right: it turned Donella around. But there was no need for anyone else to know we were trying. If it hadn't worked we wouldn't have needed to say anything to anybody.'

'And how are you all ... coping?' Her worried gaze flicked from one to the other, coming to rest on Donella.

'I'm fine. The vomiting's bad this time. That's why we've told you this early. We didn't want you finding out by accident. But otherwise fine. And this feels so right. I *know* it's right.' Her calm confidence was utterly convincing.

Roberta's enquiring look moved to Heidi.

She sat bolt upright, her hands clenched tightly in her lap. It was the first time she had spoken, but a mounting sense of horror had been growing within her.

'I cannot explain how I feel for Donella. I do not have the English. She is so ... brave and so much loving us. Nicholas and I – we want very much a baby. No-one else can give us one. No-one else can help us.' She swallowed hard. '*She* does this for us. But she does not make it a ... duty?' She tested out the word. Nicholas nodded confirmation. 'She does not make it a duty. She makes it a present from her love. It is a more wonderful thing than we have ever seen before. I do not like to see that it does not make you happy. If you are cross, you must be cross with *me*, not with her.

It is all *my* fault. It is not her fault. And Michael and Nicholas, it is not their fault. They do this thing for me too. Because … I cannot do it for myself.'

Her words ended in a whisper, the tears rolling down her cheeks.

She felt Nicholas reach across to draw her back against him, but sat rigid still.

'No, darling. It is *not* your fault,' he said simply. 'You are not to blame for your health. And we *all* made the decision for surrogacy together. But of all of us, you are the *least* to blame. You've been fantastic throughout the whole thing.'

She felt him bristling, and his voice was suddenly hard.

'None of you know what she's been through. She insisted you shouldn't. But *I* know and, believe me, she deserves your admiration a million times more than she deserves criticism.' He was looking fiercely at his parents.

Heidi saw Roberta's eyes too sparkled with tears. Her words were peppered with swift intakes of breath as she struggled with her emotions.

'Heidi – all of you … I'm so sorry. I feel terrible. You've all been … through so much. … This you don't need. If you're all OK with this … we'll learn to accept it. Just forgive … two old fogies … struggling to keep up … with you more enlightened people.'

'Mum's right.' Dick blew his nose hard. 'If you're all OK, it's not for us to give you a hard time. I apologise.'

Heidi felt a suffocating wave of emotion rising within her. She rose swiftly to her feet.

'Please, excuse me. I have to finish little things before we eat.'

Nicholas leaped up to offer assistance.

She drew herself up to her full height. She would not let them see she was running away.

'Thank you, but I should like to be on my own. I have only tiny things to do. You have much to say and – perhaps you say it better if I am not here.'

A heavy silence remained behind her.

Her dignified exit left them all feeling guilty. There was nothing they wished to say which she could not hear, but they had given her the impression there was.

For a long moment no-one moved. Then, without a word, Dick rose and left the room, raising a hand to stop Nicholas following him.

He found Heidi in the kitchen wiping her eyes on a towel. Perching on the edge of a nearby stool to bring him closer to her eye level, he began hesitantly.

'Heidi. Forgive me for intruding in your private space but I can't let this pass.'

She stood politely listening but her wary expression gave him no encouragement.

'You know that I don't approve of surrogacies. I never did. I still don't … because I've seen too much of the potential for trouble. I've made no secret of that fact. But I've spent my working life with women who have fertility problems, and you must believe me when I say I have the most enormous sympathy for them – for you. It's one of the saddest problems we doctors have to deal with.'

He paused looking at her enquiringly.

'Thank you. It is kind of you to tell me that.' Her words sounded stiff.

'When Nick first told me about your difficulties, I wanted desperately to help you both. But when I heard that it was surrogacy or nothing, I couldn't. I *couldn't* do something I know to be fraught with difficulties. But you – the four of you – have made this decision for yourselves. It's none of my business any more. I'm just a dad here. Not a doctor. It's not my place to interfere. And right now I'm bitterly regretting saying anything at all against it. You're all grown-up people. You're mature and thoughtful, and I know you haven't gone into it lightly. And heaven knows, you've all been through the mill to get to this point. It's done. It can't be undone. There's a long and difficult road ahead. You need all the support you can get. I want to help in offering that support. So can we start again? Please?'

She looked at him uncertainly.

He ploughed on.

'Our boys have always been special to us. They know we love them – whatever they do. But you, perhaps we should have told you – more – how much we've come to love you too. I suppose it was so obvious to me; I just assumed you knew. You're like another daughter to us. We've watched how Nick has changed since he found you – changed for the better. We're grateful to you for being such a good influence on him. He's a lucky man to have you. So will you forgive me and let me love you – like a father – again?'

The silence seemed interminable as he watched the play of emotion across her face.

'I should like that. Very much,' she said, suddenly shy with him. 'It is special, being in your family.'

'You're a special part of it.'

'To me it is sad that we are not happy tonight. Your family – it is very much loving of children. But not tonight.'

'I agree. It ought to be a celebration of a new life, just beginning.'

'We think it is a thing to celebrate.'

'I'm sorry it took me so long to see that. But now, can we start again? And be happy with you all?'

'It would be nice – very nice – if you could be happy too. And Nicholas and Michael would be glad if you were not cross with them.'

Dick shot her a strange look.

'Meaning what exactly?'

191

'It is important to them that you – I do not know the word – to think they are good?' Heidi paused for help.

'To approve?'

'That you approve of them.'

He stared at her for a long moment.

'You are a very shrewd young lady.'

She shrugged.

'It is obvious. All their lives they look up to you. You are a special kind of man. And a very good father, I think. They want to please you. They want you to be proud of them.'

'I *am* proud of them. Of all of you. But I'm not always a very good father. I'll try to do better in future. Promise.'

She smiled warmly this time.

'They love you very much.'

'Thank you, Heidi. I don't deserve that tonight but it's comforting to hear it. And now may I hug you to seal that promise?'

She smiled again.

'I think I should like that too ... Dad.' It was the first time she had ever used the name. Dick smiled in acknowledgement.

Hearing the door open Dick turned, but didn't remove his arm.

Nicholas stood hesitantly looking from one to the other.

'And you, Nick, will you forgive me too?'

'I've nothing to forgive, Dad, if you've made your peace with my wife.'

The constant nausea persisted. Donella looked and felt exhausted by its unrelenting toll.

After one particularly gruelling day Michael found her slumped in the bathroom with her head between her knees, crying.

He perched on the edge of the bath beside her.

'Don, what is it? Have you ...?'

'No. It's still there.'

'So ...?'

'I'm not sure I can go through with this, Mike.'

'You must be exhausted with all this vomiting. You'll feel better when that stops.'

'*If* it stops. I'm beginning to think I'm going to spend the rest of my life with my head down the pan.'

'Will it end soon? Isn't it supposed to ease off after the first trimester?'

'This kid hasn't read the right books,' she said with an attempt at humour.

A renewed bout of vomiting stopped further discussion.

'Can't you take something to stop it?'

'Nope. There's no way I'm taking any chances with this precious creature.'

THIRTY-FOUR

Ten days later Michael found her in tears again.

'Still bad, sweetheart?'

'Yeah, but it's …' She started to sob more pitifully.

He rocked her soothingly.

'Ssshh. Sssshhh. It'll be OK soon.'

'I can't do it, Mike.'

'Sssshhh. What can't you do, darling?'

'I can't go through with this.'

'You can't …' He released her enough to see her face. 'What d'you mean? You aren't …?'

'I'm going to terminate it.'

He stared at her in silence. His every instinct was to scream at her, remind her of what they'd gone through to get this far. But he knew her emotions were fragile, she was physically exhausted, her hormones chaotic.

'Wowwa. Slow down a bit. Tell me what's going on here,' he said in a calming voice.

'I'm scared, Mike – scared there's something wrong with it. All the vomiting … What if we lose it again? What if we go to *term* and there's something wrong with it?'

'Hey, your imagination's in overdrive. You're just overwrought. There's no reason why there'd be something wrong. Loads of women vomit their hearts up. You told me so yourself. I'm sure it's OK.'

'You *can't* be sure,' she snapped.

Of course. It was a senseless platitude. He kept quiet.

She grew increasingly agitated. His attempts at comfort fell on deaf ears.

'My mind's made up. You told me. You *promised*. You said … if I changed my mind …'

He was silent.

'I must tell Nick.'

'No, Don, we must think about this.'

'I must. It's his baby. He has to know.'

'Donella, you *can't*. Think what it'd do to him. To Heidi.'

'I *can*. If it was an ordinary pregnancy, I could. Why should anybody deny me the same rights now? It's my body … my baby. And you *said*!'

The voice inside him was screaming again. It wasn't her baby. They'd agreed it wasn't. It was Heidi's.

But they both knew none of this fiction was true. Deep down they knew. It *was* hers. It was her body. They had no power to stop her if she remained adamant.

When Michael phoned Nicholas he was so shocked by the news that he left at once with a terse instruction to Heidi to make excuses to their dinner guests – 'Tell them it's a medical emergency!' – and drove straight over to Donella.

'She wants to tell you herself. I'll be in the kitchen. Shout if you need me,' Michael said, grimly.

She sat stony-faced in the drawing room.

'Donella! Oh, you poor thing!' It was a shock seeing her so forlorn.

Nicholas dropped down on the floor beside her chair, taking her hands in his.

'I can't do it, Nick. I'm sorry. I thought I could. But I can't.' Her voice was flat.

'OK. Let's take it one step at a time. Help me to understand. Why the change of heart?'

'I'm scared. I think there must be something wrong with it. I can't go through … all that. Not again.'

'Of course you can't. It's too much even to contemplate. But what makes you think there's something wrong?'

'All this vomiting? And losing it last time. You and I – we aren't meant to have a baby. It's not right.'

'But last time – you said – the baby was perfect.'

'She *looked* perfect. But something made me lose her. There must have been something wrong.'

'But not necessarily an abnormality.'

'But maybe. Maybe we don't make good babies – together.'

He glanced behind him. The door was still firmly shut.

'And Rachael? Isn't she … perfect?' he breathed the word softly.

She was silent. There was no denying that.

'I understand your fears, but – there's *nothing* to indicate that you and I aren't compatible.' He stroked her hand as he spoke, trying to soothe her doubts. 'Rachael *is* perfect. And the other one – you said she was too.'

Donella stared stonily ahead.

'Is it … because of … what we did?' he whispered fearfully.

She shook her head.

'No. It's not that. It's because … I can't face … losing another one.'

'I can understand that. But … if you get rid of it now, you'd have to face that anyway, wouldn't you?' he reasoned gently.

'But if I do it now – this early on – it won't be so hard. It won't be so real.'

'OK. I see that. But if you find it's perfect … how will you feel then?'

194

Her frozen façade crumpled and the tears came.

'Help me, Nick. Help me.'

Relieved to see a natural reaction, he moved to sit beside her, rocking her in his arms as she wept. He made no effort to speak further until she was calm again.

'Oh Donella. This is too high a price. We shouldn't have let you do it. I knew we shouldn't.'

'You should. I wanted to. I needed to.' Her voice was muffled against his shoulder.

'And now you don't feel that need?'

'I do. I still do.'

He let her own words settle around them, holding her still but saying nothing. Eventually she stirred and moved away from him. Her watery smile was sheepish.

'I'm sorry. I don't know what's got into me. I'm not usually so weepy.'

'I know you're not. But ... allow me to give a little medical advice. When a woman gets pregnant, her hormones are all shot to pieces ...'

His patronising voice made her smile again.

'Give yourself a break!' He deliberately made his tone more bracing. 'You're allowed to feel weepy without thinking you're losing the plot!'

He moved to face her more directly.

'Actually, you know, it's heartening for me to see a chink in the old armour.'

'Meaning?'

'You're so self-sufficient, so strong about these things – you know, emotional stuff, sensitive stuff. You make a bloke feel pretty inadequate at times, you know.'

'Rubbish.'

'Not. It makes me feel a wee bit less useless when you show a "tinsy winsy" bit of weakness – as Rachael would say.'

She smiled faintly through her wet lashes.

'I'm sorry – to be so pathetic. Sorry I scared you too. And Mike.'

'So the verdict now is ...?'

'Go on with it. But I'll need you both to help me with this.'

'Which of course we'll do. You'll be the most supported pregnant woman in the city!'

Her instant retort both surprised and heartened him. 'Oh no! Spare me!'

'Sounds more like a threat than a promise, eh?' He grinned, easing himself away from her.

'Too right it does!' The words wobbled but she returned the grin, brushing a hand impatiently across a wet cheek.

She blew her nose hard, giving Nicholas a chance to consider his next move. He began cautiously.

'Donella … about the anxiety? You know, the abnormality thing? D'you want to go for tests?'

The fearful look was back.

'We decided I wouldn't.'

'Well, things change. It's not written in tablets of stone. I'm sure we can negotiate a change if it's bugging you. And we *certainly* don't want you to go through months of this kind of agony!'

She looked at him for a long moment.

'What do *you* think? What if …? Would we …?'

'I don't know. I honestly don't know. We'd *all* have to talk about it if they did find something. But for now, it's your peace of mind that's important.'

'Am I just being hysterical, d'you think?'

'No, you're not hysterical. Emotional maybe, but that's only to be expected. And they're perfectly natural fears. There's *probably* nothing to worry about, but if it's troubling you, maybe you'd feel better if you had some sort of outside confirmation. But hey – this is outside my area of expertise. How about talking to your Mum – or my Mum even – about it? They both know more about this stuff than I do. Would it be helpful – weighing up the risks and benefits with them?'

'I see your point. But would that be fair, d'you think? When they don't approve of what we're doing?'

'I don't see why not. We aren't asking them to make any decisions. Or even to condone what we're doing. We're all adults. We have to make our own choices. But they could give us the benefit of their experience and knowledge. I guess you and I – we're a bit too close to this for comfort, eh? Much as we try to kid ourselves we're hard-nosed professionals! The grand-mothers might be a better bet.'

'Dr Halley, I think you have just made a sound medical judgement,' she said in her professional voice.

'Well, Dr Halley *junior*, don't sound so surprised. I am always happy to give colleagues the benefit of my vast, not to say, encyclopaedic wisdom. And moreover and notwithstanding, speaking as something of a world-renowned expert in making snap judgements of mental competence, I can confirm that this particular patient is of sound mind and coping extremely well in very trying circumstances. Indeed, I personally think she deserves some kind of an award.'

He stood up abruptly before she could respond.

'Can we let Mike out of his misery?' he asked lightly, raising his eyebrows.

'Oh Mike! The poor thing. Yes, of course.'

He reached down to take her hand and haul her up to her feet. But as he made to leave the room to find his brother, she stopped him with a light hand on his arm.

'Thanks, Nick. Thanks for understanding.'

'You're welcome. Even the male of the species gets it right once in a blue moon, eh?' he said teasingly. He mustn't let the emotions get too intense.

Safely out of arm's length, he dropped his voice to a murmur, and looking straight at her said, 'And just remember – while you wait for that confirmation – *Rachael is perfect.* Hang onto that.'

She nodded.

'I will.'

Seeing their faces was enough to tell Michael another crisis had been averted. The two men exchanged a look of relief over her head.

Donella approached her own mother with some trepidation. Although little had been said, Judy's disapproval and dismay at yet another surrogate pregnancy were obvious. Understanding her mother's reaction, Donella had stayed away to give her space to adjust to the reality.

Broaching the subject so openly now she was unsurprised by Judy's hesitation.

'It feels cheeky I know, Mum, asking you when I know you don't approve of what we're doing. But I really would value your advice. Please.'

'Well, then, I personally think it might be a good idea to go for tests.'

'You didn't say so before.'

'You didn't ask me before. I'm only saying now because you specifically asked me.'

Donella heard the hurt below the words but let it pass.

'You don't think I'm being ridiculous?'

'No, I don't. I actually wished you'd go last time. But I didn't want to interfere. You're an adult now. *And* you're a doctor. You probably know more about these things than I do.'

'Not obstetric things. You midwives have loads more practical wisdom than us doctors who float through labour ward for a few months and float out again. But why did you want me to go last time?'

'Because of Bethany.'

'Bethany? But I thought she had an autosomal recessive condition.'

'Yes. She did.'

'Because you and Dad carried the same faulty gene.'

'Yes.'

'Which I don't have. So why …?'

'Well, it's just made me conscious of all the hidden things that can complicate pregnancies, that's all. But look, I don't want to worry you. This isn't the time to be worrying about things that'll probably never happen. I'm just super-sensitive about genetic problems.'

'No actually, Mum, it's *exactly* the time to talk about it. Now's the time to go for screening. OK, I didn't last time – we all decided we'd take our chance. And we wanted as little intervention as possible.' Donella paused, remembering. Heidi's reaction to medical assistance had influenced them all powerfully. 'But losing it when I did – it was just so awful …' She stopped, unable to continue.

'I know, dear. It is.' Her mother said quietly.

'It was worse for you, I know, with Bethany being full term and you knowing her as a real little person,' Donella said quickly. 'But even the pain of the miscarriage in my case – it's made me scared about losing this one. And I know, if I've got to lose it, I'd cope better if it was sooner rather than later – when I've got more attached to it.'

'Aren't you supposed *not* to get attached to it – if you're going to give it away?'

'That's the theory, but I know in practice I'm bound to get attached to it to some extent – with it growing inside me, giving birth to it.'

'Oh Donella …'

'Don't worry, Mum, I've got a careful plan for staying sufficiently distanced to be able to give it to its father. Not quite the same thing as handing it over to strangers. And I know Heidi and Nick will be brilliant parents. And I'll see it growing up and everything.'

'I hope you're right, love. I really hope you are.'

'But …?'

'Well, I must admit I'm scared for you. It won't be easy.'

'Lots of things in life aren't easy. But I want to do this.' This was one area of the process that was not for discussion.

'I'll say no more.'

'But, what you said before … You think I might carry something we don't know about? Is that what you mean? Because of you and Dad. And Bethany.'

'Well, probably not but … well, you might. Or Nicholas might. Or it might be something recessive that only comes out occasionally if the wrong genes come together … or something.'

Donella sensed that her mother was desperately trying to tone down her fears. Her own unease seeped through her defences.

'But I've had three perfect children already. And Nick is Mike's identical twin. So you'd think … odds on … it'd be OK … wouldn't you?'

'It probably will be, sweetheart, it probably will. Look, let's change the subject. I didn't want to talk like this. There's no point in worrying yourself sick – about something that might never happen.'

'No. Pretending won't stop me worrying. You know me. I'm a practical person. Best to face up to things fair and square. We have to be sensible about this. And that's why Nick suggested I talk to you. And to his Mum. To get the benefit of your advice – one step removed, so to speak. So tell me straight, Mum, would you recommend I go for screening?'

'Put like that, yes, I would. And I think you might find it'll put your mind at rest. I had a CVS for you two. And it was a huge relief to know you didn't have what Bethany had. I could enjoy the pregnancy more after that.'

'But there are still no guarantees. The tests are only for specific things. There might still be something else wrong.'

'Well, of course. But that's a risk for every pregnancy.'

'And would you have aborted us if we *had* been affected?'

'It sounds so heartless put like that. But yes, we would have. I wept buckets thinking we might have to go through that. But it was Dick – Michael's Dad – who helped us decide to go for a termination if you were affected. He said we'd be doing it for the *child's* sake not our own. We'd seen Bethany suffering. It was a responsible thing to do to prevent another child – or children in your case – going through what she went through. That made it just bearable to think of doing it. But of course, it was an enormous relief *not* to have to make that decision.'

'When you look at it like that – yeah, it makes the idea more bearable. He's a wise chap, Mike's Dad.'

'He is. He was brilliant – helping us when we lost Bethany. But I've told you all that.'

'It's not so easy for him now – with Mike and Nick – this baby – you know.'

'I can understand that. It's never easy when it's people you know and love,' Judy said quietly.

'I know, Mum. It's hard for you and Dad, I know. And Graeme.'

Her mother looked at her sharply.

'Oh yes,' Donella nodded. 'I know what he thinks. He told me himself when I finally got him on the phone. He thinks I'm totally irresponsible. Mike and Nick are a thoroughly bad lot.' She broke off.

'As far as I'm concerned, I don't have a sister now,' Graeme had ground out, before slamming down the phone.

It hurt.

'I'm so worried about him, Donella. Sometimes I think he's …' Judy stopped suddenly. 'But don't you worry about him. Not now. You've got more important things to worry about.'

'He's what, Mum? Come on. He's my brother. I want to know if there's something going on.'

Judy just stared at her with fear in her eyes.

'Tell me, Mum. What do you know? I haven't seen him for ages and he won't even talk to me at the moment. But I still care about him.'

'Well, Dad and I saw him last month and he seemed … I don't know … sort of manic one minute and dazed the next. And sometimes he sounds so wild when he's talking. He gets so worked up about little things and his reactions seem so … extreme. I fear for him, I really do. I think he's not quite right – mentally, you know?'

'Have you said anything to him? Have you suggested he goes to see the doctor or anything?'

'I tried. I asked him if he was stressed about anything. Or perhaps he needed a holiday or a check-up. But he just snapped my head off and flounced out of the room.'

'And what does Dad think?'

'Oh, he agrees there's something not right but he thinks we have to let you both do things in your way. It's not our place now to insist he goes for help – any more than it was our place to interfere in what you're doing. We might not always like what happens but you're both grown-up now, and you have to do things your way.'

'But if he's needing psychiatric help he probably can't see he does himself.'

'That's as maybe, but there's nothing definite that I can pinpoint that says he's clinically disturbed. It's just a general sense.'

'Oh Mum, what a worry for you. And I haven't exactly helped.'

'Don't you worry about that. I wasn't going to tell you actually. You need to concentrate on your own problems. Dad and I have already decided we'll go down again in a couple of weeks – we'll make some excuse or other – and just check things out again. Don't you worry about it – we'll keep an eye on him.'

'And you'll tell me? Let me know if I can do anything? I might be *persona non grata* with Graeme but I do know people in the business.'

'I will. But I hope it won't come to that. Hopefully it was just a bad spell for him.'

There was a sudden silence and Donella turned wide eyes on her mother.

'Are you suggesting … it's to do with me – with this baby?'

'No! I wasn't even thinking that. Honestly. I don't know what's going on in his life but he's not a happy man. He hasn't been for years, I'd say. He's just … I don't know … so moody, withdrawn, *angry* about things. And he seems to be getting worse. He really frightens me sometimes – he gets into such a state. I used to think it was something to do with him being on his own, and seeing you happy with your family just rubbed it in. But lately I've begun to think it's – something more than that. I don't know. But we'll keep an eye on him. Don't you worry.'

But Donella did worry. The more so when Graeme sent a message saying categorically he did not want to see her. Ever again.

THIRTY-FIVE

Roberta was touched that Donella had come to consult her about screening. Hearing that Nicholas had recommended she did so was balm to her maternal wounds.

But she was cautious.

'Are you asking for my professional opinion or my personal opinion?'

'Both, I think. Perhaps, start with what you'd say if I was one of your patients?'

'I'd ask you if you had any specific reason to worry about abnormalities. I'd tell you the risks as far as I knew them – for the abnormalities you wanted tests for, and of a miscarriage or any other complication from the screening processes too. I'd want to know how you felt about having a child who needed extra care, how your husband felt, about how much support you'd get from family and friends. I'd ask you what your own views and feelings were about abortion. I'd be looking for some kind of sense of where you were in thinking through the consequences of either course of action, and getting you to weigh up the arguments, so that you came to the best decision for you – and your husband. The one you could live with most easily.'

She was deliberately distancing herself, not asking for answers.

'Fair enough.' Donella paused. 'And your personal opinion?'

'It's difficult ...' Roberta hesitated.

'I shan't take it the wrong way. I know you have reservations about this whole thing. But I really would value your advice about screening. And so would Nick.'

It felt all wrong, Donella speaking of Nicholas rather than Michael. Roberta felt again the surge of anxiety. Were they really as strong as they believed they were? There were two marriages at stake here, four hearts to be broken, a child's life in the balance, the happiness of three little girls – her own granddaughters – in jeopardy. She dragged her thoughts back to the question.

'Given what I know of you all, and what you've told me of your own fears, yes, I think, on balance you'd be better to go for screening.'

Donella blinked.

'You look surprised,' Roberta said.

'I guess I wasn't expecting so direct an answer.'

'Oh dear, am I usually so woolly?'

'No, not woolly. But you're very careful about not telling any of us what you think we should do.'

Roberta shrugged.

'Do you think … there might be something?' Donella was looking straight at her, watching her reactions.

'I can't say either way. It would be false reassurance, as you know, to say I'm sure it's fine – much as I'd like to be able to tell you that. I don't know. No-one knows. And, again as you know yourself, even if we do *dozens* of tests there's still no guarantee of a perfect baby. But since you're obviously worried yourself, you could rule out some things.'

'This business of my sister – the autosomal recessive metabolic thing?'

'Mmhhm.' Roberta had to concentrate on keeping her face impassive.

'Is it something I should worry about?'

'Well, I'm no geneticist, but from what you've told me, you tested negative when your Mum had screening in pregnancy, yes?'

'Yes.'

'So you don't have to worry about that.'

'And other recessive characteristics? Or … anything else? Should I be worried about anything else?' Donella was watching her closely.

'I don't know. I'm sorry. I can't say, one way or the other.'

'"Can't" – as in you don't have enough information? Or "can't" – as in you're not in a position to say what you know?'

'I'm not sure what you mean.' Roberta felt she was on dangerously thin ice.

'Is it OK if I'm really upfront?'

'Of course.'

'And will you be honest with me too?'

'I'll try to be,' Roberta said cautiously. What was she letting herself in for? But what other response was there?

'You've always been lovely to me. And everyone has made me feel part of the family. But I know – because Mike told me – when I met him soon after Nick went to Brazil – that it was you who persuaded Nick to drop me.'

Roberta nodded. She remembered only too well.

'I was upset and Mike was just trying to comfort me, to make me feel it wasn't my fault Nick had gone off like that.'

'And he was right. It wasn't your fault.' Roberta owed her that.

'He said it probably because Nick was too young and you wanted him to get on in his career. And you probably didn't know how involved we were. And he thought … Nick probably didn't realise either, how much … I was involved.' It was clearly hard for the girl to voice these thoughts even now so many years later – especially to her, their mother.

She nodded again.

'I think Mike was right. Nick *was* more in love with you than I certainly realised. I've felt terrible about it since – but I didn't know it had gone so deep. I'm so sorry, Donella.'

'Don't be. I'm sure you did it for the best. I know how much you love the boys.'

'But,' Roberta said hesitantly, 'do you regret … not being with Nick … now?' The question was only just above a whisper but it hung between them with leaden weights. Roberta held her breath. How had she dared so much?

Donella was looking down at her hands, twisting her wedding ring. There was a long pause.

'Not now. No.' She looked up at last. 'Mike and I are right together. And Heidi is brilliant for Nick. I admit, I didn't think so at first, but as we've got to know her, I think she's exactly what he needs. Much better for him than I would have been.' Her words gathered conviction.

Roberta let out her breath slowly.

'Thank you. Forgive me for being impertinent enough to ask outright. But I've wondered sometimes if …'

'I understand.' Donella stopped her voicing the thought. 'But it's OK.'

'I'm glad. Because having this baby with Nick, it could be …'

'We know. And we've all – all four of us – talked about that. Along with everything else. And it's OK,' Donella said, 'I'm having it *for* Nick – not with him. It will be Heidi's baby.'

If only it were that simple.

'You're amazing, Donella. I can only admire your courage and strength.'

It was Donella's turn to shrug.

'Anyway, back to the reason for Nick dropping me.'

Roberta's heart plummeted again.

'When Mike and I got together I remembered you'd warned Nick off, and I made him check with you – to see if you had anything against me – for *him* too.'

Roberta nodded. This was getting dangerous.

'He said you told him you didn't have anything against *me* – for myself, I mean. But – I can't remember the exact words now – but you had some sort of confidential medical information that might affect me. Right?'

Roberta nodded dumbly.

'We talked about it. Carefully, you know. Well, as carefully as young-sters in love do talk about things!' Donella smiled wryly. 'But then, we were so happy, and you seemed to accept me, and it all sort of faded into the background. If you didn't like me as a daughter-in-law, you covered it up – so well, I thought perhaps you *did* accept me.'

'Oh, Donella, it wasn't a cover-up. I do love you – very much indeed. You've been amazing – for Mike, for Alex when she had her cancer scare, and now for Nick and Heidi. And you're a super mother. I couldn't ask for a better daughter-in-law. I mean it. Sincerely. It's not an act.'

'Thank you for saying that. You've been lovely. And I do feel a real part of your family.'

'And so you should. You are. A very special part of it.'

'It wasn't really until we lost the baby … Well, I was desperately upset and I kept going over and over things in my head, trying to find a reason for it. After three perfectly normal pregnancies, why did I lose this one? I know – my normal sane self told me – there's often no reason. It just happens. But things get out of perspective when you're distressed, when your hormones are all over the place. *You* know about all that. And I got this dreadful feeling that it was my fault in some way. It just wouldn't go away. I felt I'd been responsible for letting everyone down.'

Roberta's heart went out to her. As if she hadn't done more than enough to absolve herself from any blame. But she understood the thinking. It rang familiar bells.

'I gave Mike a hard time, I know,' Donella went on. 'He was brilliant. Even though it wasn't his baby. He was so good about it all. So patient. But I plagued him with questions. About all sorts of things. And I remembered again him telling me you knew something about me. So I kept on at him to tell me exactly what you'd said. He couldn't remember the details. He just kept telling me: it *couldn't* be anything to worry about; it was *obvious* there wasn't anything; we'd shown that; we were so happy together; everything had gone so well for us. But it still niggled with me. What if *you* knew something that meant I wouldn't have healthy children? Of course, Mike poured scorn on that idea. What about Rachael and Fiona and Emily, he said; weren't they living proof that I was worrying ridiculously? I *wanted* to believe it, but the thought wouldn't go away. I kept thinking about one-in-four chances and all that sort of stuff. And because of my sister, I suppose I'd always been that bit more aware that things do sometimes go wrong. If Dad and Mum had had a problem, well, I might too.'

Roberta watched the flickering emotions playing over Donella's face as she lived through her doubts again.

'OK, I'd had three lovely children – no problems at all. But then this. Was it that one-in-four thing? Or was it because it was a different father? Were Nick and I incompatible in some way? Was that why you warned Nick off? You told me the first time we met that you'd worked as a locum in the Roslin practice – the one where Mum and Dad were patients. I thought maybe you knew something about their medical history, you know? So I asked Mum outright if there was anything I should know about. But she assured me there was nothing.'

So Judy didn't know. Or else she was an extremely convincing liar.

'So can I ask you? Is there something I should know about?'

A direct appeal. No escape.

'Donella,' Roberta began slowly, 'this is difficult. But you're a doctor. You understand about confidentiality.'

'Of course. And I don't expect you to go into details. But couldn't you tell me if there's something? Something to worry about for … this baby?' She was close to tears, Roberta could see. 'It's our last chance. We've agreed. But if it's going to end … like last time … or worse … I'd rather know. I don't think I could bear it if we got to the end … and then …' The words were a hoarse whisper dragged unwillingly from her heart. Two tears escaped, rolling unheeded down her cheeks.

'Oh my dear, after all you've been through. I understand. Believe me, I do.' Roberta leaned forward to lay a hand on her daughter-in-law's arm. Her mind was seething. Should she tell her? What would the knowledge do?

Donella was waiting, watching her.

'You're right, I did learn something about your family's medical history. But it isn't mine to tell. You'll understand that. We hear all sorts of things – in confidence, don't we? But I *can* reassure you that you're at no more risk of having a child with problems this time than you were with Rachael and Fiona and Emily. And look at them!'

'No? You really mean it?'

'Absolutely.'

'And having Nick's baby? Is it more risky than with Mike?'

'Not as far as I know, no. And I'm only qualifying my answer because we none of us know exactly what we've inherited or what mutations we carry. And we don't know about Nick yet, because he hasn't had children yet.'

'So, whatever this thing is that you know, there's no more risk for this one than any of the others?' Donella was persisting.

'That's right.'

There was a long silence. Then Donella looked at Roberta squarely.

'If I ask you an outright question would you be able to answer it?'

'I'll try to.'

Again Roberta felt she was teetering on the brink of a yawning crevasse.

'Is it something like a risk of … Huntington's or a form of hereditary cancer or some other … progressive or fatal disease I might have inherited?'

'No. It's definitely nothing like that.' Roberta's heart went out to her. To have harboured such fears! At least she could be reassuring on that score. 'Absolutely not.'

'Thank you for being honest. I won't press you for more. I understand. Except …' She paused. Roberta froze inside again. 'Do Mum and Dad know?'

'I honestly don't know. I'm sorry. I'd tell you if I could. But I just don't know. Remember I was only a locum there. And it's donkey's years ago.'

'Does Graeme know?'

Roberta frowned.

'Graeme?'

'My brother, Graeme? It's just that he seems to be ... well, Mum thinks he's having some sort of mental problems, so I just wondered if he maybe knew something that was troubling him but he couldn't share it ... and I also wondered if maybe that was why he's never married or had kids.'

'I'm so sorry to hear that – about his problems, I mean. But I can't say if he knows or not. I just don't know if anyone else knows.'

'OK. Thanks. That's fair enough. I just wondered. So you think I should go for screening. Can you suggest what we should look for?'

'Well, I'd go by what you're worrying about. From what you say it's the things to do with Bethany's problems. So ... recessive disorders? And probably the usual things like ... Down's? Whatever you'd like to know, I think. You'll know which conditions might affect your decision about termination. Stick to those.'

'Thanks. It's been really helpful talking to you like this. I hope I haven't made things awkward for you.'

'Quite the reverse. You've made me realise – even more – how seriously you've all taken this step. But also what it's cost you. You deserve a happy ending.'

'Unfortunately we don't always get what we deserve in this life,' Donella said sadly. How true it was. 'And believe me, we're absolutely aware of the potential problems. We're just trying to think positively and pray that it all works out.'

'Nick and Heidi are very fortunate to have you on their side.'

'Well, as I hear it, you offered something similar yourself.'

Roberta looked sheepishly at her.

'That's different. I'm their Mum. We'd do pretty much anything for our children, wouldn't we?'

'And that's why I'm here today. Because I know you want the best for your boys.'

'And for you and the children.'

Nicholas was taken aback by the private reaction of Heidi to the decision to go for tests.

Outwardly she agreed: 'If that's what you and Donella think. You are doctors. You know these things.'

Inwardly, he knew, she was anything but in agreement.

He felt sick. Had she somehow learned about this child's conception? Full of foreboding he eventually pressed her into talking.

'Heidi, you *must* tell me what's bothering you. You've been brilliant about this whole thing up to now. What's changed?'

She shook her head, compressing her lips obstinately.

'Are you having second thoughts about having this baby?'

'Oh no. I do want the baby. Very much I want it.'

'Are you still worrying about how I feel ... about Donella?'

She shook her head but did not answer.

'Has something been said … to upset you?'

She shook her head again.

'But something *has* upset you. Try to tell me what it is.'

Still she remained silent.

'Remember before, when you couldn't talk to me, how unhappy it made us? Don't let's do that again. *Please*, Heidi. Things have been so good between us lately.'

'I am afraid,' she whispered. He saw the fear in her face.

'What are you afraid of?'

'That they will make the baby not all right?'

'Who?'

'The people at the hospital.'

'D'you mean the people who do the screening tests?'

She nodded, looking at him anxiously.

'They'll be really, really careful. There *is* a risk of miscarriage, you're right. But it's a very, very small risk.'

'But will they make the baby … I cannot remember how you say it … not right? Not like other people?'

'Damaged?'

'Mmmm, maybe … but things really wrong inside too?'

'Abnormal, d'you mean? Make the baby abnormal?'

'Yes.'

'No. They won't do anything to harm the baby at all. They might *find* an abnormality, but they won't *cause* it.'

'You can be sure?'

'I can be sure.'

'And they will not make things wrong inside Donella?'

'No. They won't hurt her either.'

'You know these people? You know they are *good* people?'

'Well, I don't know them all *personally* but I know they are good people. Yes.'

'And they know your father? That he is the Professor, the chief man for having babies?'

'They will do, yes.'

'And that will make them be careful with Donella? Because she is his family?'

'They would be careful anyway. But yes, they'll want to give Donella the very best of care.'

'And you do not worry about her having these tests?'

'No. I'm sure she'll be fine. They're routine kinds of things.'

'Then that is OK for me too.'

'Where is all this coming from, Heidi?' asked Nicholas, completely mystified by her line of questioning.

'I cannot tell you why I ask. It is enough that you tell me she will be OK. And the baby will be OK.'

'Well, I can't promise you the tests will all be OK ...' Nicholas said quickly.

'Oh I know you cannot do that. If you could, she would not need to have the tests. But it is enough – what you tell me. We will not worry any more.'

She would say no more.

But Nicholas felt his own secret dread ease for the time being.

Dick had much to brood over.

He'd watched with satisfaction Donella's spirits lift with the reassurance of good test results. But it had come as a shock to learn from Michael how much Roberta's commendation had meant to her – as a wife for their son, and a mother for their granddaughters.

Until recently it had never occurred to him that both his daughters-in-law had worried about what he and Roberta felt about them. Was this a reflection of the twins' need for his approval? Were they really intimidating parents?

Alex and Jo were much less intense about his reactions. Had he been softer with his daughters? Had he been afraid to relax with the boys? Did he have different expectations of them?

Or was it a male thing? He smiled ruefully at the thought. Perhaps. Subconsciously he'd seen himself as the undisputed leader of the pack. But the cubs had grown imperceptibly, matured, acquired their own females, their own cubs, their own territory. They were the ones – swifter now than he – to chase off marauding predators, ensuring the safety of their young.

It had taken his Swiss daughter-in-law with her perceptive eyes and her hesitant English to make him see that. And Nick's defence of Heidi on that dreadful evening had shown him that they could be more sensitive than he was. He groaned inwardly remembering. It had been a thoroughly chastening experience, and he had to admit, he was still smarting from those half-veiled criticisms.

But in a perverse way, it had made him realise how proud of his sons he was. Even though he was still full of foreboding about the surrogacy, he had to concede they had shown great maturity, and great strength going through with it, even in the face of his disapproval.

Yes, he'd have to move over and let the young people take their rightful places as the dominant males.

THIRTY-SIX

It was a relief to all concerned to have Donella regaining her usual cheerful, brightly positive approach to life.

The meticulous diary Heidi kept was crammed with details only a mother could divulge. This time Donella asked her to sing to the child at regular intervals; the growing fetus must recognise Heidi's voice, and know the calm feelings that music could create, she insisted. And Heidi must feel the child moving, listen to its heartbeat. In turn Donella shared with amazement the creation of a supply of beautiful garments and bed linen, the work of Heidi's nimble fingers.

But only in Heidi's presence did she offer paternal liberties to Nicholas.

As they had predicted, telling people that she was not keeping this baby proved something of an ordeal. There were few outright criticisms, even fewer distasteful references to the conception, than Donella had expected, but she was still left with an uneasy feeling of general disapproval and incomprehension.

But it was Nicholas who was most shocked by the opprobrium the pregnancy attracted.

Donella was seven and a half months pregnant when Nicholas and Michael received invitations to bring their wives to the wedding of a childhood friend from the Borders. Predictably the identical twins, in identical morning suits, occasioned much comment: they made a striking pair, and their stylish wives drew admiring glances. Even in late pregnancy Donella carried herself well, her height and elegance giving her an air of distinction, but Michael hovered protectively close to her. Dialects and strong accents still bewildered Heidi and it suited her to remain a little aloof, with Donella and Michael as well as Nicholas to shield her from awkward situations.

Nicholas recognised neither voice but he couldn't help overhearing the conversation between two closed cubicles in the gentlemen's lavatories.

'She's a bit of a dish, isn't she?' Obviously a local.

'Whichsh one, dch'ye mean?' It was early in the proceedings for that level of inebriation, Nicholas thought idly.

'The tall one. In pink.'

'The pregggnant one?'

'Yeah. Dishy, eh?'

'Ssshuppose ssshe isss. Don't go for pregggnant ones myssself.'

'But *she* must be something else. Wouldn't mind having a round with *her*.'

'How dch'ye mean?'

'Well – don't you know? She's the three-in-a-bed bird. For all she looks so snooty and fancy. She has it off with two guys at once.'

Nicholas froze. He clenched his fists wanting to smash down the door and beat the unseen face to a pulp.

'Uhhh?'

'Does it with both the brothers. Having kids with both of them too.'

'How dch'you know thhhat?'

'Common knowledge. Seems she tells folk herself she's giving the kid to the brother.'

'Ttthat'ss the twin, uhhh? Can't tell whichhh isss whichhhh myssself.'

'Neither can I. Maybe the bird in pink can't either, eh?' There was coarse laughter.

'Getsssh 'em mixsshed up, y'mean?'

'Or maybe they take turns, eh? Probably can't tell which is which in bed either.'

Nicholas closed his eyes, clamping his teeth together.

'Funny ttthing for ttth'ottther wife, uhh? Ssshe'ere too?'

'Yep. Little thing. Blonde. Wearing blue. Dishy too. Know how to pick 'em those guys.'

'Ssshe the foreignnn one?'

'Yeah. German – Austrian – something like that. Foreign anyway.'

'Sssshe know whhhat ttthey geddup to?'

'Looks like it. Very matey all of 'em. Probably at it too. Probably used to that sort of thing where she comes from. Wife-swapping. Kinky sex. Wouldn't mind getting tangled up with *her* either. Corrrrrrr!'

'Donnn't loouuk like tttthat kind, eh? Loouuuk preddy uppa classsshhh typessssh.'

''S'pose it's only the upper classes who can afford those kinds of orgies. Plenty brass. Time on their hands. Posh frocks and the classy suits, maybe, but steamy underneath, eh?'

'Tttthink ah'll go'n 'ave anottther sssquint a' tttthesssshe damesssh.'

The sound of the water flushing prepared Nicholas for his exit.

'Leave the tall one for me then.' The request was shouted above the noise.

The young man who staggered unevenly from the cubicle looked so surprised to see one of the 'upper class' men he'd been discussing, standing stock-still waiting for him, that he remained speechless as Nicholas grabbed him by his lapels and hauled him towards the door. With his face only inches from the nose of the spluttering guest Nicholas hissed through clenched teeth, 'Don't you ever – *ever* – speak of my wife or my sister-in-law in that disgusting way ever again.'

'OK. OK. Keep yerrr hhaaair on. Only a jchhoke. Diddn't mmean it.'

Nicholas flung him away to be ready for the real culprit. The young man slunk out while the going was good, holding onto anything he could to keep himself upright. The door slammed behind him.

In the sudden quiet the second man emerged rather more cautiously. Nicholas saw that he was a small, greying man in his early forties, his tie dragged down from an opened shirt collar, a cigarette hanging loosely from his slack lips.

Impeccably dressed himself, icily controlled, Nicholas advanced until he was towering above him.

The next minute the man's head was being held under the tap and freezing cold water was deluging him. He gasped and struggled but Nicholas kept up the remorseless grip on his neck. Not until he was totally sodden did Nicholas turn off the water, and throw the man into a corner, and only then did he speak.

His voice was colder than the water.

'I do not intend to sully my hands by so much as touching you, you filthy, contemptible little skunk, though you deserve to be beaten from here to kingdom come. Vermin like you will always have cesspits for minds and sewers for mouths. You're not worthy to even *think* about my family, much less speak about them. If you so much as *mention* my wife or my sister-in-law again – to *anyone* – you'll have me *and* my brother to answer to. Is that clear?'

'Yes, sir.'

The trapped man was shivering; Nicholas hoped it was with fear as much as cold.

There was a sound of approaching voices outside in the corridor. They passed by but it was enough to remind Nicholas of the occasion.

'Get your despicable person and your filthy, scurrilous lies out of here and stay right away from my family or I won't be answerable for the consequences,' he ground out.

He moved back just a pace to allow the other man to escape, his fists still clenched at his side, his snarl conveying his disgust and contempt. The man edged away, the water still running off of him, leaving a conspicuous trail. He stayed close to the wall, never taking his eyes off Nicholas until he was out of the door.

In reality Nicholas knew he was so shaken himself that he was probably incapable of violent action. He slumped against the wall, breathing deeply. He needed time, space to calm himself, but it was a matter of urgency that he get back to his party soon – give them his protection. He dried the water off his sleeve and washed his face with trembling hands.

Ten minutes later he strolled back to Heidi with a smile, and slipping his dry arm around her, took his glass of champagne in steady fingers and silently toasted her. She smiled serenely up at him.

There was no sign of either of the men he had threatened. Presumably they'd left the reception early. The short wet one had little alternative, he thought ruefully. The drunk one probably wouldn't remember he'd even been to a wedding.

But Nicholas couldn't forget what he'd heard. The rumours and speculation must be widespread. He could only pray it was a seven-day wonder and the nasty minds would soon turn to other victims.

Heidi surprised him greatly with her own robust approach.

Under close questioning she admitted people had said hurtful things to her. Variations on a theme mostly: did she mind her husband sleeping with his brother's wife? Nicholas felt his heart miss a beat. If she only knew. But she never would.

'And you said?' he asked.

Heidi drew herself up with dignity, her grey eyes bright, remembering her anger.

'I said, "It is a dangerous thing to talk about things when you do not know what you are talking about. It was not like that at all. But I do not choose to tell you what *did* happen because it is none of your business."'

She confessed she'd then turned the tables on them with a question. 'I said to them, "Do you love anyone in your family enough to have a child for them as my brother- and sister-in-law are doing for my husband and me?" Of course, they could not say yes. So I said – and it was not a very kind thing to say but they make me angry, you know – I said, "I am glad I did not marry into *your* family!"'

'Brilliant tactics, Heidi.' Nicholas whooped with delight. 'You're a genius. I'm sure they felt like crawling under a stone. Well done!'

By contrast, telling the children proved less hazardous than any of them had anticipated.

It had been the most harrowing part of Donella's deliberations and she knew she was procrastinating, repeatedly deferring the moment when she must explain things to them. Not until she started to develop a visible bump did she tell the older two girls about the coming child, and she waited a further month before introducing the idea of giving the baby away.

Emily was satisfied with the simple facts of the baby growing inside her mother's tummy. Fiona initially merely nodded, patted the bump, and wandered off to play with her toys. As time went on she squealed when she was on her mother's lap and the baby kicked, and she loved to lie on Donella's abdomen and listen to the sounds within through her stethoscope, but otherwise she took little interest in the forthcoming arrival.

Rachael predictably proved more inquisitive and taxing. She was mystified by the complexity of the relationships when Donella tried to warn her that they wouldn't be keeping this baby.

'It's not *our* baby this time. Not like you and Fiona and Emily were our babies – Daddy's and mine,' Donella explained quietly.

'Whose baby is it?' Rachael asked, not looking up from the card she was colouring in for Michael's birthday.

'Well, you know Uncle Nick and Aunty Heidi don't have any babies?'

'Uhhhuhh.'

'They'd really *like* a baby, but Aunty Heidi can't have one herself.'

'Why not?'

'Because she's got something wrong inside her tummy where babies grow so a baby can't grow inside her.'

'Does it hurt?'

'Sometimes. But Aunty Heidi's very brave.'

'Does she cry?'

'I expect she cries sometimes because she doesn't have a baby.'

'Oh.'

'And we don't want Aunty Heidi to be sad, do we?'

Rachael shook her head vigorously, digging the green pen hard into the paper as it started to dry up.

'So that's why *we're* having this baby for her. I'm growing it in my tummy and then when it's born we'll give it to Aunty Heidi and she'll be happy again. She'll be a Mummy. That'll be nice, won't it?'

'And can I hold it?'

'Oh yes, I'm sure Aunty Heidi will let you hold it and put it to bed and play with it.'

'And will Uncle Nick be its Daddy?'

'Yes, darling.'

'Will he still be *my* Sunday Daddy?'

'Oh definitely. You'll *always* be his special Sunday girl.'

'Will Daddy be its Daddy too?'

'No. Babies don't need two Daddies, do they? Our Daddy will be Uncle Mike and I'll be its Aunty. Just like Uncle Nick and Aunty Heidi are *your* uncle and aunty.'

'Will you be sad when you don't have a baby?'

'I might be just a little bit sad. But I've got three lovely children already – you and Fiona and Emily – so I shan't be *really* sad – not like Aunty Heidi's been sad having no babies. I shall be happy if Aunty Heidi's happy. And we can still see the baby, and love it and do things with it.'

'Will it be a girl baby or a boy baby?'

'I don't know yet, sweetheart. We'll have to wait and see.'

'I hope it's a boy baby. Amelia in my class – she's got a baby brother. If we have one too, *I* can say what *he* does.'

'But this baby won't be your brother, Rachael. It'll be Aunty Heidi's baby, not ours. It won't live with us.'

'But I want a baby brother, Mummy.'

'You've got two sisters already. We mustn't be greedy. It's Aunty Heidi's turn to have a baby.'

The child stood thinking about this for a long moment.

'But *next* time it's our turn.'

Donella reached across to rumple her curls.

'We'll see.'

There seemed no point in dashing hopes at this point. It was enough for Rachael to cope with for now.

Typically Rachael reserved the most awkward questions for a more public occasion. Nicholas and Heidi were sitting at the dining room table playing a game of ludo with the two older girls when she suddenly turned to Heidi and asked her first question.

'Aunty Heidi, can I play with your baby? Please?'

'Yes, of course. I shall need you to help me to look after it,' Heidi assured her with a smile.

'Good. Mummy said you'd let me. I like babies.'

The game resumed. Fiona threw a six and there was a shriek of delight from around the table. She carefully moved her counter six spaces.

'How did your baby get in Mummy's tummy?' Rachael's question fell into the spaces between the dull thuds of the moving counter.

There was a breathless silence.

Then Nicholas leaned across the table towards Rachael.

'You know that babies grow inside mummies' tummies when daddies put seeds inside them?' How glad he was he'd checked with Donella how much each of the girls had been told about reproduction, in anticipation of just such a moment.

'Uhhuhh.'

'Well, your Mummy's a doctor, isn't she?' The curls bobbed. 'And I'm a doctor. So we knew how to put the seeds inside your Mummy so that she can have a baby for Aunty Heidi.'

'And where did you get the seeds from?'

'They were my seeds.'

'Not Daddy's seeds? This baby didn't grow from Daddy's seeds?'

'No, darling. Not this baby.'

'That's all right then.'

'Yes?'

'Yes, Aunty Heidi can have it if it isn't *Daddy's* seeds.'

'Oh good. Thank you very much,' he said, struggling to keep his face serious.

'*Come* on, Uncle Nick – it's your *turn!*' Rachael cried impatiently, sighing at his inability to talk and play at the same time.

He had moved his counter four spaces up the home straight. Only when Fiona was shaking the pot noisily did he dare to glance at Heidi. Though she too maintained a perfectly composed façade, her eyes were alight with laughter. But not until Rachael dived under the table to retrieve the die did they allow their mirth to show.

'Well done!' Heidi whispered under her breath. 'I was impressed.'

'Just pray that's all we get!' he muttered back before the child emerged red-faced but triumphant, and play resumed in earnest.

THIRTY-SEVEN

Labour started three days before the expected date of delivery. As soon as Donella was sure that this was no false alarm the well-rehearsed plan went into action. This was no time for knee-jerk reactions, or emotional discussion.

She rang Michael. He had already arranged for a colleague to take over his teaching commitments for that week and the next, so was able to slip unobtrusively from his office.

Michael rang Nicholas. The registrar he called in to take over his duties knew the Halleys were expecting a baby any day; the changeover was swift and wrapped in a welter of good wishes.

Heidi had already left her job to be ready for full-time motherhood, so it was a simple matter for Nicholas to collect her from home.

Each knew their role. There would be no confusion, no competition.

Donella had taken the midwife, Catriona Higgins, into her confidence from the outset, and during the eighth month introduced her to Nicholas and Heidi. It would give her time to think about how she would deal with the potential awkwardnesses.

To her surprise, Donella found she was perfectly relaxed, and being in her own home surrounded by familiar things helped. She remained ambulant as long as possible, only moving to the guest bedroom for the delivery itself, and not until she was comfortably settled and covered with the top sheet did Catriona admit Nicholas and Heidi.

Without a word Nicholas slid into the chair at her head. Donella watched as Heidi took her place alongside the bed, on the opposite side from Michael but in a position to watch the child being born. She saw the nervous eyes flicker from place to place, and reached out to squeeze Heidi's hand briefly, smiling her encouragement.

Nicholas was struggling.

With no active responsibilities he had far too much opportunity for reflection. This atmospheric music Donella had chosen to welcome her baby – their baby – was churning his emotions, threatening his control. He must focus on external things.

It felt unreal being back in the room he and Heidi had used for the conception process, dimly lit now as it was then, but this time the backdrop to a very different scene. No pretty embroidered sheets; these were utilitarian, plain, white. No flowers, no pot pourri: only a tray of instruments laid out in readiness. Not just Heidi – sensuous, giving Heidi

– alone with him, but five adults caught up in a suspense that was palpable.

He sat with closed eyes, willing his brain to concentrate on the present. The occasional low voice of the midwife encouraging, instructing – Donella's hard breathing – fragmented his efforts. The silence hanging between each contraction was deafening in its intensity.

There was a sudden movement.

'I need to push.'

His eyes flew to Donella.

Now in the end stages of labour, her face contorted with the effort, her long chestnut hair tied back loosely, damp with sweat, she was hardly recognisable. A vivid picture of her lying in that other bed nine months ago coalesced with the image of her telling him she was carrying his child. No … he must not …

His eyes swivelled to Michael.

He watched the confidence of a man sure of what was expected of him, holding Donella through each contraction, wiping her face afterwards, dropping kisses on her forehead. He had been so steady through all this nightmare. Yet none of this was for his benefit. If Michael knew how his brother had repaid his generosity … Oh, if only he'd been there, that last time – the time when this child had been conceived – ensuring there were no deviations from the agreed plan, fiercely protective of his wife, as he was now.

Nicholas felt his teeth clench.

It was Heidi who dragged his thoughts back to the present. She was looking at him anxiously. He summonsed a brief smile; she looked away again. He stared at her rigid form. She had made the unthinkable possible, here in this very room. She had overcome scruples that he could only dimly understand to give him the child he craved. For him. And now? The gulf between them felt unbridgeable in that moment. An invisible barrier set limits to what was seemly today; her innocence separated her as irrevocably from his guilt. Knowing nothing of what had brought them to this moment, she waited only to receive his child.

Donella, Michael, Heidi – but for him they would never have met. And yet here they were, inextricably linked in a birth that challenged the limits of what was acceptable, what was forgivable.

A flurry of activity dragged his eyes back to the bed.

'Pant, Donella … Good. Just pant … Pant. Lovely … Gently now. Keep panting.'

Nicholas felt his own breath suspended.

'Right, Heidi. Put your hands here, like this. Good. Lift … gently.'

The sound of a child taking its first surprised breath took him by storm.

'It's a boy,' Catriona said to no-one in particular.

Who said silence was golden? This was jagged and painful and full of purple. It hung uncertainly, uncomfortably, over the miracle of this event. No smiles. No tears. No congratulations. Not yet.

Nicholas saw Donella raise her head to look down at the baby briefly but turn at once to bury her face in Michael's shoulder. He continued to hold her tightly but he was staring at the baby, his jaw set, his eyes unsmiling. Catriona mechanically clamped and cut the cord, wrapped the child in the warmed blanket with practised hands, and handed him to Heidi. Nicholas watched her walk quietly out of the room.

It was his cue. Stooping momentarily to kiss Donella's averted head, he followed without a backward glance, closing the door softly behind him. His emotion, his kiss, had been the only spontaneous moves in the well-ordered procedure.

There was silence as they waited for the placenta. Catriona did her best to ease the discomfort hanging around them by asking Donella about her research findings. Donella answered mechanically.

Only when Catriona had gone to make a pot of tea for them did Donella look at Michael.

'Hold me tight, Mike.'

There were no sobs, no cries, just a voiceless pain too great to speak.

His name was Andrew Edward Halley. In the end Donella had declined to choose; she wanted them to feel the child was totally theirs. Would she be happy if they chose Rebecca Alexis or Andrew Edward, Heidi had asked tentatively. She'd be happy with whatever they chose, Donella had assured her with a smile, as long as they didn't use Hayley Halley for a girl!

He was the image of his father. Except for his eyes: those he had inherited from his mother.

Catriona had gone. Each couple sat in a different room. Only then did they stray into uncharted territory. Who should make the first move? When? It had not been discussed.

Donella decided. She took so long in the shower that Michael became anxious. But when she eventually emerged – fresh, calm, fragrant – she told him she was ready to go through to see the family.

The baby lay in the basket in which he would be conveyed to his new home. Nicholas and Heidi sat close together looking at him but they sprang to their feet as she entered the room.

'Congratulations!' she said. She heard her voice, perfectly even.

A stunned silence answered her. The scent of Donella's perfume filled the room.

She lowered herself gingerly onto the seat beside the baby. The other adults stood uncertainly.

'And now may I hold Andrew?' she asked, moving to peer into the basket.

No-one spoke. She looked round, eyebrows raised, her eyes coming to rest on Heidi.

'May I?' she repeated.

'Of course,' Heidi whispered.

Donella lifted the child up and held him in her left arm, close to her heart, while she ran her fingers over his head, examined his arms and legs, fingers and toes.

'I'm pleased to see he's a Halley to his fingertips,' she said lightly. 'The Halley males are all handsome heart-throbs. No doubt you'll break a few hearts in twenty years time too, eh, young man?'

Nicholas left the room precipitately.

Donella remained rocking Andrew gently, looking steadily down at him blinking in the unaccustomed light.

Not until she was confident of her composure did she turn back to Heidi.

'He's lovely, Heidi. And he's yours.'

She stood up then and placed the child tenderly in Heidi's arms, her hand lingering on him for a long moment. Then stepping back, she added quietly, 'I'll go and find his Dad.'

'Donella …' Michael moved towards her.

'It's all right, Mike. I'm OK. It's best I go. You stay here with Heidi and the baby. I'm OK.' She *was* – as long as she kept doing things – as long as she concentrated on caring for everyone else.

She found Nicholas standing staring out of the window in the drawing room, taking big gulping breaths.

'Nick,' she said softly.

He turned, his face streaked with tears.

She took him in her arms, feeling the waves of emotion engulfing him, stroking his head softly, maternally.

She staggered slightly as he suddenly jerked his head up and released his hold.

'Good grief! What am I thinking about? Shouldn't you be sitting down – lying down – or something?'

'I'm fine. But I must admit I'd quite like to sit down,' she smiled.

He knelt on the floor beside her chair.

'How do you *do* it, Donella?'

She held his eyes steadily.

'This is what we've been working towards for the last year. I've had lots of time to prepare.'

'You're unbelievable.'

'No, not really. This is what I needed – remember? I've waited all these years … to hand you your child.'

He shook his head slowly.

'There just aren't the words to tell you what I'm feeling right now.'

'I know. But we don't need words. You will love him and care for him for me, just as I've loved and cared for Rachael for you. That's all I ask.'

'I will, darling, I will.' She heard the choked endearment, and understood.

The silence felt right. She was loath to break the spell.

'Nick, I handed him to Heidi just now. It would feel right – if I could give him to you. Could you bear it?'

He covered his mouth with his hand, but not before she'd seen his quivering lip.

'It's OK. They'll understand if you're emotional,' she reassured him.

He nodded.

'You stay here. Give yourself time to prepare. We'll – *all* – come to you.' Her hand moved gently down his wet cheek. 'It's time for those first family photos.'

Wiping his eyes again on a fresh tissue, he rose to his feet and helped her up out of the chair. When she was steady he placed his hands on her shoulders and quite deliberately bent to kiss her full on her lips.

'Thank you – more than I can ever tell you.'

'You just did. In true Nicholas fashion.' She smiled.

Heidi and Michael both looked up anxiously as she re-entered the room. 'OK?' he asked.

'Everything's fine. A certain Master Andrew Edward Halley needs to go to his father. But Uncle Mike, would you get the camera first? We'll wait here till you've got it, then we'll all go through to the drawing room.'

'Of course. Won't be a jiffy.'

'Take your time,' she said firmly, and saw that he understood.

Left alone with Heidi, Donella sat down beside her. Heidi turned to face her, pale but earnest.

'Donella, I cannot – it is not possible ...' She gave up the attempt to express the impossible. 'You will always be the most special person for *me* as well as for Nicholas.'

'Thank you, Heidi.' To her dismay Donella felt tears welling up. Her voice sounded strangled. 'Love him for me.'

'I will love them *both* for you. Always.' Heidi said softly.

The two women held one another close for a long moment.

But Donella needed to be active. She walked across to pick up the baby again, not seeking permission this time. His father had already given it. Gently she unwrapped him again and together they exclaimed over his perfection.

When Michael returned with his camera they were sitting calmly waiting. Holding the child close against her, Donella led the way to the drawing room, where Nicholas stood by the window facing the door, pale but dry-eyed now.

Laying the child in his arms, she whispered, 'With my very special love,' then turned instantly to Michael.

'And now – those first family photos, Uncle Mike.'

As Michael moved into action, Donella slipped out of the room.

In the kitchen, she made another pot of tea. While it cooled she took the cutlery out of the drawer piece by piece, sorting it neatly, replacing it. Sipping the tasteless brew slowly she repeated her mantra: 'This is Heidi's baby. This is Heidi's baby.' The knives, forks and spoons reproached her in their orderliness.

Footsteps approached. She took a deep breath. Michael entered the kitchen.

'You coming for a photo, darling?'

'No, Mike. This is their time. I'll stay here till you've finished. Take lots.'

He looked hard at her, then took a step towards her.

'Please, Mike. Not yet. Later. *Please.*' It was through clenched teeth.

He backed away, reluctantly.

Carefully walking back upstairs she began re-ordering the room where she had given birth. In the silence, as she padded this way and that, replacing ornaments, selecting bed linen, shaking cushions, she became aware that her knees were shaking. She sank down onto the stool, feeling the trembling creeping over her body.

Walking slowly back downstairs she slipped silently through to the study, where she curled herself up in a chair, drawing her dressing gown tightly round her, hugging herself, rocking to and fro. She heard doors opening, Michael looking for her.

The curtains were drawn and it was almost dark in the room. He crouched down beside her.

'They should go home now,' she said carefully. 'I'm shattered. I won't come out to see them go. Say goodbye from me.'

She shrank from his look. Not yet …

The departure was so protracted. But only when the car engine faded out of earshot did she give vent to the heart-rending cries racking her body. The desolation of her yearning brought Michael instantly to her side and he took the full force of her inconsolable weeping.

He made no effort to search for comforting words. There were none.

THIRTY-EIGHT

It had been agreed that Donella would be the one to decide when she was ready to see the baby again. For the first few days, as arranged, her midwife brought regular brief professional reports that all was well, and Nicholas sent personal reassurances through his twin. But it was three weeks before she saw Andrew again herself.

She had arranged for a month off work but also taken the precaution of drawing up a list of domestic tasks to keep herself constantly busy and focused. She found solace too in being much in demand with her three girls. To her surprise their innocent questions eased away something of her dread.

But she watched her eldest daughter carefully.

On the third morning after Andrew's birth Rachael sat at the breakfast table, clearly preoccupied.

'Amelia's baby's got teeth,' she said pensively.

'Uhhuh,' said Donella, wiping smears of Marmite from Emily's face.

'Our baby hasn't got teeth, has he?'

'We haven't got a baby, Rachael. D'you mean Aunty Heidi's baby?'

'Yes,' Rachael sighed wearily. 'You *know* who I mean. Baby Andrew.'

'No. He's too new to have teeth. He doesn't need them yet.'

'But he *will* get teeth when he grows bigger.'

'Yes.'

'I wish he lived here and I could see when his teeth come.'

'But you'll see him often and you can watch them coming.'

'But I might not be there when they *come*.'

'You could ask Aunty Heidi to let you know when they come, and go over and see them straight away.'

'But it's not the *same*,' Rachael said with another heavy sigh.

'But you've seen Fiona and Emily getting their teeth.'

'But that was *ages* ago. And anyway, they're *girls*.'

'Boys get teeth just like girls.'

'Well, Amelia says it's different. And she knows cos she's got a sister *and* a baby brother.'

'Oh.'

'I told her about Emily but she says, "Oh that doesn't count. She's only a *girl*."'

'Well, I think you just mustn't take too much notice of Amelia. Sounds to me as if she's saying silly things to annoy you. *You* know girls count. Fiona counts. Emily counts.'

'I still wish *I* had a baby brother. I wish Andrew lived with us. I wish he was my brother.'

'Well, he's your cousin. That's good too, isn't it?'

'I know!' Sparkling dark eyes turned to Donella. 'He can be my *Sunday* brother! Like Uncle Nick's my Sunday daddy.'

'That sounds like a brilliant idea. But you'll have to ask Uncle Nick and Aunty Heidi if that's OK with them.'

'I'll tell Amelia and then she *can't* say I don't have a baby brother. I bet she doesn't have a Sunday daddy *and* a Sunday brother!'

'I bet she doesn't!'

Donella smiled. Problem solved.

For their first meeting after the birth, Donella suggested a rendezvous in the Botanical Gardens.

When Nicholas' car arrived it was suddenly imperative that she should tie Fiona's laces and she stayed crouched down, reminding the excited little girl of the need to be careful if she was near Aunty Heidi's new baby. She missed seeing the pram being unloaded and the baby settled in it.

With a wave in their direction, she turned to Rachael.

'Race you to the red tree!'

Letting her daughter win by a small margin, she caught her up in a big hug before suggesting Rachael should now race Fiona to the next landmark. She strolled back to the adults slightly out of breath.

'Not exactly in peak condition!' She grinned. 'All downhill after thirty!'

'I've a nasty suspicion you'd still beat me,' Michael said teasingly. 'All this training you do with the children.'

'Well, I'm not going to put *that* little theory to the test, but hey – you two. Let's see you have a *dad's* race. Come on! Toe the line here. OK? To that far greenhouse and back. On your marks. Get set. Go!'

The children shrieked with delight as the two men shot down the path past them, neck and neck. Their enjoyment was infectious and Donella found herself laughing with them naturally. She was ready to turn to Heidi and the baby. Her composure held until Andrew demanded a feed; the sight of the bottle brought waves of emotion.

Michael was suddenly at her side, elbow extended in mock courtesy.

'Madam, may h'I seek the pleasure of a swift peripheral perambulation whilst certain members of h'our party h'are h'otherwise h'engaged?' he asked in an affected voice.

'Why, sir, nothing would afford me greater pleasure than a promenade on the arm of such a dashing young blade.'

'Why, thank you kindly, ma'am. It will be a high honour h'indeed. To be seen with such a beautiful and charming young lady on my h'arm – a very high honour h'*indeed*.'

She grinned broadly at him and they minced off along the path, Fiona and Emily skipping along on either side of them. Rachael remained perched on the bench between Heidi and Nicholas, watching the proceedings with fascination.

It was a further two weeks before Donella felt ready to test herself again.

Work was her salvation. She applied herself to writing a new research proposal with single-minded determination. Even the questions about the baby were less taxing than she had expected. Her response was automatic: it was a boy and he was actually living with his father. It sounded so straightforward. Just like a couple splitting up.

Only at night, in the safe arms of her husband, did she give vent to her true feelings. Expecting it, he accepted it. On no occasion did he say anything to diminish her pain or try to speed her recovery. Not once did he remind her that he hadn't wanted her to do this thing. He was simply there for her whenever she needed his comfort. She tried twice to find out how *he* was feeling. He assured her his only trouble was her distress.

But it was Heidi who managed to slip under her guard on one memorable occasion. She suddenly handed Donella a flat square parcel wrapped in soft blue tissue paper.

'I am going upstairs to sing with the girls,' she said quietly. 'Please open this while they are not here.'

Donella smiled at the sounds of running feet and thumps overhead, the sudden silence as the haunting chords flooded the house. Listening as the three piping voices joined in, she was hardly concentrating on the unwrapping.

But as the paper fell away she stood stock-still and then crumpled into a chair. She was dimly aware of Michael's swift intake of breath beside her. The exquisite embroidered picture of a mother – a chestnut-haired mother – and child lay in her lap. And there in one corner were a neat row of numbers sewn in golden thread, as though commemorating the date the work was completed. The date of Andrew's birth.

Michael's hands moved the picture out of reach of her tears. He turned it over to protect it.

In loving recognition of your own most perfect creation.

It was Nicholas' hand.

That evening when the baby woke, it was Donella who went to pick him up, carrying him through to his parents with a composed face and a grateful heart. It was not so difficult to hand him to Heidi today.

But when she eventually asked if they could babysit one evening so that his parents could go out alone together, Heidi hesitated.

'Are you sure, Donella? We do not need you to suffer more.'

'I'd really like to. I'm not asking because I think I *should*. Honestly.'

'Of course, there is no-one we should like better to have him. If you are quite sure.'

Donella was sure of her intentions, less sure of her stamina. It would be best to test herself away from the anxious eyes of his parents – anxious for *her* welfare, not the baby's.

She waited impatiently for the baby to wake. The crying stopped instantly when she nestled him on her shoulder. His soft breathing against her neck, his warm skin against her own, the baby smell he exuded, made her close her eyes the better to savour the moment.

She only became aware of Michael's close scrutiny when she began to change the nappy.

'Is it harder because it's a boy this time, Don?' he asked softly.

'It's a strange thing but … no. I thought it might be. But it sort of makes him different. Not familiar. Not like our three. It makes it easier to feel he isn't mine. Just borrowed.'

'Does it make you feel broody?'

'I just love the feel of them, the smell of them. That makes me feel clucky, I will admit. I just want to cuddle him close. But no, it doesn't actually make me feel broody. Surprisingly.'

'Did you expect to?'

'I wondered if I might. But no. Three's right as far as I'm concerned. Rachael won't be pleased. But hey, I don't intend to go through another pregnancy for *her*!'

He grinned back at her. 'Phew!'

'No. My days of having babies are done.'

The steady rhythmic sucking was soothing. Donella found her thoughts straying. Strange to think that if she so chose she could apply to the courts and claim this child for her own. Her egg had created him; her body had nourished him. She had suffered all the horrors of pregnancy and birth, of having him taken away from her. The lawyers, the judges, they would be sure to give her – the birth mother – custody; there would be no dispute. Of course there wouldn't. Heidi and Nicholas would never contest her claim.

But she would make no such a demand. She smiled softly. It was all based on trust – a trust and a depth of loving they could all depend on. That was why it had worked.

Feeling Michael's eyes on her, she spoke without looking up.

'I'm so glad he looks so much like a Halley.'

'It's nice for Heidi if he does.'

'*If* he does? Don't you think he does?'

'Never do see likenesses myself.'

'He's a Halley all right. His chin, the shape of his head, the length of his legs, his colouring. Everything except his eyes, really. Yes, you're a miniature version of your Dad, aren't you, honey?'

She sat quietly studying the now sleeping child.

'Are you all right, sweetheart?' he ventured cautiously.

'I'm fine. I'm so glad I could do this without the others watching. I can be myself, just look at him, let him feel my love, without worrying what they're thinking.'

'What d'you feel they're thinking?'

'Is she OK? Is she going to burst into tears? Is she thinking: he's mine?'

'They're concerned for you, that's all.'

'I know. But it's still nice just to be myself and not think all the time: what's my face telling them? What's my body language conveying? I can just enjoy it. And if I do shed a tear it won't upset anyone.'

'Does it still make you want to cry?'

'Sometimes. But not just now.'

'And what about what *I'm* thinking?'

Her eyes flew to his face.

'Are you worrying all the time too?'

'Not *all* the time.' He smiled wryly.

'But – you're still worrying?'

'Not about whether you'll burst into tears or anything. I can handle that. But I am worried about how much this is all taking out of you.'

'Am I giving you a hard time?'

'No, you're not. But are you doing as well as you seem to be, Don? Or are you hiding it from me too?'

'Certainly not from you. You're the only person I *can* be myself with. I do watch myself with everyone else, of course. I *have* to. But not with you. Goodness, Mike – you must be fed up with me weeping all over you!'

'Of course I'm not. That's my job!'

'Well, you're a huge comfort. I couldn't have done it without you. Just knowing you're there – and you'll understand – and not tell me to get a grip – it makes all the difference.'

'I'm glad. But you're fantastic. I don't know how you do it. I feel so … *proud* of you.'

Donella's conscience smote her physically. If he only knew … But he must never know.

It was some time before she could speak again.

She looked at him hard. 'Are *you* OK with this? Do *you* mind? Me holding Andrew? And everything?'

'No. I mean, yes, I'm OK; no, I don't mind. It's just a relief that you can do it and not go to pieces. I was afraid you'd find it all a lot harder than you seem to.' He held her gaze steadily. 'I know you'll have bad moments but … are we over the worst? Or is it still to come?'

'I think we are. I really believe we are, Mike.'

THIRTY-NINE

The house was silent. Heidi sat perfectly still looking down at the sleeping baby in her arms. She still found it hard to take in the reality.

Andrew's likeness to Nicholas was a bonus she hadn't let herself hope for. Since both she and Nicholas were so fair, a fair-haired son seemed too good to be true. He had Donella's eyes but they were so beautiful she couldn't feel dismayed by that. But best of all the whole family treated him as hers.

Curiously it was she herself who generated the doubts and questioned her motherhood most. She was all too conscious of the reality. Almost everyone else connected with them was his blood relation – everyone, that is, except her. His aunt was his mother. His cousins were his half-sisters. His father, his uncle, his grandparents were exactly that. Even Donella's parents and her brother, with no acknowledged kinship, had greater biological ties to him than she had. And yet she, jointly with Nicholas, was legally his next of kin. She could only hope that in time this sense of insecurity would fade.

Nicholas' devotion to the child was tangible, but she had to admit secretly to herself that seeing them together was a bitter-sweet experience at times. Was he thinking of Donella, looking for traces of her in the child? Did he see resemblances she could not? Nothing in his words or behaviour suggested anything untoward but she could not entirely banish the anxious thoughts.

Only once was she betrayed into voicing her concern. They were standing looking down at the baby lying fast asleep in his cot after the last feed at night, when Nicholas said casually, 'Funny how he always curls himself up in the same way. His fetal position, I guess.'

She said nothing as they crossed the landing to their own room. But Nicholas must have seen her set face.

'Heidi?'

'It is nothing.'

'Come on. Tell me.'

'Do you think of him inside Donella? When you see him now?'

'Not usually, no. But seeing him always curled up in the same way, I just wondered if he was simply reverting to how he used to lie then. That's all.'

'Oh.'

'Heidi? What is it? Come on. Don't play games. Just say what you're thinking.'

'Do you think of him as Donella's baby?' She felt ashamed of her jealousy.

'No, I don't. I shall always feel indebted to her, of course – I'd be a poor sort of person if I didn't, wouldn't I? But no, I *don't* think of Andrew as hers. He's *ours*. Yours every bit as much as mine. Honestly.'

'Yes?'

'Emphatically yes!'

'I'm sorry.' She looked shamefaced.

'And so you should be!' His tone changed. 'I must tell you that I am far from satisfied with the example you are setting our son and heir. I cannot allow you to let him think for one second that his mother doubts his father's integrity in this way. It would be grossly unfair to me, when I've done *nothing* to deserve such a fate, and a shocking start for one so young and innocent.'

She couldn't help but smile.

'That is *more* the sort of face I wish him to copy. But you must try harder still. Do I still see a hint of doubt in that right eye?' He peered at it as if he saw something tangible, moving in closer as an optician might do, until she giggled spontaneously.

'You, Heidi Lisbet Halley, are a hard woman to please!'

Heidi knew he was right. He never did give her any reason to fear his allegiance to Donella was anything other than what he said it was.

Nicholas leaned back in his chair, watching the light reflect off his glass as he swirled the whisky gently round and round in his hand. In all the excitement, busyness, and pleasure with Andrew, he had scarcely had time to think of his own emotions.

The strength of his feelings for Andrew stirred him profoundly. This was his own son. There was no doubt he loved him totally.

Heidi's happiness was his happiness. Observing her growing content-ment he had found a peace he had feared would elude him. Yes, they had been right to pursue this course.

And Donella? What did he feel for her? A curious awareness crept over him: his predominant feeling now was one of anxiety. Was it hurting her to see them with the baby? Was she regretting what she had done for them? Would every milestone keep the hurt alive?

But what else did he feel? The thought sprang out of nowhere: if someone were to ask him how many children he had fathered, the cor-rect answer would be three. And Donella – *his brother's wife* – was the mother of them all. Her life was inextricably woven with his; he had felt for her emotions which no other woman had aroused in him. He had loved her once – deeply, passionately. Even since her marriage to Michael he had adored her – from a safe distance – most of the time from a distance anyway. He had been as close to her as a man can be with a woman. She shared secrets with him no-one else in the world even suspected.

But now?

It was too soon to be sure. The anxiety for her was always dominant.

Nicholas continued to watch for any sign of trouble in Heidi. But he was completely unprepared for what she had to tell him.

Quite unexpectedly she turned to him one evening and said she would like to explain something to him, but first she must check something with him.

'Fire away,' he said.

'Andrew is quite normal? There is nothing wrong with him?'

'As far as we can tell, he's absolutely normal. Perfect in every detail,' he smiled.

'And Donella – she is not hurt because she grew him inside her?'

He nodded slowly, guarding his thoughts.

'She's fine. Everything is normal there too. Being a doctor I took the liberty of asking her – not in detail, you understand,' he added hastily. 'Just in general. And she assured me, she's fine. Back to normal. And Mike said something along the same lines.'

'I am glad to know this.'

'But?'

'I should like you to understand something about me. To understand why I made you unhappy. It made me sad to make you unhappy but I could not help it. I could not speak of these things. Not then.'

'You don't make me unhappy, Heidi. Quite the reverse.'

'But I *did*. When I would not talk about what happens inside when we make babies, I know I *did*.'

'Oh *that*. Well, we were both very tense then. It was a hard time for us. But it's all forgotten now. So you don't need to explain. Some people just are squeamish about these things. It doesn't matter.'

'But it was not like that for me.'

Her earnest expression arrested his full attention.

'Please. I need to tell this thing. But do not stop me. Please. If you stop me I shall not say it all. It will not make you see.'

'I'll be quiet. Promise. Take your time.'

'When I was growing up in Switzerland, my mother took in a … a man who pays to have a room?' She was clearly searching for the word.

'A lodger?'

'A lodger. That is it. A lodger. His name was Hans Friedel. I did not like him. He frightened me. When my mother was not in the room he would tell me things – about the war. About the things they did to people. Especially to girls. Things that hurt them – inside. He knew it made me frightened. But he liked to see me scared, so he told me many things – like that. Horrible, *horrible* things.'

She shuddered, seeing again the hated face close to hers whispering shocking facts.

'He said there were many doctors in our country who did these things still. They liked to get girls into their hospitals, and do things to them. Horrible things. Things to stop them having children. They *could* do such things, he said, because people trust doctors. They do not ask questions.'

Her grey eyes were dilated with the fear she had felt.

'He told me they would do such things to *me* because … because … they liked the … pretty ones.' Her voice sank to a whisper. 'But I was not ill, I did not have to go to hospital, so I did not have to worry for myself. Until … '

She was struggling with her emotions. Nicholas fought the instinct to reach out to her.

'When we did not have a baby – you said I *must* go. I was afraid. You know I was afraid. Very much afraid. But you told me – you *told* me it was all right. I would be safe. Of course they did things inside me. And then … then they told me I could not have a baby. It was not possible now.'

It was so hard to just sit there, not help her. But she had to do this.

'I thought it must be the doctors who did this thing to me. They said it was not so, it was already so inside me. And then they said it was too late for me; I could not be right inside again. And you told me, what they said, it was right. But inside my head I could not trust such men any more. I *could not* let them do anything else to me. And that was why I could not let them make me have a baby.'

He nodded mutely.

'But then you said someone else, another girl, she might help us. At first I could not let such a person do this thing. They might hurt *her* too. But you I could trust. And I thought – you told me – I could trust your father. You told me I could trust all your family. So that is why I said, we will come to Scotland. *He* will do this thing for us.' Her voice had brightened but now it sank back into flat despair again. 'But then he could. He says he will not. He loves you, we trust him, but he cannot do this thing.'

Nicholas felt her hopelessness acutely.

'But then Donella says *she* will do this thing for us. You told me, no doctors will be needed. She is a doctor. You are a doctor. But we do not need a doctor we do not know. It is OK. We can do this thing. She will not be hurt. I know *you* will not hurt her. And Michael if he does this thing to her, he will not hurt her.'

She could have not the remotest idea of what her words were doing to him.

'And when Michael cannot do this thing any more, she says she will do it herself. She is safe. I do not have to worry for her. And then – she has this baby. And he is born. We all see him arrive. No-one hurts her. We see him born. She is safe. The baby is safe. The midwife does not do anything to hurt her inside. You tell me she is not hurt now. Everything is OK inside her still.'

Nicholas waited still, unsure if she had finished.

'So that is why I made you unhappy. I am truly, truly sorry. I tell you now because we will not do this thing again. And I do not like that you think I cannot talk to you – about everything.'

He held her tightly to him without speaking for a long time. Then step by step he dealt with each issue she had raised – medical integrity, her own endometriosis, and the safety of them all.

Nicholas felt her relax as the ghosts were laid to rest, one by one. A sense of peace crept into his heart too. They had never felt so close.

FORTY

It was Heidi and Nicholas who suggested that Donella's parents should be known to Andrew as 'Sunday Grandpa' and 'Sunday Granny'. Donella requested time to consider the implications of this. Would it throw up unnecessary awkwardness? Would her mother harbour feelings of resentment? Would it confuse the children further? Nicholas had assured her their only wish was to include Andrew's biological grandparents in the warm circle of his family, but only Donella and Declan knew how much her mother still struggled with what they had done. In the end she asked her parents outright and was surprised and pleased by the alacrity with which both accepted their new titles.

Their official inclusion drew the family closer together, but just as Donella had started to relax again with her mother, Declan brought disturbing news which introduced different tensions, threatening the fragile peace: Graeme had been admitted to a psychiatric hospital following a complete breakdown. Donella's every instinct was to go to him but Declan told her gently, not yet. In time he was sure she could see her brother, but not yet. Judy had gone down to Oxfordshire and would stay there indefinitely; she would keep them informed. Declan travelled down once a fortnight and gave Donella first-hand reports.

But as the weeks went by Donella became increasingly suspicious. She demanded an explanation. Reluctantly Declan admitted the truth: Graeme was fiercely opposed to seeing her. She mustn't take it personally, his mind was seriously disturbed, but she really mustn't attempt to see him. Upsetting him at this stage could do untold damage. They must all tread carefully. He was very vulnerable, the doctors said.

Donella raged against the edict. Graeme didn't know what would be good for him; he was too disturbed to know, she protested. She must see him. He would want to see his sister, his twin; they had been so close. No, her father insisted, the psychiatrist too had said she shouldn't go. Not yet. Not until Graeme was more mentally robust. Just now he was sedated and even they, his parents, must limit their visits.

Donella fought against the control. She was a grown woman, a doctor. She wouldn't do anything to set back her own twin. She'd be careful.

But they were adamant.

New gaps yawned between herself and her parents as they continued to keep her away from him. Even her father, her closest ally, was guarded in what he told her about Graeme.

He, for his part, continued to watch his daughter with anxious eyes. It seemed inconceivable that she could relinquish her son without considerable trauma. The strained relationship with her mother had added to her burden. To be kept away from her brother too – would that be too much for even Donella to bear?

When Andrew was four months old, Declan contrived – with Michael's assistance – to get Donella to himself by inviting her to go for a walk with him one Saturday – 'like old times'. Father and daughter set off into the Pentland Hills.

It was a beautifully clear day and they stopped often to admire the view. But it was not until they neared the highest point of their climb that Declan ventured onto difficult territory.

'Don, I really am sorry about Graeme – you not getting to see him, I mean.'

'So am I, Dad. And I still don't think it's the right decision. But I'm not blaming you. I know it's not your fault. Sorry I've been so prickly lately.'

'I'll keep checking for you. I promise. As soon as the psychiatrist says it's OK, I'll let you know. But, you know, Graeme's like a zombie half the time. I doubt he even takes in who sees him. It is *so* distressing to see him like that. It really is. It's killing Mum.'

'It must be just ghastly for both of you, seeing him, in that sort of state.'

'Well, maybe it's a blessing it got to this stage. He's been struggling for ages. Now it's reached crisis point at least he's getting help. Let's just hope he comes out of it stronger and happier.'

'Are they still saying it's paranoid schizophrenia?'

'Yes. Although he doesn't show all the classic symptoms, the doctor told Mum.'

'Poor Mum. She suspected years ago there was something wrong.'

'She did indeed, but she says she never imagined anything as serious as this. But then, we saw so little of him in recent years. How would we know he was getting so much worse?'

'You mustn't blame yourselves, Dad. It was Graeme's choice, keeping himself to himself.'

'Maybe.'

'It was. But even so it must be grim for Mum now. Now she knows. This is one of those times when a little knowledge is a dangerous thing. She'll know a bit too much about mental illness for her own peace of mind, but not enough to help her cope with it.'

'How *do* you cope with something like this? I don't know.'

'No. It's depressing whichever way you look at it.'

'And we're going to worry about him for the rest of his life.'

'But antipsychotic drugs are so much better nowadays, Dad. I talked to one of the doctors from the Royal Ed, and he said that.'

'If he takes them. You probably know already, but Dr Amos – you know,

Graeme's psychiatrist – told us, these people aren't reliable. If he's paranoid and thinks somebody's trying to poison him … well, you must have read about it.'

'I do know, yeah. But they'll be monitoring him closely. They do. Jack said.'

'While he's in hospital. But he'll need to be closely watched even when they've stabilised him, Dr Amos says. Mum's already saying he'll have to come and live with us so she can keep a close eye on him.'

'And is that what you want too, Dad?'

'If it stops him going off the rails again, of course we'll do it. Who else is there to look after him? But I can tell you, Don, I'm worried about Mum. Is she strong enough to take this on? She gets upset when Graeme's bolshy normally. How will she cope with this kind of behaviour?'

'We'll all need to be vigilant and take some of the strain. You know Mike and I will do everything we can to be supportive.'

'I know you will. And thanks, Don. It helps having you nearby and so … normal!'

'Not quite what Mum was saying a few months ago,' Donella said ruefully.

Declan acknowledged the truth of this with a half smile.

'How are you coping – really, Don – with giving up the baby and everything?'

'Most of the time now, I'm fine. Yep.'

'Still hard sometimes?'

'Occasionally. But I guess there'll always be odd moments. Like there is with any significant loss.' Her voice sounded calm.

'You're such a self-sufficient person. But … do you ever regret doing it?'

'No. No, I honestly don't, Dad. I know it was the right thing to do. The hurt now is just part of the price we pay for loving him.'

'You're amazing. You're just so strong.'

'No. I'm not actually. I've just got a fantastic support team!'

'Well, I know better. You're stronger than the rest of us, I do know that. Mum and I – we couldn't have done what you've done.'

They stood on the top of the hill looking around them at the spectacular views on all sides.

'Dad, can I ask you something?'

'Uhhuhh. As long as it's nothing too difficult!' He grinned at her.

She leaned on her walking stick, looking at him. 'Have you ever had secrets from Mum?'

Declan was caught off guard.

'Aha. You have! I see it in your face!' she exclaimed triumphantly.

He gave a half smile. 'Why d'you ask? Don't you have any secrets from your husband?'

'I do, as it happens. But that's another issue.'

'So? What's so special about me having secrets from Mum?' he asked, keeping his tone light.

'Well, I asked Mum something once and she couldn't answer me. But I've wondered of late if maybe you knew something she didn't.'

'Mmhmm.' Declan kept it non-committal.

'Remember when Nick dumped me, I talked to you about it? I told you I couldn't understand the sudden change?'

'Yes. I remember.' He looked across the hills. Give me strength, he prayed. Give me the right words.

'Well, I've found out since, his Mum *did* know something about me. Something in our medical history. Something she found out when she worked in the Roslin surgery – as a locum. Something to make her uneasy about Nick being involved with me. She deliberately intervened.'

He kept his face slightly averted.

'And then, when Mike and I got together, she tried to dissuade *him* too. But by then … well, it was the real thing. We were in too deep and Mike just wouldn't drop me. He just told her if she couldn't tell him what it was, and if it wouldn't hurt *me* to marry *him,* he was going to marry me anyway. And the rest, as they say, is history.'

'And Dick – his Dad?' Declan needed to know just who knew. And he wanted to stall for time.

'He didn't know the first time – when it was Nick. Mike's Mum's scrupulous about medical confidentiality. They *both* are. And I admire that – even though I wanted them to tell us what they knew. But that first time, his Dad just assumed his Mum was protecting Nick's career interests. But then when Mike *wouldn't* be persuaded to give me up, his Dad said they should decide *together* whether to tell Mike. So she told him then. His verdict was, because Mike's feelings for me were so serious, he didn't think they should stop him from marrying me, but Mike was better not to know this confidential information. They could only tell him that they had nothing against me – for myself.'

No, indeed. But it was kind of them to give her that assurance – given what they knew.

'And to be honest we hardly gave it a thought for years. And when we *did* it was with a sort of smug feeling. Ah, we've shown them! We're happy. Nothing terrible came of Mike marrying me.'

Declan saw a shadow flicker across her face.

'But then with the surrogate pregnancy – the first one – when I miscarried – it made me start to wonder. Was it because Nick was the father? Were he and I incompatible in some way? Of course, I know it seems unlikely, with them being identical twins but we were … doing something unusual. Anyway then I got so depressed about it all and I just knew that I needed to try again – try to make it OK. I felt such a failure.' Her voice dropped.

He heard the misery.

'Sweetheart, it wasn't your fault. You've never been a failure,' Declan said, moving to slip an arm around her. She rested her head on his shoulder for a moment.

'Thanks, Dad. In my brain I *knew* it wasn't really my fault, but it *felt* like I'd let everybody down. I just had this tremendous need to put things right. The boys didn't want me to do it again. They *really did not*! But I must confess, I gave them a hard time until they relented. You know how persistent I can be when I *know* I'm right!' Her self-mocking tone lightened her words.

'Which in your terms is most of the time!' he smiled, taking his cue from her. Yes, he knew her very well. It wasn't surprising to him that the men had succumbed.

'And it *was* the right thing to do. Only then I started vomiting. It was relentless, all the time. It really dragged me down and I started to feel really depressed again. Then I convinced myself there was something terribly wrong with this baby, and all the old fears came to the surface again. I even considered aborting it. Imagine! After all we'd gone through! But the boys were both great and helped me through that. And Nick suggested I talk to Mum, and to his Mum, about screening. Just to get their advice. So I did.'

Declan recalled Judy telling him about that conversation. How worried she'd been in case Donella's hunch was right, and this was a repeat of their sad experience with Bethany.

'I asked Mum outright if she knew of anything in our medical history. But apart from Bethany, she said she didn't. Funny thing – it didn't occur to me *then* that you might know something she didn't know. Mum being the midwife and everything. And I suppose I never imagined that you and Mum might have secrets from each other. You've always been so close.'

Declan stirred the leaves at his feet with his stick, not looking at her.

'I talked to Nick's Mum, too. I knew, of course, that she *did* know something, but I couldn't make her break a confidence. So I just asked her outright, did she know of anything that might make it likely there was something seriously wrong with this baby? She was great, actually. Basically said if I was worried it would be sensible just to have some tests done. To set my mind at rest. By that stage I'd convinced myself that the deep dark secret was something horrible – some progressive disease or something that was lurking in the shadows, ready to strike us down. But she was super. Reassured me that it was nothing like that at all. And there was no reason why this fifth baby was at any more risk than any of the others.'

Declan let out his breath slowly. Maybe she wasn't going to ask for that secret knowledge.

'And of course I had the tests,' Donella went on in a brighter voice, 'and they were all fine. And Andrew *is* perfect.'

'And I thank God for that. You deserved that. After all you'd gone through.'

'But can you tell me, Dad – what this family secret is? This thing that even Mum doesn't know? *You're* not bound by the old professional code of ethics. And I *am* a doctor. Not much shocks me.'

He was silent for a long time, leaning heavily on his walking stick. What would it do to her to know this? He trusted her capacity to keep it secret, but what would she think of him – or about herself – if she knew?

'Are you quite sure you're not going to have any more children?' he began cautiously.

'Positive.'

'And will you promise never to tell Mum? Or anyone else come to that?'

'Not even Mike? If it affects him?'

'I'd rather you didn't. Although I'm not generally in favour of wives having secrets from their husbands.'

'Just husbands keeping secret from their wives, eh?' she teased. 'OK. I can keep a secret.'

'I know you can. But you're the only person I *would* trust with this particular one. Mum's not as strong as you.'

'Does Graeme know?'

'No. And I don't think he *should* know. I don't think he could handle it. Even before all this happened … he's not as robust as you. And he doesn't share your understanding of these sorts of things. And I certainly wouldn't trust him not to tell Mum.'

'OK. I promise. I'll keep it to myself. Goodness, if *you've* kept the secret for over thirty years, and Mike's Mum and Dad have too, I surely can!'

Declan took a deep breath. Not looking at her he began the story, keeping it brief, steeling himself for her reaction.

'I told you once about both Mum and me being the product of artificial insemination. But of course if we hadn't had Bethany, we'd never have known, and we'd never have found out that we both carried this faulty gene. But once that came out, people started looking at our genetic history and our genes and everything, and our GP started putting the results together. She already knew we both had Gilbert's Syndrome.'

'Is that significant?'

'Not as far as we're concerned – *medically*, I mean. But it's an inherited dominant condition.'

'I didn't know that.'

'Neither did Dr Farnham – our GP. But when she *did* find it out she started asking awkward questions. Oh, not asking *us*. Other people – professional people. And eventually she put two and two together.'

'And that made?' Donella still didn't understand. 'We've all got these funny things on our genes, haven't we?'

'Yes, but not quite in the way Mum and I have. So many of the *same* funny things. We have the same unusual eyes too. Like yours. Like the girls'. And Andrew's. The GP – she told me that we – Mum and I – were … almost certainly …' It was so hard to say it aloud. 'We almost certainly had the same … sperm donor. The same father. And she let it out one day, thinking I'd already been told by the geneticist. It had never entered my head!'

There it was said.

Declan didn't dare look at her. He kept his unseeing gaze on the end of the walking stick as he turned it round and round in his hand.

'And you've known … *that* – since before I was *born*?' The words sounded incredulous.

'Yes. But when I found out, you'd already been conceived,' he said quickly. She had to believe he hadn't deliberately put her at risk. 'I'd *never* have had children with Mum if I'd *known*. I wouldn't have *married* her if I'd known. But by the time I found out, it was too late.'

'And you've carried that knowledge around with you all these years? Alone?'

'I *had* to. Mum just couldn't have handled it.'

'Well, I don't know *how* you've done it. And you call *me* strong!'

He slowly turned to face her. 'You aren't disgusted? Shocked? You aren't going to condemn me completely?'

'Oh *Dad*! Why should I? I know you; you'd never have done anything like that *deliberately*. My goodness, I don't know *anyone* with higher principles of conduct than you! You make *me* feel positively decadent! But to *know* and to stick by Mum – and, well, everything. That takes guts. And you must have known it could come out – any time.'

'At first I couldn't think of anything else. I watched your Mum like a hawk. If she was the least bit down or unhappy, I thought, she knows – somehow she's found out. Because of course, I had no idea *who* knew. Apart from our GP. Oh, and a few other people she told me about. She'd talked to the geneticist, some researchers somewhere, and a locum doctor – and that must have been Roberta – Mike's Mum. Incredible, eh? She was one of the few people to know. And you have to fall for her son!'

'Or *sons* plural, even! *She* must have found *that* incredible. Just managed to deflect trouble once, and then – wham – it comes back like a boomerang and strikes again. But Dad, you have to admire her for keeping her own counsel. She's never told me. Or Mike, or Nick.'

'Yes, that took courage. And strength.'

'And she's been lovely to me. They *both* have. Even though they *knew*. They've never let it make a difference.'

'They're a very close family, aren't they? Unusually close, I'd say. Although they *must* have worried about what might come out in the children. Just like I did every time. I *couldn't believe it* when you not only had children with Mike – but deliberately with Nick too! What that did to their parents I can't begin to imagine, knowing what they know, and it being *both* their sons!'

'No wonder they were shocked into expressing their disapproval!' Donella said ruefully. 'They're normally so supportive, but we knew without a shadow of a doubt they didn't approve of what we were doing. We thought it was simply the surrogacy thing they objected to. But I guess it was this on top of the obvious hazards of surrogacy too. A complete recipe for disaster.'

'But, thank God, the children are all perfect. It's a great relief to hear you say, no more. That's one worry we can leave behind us. Do Dick and Roberta know you've decided that?'

'They do now. Yes. But I see what you mean. It must be a *huge* relief for them, because, of course, they know better than most people the risks of inbreeding.'

Declan moved to lean against a rock, suddenly very weary. It was a risk he'd lived with for almost all his married life.

'Don ... d'you think ... is Graeme ... like he is ... because ...?'

'I don't know. I wish I could reassure you, Dad, but really I don't know much about psychiatric illness.'

'Well, they do say that inbreeding caused some of the madness in the royal family way back, don't they?'

'I've heard that said, but I have no idea whether it's based on any scientific evidence. But in our case – well, Graeme's always been an intense kind of a guy, hasn't he? I mean, remember how jealous he was of my friends when we were kids? He's always resented anyone I've been close to. And he's been really off with the Halleys. And now he won't even speak to *me*! Don't beat yourself up on that score, Dad. I'm sure it's not your fault. It's just Graeme.'

There was a long silence.

'I always dreaded you children finding out. I thought you'd hold it against me, think I should have annulled the marriage or something – whatever you're supposed to do in these circumstances. I went over and over it all – till I was sick with the worry. But in the end I couldn't do it to Mum. She couldn't have coped with something like that. By the time I knew, she'd already lost Bethany, *and* she was pregnant with you two. I couldn't pile any more agony on her by leaving her, or telling her she must terminate the pregnancy. I just *couldn't*. And besides I loved her so much, I didn't *want* to give her up.'

'I can understand that, Dad,' Donella said with conviction.

'But you have to believe me, Donella. I wouldn't have agreed to have children *at all* – after we found out. But it was too late. And Mum really couldn't have dealt with aborting you.'

'Especially after Bethany. I *can* believe that.'

Of course she could; she too had known the pain of loss.

'I managed to persuade her not to have any more. I didn't tell her why, of course. Just said we had to remember that every time there was a one-in-four chance of a problem like Bethany's. She'd found it terribly traumatic waiting to be tested, waiting for those results with you. I told her I loved her too much to watch her torturing herself again, and anyway I was content with you two. I think she knew in her heart it would be too much for her. Anyway she accepted it. And we never talked about it any more.'

Donella suddenly moved across to him and threw her arms around him. She held him tightly without saying a word. He felt a burning sensation in his eyes but blinked rapidly.

'Thanks, love. I know I can trust you not to tell a soul.'

'I won't, Dad. I won't.'

They began the return journey.

'I've always been glad that you've got Mike, if ever anything of this came out. He's a good man. And I'm sure he'd stick by you.'

'He would. I know he would. He's strong. He's been brilliant through all this surrogacy stuff, Dad. I'm glad you like him too.'

'I do. Very much.'

'I wish Graeme did,' Donella said sadly. 'It's spoiled things. We used to be so close.'

'I know. It'd be better, I think, if Graeme had someone of his own. He wouldn't be so jealous of the men in your life then, I think. It's the twin thing, I know, as you say. You're close because you're the same age, do so much together, share so much. But that makes it tough on the one who's left when the first one finds a partner.'

'I wish he'd make more of an effort though. I mean, Mike does his best to be nice to Graeme. And we've been together long enough now for him to be used to seeing us together. And we both try really hard not to do – you know – all the little loving sorts of things that exclude other people, when he's around. But he just doesn't seem to *try* to reciprocate.'

'I'm sorry, love. But unfortunately I don't see things improving in the foreseeable future. He doesn't show any sign of being interested in girls at all. I haven't heard of any girlfriends – ever. Have you?'

She shook her head.

'Nor have I heard of boyfriends,' Declan went on. 'So I presume it's not because he's gay. Although he might be. I don't know. He just seems to be a loner.'

'Maybe the treatment he's getting now will help to get to the bottom of his problem. If he's getting therapy maybe they'll help him to see why he feels bad about things and perhaps he'll come out the other end a stronger person.'

'I hope so. I really do hope so. I hate to see your relationship deteriorating like it has done over the years.'

'Me too. But it's not for want of trying on my part, Dad.'

'Oh, I know that, love. I'm not blaming *you*. No, it's Graeme, I'm well aware of that. Though it grieves me to say it, he's never been an easy lad.'

The silence between them was heavy as they stomped along the rough path.

'But it's good to see you getting on so well with Michael's family. *That* twin relationship has stood the test of time. Nicholas hasn't resented *you*. At least he doesn't appear to.'

'That's true,' Donella said, looking away from him to check their route. 'The boys are still very close. Although, of course, Nick's got Heidi too. And she's a treasure.'

'But their relationship – Mike and Nick's, I mean – that must be strong. It's survived a lot. Even falling for the same girl!'

'Probably comes from being two parts of a whole in their case – identical twins,' she said lightly. 'Both attracted to the same crazy kind of humour! And the same obsessive workaholic, pathologically tidy, restless kind of personality, eh?'

'And the same wonderfully warm, understanding, beautiful kind of person.'

'Thanks, Dad.' She shot him a smile. 'You are, of course, horribly prejudiced!'

'Me? Never!' He laughed.

'But Nick's better off with Heidi than he ever would have been with me. She's exactly right for him. And she's completely different from me.'

'It's lovely that the four of you get on so well together. Makes up a bit for Graeme being so jealous and ungiving.'

They tramped for a long time in companionable silence. Only when they were nearing home again did Donella return to the earlier disclosure.

'Thanks for sharing that with me, Dad. And, for what it's worth, I came to the conclusion some time back that sometimes it's a greater love that keeps a secret than one that destroys someone else's peace of mind by insisting on sharing it.'

'Did you? You're a wise woman.'

'No, I'm not. I'm just a very fallible and flawed one.'

Not until he was discharged from hospital and living, albeit reluctantly, at Roslin with his parents for a convalescent period did Graeme relent and finally agree to see his sister – on her own – only on her own. He was morose and hostile at first but she persisted and soon became a regular visitor. Eventually something of their old ease crept back into their exchanges.

Judy was grateful for another professional eye on his progress, and a shared sense of responsibility restored the bond the two women had always felt until Judy's disapproval had driven a splinter between them. The return of outwardly harmonious relationships lifted a weight from the collective shoulders.

But after ten weeks with them Graeme grew increasingly restless and insisted he was ready to pick up the reins of his old life back in Oxfordshire. The administrators at the college which had employed him to teach English as a foreign language were cautious but agreed to a trial part-time contract. With a new energy and application Graeme quickly proved he was equal to the task and gradually began to assume additional responsibilities for various evening classes. The psychiatric team expressed themselves well pleased with his progress; Judy reduced her trips south, and the family began to breathe more easily.

Instinctively it took Donella longer to trust his more benevolent manner towards her, but over time the suspicions subsided and little by little Graeme resumed his old pattern of infrequent visits and long silences.

The years passed and their busy lives made the long absences less noticeable.

FORTY-ONE

It was August. The house was bathed in sunlight as Michael turned in from the road. He really must do something about those overhanging trees this weekend. If he left it much longer, he'd have to duck his head to pass under them.

It always gave him a good feeling returning home. They'd both grown to love this house. It had seen so much happiness over the years. And tonight was even more special than usual. He smiled as he drove up to the door.

Seeing the grey Citroën standing in the drive he cursed under his breath. It was their eleventh wedding anniversary. The girls had gone to Dick and Roberta's, he was taking Donella out for a meal, and he'd wanted to surprise her by arriving home earlier than she anticipated. Now it looked as if she had an unexpected visitor.

Inwardly annoyed by the thwarting of his careful plans, he picked up the bouquet of lilies he'd bought her, and his briefcase, and locked the car.

He lightly touched the bonnet of the visiting car; it was cold. Whoever it was had been here for a while. Hopefully they'd go now he was home. What he had in mind didn't involve third parties.

His key turned in the lock. Strange – the front door wouldn't open. It seemed to be bolted on the inside. He grinned to himself. So Donella had surprises in store for *him*! On tiptoe he sneaked round to the back door. He peeped round the corner cautiously, expecting to see her waiting in the conservatory, or in the garden. No, no sign of her. She'd be planning to surprise him inside then. Anticipation made his skin tingle. He turned the handle. Odd – that door was locked too. He tapped on the glass. No answer. The plants looked as if they needed water. They got very hot with the conservatory all closed up at this time of day. Funny – Donella usually opened it all up if she was home first. Her visitor must have arrived before she'd had time.

He walked back round to the front and rang the bell. No answer. He rang again, more persistently. Presumably she was home. He checked in the garage. Yes, there was her Renault.

He rang the bell more insistently again. Still nothing. Walking backwards he looked up at the windows, expecting to see her grinning down at him, tantalising him. But no. Nothing.

He took out his mobile phone. It rang, and rang. She *must* be there. This was getting silly. On the point of ringing off he heard the receiver being lifted.

'Come on, Donella. Let me in. We'll have the neighbours reporting me for loitering with intent in a minute!' he said, laughing.

She didn't reply.

'Donella?'

Still nothing.

'Donella – speak to me.'

Still nothing. He felt his skin crawling.

'Donella? Are you OK?'

This was getting scary.

'She's safe now. You can't hurt her any more.' It was a curiously flat male voice. Certainly not Donella.

'Hello? Who's that?' he said urgently.

The receiver was replaced. He rang again – letting the phone ring for ages – but there was nothing.

Seriously alarmed now, he thought rapidly. He couldn't identify the voice. It sounded robotic, devoid of any emotion. He didn't recognise the car. Peering into it he could see nothing to identify it as one he should know.

Standing inside the porch, he rang the emergency services.

'Which service, sir?'

'Police.' His voice was low but urgent.

It seemed to take an eternity for anyone to arrive. While he waited he tried windows, looking for any means of entry, but they'd always been careful about security. No, there was no way he could sneak in without alerting whoever was inside with Donella.

As in a film, tyres scrunched as the patrol car swept up his drive, two constables got out, donned their hats, walked towards him, arms bare in the hot sunshine. Radios crackled.

'Dr Halley?' Michael nodded. 'I'm PC Jim Langley. This is PC Paddy Norton. Lothian and Borders Police.'

'There's someone in the house – with my wife.' The words choked him. Saying it made it real. 'The doors are locked. I can't get in.'

Jim had the weary look of a man who'd seen it all before.

'Could we try, sir?' Paddy took his keys and moved away towards the house.

'Any reason why your wife might lock herself in?' Jim asked conversationally.

'No. Of course not.'

'No arguments? Anything …'

'For goodness sake,' Michael snapped. 'My wife's in there with some lunatic. I didn't call you out because I'm locked out of the house!'

'It is your house then? You live here normally?'

'Yes! It *is* my house! I live here normally – *with* my wife and we've *not* had a domestic argument! For goodness sake, get in there and make sure she's all right!'

244

Paddy returned from the back of the house, trying windows as he went. 'All locked,' he reported flatly.

'I *told* you that! Now will you *do* something!' Michael's patience was paper thin. 'I *heard* the guy! I know there's someone in there with her.'

'D'you know who it is, sir?'

'No. Only that it's a man. He answered the phone.'

'And you didn't recognise the voice?'

'No.'

'Any reason to think she might have a ... *friend* in – not want you to know who it is?'

'None whatever! Look, I know where you're coming from but you're barking up the wrong tree. There's something wrong. I know it. She might be in danger. Will you get in there, and *do* something!'

'You say you heard the man. And did you speak to your wife, sir?'

'No, I didn't. Whoever it is in there just put the phone down and he didn't answer it again after that.'

'So we don't know for sure she's in there.'

'Well, not for *sure*, I suppose. But her car's here. And we're going out tonight and she'd be getting ready.'

'So you've only spoken to the man.'

It was as if the constable could only absorb one fact at a time, had to think about it, process the information slowly. It was infuriating, frustrating. Why didn't they just act on what he knew? He gritted his teeth, clamping his mouth shut. No point in antagonising them. They were only doing their job. And they didn't know him from Adam. They weren't to know he wasn't some abusive husband, locked out by a terrified wife. They weren't to know Donella would never cheat on him.

'Yes. I've only spoken to the man. But I know he's got Donella in there. I know it.'

'Did he say so?'

'Not exactly, but ...'

'Can you remember, sir, what did he say – exactly?'

'He didn't say much. But his voice sounded ... like a recording ... sort of flat.'

'It'd help if you could tell us – just what he said.'

'Something about her being safe ...'

'Can you try to remember exactly what he said, sir? Might be helpful.'

'"She's safe" ... That was it. "She's safe now."'

'That's good. She's safe. OK. And that was all?'

'No. There was something else.'

'Take your time, sir. Try to think exactly what he said.'

Michael wanted to scream at him – there *isn't* time – just get inside. She'll be terrified. Find her – protect her. His brain was like pulp. Everything was in slow motion. What had the man said? What did it matter? That wasn't important. He needed to get to Donella.

'She's safe now ...' Jim prompted.

Michael closed his eyes, straining to remember. The policeman wasn't going to let up.

'"She's safe now ...,"' he repeated slowly, mimicking that flat voice. '"She's safe now. You can't hurt her any more."' His eyes flew open. 'Yes, that was it. "She's safe now. You can't hurt her any more." That's what he said.'

'"You can't hurt her,"' Jim repeated carefully. 'And why would he think you'd hurt her?'

'I've no idea! I've never hurt her in my life!' This was getting ridiculous.

'So why would he say that, d'you think?'

'I haven't a clue! I don't know who he is. Or what he wants. But I *do* know my wife is in there and I'm getting increasingly worried, so will you *please* stop all this questioning and *get in there!*'

'I understand, sir.' He didn't, or he wouldn't stand there asking his stupid questions, implying things! 'D'you recognise the car?'

'No, I do not,' Michael snapped.

'Paddy, run a check on the vehicle, will you?'

'Righty-ho.' The radio crackled again. The registration number vanished along the airwaves. Surely they weren't going to wait again till they heard back on that! How many other numbers were in the queue ahead of this one on that screen somewhere in the police station? Why could nobody see this was urgent?

He saw PC Norton start banging on the door, peering in the down-stairs windows, shouting up at the windows. He cringed. All that noise – didn't they realise it might make whoever was inside agitated?

'Hello! This is the police. Will you open the door, please?'

More banging.

Still watching his colleague hammering on the door, shouting his requests, Jim spoke again. His voice was politely enquiring. As if they were guests at a dinner party, trying to make polite conversation.

'Anyone got a grudge against your wife, Dr Halley?'

'Not that I know of,' Michael ground out. No, he would *not* be the polite guest; he would not encourage this farce.

'Any ex-lovers? Any patients with a grievance? Anything like that?'

'Not that I know of.'

'Anyone with a grudge against *you*, sir?'

'Not that I know of.' Michael felt he was on automatic pilot. OK, if that was the game to play while they waited.

'Ever had any threats made against you?'

'No.'

'Or any of your family?' Ahhhh ...

'Well, my father used to take precautions.'

'Can you tell me about that, sir?'

Michael felt a glimmer of hope. His tone moderated.

'He's the head of the Centre for Reproductive Medicine here. Different members of the team are into various kinds of research – they use tissue from abortions and sometimes the work involves animals. So they all have to be careful.'

'Is he Dr Halley too?' Constable Langley asked, his attention fully arrested now.

'He was. He's *Professor* Halley now.'

'That's very helpful. Thank you.'

'D'you think it's connected?' Michael was finding it hard to believe anyone would target *his* family because of things done in his father's place of work. But you never knew with some of these fanatics.

'I can't say at this point, sir. But we'll bear it in mind.'

Paddy Norton returned from the back of the house.

'No sign of forced entry, Jim.'

'OK.' Jim nodded. Then turning to Michael he ushered him towards the patrol car. 'Can I suggest you sit in the car, sir? I'm going to radio the station, talk to my Inspector.'

Michael felt robotic himself, obediently climbing into the police car. He looked out at the familiar house, tranquil in the sunshine. From inside the car it was like being behind a screen – seeing out but not being seen. Still the two policemen stood talking. They seemed to be just waiting. What were they waiting for? How could he get it across to them? This was no domestic incident. Donella was inside – with some stranger!

There was a sudden flurry of activity. Another police car ground to a halt behind him. An Inspector, braided cap, serious face, older, got out. PCs Norton and Langley crowded round him, voices too low for Michael to catch what they said. More scrunching as the Inspector's boots came towards him.

'Dr Halley – Inspector Rod Campbell. Dalkeith station. I understand there've been threats against members of your family.'

'My father, yes. In the past.'

'Might be relevant. My officers can't get the person inside to open the door. Or your wife. I think we might need to force entry. Any objection to our breaking in? I could try to contact a joiner …' At last!

'Do whatever it takes! I don't care about the door! Just get *in* there.'

The Inspector moved out of range before barking orders into his radio.

In disbelief Michael watched him go off towards the house with Jim Langley and himself start to peer inside, try windows. Paddy leaned into the car.

'Just waiting for the Community Support Unit, sir. Won't be long now.'

Community Support?! Sounded like social work jargon! He didn't need support. He just wanted to know Donella was safe.

The Inspector filled in the time periodically calling to the man inside, asking him to open the door. Would whoever it was be intimidated knowing the big guns were moving in? No. Still nothing from inside the house. Well, if it was some joke that had gone wrong it'd be even more embarrassing knowing there was a police inspector to be faced!

A dark van shot into the drive, slammed to an abrupt halt. An army of identical figures in identical overalls spilled out – like mass-produced figurines. Six of them. Swarming. Chips of gravel flipping erratically beneath their big grinding boots. Inspector Campbell spoke to them briefly, gesticulating, pointing.

Michael looked on incredulously. It looked like a crime scene from a police drama. There were now two civilian cars, three police vehicles, nine police officers in the drive. But this was *Dalkeith*. It was *his street*. It was *his house*. Whatever were the neighbours thinking? First the shouting, now this concentrated police activity. He wanted to wake up from this nightmare.

He saw the figures disperse, three overalled men vanishing round the back of the house. Inspector Campbell moved to stand between the car and the front door, cupping his hands to his mouth. His voice was calm, even, undemanding, just requesting.

'This is the police. Inspector Campbell. Would you open the door, please?'

Nothing.

'This is the police. Open the door!' Louder, sharper.

Still nothing. Michael's eyes darted from one window to another, willing Donella to appear shamefaced, to tell them it was all a silly joke.

Inspector Campbell stayed calm, steady, waiting. It seemed like forever.

Then suddenly there was a movement. A face appeared at an upstairs window – their bedroom window! It was a flat white blob from where he sat. Thank goodness! She was OK. She must have fallen asleep in the bath. Inspector Campbell had seen it too. The face came closer. But ... it wasn't Donella. Who was it? Michael strained forward to see.

It was ... it was ... No! It couldn't be. Graeme? Donella's twin brother? What on earth was he playing at to scare them half senseless with this kind of joke?

'Graeme?' he muttered under his breath.

'You know the man, sir?' PC Norton's head was immediately inside the window of the car.

'Yes. It's my wife's brother. Graeme – Graeme Robertson,' he exclaimed, still leaning forward, staring, uncomprehending.

Paddy told him please to stay where he was. He approached the Inspector, murmuring something in his ear.

Michael stared at the scene before his eyes. It didn't make any sense. Why didn't Graeme come down and let them in, tell them it was only he?

He must be able to see this thing had got quite out of hand. He must have seen all the policemen, the cars. Why didn't Donella come to reassure them she was OK? The voice had said she was safe. Why didn't she come?

Rod Campbell leaned in through the window.

'Can you tell me about your brother-in-law, Dr Halley? Anything at all. It might help.'

Michael explained rapidly, in disjointed phrases – about his twinship, his job, his home address, his parents. He was unmarried. Lived alone. Must be a new car – he didn't recognise it. But he hadn't seen him for – must be at least eight months. Yes, it was last Christmas. But the voice on the phone – it hadn't sounded like his voice at all. Could there be someone else in there with him? Were they just trying to scare him? They were making a pretty good job of it anyway!

'And Mr Robertson's relationship with his sister?' the Inspector asked evenly.

'They were very close as children. Not so much now. Well, Donella's got a family of her own. He lives in England. They don't see much of each other.'

'No bad blood?'

'Not really. Well … he did have a bit of a mental breakdown some years back. He didn't want to see Donella for a time then. But that was all part of his condition. And it's all in the past now. He had treatment. It was ages ago.'

'OK. And with you? Does he get on all right with you?'

'I haven't had a lot to do with him, to be honest. He kept away from me for the most part.'

'Any reason – that you know of?'

'Well, he's always been a bit jealous of my wife's relationships with other men – a bit. But it's just a sort of twin thing,' Michael said hesitantly. No point in dwelling on Graeme's immaturity now. Besides no-one wanted the family's dirty linen washed in public. He just needed to get to Donella. Why didn't she come to the window?

'A twin thing?'

'Yes, they're twins. Extra close. He sort of resented her getting close to anyone else. That's all. It happens.'

'OK. Thank you, Dr Halley. That'll be a great help. It gives us a better idea of what we're dealing with. I must ask you to stay out of sight for the time being. Thank you, sir,' Inspector Campbell said, moving away, back to the house. Good thing the police had a better idea, Michael thought – it was a complete mystery as far as he personally was concerned. Whatever was Graeme playing at?

The Inspector called up to Graeme by name this time. More talking – asking, encouraging: 'Open the door, please.' 'Just come back to the window and talk.' 'We just want to talk.' After six minutes of the monologue, the face re-appeared. But Graeme didn't open the window. No amount of persuasion had any effect. He stood motionless, just staring down at them.

Michael, afraid to blink in case he missed something, saw the Inspector give a signal. Immediately the motionless figures outside the front door came to life. Suddenly the door was open. The figures slid inside like liquid seeping through a drain. They were gone. It was bizarre – these strangers melting inside *his home* – uninvited – in full view of him! Other officers emerged from behind him, taking up positions at different angles, as if they were figures in a game, moving from square to square. Like chessmen. Moving into defined positions – diagonally, two steps forward, one to the side. Then stationary, motionless, like spring-loaded models.

And all the time Graeme remained motionless himself at the window. Then suddenly two of the overalled officers appeared behind him. All three disappeared. Silence. The scene in front of Michael's eyes was frozen. It seemed impertinent of a swallow to dip down under the eaves.

One of the men appeared in the doorway, beckoning. Inspector Campbell moved forward in big strides. He paused for a moment listening, then they both vanished inside the house.

Michael made as if to get out of the car – every fibre of his being straining to go to Donella, to find out what was going on. PC Norton laid a hand on his arm.

'Not yet, sir, sorry. We'll have to wait for the Inspector to tell us it's OK to move.'

'For goodness sake,' Michael snapped, 'I have to know she's all right.'

'I understand, sir. But we don't know if it's safe to go in yet. Inspector Campbell will tell us the minute it's OK. Please just try to be patient a few minutes longer. I'm sure he'll be out soon.'

Michael became suddenly aware that he was still clutching the lilies. The police car was full of their perfume. He would hang onto them now – give them to her as soon as he saw her. Eleven stems. One for every year of marriage. She loved lilies, said the heady scent made her feel intoxicated. He wanted her to feel intoxicated tonight.

FORTY-TWO

The waiting was interminable. Radios crackled intermittently. PC Norton paced beside the car, moving away when his radio came to life, out of earshot when he replied.

Another car tried to enter the drive, found there was no space left, and juddered to a halt on the pavement. An imposing uniformed policeman strode past the car. Norton stood stiffly. 'Sir.'

'What the hell's going on?' Michael demanded, opening the door, swinging his legs out.

'Please, sir. Please. No.' Norton hustled him back inside. 'Just stay where you are. I'm sure it won't be long now. That's the Superintendent now.'

'You've been saying that for the past quarter of an hour, for goodness sake! How many more people are you going to summons before I get to see my wife? I must know what's happening! If you won't let *me* go, can't *you* at least find out what's going on? Just let me know she's all right.'

'Ah! Here's the Inspector now.' The relief in Paddy's voice was palpable.

At last! But why didn't he hurry? He walked like a man in slow motion. Inspector Campbell opened the door of the car.

'Sorry about the wait, Dr Halley. Would you come with me now?'

Michael needed no second bidding. His eyes were on the Inspector's impassive face, expectantly.

'What's happened? What's ... My wife ... is she all right?'

'Just come inside, please, sir.' The Inspector's voice was still calm. Giving nothing away. Soothing. 'I must ask you, please, just to stay with me.' His hand was under Michael's elbow as if warning him not to run off.

It was unreal. This was his home. Why should he need warnings? Why did he feel under guard?

As he allowed himself to be ushered into the house, his eyes darted everywhere looking for clues. Where was Donella? Where was Graeme? What was going on?

Everything looked perfectly normal – apart from the policemen in their dark overalls standing, one just inside the door, one at the foot of the stairs, not looking at him. A pair of Rachael's shoes lay discarded in the hall. Fiona's skipping rope – tangled *again* – was on the telephone table, waiting for him to straighten it out. A rag doll lay spreadeagled on the chair, its brassy yellow hair hanging down in two bunches from its flat pink face. He'd always hated that doll – something about the harsh colours. But it was worn threadbare by love.

Sunlight streamed in through the stained glass window at the turn of the stairs. The rainbow of light bounced off a favourite photograph of Donella with the three girls. But as he walked towards it, her smiling face came into focus. He looked towards the stairs expecting to see Donella herself, embarrassed by the fuss, telling him it was all a big mistake.

Instead the Inspector took him into the empty drawing room. Michael looked at him searchingly.

'Please, take a seat, Dr Halley.'

It was *his* home. He didn't need permission to sit down in his own home! But he sat down automatically. This big man with his grave face and his imposing uniform oozed authority.

'I'm afraid it's bad news, sir. Very bad news.'

He stared at the policeman's face, forcing himself to concentrate.

What was he talking about? Michael watched the Inspector's mouth, frowning with the supreme effort it took to listen to what he was saying. This wasn't real. His ears heard the words but they couldn't be right. Somewhere the pathways between his senses and his brain had got confused.

Donella – *dead?* She *couldn't* be dead. She *couldn't* have been murdered. This was his home – their home. It was their anniversary. He was taking her out for the evening. He'd phoned her at lunchtime. She was bright, excited, looking forward to their evening alone.

But the Inspector was repeating things. Why didn't it make sense still? He'd go and see Donella himself, ask her for an explanation of what was going on. He leapt to his feet and made to leave the room. The hand on his arm was firm.

'I'm afraid not, sir.'

'I must see her,' he insisted.

'Is there someone I can call?'

'I must see her,' Michael repeated, shaking off the restraining hand.

'I'm sorry. No offence. It's routine. We can't have anything disturbed. Not till the doctor, the forensic people, the procurator fiscal, have been. You know how it is. I'm sorry.'

Michael *didn't* know. 'I must see her.'

'Later. Yes. We'll need you to identify her. Later.'

'Why not now? Why not? I must see her.'

'We mustn't disturb anything. It's the scene of a crime. The forensic people need to do the photos, fingerprints, all that sort of thing, I'm afraid.'

There was a sound of another car, more voices murmuring out of earshot, more footsteps.

'I don't understand. Why can't I go? She's *my wife*. Why can't I see her?'

'We can't touch anything …'

'For goodness sake! My fingerprints are everywhere in this house. I *live* here!'

The Superintendent appeared suddenly in the hallway. Through a fog Michael heard the muttered fragments.

'Get Robertson out of here ... *NOW!* ... I've notified the Chief Super-intendent ... official routes demarcated ... SOCO's just arrived ... police doctor's on his way ...'

A sudden bustle of activity interrupted the monologue. Michael sprang forward, seizing the opportunity of the distraction. Behind the figure of the Superintendent – in ... in *his* dining room! – he could see two men, one woman, climbing into white suits, gloves, goggles. He made to push past the Inspector. The restraining hand was like a vice.

'*Let ... me ... go,*' Michael ground out.

The Superintendent was sympathetic. Michael heard vague smatterings of their swift exchange: 'Perhaps he could go upstairs ... do the identifica-tion now .... all right with you, Rod? ...as long as he doesn't touch anything.'

At *last*!

He was escorted up the stairs ... *his own stairs*. Past the overalled policeman. Past another one.

He paused, frowning.

PC Norton was standing in their bedroom ... *their bedroom* ... by the wardrobe ... *Donella's wardrobe*. Looking uneasy. He took a step forward when he saw Michael coming, tense, poised for action.

The room was full of her perfume. It was his favourite. The one she reserved for special occasions.

Donella lay on their bed, her navy blue bathrobe wrapped around her, chestnut hair splayed across the pillow, her huge dark eyes wide open. But ... her face – the look, the colour of her skin – no, this wasn't right. The livid cuts – he must bathe them. He must comfort her. He took a step forward. The Inspector's hand closed on his arm.

'No, sir. I'm sorry but I can't let you. Please, don't touch anything.'

'But I must ...'

He was staring at her face; something shrieked through his veins.

'No, sir. I'm afraid I can't let you disturb anything. Not yet. We must collect evidence first. I'm sorry, I do understand.'

What did he understand?

Michael stared at Donella. How could he understand? This was beyond understanding.

'You can't do anything to help her, I'm afraid,' the policeman said gently. 'It's too late. She's dead. She's been dead some time.'

Dead? *Dead?* Donella? She *couldn't* be!

His mind went blank. Nothing made any sense.

Somebody's hands guided him away from her, taking him back down-stairs. He found himself sitting in a familiar chair, surrounded by familiar things. He was still clutching those eleven lilies. He'd forgotten to give them to her.

Someone was pressing a hot drink into his hands. It was one of their own china mugs. Who was messing around in their kitchen? Did Donella give them permission? He stared down at the mug. It was one of her favourites. Why had he got it? What was going on?

'I'm sorry to have to ask it, sir, but … it was … your wife?'

Michael stared uncomprehendingly at the Inspector's concerned face.

'Yes. What … what … happened … to her …?'

'I'm afraid she's been strangled.'

'But her face …?'

'Looks like she's been slashed – a knife.' There was no way of sanitising it. 'Is there someone we could call?'

'Someone?'

'A relative perhaps?'

Nicholas. His brother. Dr Nicholas Halley. Senior Registrar in Accident and Emergency. No, he didn't know what hours he was working today. Try the hospital, they'd know. Or Heidi, his wife, she'd know. He gave both numbers mechanically. The questions stopped. He sagged.

Nicholas would sort out this mess. He was a doctor. He'd know what to do.

Nicholas was stitching a bad facial laceration when the call came. They took him to Dalkeith in a screaming police car.

He saw the Inspector do a double take as he took the front steps in one leap. So no-one had warned him they were identical twins.

Vague figures hovered discreetly in the background, but he made straight for the drawing room. Michael sat on the edge of the settee clutching lilies, staring into space. His ashen face turned as Nicholas entered.

'Thank God! What's going on, Nick. It doesn't make sense.'

Nicholas held him tightly, his own body trembling uncontrollably. Michael was rigid in his arms.

'It was Graeme. Graeme killed her, Mike.' His own voice was unrecognisable too. It sounded strangled as if there was no room for the air to pass.

'Graeme? But why would he hurt her? It doesn't make sense.' Michael was struggling in the dense fog of incomprehension.

'I don't know,' Nicholas whispered. 'I just don't know. The police are talking to him now.'

Graeme Robertson sat impassively opposite the two policemen. He answered their questions mechanically. It wasn't difficult.

Yes, of course, he remembered what had happened.

Yes, he had gone to see his sister.

No, she hadn't known he was coming. He was up here unexpectedly to visit his parents in Roslin. It was a spur of the moment thing. He'd pop in and surprise her.

No, he hadn't rung to tell her he was coming.

Yes, she'd been pleased to see him. Of course she was. But she'd told him she couldn't spend long. She was getting ready to go out. It was important she wasn't late.

Yes, she'd told him who with. Her husband. Only her husband. It wasn't really important. She saw him all the time.

No, she said she didn't know where he was taking her. It was a surprise.

How did she seem? Excited. She was taking a lot of trouble to look her best. He could see that. She'd just come out of the bath. Putting on her make-up when he'd arrived. Not dressed yet.

How did she look when he saw her at first? Lovely. She was looking lovely. But it was all for her husband. Not for him, not for her brother – her only brother. Couldn't have been. She didn't know he was coming.

Yes, she'd been pleased enough to see him at first. She'd made him a drink. Sat talking.

And later? Well, after a bit she'd started to fidget. Kept looking at her watch. Said she didn't want to keep her husband waiting.

No, she didn't seem to be scared of her husband. He didn't think so anyway.

What impression did he get? Impression? Well, more that she wanted to be ready for him. She was excited. Said it was special … tonight.

Yes, she'd said why. It was their wedding anniversary.

No, he hadn't known that himself.

Did he remember the date? No! Certainly not!

Why? *Why*?! It wasn't a happy thought for him – remembering that day, that's why.

Why not? Because she shouldn't have married Michael.

Why not? Because the Halleys – both of them – they were bad news. They weren't good enough for her. They didn't love her enough. They hurt her.

How? How did they hurt her? Physical abuse? Oh no. Nothing like that. Well, not as far as he knew anyway. Nothing so obvious. Much more subtle.

What did he mean then – hurt her? They dumped her when they'd had enough of her. They made her do things she didn't want to do. They forced her to have children. They didn't understand her. Not like *he* understood her.

Yes, he could certainly tell them about the Halleys. Chapter and verse. *Chapter and verse*. He'd *made* her tell him. He'd forced her to fill in all the bits he hadn't understood.

Yes. They'd heard right. 'Forced.' That's what he'd said.

No, she hadn't just *told* him. Said she couldn't tell him. Some feeble excuse about loyalty. *Loyalty*? To a *Halley*? Give me a break!

But he'd *made* her tell him. He'd had to. It was for her own good. To save her from these men. He was the only one who saw what was going on. He was her twin. Twins saw things – felt things – no-one else could see or feel.

What did he feel? He *knew* she was unhappy. He knew she wanted to be with him – her twin. They'd always been there for one another. Twins were. But she couldn't be with him, because she couldn't escape these Halleys. They had her in a stranglehold. They had a hold over her she couldn't get away from on her own.

No, he didn't know – when he arrived today, he didn't know what it was. He'd never understood it. That's why he'd had to force her to tell him. She needed him to help her to escape. He was the only one who could save her. But he had to know what hold they had over her. If he didn't know he couldn't ever cut her free.

Yes, that's why he had to threaten her. Force her. Because he had to know – for sure. It was for her own good.

What kind of force? He'd warned her: he'd have to cut her face. It was the only way. She had to tell him – everything – or he'd have to do it. Oh yes, he'd known she'd talk if he said that. She knew the Halleys wouldn't love her any more if she had a cut face. They only loved her while she was beautiful. They wouldn't love her if she was scarred. These handsome men were all the same. They only wanted lovely women who'd show how successful they were. He'd seen it in their faces – the lust, the scheming. That's why these two both wanted Donella. She was beautiful. A trophy. A feather in their caps. A valuable asset. They could use her looks to their advantage. *And* she was successful herself – a successful doctor. That would help them get the big houses, the flash cars, the expensive holidays. *And* she could give them children – show they were real men.

Oh yes, *both* of them. They *both* lusted after her. They *both* had children by her. They must have forced her to do it. She wouldn't have done it otherwise. Yes, Donella was just what they both wanted, both needed. She'd help them get on.

And *had* she told him? Oh yes. Oh yes. Indeed she *had*. Little by little he'd winkled it out of her. Oh, she'd been difficult at first. Refused to say it. But she'd always been a determined girl. He knew her. He'd known her all her life. But he could be determined too, just as stubborn as she was. With encouragement – just a little cut here, a little cut there – yes, she'd told the story. He knew it all now. He knew what hold these evil men had over his sister. And they were straight-out-of-hell evil these two. He *had* to save her from evil that black.

What had she told him? When he cut her, what had she told him?

The story he told was so incredible that the CID officers frankly disbelieved it. Of course, they'd have to go through the motions – ask the husband and his brother, the sister-in-law, her parents even. Truth was often stranger than fiction. They knew that – knew it only too well in their line of work. But this was something else. There was something fascinating about the product of the deranged mind. In this case it all sounded possible. Where did the boundary come between imagination and insanity? Who knew?

Rod Campbell sighed and shook his head when he heard their account. This guy'd be locked up for a very long time, if he was any judge. Criminally insane, that's what he was. Too bad they'd have to put the whole family through such an ordeal, asking all this stuff. Nice, decent folk.

They took Graeme away in an unmarked van. Psychiatrists, psychologists, they'd all work with him, unearth more of his delusions, try to get inside the head of a maniac who'd killed his own twin sister.

Inspector Campbell yawned expansively. It was going to be a long night. But first he must get back to the husband. He'd need to tell him something of this story his brother-in-law had given them. Not that it would help him understand why his wife had been cold-bloodedly murdered on her wedding anniversary. Horrendous timing. On her anniversary.

He could see tomorrow's placards. It'd sell newspapers. 'Local university lecturer's wife murdered by twin brother.' 'Doctor axed by brother on wedding anniversary.' The ghouls would flock to Dalkeith to look at the scene of the crime. Strangers would lay flowers at the gate to the house. And when the trial came – well, if even a scrap of what the murdering lunatic said was true – the press would have a field day.

By the time the Inspector arrived back at the cordoned-off house, the forensic team had left, the body had been taken away, the family had gathered. Nicholas had taken charge.

His brother steadfastly refused to leave the house, so Nicholas had summonsed his own parents to come to stay with Michael, leaving the children with Alexandra, while he'd gone to break the news to Donella's parents. He'd insisted he couldn't stand by and let a policeman tell them – tell them that their only daughter had been murdered by their own son. Used as he was to breaking bad news, he could think of no possible way of softening this communication. He could only spare them the necessity of hearing it from a stranger.

Stunned beyond reaction Judy and Declan went with him silently. They had to be there. Two parents, two parents-in-law, a husband, a brother-in-law, gathered in Donella's drawing room. They held one another in silence. There was nothing anyone could say. They sat – isolated in their own appalled thoughts – no tears, no sound – waiting for the Inspector who would explain to them what had happened.

Typical of these classy families, Rod Campbell thought. No hysteria, no drama. It made him shudder to think what went on beneath that dignified exterior.

He braced himself. For now he'd stick to the simple facts. They'd need to be interviewed one by one to try to get their individual accounts of the things Graeme claimed had taken place in this family. He didn't want any one of them influencing the others. He didn't want a varnished acceptable *family* account. He wanted – he needed – the truth. No matter how bizarre.

The scent of lilies was overpowering.

Other books in the Living Literature Series

VACANT POSSESSION

Vivienne has been in a persistent vegetative state, looked after in a Home, for years. How can she suddenly be pregnant? She cannot speak for herself, so who should decide what happens to her unborn child? What is in her best interests?

Her family, the medical team who care for her, the police investigating the crime – all have different interests, values and opinions on the best way forward. As events gather their own momentum, other people must make medical and moral choices on Vivienne's behalf – choices beset with uncertainty that profoundly affect their own relationships and futures.

ISBN 1 85775 651 7   Paperback, £11.99

PATERNITY (prequel to *Double Trouble*)

When Judy agrees to marry Declan his happiness is complete. But from the first night of their marriage cracks appear in their relationship until eventually Judy reveals the demons which haunt her. When a child dies, the questions that follow unravel a past which rocks their security to its foundations.

What have they inherited? What are they passing on to future generations? This story of love and deception challenges the morality of what is done in the name of infertility treatment today and exposes the dilemmas and conflicts which society must address.

ISBN 1 85775 652 5   Paperback, £11.99